# LOVE IN EXCESS

# LOVE IN EXCESS;

## OR, THE FATAL ENQUIRY

Eliza Haywood

*edited by David Oakleaf*

*second edition*

broadview literary texts

**Canadian Cataloguing in Publication Data**

Haywood, Eliza, 1693?-1756
    Love in excess, or, The fatal enquiry

(Broadview literary texts)
2nd ed.

ISBN 1-55111-367-8

I. Oakleaf, David, 1947-    . II. Title. III. Title: Fatal enquiry. IV. Series.

PR3506.H94L6 2000    823'.5    C00-930086-4

Broadview Press Ltd., is an independent, international publishing house, incorporated in 1985.

North America:
P.O. Box 1243, Peterborough, Ontario, Canada K9J 7H5
3576 California Road, Orchard Park, NY 14127
TEL: (705) 743-8990; FAX: (705) 743-8353;
E-MAIL: customerservice@broadviewpress.com

United Kingdom:
Turpin Distribution Services Ltd.,
Blackhorse Rd., Letchworth, Hertfordshire SG6 1HN
TEL: (1462) 672555; FAX (1462) 480947; E-MAIL: turpin@rsc.org

Australia:
St. Clair Press, P.O. Box 287, Rozelle, NSW 2039
TEL: (02) 818-1942; FAX: (02) 418-1923

www.broadviewpress.com

Broadview Press gratefully acknowledges the financial support of the Book Publishing Industry Development Program, Ministry of Canadian Heritage, Government of Canada.

Broadview Press is grateful to Professor Eugene Benson for advice on editorial matters for the Broadview Literary Texts series.
Text design and composition by George Kirkpatrick

PRINTED IN CANADA

# Contents

# Introduction

*Love in Excess* is the spectacularly successful first novel of a spectacularly successful novelist. Building on its success, Eliza Haywood wrote a novel "on average every three months" during the 1720s (Ballaster 159-60)[1] and became the decade's most popular and prolific novelist. Only five years later, she included *Love in Excess* in the first of several substantial collections of her works. She devoted the 1730s and early 1740s to an eclectic array of other activities – including acting, theatrical and periodical writing, translation, and even publishing – but then returned to fiction in the late 1740s. As William H. McBurney reminds us, she did not win her early renown by default: "In 1719 appeared the first parts of two novels which in terms of book sales share with *Gulliver's Travels* the distinction of being the most popular English fiction of the eighteenth century before *Pamela*. These were *Love in Excess; or, The Fatal Enquiry* and *The Life and Strange Surprizing Adventures of Robinson Crusoe*" (McBurney 250).

Haywood enjoyed this striking achievement in a highly competitive literary marketplace. Although literacy rates were increasing in the eighteenth century, relatively few people could read and even fewer could afford to spend shillings on books. New groups of readers alone (e.g., wage-earners or an increasingly literate female population) could not provide a viable market (see Ballaster 36-41, but cf. 170). When *Love in Excess* entered the dynamic, experimental literary scene, it won its acclaim from the same sophisticated, demanding readers who eagerly consumed the literary classics of the day. Daniel Defoe's first novel is one of the most popular novels ever printed in any language. Like *Robinson Crusoe* and John Bunyan's *Pilgrim's Progress* (a non-novelistic blockbuster two decades too early for McBurney's list), *Gulliver's Travels* won enduring popularity as well as critical esteem. Samuel Richardson's first novel *Pamela* – McBurney's standard of immediate success – is

---

1  Parenthetical citations refer to works listed in the Selected Bibliography.

itself partly in the tradition of Haywood. It was so popular that Pamela, then an obscure literary name, became and has remained a popular girls' name. *Love in Excess* earned its prominent place in this remarkable fiction explosion of the eighteenth century and regularly appeared with collections of Haywood's works into the 1740s.

Though we now know little about the private woman behind this conspicuous success, our ignorance is no proof of her obscurity. A successful actress as well as a very important writer in an impressive variety of forms, Haywood was solidly enmeshed in the literary scene of her day. We still can catch teasing glimpses of her in studies of writers now more famous, including the notoriously evasive Defoe, Alexander Pope, Henry Fielding, and the minor writer Richard Savage, who had the good fortune to have his biography written by his friend Samuel Johnson. Haywood wrote *Love in Excess* when she was a member of the bustling literary circle surrounding playwright and theatre manager Aaron Hill. Her bookseller (i.e., publisher) shrewdly dedicated her first novel to Anne Oldfield, a famous and socially prominent actress with considerable potential as a patron. Indeed, Oldfield helped support Savage, a member of the Hill circle who supplied a commendatory poem for *Love in Excess*.

Haywood may eventually have met Hill's friend Samuel Richardson, the future novelist who printed Haywood's comedy *A Wife to be Lett* in 1735 and who certainly read her work. (Margaret Doody's modern study of Richardson was until recently one of the few sources of intelligent Haywood criticism.) With another writer, traditionally thought to be Defoe although modern Defoe scholars are cautious about the attribution, she was involved in a series of pamphlets about the deaf-mute prophet Duncan Campbell. She worked with another future novelist, Henry Fielding, when he managed the Little Theatre in the Haymarket. The benefit night for Haywood, 24 May 1737, was Fielding's last production as theatre manager before the Licensing Act imposed government control on a highly political stage. Haywood herself played Mrs. Screen in his *Historical Register for the Year 1736* and the Muse in his farce *Eurydice Hiss'd*.

While there is evidence that she wanted her private life to remain private, Haywood was a very public figure. Her novels won her fame as the "Great arbitress of passion!"(see Appendix 278). Even Fielding's satire of her as Mrs. Novel in *The Author's Farce* (1730) acknowledges her fame as a novelist. When she appears in the cast list of an adaptation of *Arden of Feversham* as "Mrs. Eliza Haywood, the Author," this too may simply demonstrate her fame as a novelist (see Rudolph's introduction to her plays, ix-x). When she tried her hand at scandal novels – political fiction in the tradition of Delarivier Manley's *New Atalantis* – she did so prominently enough to provoke Jonathan Swift, who attacks her (probably) in his poem "Corinna," and Alexander Pope, who savages her in the second book of *The Dunciad*, his major satire of Grub-Street writing. Richard Savage, with whom she quarrelled in 1724, satirized her in an anonymous poem, *The Authors of the Town*, and named his prose satire, *An Author to be Let*, from her comedy *A Wife to be Lett*.

In the small, jealous, and intensely political literary scene of Haywood's day, appallingly cruel satire was almost the routine tribute to success. Pope may assert that he speaks impartially for cultural values, for example, but his cover story is the sure sign of the partisan. And if print confers the power to wound, Haywood wielded it too. She tells her own, restrained account of Savage in *Memoirs of a Certain Island Adjacent to the Kingdom of Utopia*, one of the scandal novels Pope attacks. If she resented Fielding's satire, she reserved her feeling for an incidental swipe at "F—g's scandal shop" in her 1751 novel, *The History of Miss Betsy Thoughtless* (ch. 8). After all, she worked with Fielding in that scandal shop as an actress and perhaps – the benefit night may suggest this – as a collaborator in the troupe's anonymous plays. Hurt feelings did not interfere with professional opportunities.

Haywood's professionalism makes it unlikely that, as some critics have assumed, Pope's satire or anyone else's drove her from fiction in the decade after *The Dunciad* appeared. That decade was the period of her greatest theatrical involvement. In addition to acting steadily and possibly adapting or collaborating in plays for her troupe, Haywood wrote two plays. *Fred-*

*erick, Duke of Brunswick-Lunenburgh* was performed and published in 1729 ("an indifferent success"). But it was in collaboration with actor and playwright William Hatchett, her lover, that she achieved her greatest theatrical success with *The Opera of Operas.* This musical adaptation of Fielding's *Tragedy of Tragedies,* a version of the Tom Thumb story, in turn received the compliment of a one-act adaptation by Theophilus Cibber with music by the famous composer Thomas Arne. In addition, she drew on her theatrical knowledge to write a major work only recently ascribed to her (Blouch 541 confirms the attribution by Marcia Heinemann). *The Dramatic Historiographer; or, The British Theatre Delineated* (1735) was a valuable and popular survey of the British theatre later retitled *The Companion to the Theatre;* Blouch counts seven editions between 1735 and 1756 alone! Almost incidentally in this busy period, she also produced *The Adventures of Eovaai* (1736), her Oriental tale satirizing the government of Sir Robert Walpole.

Haywood's writing is as impressive for its variety as for its striking quantity. With at least some success, she wrote different kinds of drama. Between *Love in Excess* (1719-20) and *The History of Jemmy and Jenny Jessamy* (1752) she produced several kinds of fiction, much of it especially directed to the woman reader. Like many other writers, she parodied *Pamela.* She translated French fiction and drew on French sources to write a life of Mary, Queen of Scots, wrote theatre history and criticism, and ventured briefly into publishing. Between April 1744 and May 1746, she wrote monthly issues of *The Female Spectator,* the first English periodical written by a woman for women. She was writing another weekly periodical for women, *The Young Lady,* when she died on 25 February 1756.

It is to be hoped that current research leads to fuller knowledge, perhaps even a full biography, of Eliza Haywood. We could learn a lot from her life about the crucial transformation of writing from a gentlemanly accomplishment into a profession open to women as well as men. Even so, the professional writer earned too little to escape the next urgent deadline. Haywood herself long wrote from the surest of spurs to professional industry: she had to support herself and two children. When she apologizes in the last issue of *The Young Lady* that she is too ill to continue writing, she reveals starkly the unremitting demand to produce that shaped the professional writer. But she also suggests the courage and the vitality she needed to maintain for so long a high place in this literary world. What the gentlemanly critic deplores as opportunism and hack writing, the rest of us can profitably admire as energetic professionalism finely attuned to the precarious commercial marketplace that was displacing aristocratic literary patronage. Naturally enough given its circumstances of production, her writing is sometimes pedestrian. But it is more commonly lively, and it is necessarily deeply engaged with the changing demands of an emergent readership.

An equally keen engagement with Haywood's fiction is the best antidote to a patrician disdain. Some of the reasons for Haywood's success are obvious. Eighteenth-century readers looked for variety, and *Love in Excess* is exuberantly various. It also celebrates sexual desire, a topic its competition fastidiously avoids. Bunyan's Christian fixes his eye resolutely on the next world. Swift's Gulliver solemnly denies a rumour that he had an affair with a woman five inches tall, asserts his rationality by spurning an eager female Yahoo, and distances himself from his long-suffering wife. Stranger still, Defoe's Crusoe domesticates the desert island he is marooned on and then reflects that, apart from a few conveniences like a tobacco pipe, "I had no room for Desire" (129). But Haywood never forgets that desire does not usually content itself with goats, grain, and grapes. Writing in the tradition of passionate but more overtly political predecessors like Aphra Behn and Delarivier Manley, she elaborates her basic narrative situation, the love triangle, to present an impressive variety of female roles and fates.

Of course *Love in Excess* does, like *Robinson Crusoe*, inscribe a significant eighteenth-century cultural pattern. Defoe's novel articulates the definitive paradigm of self-activating bourgeois identity, for its hero disciplines himself in order to discipline his environment. *Love in Excess* works within this paradigm while it articulates the related cultural shift toward a companionate model of marriage. It begins with ambition, which is public and culturally male, but it ends with "conjugal affection" (266), which is private and culturally female. In between, Haywood confronts directly the social conventions which, by making female sexual desire unspeakable, silence her protagonists. Indeed, Haywood won praise precisely for finding a language through which to express passion. As the congratulatory poems in the second volume show, she was praised for both strength of feeling and force of language. She strikingly crafts a public space for subjectivity, especially for the desiring female subject.

Although *Love in Excess* is memorable for its women, its narrative follows Count D'elmont. A male version of the cruel mistress whose mere sight inspires hopeless passion, D'elmont routinely attracts sexual propositions from women to whom he is indifferent. Haywood traces his progress from total insensitivity through suffering passion to happy marriage. Inset narratives tell the amorous stories of his brother Brillian and his future brother-in-law Frankville, but D'elmont himself is active in most of the love triangles. This causes confusion, but Haywood's narrator helps the reader's memory (and signals her controlling design) through alliterative doublings. The first volume places D'elmont between Amena and Alovisa, whom he marries for money at the end of the volume. The second volume retains Alovisa while placing D'elmont between the flirt Melantha and "the matchless Melliora," whom he loves. Doubling D'elmont with Melliora's brother Frankville, the third volume surrounds them with Ciamara (a lecherous aristocratic widow), Frankville's love Camilla, Frankville's friend Cittolini, and Violetta (a woman whose break with the alliterative pattern marks her as the odd one out in other ways too). Ingeniously elaborating a basic pattern, these complications allow Haywood to explore varieties of female subjectivity.

In *Love in Excess*, Haywood situates that subjectivity in an aristocratic society that demands the public display of status and wealth. Such a society inevitably subordinates love to ambition. While one of her most important modern critics feels that her hero's "military and social status is part of the automatic embroidery his character needs" (Richetti 184), D'elmont's rank and valour express the class imperative that dictates his marriage to Alovisa: "Ambition was certainly the reigning passion in his soul, and Alovisa's quality and vast possessions, promising a full gratification of that, he ne'er so much as wished to know a farther happiness in marriage" (76). Her poverty and modest rank, not her personal deficiencies, explain D'elmont's "disgust" at the thought of marrying Amena (51): such a marriage "would in no way agree with his ambition" (59). An inherited title and estate define D'elmont's social identity, and he calculatingly supports his family honour by marrying to replenish the family coffers.

When he is evidently no longer infatuated with her, Alovisa complains that D'elmont's "well nigh wasted stream of wealth had dried, but for [her] kind of supply" (128). But she is no less aristocratic and no less ambitious than her husband. When he responds to her first anonymous love letter by mistakenly courting Amena, she sternly exhorts him in a second letter to aim higher: "If ambition be a fault, 'tis only in those who have not a sufficient stock of merit to support it" (45). D'elmont, of course, has already displayed his merit in the manner that traditionally justifies aristocratic privilege: he has served his king in battle. Alovisa feels attracted because he has thereby won "more than ordinary reputation" and been "received by the King and Court, after a manner that might gratify the ambition of the proudest" (37). In short, D'elmont has earned his ambitious marriage to the "co-heiress (with her sister,) of a vast estate" (38), "one of the greatest fortunes in all France" (75).

In *Love in Excess*, this aristocratic pride is a persistent threat to the private world of desire. A doting father's ambition places Amena in the dangerous situation that fascinates most early novelists; it places her, that is, where she will attract sexual attentions that cannot lead to a socially sanctioned marriage. D'elmont's careless dalliance with her is echoed by the Baron D'esparnay, who assaults Alovisa, and by the proud Italian widow Ciamara, who assaults D'elmont himself. D'elmont's ambitious marriage is echoed by Ciamara and her brother Cittolini, aristocrats impoverished – paternal lapses are a persistent theme – "by the too great liberality of [their] father" (188). Attracting a rich but old suitor, Ciamara "married and buried him in a month's time." Left "mistress of all he had in the world," she plots the marriage of his daughter, now her step-daughter, to her ugly and older brother, Cittolini. Naturally enough in this context, Cittolini glibly promises his own daughter to Frankville in marriage without consulting her (189). And though Alovisa admittedly opposes rather than arranging her sister Ansellina's marriage to D'elmont's brother, she too subordinates other people's desires to her aristocratic pride.

Love, in short, does not follow ambition. Alovisa quickly marries the man she chooses, but she is not courted: "she took care that if he should be wanting in his kind expressions after marriage, he should not have it in his power to pretend (as some husbands have done) that his stock was exhausted in a tedious courtship" (77). Not surprisingly, a month – the newly-weds' traditional "honey" moon – completes D'elmont's love (141). Amena on the other hand is courted but not married. She flees to a convent, the definitive literary refuge for thwarted feeling at least since the late seventeenth-century vogue for *The Portuguese Letters*, a popular collection of five letters allegedly written by a nun to the cavalier who seduced and abandoned her. Only Alovisa's accidental death by his own hand and his passion for Melliora finally chasten D'elmont's ambition: "*Ambition*, once his darling passion, was now wholly extinguished in him by these misfortunes, and he no longer thought of making a figure in the world; but his *love*, nothing could abate ..." (163-64). Apparently "wholly dead to gaiety," the count forsakes society and the retinue appropriate to his social importance, preferring a setting appropriate to love – "a solitary walk, a lonely shade, or the bank of some purling stream" (165-66).

To the extent that they too must create a space for subjectivity within this public, aristocratic society, Haywood's characters share their situation with the novelist. Alovisa speaks for her author when she laments that women cannot, like men, express their desire directly: "whilst those of [D'elmont's] own [sex] strove which should gain the largest share in his friendship; the other vented fruitless wishes, and in secret, cursed that custom which forbids women to make a declaration of their thoughts"

(37). Even though Amena retains, barely, her virginity, she is ruined socially because her retreat to the Tuileries with D'elmont makes her love public. To her father, her great crime is to have expressed her passion: "'But is it possible,' cried he, quite confounded at these words, 'that she should stoop so low to offer love?'" (64). The novelist commits the fallen maiden's crime: she breaches the discursive decorum that forbids women to express their desire.

Not surprisingly, this constraint is a prominent theme of eighteenth-century women's writing. Custom required a woman to attract and marry an eligible man, but the same custom forbade her to show her interest in a man until he had formally declared his love for her. Amena's obvious delight in D'elmont's addresses (46) makes her vulnerable to seduction. Violetta regards as a "shameful declaration" (265) her deathbed confession of her chaste and hitherto concealed love for D'elmont. These women share the frustration of silence with the narrator of Jane Barker's 1713 novel, *Love Intrigues*, who remains baffled that her virtuous decorum should have thwarted her desire for Bosvil. They also share their frustration with Jane Bennett in Jane Austen's 1813 novel, *Pride and Prejudice*, another woman whose decorous serenity almost costs her the man she passionately loves.

Eighteenth-century discourse subjected even books to the social decorum that would apply to the author's speech. Defoe crafted his prefaces to confront the respectable reader's unease at the low representation of low lives. Much later than *Love in Excess*, Owen Ruffhead looked back to Thomas Hobbes in order to accuse Laurence Sterne's *Tristram Shandy* of violating in discourse the grid that maps social distinctions onto space: it associated a clergyman's public dignity with a bawdy text, he charged, and it brought into the salon the private thoughts appropriate only to the private chamber. Even Fielding's *Tom Jones*, which is intermittently sexual even though, as Henry James observed, it is strikingly free of the rhetoric of private experience, risked censure. It mixed the socially high with the socially low, an activity always open to polite disapproval. Fielding solves his problem by presenting *Tom Jones* as a stagecoach journey with stops at various inns. He thus assimilated his text to a familiar social situation that permitted such potentially transgressive social mixtures. Writers had to adapt their language to potentially hostile social scrutiny.

Social decorum weighed especially heavily on the woman novelist of sexual desire. As contemporary praise for Haywood acknowledges, social decorum had no place that authorized – i.e., conferred social authority on – private desire. Certainly the notion that desire should on its own legitimate an action is alien to a society based on landed inheritance. Such a society validates stability and stigmatizes change as instability. Even Robinson Crusoe's definitively bourgeois father rebukes his son's desire to wander, preaching contentment with the achieved middle station of life. The amusement that colours John J. Richetti's influential discussion of *Love in Excess* shows how readily even a sympathetic reader can shift from Haywood's subjective discourse of the body to its opposite, a socially-grounded bawdiness that scrutinizes intimacy from without: "We wonder just what sort of picture Mrs. Haywood's readers drew for themselves when they were told that Melantha interrupted the lovers again just as D'Elmont 'was preparing to take from the resistless Melliora the last, and only remaining proof that she was all his own'" (Richetti 201).

Haywood's narrative challenge, therefore, is to situate her reader where she or he will forget such social judgment and instead accept the authority of desire. Haywood faces that challenge explicitly when she identifies herself with her erring lovers in defiance of their critics:

> Wretches! We know all this as well as they; we know too, that we both do, and leave undone many other things, which we ought not; but perfection is not to be expected on this side the grave. And since 'tis impossible for humanity to avoid frailties of some kind or other, those are certainly least blameable which spring only from a too great affluence of the nobler spirits. *Covetousness, envy, pride, revenge,* are the effects of an earthy, base, and sordid nature, *ambition* and *love* of an exalted one; and if they are failings, they are such as plead their own excuse, and can

never want forgiveness from a generous heart, provided no indirect courses are taken to procure the ends of the *former*, nor inconstancy, or ingratitude, stain the beauty of the *latter*. (186)

To the generous heart – and who admits to any other? – elevation of feeling authorizes even a moral fall. Love is an exalted private desire equivalent to ambition, the exalted public desire for distinction cherished by an aristocratic society. A "vast and elegant passion" (101) defies expression in something as public as language, but it partakes of an aristocratic elegance. Low desires characterize lower-class characters like Anaret, Amena's mercenary servant, or aristocrats corrupted by pride of rank, like Ciamara, whose lust is mean-spirited and hence unworthy. Haywood's narrator validates private experience by ennobling it, creating a privileged community of desiring subjects: "we" lovers, "we" readers.

Of course, a new community requires a new decorum. Much as Fielding exploits the trope of the stage coach journey to express his anxiety about social mixture, Haywood exploits images of liminal situations to address unease at the public expression of private feeling. Of course she can charge any action or space with emotion. Alovisa's death by a careless thrust of her errant mate's sword is, surely deliberately, a grim bit of comic symbolism. Amena's house so smoulders with passion that when Alovisa's servant raises the cry of fire to alarm her father, Haywood's most comprehensive modern reader, true to Haywood's subjective focus, recalls the image as a narrative fact: "the lovers return to find their absence noted, Amena's house smouldering, and their return to her garden blocked" (Schofield, *Eliza Haywood* 19). But Haywood's most suggestive symbolic space is a liminal "plot" inherited from romance. In *Love in Excess*, she situates desire in the walled garden that has been an image of the female body at least since the Song of Songs.

Specifically, she situates her lovers in the garden between the house's private chambers and the public world beyond. Striking for her "beauty and sweetness" (41) and courted in such a garden, Amena may even take her name from the seductive *loca* amoena ("attractive places") of pastoral romance: she meets her disgrace not here but in the Tuileries, the fashionable palace garden beyond the walls of her father's house. D'elmont courts Melliora too in enclosed gardens, and when Frankville courts Camilla in Ciamara's garden, their sexual union brings not disgrace but eagerness to marry and publish their mutual desire. Ciamara, by contrast, stages her lust not in a *locus amoenus* but in a version of the House of Busirane, the castle of unlawful love in Edmund Spenser's *Faerie Queene* (see especially *F.Q.* III.xi.29ff.). Ciamara's "splendidly luxurious" (206) room depicting the transgressive loves of immortals for mortals reveals that she is a calculating aristocrat devoted to art rather than nature. Melliora's bedroom, by contrast, is a chamber of the mind. There D'elmont naturally discovers subjective truth – Melliora loves him – through the artless (and guiltless) medium of her dreams.

As her lovers slide gradually into increased intimacy, Haywood creates for them a vast new terrain where society decrees only the sharp divide between "wife" and "whore," the alliterative opposites that defined women's sexual choices. (A wife who lost her husband entered an alliterative third category – "widow"; since a widow was an unmarried but sexual woman with an anomalous degree of social power, society reaffirmed its boundaries by representing her as a sinister lecher or a randy figure of fun.) Haywood's garden between the private chamber and the public world blurs these distinctions, substituting a rich subjective space with its own imperatives. Here lovers share subjectivity as well as sexual intimacy, and Camilla remains a desirable as well as a desiring subject. Here Frankville must reject suspicious appearances for love. Though Ciamara may tempt D'elmont in Camilla's name, and though prudence may dictate marriage, Camilla also retains her freedom to reject a lover too ready to reject subjectivity and scrutinize her critically. Here D'elmont must learn to despise D'espernay's cynical counsel of acquaintance rape and attend instead to shared feeling. All lovers, and only lovers, are subjects.

That is why Haywood's narrator promiscuously confers her narrative favours on all of them. Her women may plot against women, but Amena's despair, Violetta's adoring denial of self, and Ciamara's lust all receive their due. Alovisa's jealousy receives as much attention as Melliora's futile struggle against her passion. The narrator rewards even Melantha's mischievous sexual encounter with D'elmont. After mocking D'espernay's sexual double standard – "Few men, how amorous soever themselves, care that the female part of their family should be so" (144) – she grants Melantha the marriage that ends the second volume conventionally but ironically: "not of a humour to take any thing to heart, [she] was married in a short time, and had the good fortune not to be suspected by her husband, though she brought him a child in seven months after her wedding" (159). Her child by D'elmont may, if he is male, inherit her childless brother's estate as well as her husband's, but the narrator indulges no patrilineal anxieties. Provocatively refusing to gender Melantha's child, she maintains her narrative focus on a lover's good fortune.

Such transgressive subjectivity finds its natural expression in what we could call liminal relationships – sexual relationships that transform socially sanctioned ties. Challenging ties of obligation or friendship, transgressive love acquires the intensity of friendship. D'espernay is D'elmont's unsuspected sexual rival as well as confidant, as Melliora is Alovisa's. Most transgressive of all is D'elmont's passion for Melliora. Legally empowered as her guardian, D'elmont initially abuses his power to harass the powerless Melliora – as she recognizes: she had "not even an acquaintance at Paris, or friend, but him who but newly was become so, and whom she found it dangerous to make use of" (88). But his transgressive role also defines the intensity of his passion: "'Friendship! did I say?' rejoyned he softning his voice, 'that term is too mean to express a zeal like mine, the care, the tenderness, the faith, the fond affection of parents, – brothers, – husbands, – lovers, all comprized in one! one great unutterable! comprehensive meaning, is mine! is mine for Melliora!'" (89). The subjectivity of Haywood's novels infuses into sexual relationships the potent feelings appropriate to the authoritative relationships of patriarchal society.

Appropriately enough, then, the garden in which Haywood stages so much passion is just inside the realm of public scrutiny. Even if it is only Melantha who stumbles upon the lovers or

Alovisa who glances out a window at them, their private intimacy will become public knowledge. As April London argues of the gardens common to pious and amatory novels, "the garden retains its material status as property, with the attendant issues of ownership, consumption, productivity, and improvement" (102). Haywood writes within, and about, the society in which the male landowner/gentleman possesses and controls the garden/female body; hence the passivity typical of the woman seduced in the literary garden. A landowner – a father – may oversee rather than overlooking the lovers' passion.

That may be why female agency is far more equivocal than female subjectivity. Haywood offers not so much a new social structure as a new way of inhabiting an existing patrilineal structure. Indeed, social anxiety was so strong that, on the question of choice, eighteenth-century fiction finally contented itself with an uneasily shared balance of power: a child should marry only with parental consent, but a parent should arrange a marriage only with the child's consent. In *Love in Excess*, however, Haywood presents women free to choose. Amena chooses, unhappily, against a careless father's preference. Melantha chooses, rebelliously, to act as her brother acts rather than as he would advise. Though Alovisa chooses unhappily, she and Ansellina are heiresses free to choose for themselves. Camilla chooses love but feels free to reconsider her choice when her lover seems unworthy. Denying sexuality rather than indulging it, Violetta too chooses love, contributing to her unworthy father's death. And though the novel ends with submission to paternal authority, Melliora is the Prospero who engineers a return to social order entirely in accord with her desires.

Articulating the desire of the woman whose body it represents, a landowner assumes control of his garden. Transformed by feeling, D'elmont will no longer abuse his social power. The powerless captive of a transgressive lover, Melliora asserts her will by relinquishing it – "'since heaven has restored them ['my brother and Count D'Elmont'] to me, all power of disposing of my self must cease...'" – and deferring to patriarchal approval: "'I am still ready to perform my promise, whenever these gentlemen shall command me. – The one my brother, the other my guardian, obtain but their consent, and –'" (261). The guardian who acts for her father and her brother is also the lover who can speak her desire as well as his own. Even public honour is appeased:

> when they came to Paris, they were joyfully received by the Chevalier Brillian and Ansellina, and those who in the Count's absence had taken a liberty of censuring and condemning his actions, awed by his presence, and in time won by his virtues, now swell his praises with an equal vehemence. Both he and Frankville, are still living, blest with a numerous and hopeful issue, and continue, with their fair wives, great and lovely examples of conjugal affection. (266)

Exemplary lovers win even the praise that gratifies ambition.

Haywood won such praise as a novelist. Of course poems of praise may be no more sincere than other paid commercials, but even a puff has to use a credible language of praise. Richard Savage praises Haywood for both her devotion to love and her mastery of language: "For such descriptions thus at once can prove / The force of language, and the sweets of love." She deserves a crown of both myrtle leaves, sacred to Venus, and laurel leaves (bays), sacred to poetry: "The myrtle's leaves with those of fame entwine, / And all the glories of that wreath are thine!" Writing the fires of love, she provokes from Savage complex comparisons with heat, the eagle that can proverbially gaze directly at the sun, the sun god Phoebus (Apollo) who is also the god of poetry and learning, and the immortal light of the skies.

Some of the praise explores Haywood's destabilization of gender categories with striking ambivalence. Especially revealing is the poem "By an Unknown Hand, To the most Ingenious Mrs. Haywood, on her Novel Entitled, *Love in Excess*." A woman could have written this anonymous poem, of course, but since Unknown Hand finds a reflection in D'elmont and praises Haywood in the language of gallantry, I will call her "he" and "him." He claims that he was an unbeliever in women's strength of soul (their power as writers) until Haywood converted him. Like D'elmont, he was also an atheist to Love's power. Drawing on the cliches of anti-Moslem writing, he presents Haywood as at once a beautiful woman, a writer, and a Christian champion like St. George. As Christian champion, she conquers the "Unbeliever," the "atheist" (the infidel ignorant of love, especially the Moslem unbeliever in Christianity who denies that women have souls). As writer, she is blessed by the poetry god Phoebus, who enables Hand to develop the appropriate conceits even more elaborately than Savage. In Hand's version of Phoebus' roles, the conquered Moslem infidels are comprehensively Oriental. They are at once suntanned ("tawny Sons of a luxuriant Coast," that is, the eastern Mediterranean), amorous ("luxury" suggests the lechery as well as the wealth of a hotter clime – the orient of harems), and poetic (they boast the origin of poetry, for Phoebus, the sun, rises in the East of the Song of Songs).

Before his conversion by Haywood (whose first play would be the 1721 harem drama, *The Fair Captive*), Unknown Hand was, by contrast, typically English; that is, he was pale, cool to love, and (hence) unpoetic. But now he is playing with fire. By his account, Haywood is anomalously both Eastern/Moslem and English/Christian, both female and male. She may be a St. George, but as "Champion for the Sex" she warms his English coolness with foreign heat. The blazing source of welcome heat brings to Hand's "blest" western isle what it most lacks, "more than Eastern heat." As a writer, she is also Phoebus himself – the source of light and warmth. As an amorous woman, she is the source of love's fires: "Love's shafts new pointed fly," he tells her, "Winged with YOUR Flame, and blazing in YOUR Eye." She has brought England a literature of passion and, perhaps consequently, the lechery that characterizes the East of the English imagination. It would be hard for a poem of praise to register Haywood's transgression of cultural boundaries more directly.

"Amatory fiction," our received term for the fiction of Haywood and her predecessors, betrays a similar ambivalence. But no other term will do. "Romance" is dignified but misleading

– an aristocratic narrative form to the critic but a love story to readers less professionalised. "Love stories," on the other hand are *infra dig.* – likely "girlish," lower class, or (horrors!) both: "love stories" are stories to read, not texts to study – by no means "mature" or "sophisticated" fiction. "Erotic fiction," by contrast, suggests *Fanny Hill* rather than *Love in Excess*. Since it describes the gentlemanly or merely male objectification of female sexuality, including pornography, it is the opposite of Haywood's "subjectification" of sexuality. So the gentle critic refers to "amatory" fiction, hoping that the safely donnish term will steer the reader with some dignity between extremes. "Amatory" does suggest sexual love, but so Latinate a term also gestures reassuringly toward the late-Classical romances and hence toward a genealogy appropriate to the novel's cautious rise to literary respectability.

"Amatory novel" will therefore do for Haywood's narrative of desire. In part, *Love in Excess* is a sophisticated development of the Ovidian verse epistle from a woman to her absent lover, a form that shaped fiction directly and through prose variants like *The Portuguese Letters* and Behn's *Love-Letters between a Nobleman and His Sister*. Partly set in Italy like a Jacobean tragedy, however, it also tells tales of transgressive sexual desire on the theme of "women beware women." Partly centred on women united by common feeling if not by alliances, it is a covertly feminist critique of the subordination of women. Partly centred on a hero, it is a Bildungsroman representing its narrowly ambitious hero's education in the ways of the heart. Partly centred on a beleaguered heroine, it is a young virgin's erotic fantasy about her surrogate father. More bluntly, it is a bodice ripper. It is also an emotionally charged soap opera of brutal ambition, adulterous passion, and abuses of power. Again, it is a cautionary young-adult novel tracing the love-lives of impressionable young women in a violent, male-dominated world.

And so on. Any novelist would kill to write a novel with such broad appeal. Certainly her publisher would kill to publish it! For Haywood appealed to very different readers, as she had to, and some of her conventions have proved remarkably durable. She did educate the newly affective male reader, the reader who comfortably inhabited the language of gallantry but who was nevertheless also curiously turning Haywood's pages. But at the same time and more urgently, she was constructing the modern female reader of women's romances (see Ballaster 169ff.) Now that narrow literary canons and still narrower gender roles are commanding scrutiny, the versatile writer who contributed so much to an emerging genre and an emerging profession deserves renewed attention. And there is no better place to begin or renew an acquaintance with Haywood than *Love in Excess; or, The Fatal Enquiry: A Novel*, the book with which an aspiring actress and playwright first caught the attention of her contemporaries.

# A Note on the Text

This text is based on the first edition, published in three separately paginated volumes in 1719-20. Obvious printers' errors are silently corrected, but most changes involve modernization. Published before the mid-century simplification of typographical conventions, *Love in Excess* bristles with initial capitals, routinely marshals italics or large and small capitals to dignify proper nouns like *Paris* or MELLIORA, and regularly marks with italics quoted letters and a few other brief quotations. Flocks of apostrophes silence letters we never pronounce, like the "*l* " in "*should*" or the "*e*" in "*ed*" endings. Direct speech merges unmarked into the surrounding prose, signalled only by tag phrases like "interrupted she" – phrases that are sometimes but not always placed in parentheses that sometimes but not always coincide with the phrase's actual syntactical boundaries.

Since these conventions can daunt modern readers, lending an air of remoteness to even this most accessible of novelists, this edition modernizes routine printers' conventions. Most capitals and italics vanish. *Shou'd* gives way to *should, sigh'd, rely'd,* and *beg'd* to *sighed, relied,* and *begged.* The use of italics for quoted letters and postscripts, Roman for their beginning and ending formulas, is regularized. Quotation marks are added to direct speech, and the accompanying punctuation is nudged in the direction of modern practice. Where it seemed a reader might get lost, other punctuation is lightly modernized to highlight the units of Haywood's prose. But other conventions of the day work remarkably well, notably the shifts from one character's speech to another's within a single sentence, shifts that suit Haywood's intersubjectivity and deliberate blurring of boundaries.

Unless they seem likely to mislead a modern reader, local variations are preserved. *Then* and *than,* then interchangeable, are not normalized except where a contrast of *now* with *than* might cause brief confusion (155). *Tho'* and *'em* remain, the latter possibly capturing a feature of Haywood's speech, as do some colloquial grammatical lapses; e.g., *there was no hopes* (59) or *a kind of pleased expectations* (230). Variant spellings of characters' names also remain: *Alovisa* also appears as *Alovysa* and even *Aloisa; D'elmont* (or *D'Elmont*) meets the *Marquess* (or *Marquese*) *De* (or *D'*) *Saguillier* (or *Sanguillier*). Past tenses like *vyed* remain unaltered, as do irregular possessives (e.g., *baronesses* or *ladies* for *baroness's* or *lady's*) and unusual apostrophes (e.g., *her's* or *see's*). The reader will find *would'st* and *couldst* in the same sentence, *beleive, recieved,* and *perceiveing* as well as the modern spellings of the same words. Editorial changes consider but do not invariably follow the 1722 edition ("The fourth edition corrected"), which shows no signs of authorial revision but corrects some obvious slips. Textual cruxes and striking substantive changes (e.g., "she" for "he") receive comment in footnotes that sometimes cite the 1722 edition as "4th ed."

Local variation was part of the adventure for Haywood as well as her reader, for bookseller and printer would have a say in the book's appearance. (Haywood's bookseller dedicates her novel to an actress whom he praises for freely altering the texts of plays!) Capitalization, typefaces, and punctuation were seasonings stirred liberally into the prose by the printer just before serving hot to an eager public, and even the different volumes of *Love in Excess* follow distinct recipes. The third volume, for example, prefers *D'Elmont* to *D'elmont* and accents rhetorical contrasts by changing typefaces: "Her *real perfidy*," Frankville says of Camilla, "shall be repaid with *seeming inconstancy* ..." (215). Such variations may reveal early readers trying to capture the rise and fall of Haywood's voice, and even where they suggest only quick commercial publication, they remind us of Haywood's engagement with a demanding marketplace. Excessive modernization would spoil the flavour.

Footnotes to the text gloss allusions and unfamiliar vocabulary as well as occasional textual problems; "Johnson" in parentheses after a quoted phrase indicates a definition from Samuel Johnson, *A Dictionary of the English Language* (1755), also cited for flavour.

I gratefully thank those who aided and abetted my efforts. As ever, Anne McWhir mixed practical help with encouragement to persist in my folly. Suzanne Gibson, April London,

Lorne Macdonald, Jay Macpherson, Murray McGillivray, J.E. Svilpis, and Earla A. Wilputte all offered aid or encouragement. Dominique Berthiaume, Chris Frey, Katie Harse, Susanne Heinz, and Renée Lang confirmed my hunch that Eliza Haywood has something to offer bright contemporary students.

My thanks to the staffs of the Newberry Library, the British Library, Special Collections at the McKimmie Library of the University of Calgary, and the inter-library loans department of Pennsylvania State University (where Shane and his colleagues handled an urgent telephone request with impressive promptness and courtesy). Thanks too to Don LePan and Barbara Conolly of Broadview Press for allowing me, during reprinting, to augment the text with an appendix.

The second edition makes a few corrections, updates the selected bibliography, and substantially expands the Appendix. I owe special thanks to Christine Blouch and Broadview's Risa Kawchuk for calling my attention to *The Ladies Journal* and to Howard Weinbrot for speeding a copy my way. Further experience has deepened my gratitude to the staff of the McKinnie Library and to Don LePan, Barbara Conolly, and the staff at Broadview Press.

# Eliza Haywood: A Brief Chronology

[We know little about Haywood despite her importance and her connection with writers we know well. A chronology reveals the pattern of her literary career, but treat assertions and dates, including publication dates, with caution. Christine Blouch's article – see Selected Bibliography – is at present the best source of biographical and other information; Mary Anne Schofield's *Eliza Haywood* offers the fullest survey and discussion of Haywood's varied career; and George Frisbie Whicher's book is still the only full biography.]

?1693     [1689 has also been suggested] born Eliza Fowler, traditionally to a merchant family in London but just possibly as sister to Sir Richard Fowler of Harnage Grange, Shropshire, with whom EH claims in a letter to be "nearly related"

1715     in Dublin as Eliza Haywood: EH acts part of Chloe in Thomas Shadwell's Shakespeare adaptation, *Timon of Athens; or, The Man-Hater*. Her husband's identity is not known (Blouch disproves Whicher's conjecture that EH was the eloped wife of Reverend Valentine Haywood); in a later letter, EH gives "an unfortunate marriage" as the reason she writes to support herself and her two children

1719-20     *Love in Excess* published to great acclaim in three parts; *Letters from a Lady of Quality to a Chevalier* (trans.). EH is part of the literary group surrounding Aaron Hill, playwright and manager of the Little Theatre in the Haymarket (1720-33); meets Richard Savage, who supplies a prefatory poem for the second part of *Love in Excess*

1720-25     as well as acting and writing plays and novels, EH involved in pamphlets featuring the deaf-mute prophet Duncan Campbell; these include *The Life of Duncan Campbell* (allegedly by Defoe), *A Spy Upon the Conjuror* (1724), *The Dumb Projector* (1725), and

The Friendly Daemon (1725; rpt. 1732 as Secret Memoirs of the Late Mr. Duncan Campbell)

1721 The Fair Captive, tragedy, acted

1722 The British Recluse; The Injured Husband

1723 A Wife to be Lett, comedy, acted; Idalia; Lasselia; The Rash Resolve (with a prefatory poem by Savage); The Works of Mrs. Eliza Haywood, consisting of Novels, Letters, Poems, and Plays, 4 vols. ( vol. 4, Poems on Several Occasions, 1724)

1724 quarrel with Savage (& Martha Fowke Sansom), who later satirizes her; EH's account of Savage appears in Memoirs of a Certain Island adjacent to the Kingdom of Utopia (vol. 2, 1725; 2nd ed. 1726), a scandal romance in the tradition of Delarivier Manley's New Atalantis
The Masqueraders (pt. 2, 1725); The Fatal Secret; The Surprise; The Arragonian Queen; La Belle Assemblée (trans.; vol 2, 1726); Bath-Intrigues; Fantomina; The Force of Nature; Memoirs of the Baron de Brosse

1724-25 Secret Histories, Novels and Poems, (4 vols., eds. in 1732, 1742)

1725 The Lady's Philosopher's Stone (trans.); The Unequal Conflict; The Tea Table (pt. 2, 1726); Fatal Fondness; Mary Stuart (life of Mary Queen of Scots)

1726 The Distressed Orphan; The Mercenary Lover; Reflections on the Various Effects of Love; The City Jilt; The Double Marriage; The Court of Carimania, a second scandal romance; Letters from the Palace of Fame; Cleomelia

1727 The Fruitless Enquiry; The Life of Madam de Villesache; Love in Its Variety (trans.); Philidore and Placentia; The Perplex'd Dutchess

1728 The Padlock; or, No Guard without Virtue (with 3rd. ed. Mercenary Lover); The Agreeable Caledonian (pt. 2, 1729; reissued as Clementina in 1768); Irish Artifice (in The Female Dunciad); Persecuted Virtue; Some Memoirs of the Amours and Intrigues of a Certain Irish Dean; The Disguised Prince (trans., pt. 2 1729)

1729  *Frederick, Duke of Brunswick-Lunenburgh* acted ("an indifferent success"); *The Fair Hebrew*

1730s  active in theatre, both acting (often with William Hatchett, apparently also her lover) and writing plays

1730  *Love-Letters on All Occasions*

1733  *Opera of Operas*, by EH and William Hatchett, with music by John Frederick Lampe, runs for eleven performances (a hit!) and is then published

1734  *L'Entretien des Beaux-Esprits* (trans.)

1735  *The Dramatic Historiographer; or, The British Theatre Delineated* (later retitled *The Companion to the Theatre*); 7 eds. by 1756

1736  *The Adventures of Eovaai* (rpt. 1740 as *The Unfortunate Princess*)

1737  adaptation of *Love in Excess* acted (Stanton 346) 23 May: benefit night for EH at Little Haymarket

1741-42  publishes (& probably wrote) *Anti-Pamela; or, Feign'd Innocence Detected*; publishes (and trans.) *The Busybody; or, Successful Spy; The Virtuous Villager* (trans.)

1743  *A Present for a Servant Maid*

1744  *The Fortunate Foundlings; The Female Spectator* (monthly periodical, April 1744-May 1746): the first English periodical written by and for women

1746  *The Parrot* (weekly, 2 August to 4 October)

1747  *Memoirs of a Man of Honour* (trans.)

1748  *Life's Progress through the Passions; or, The Adventures of Natura*

1749  *Dalinda; or, The Double Marriage; Epistles for the Ladies*

1750  *A Letter from H— G—g, Esq.* (a pamphlet-letter supposedly by the Gentleman of the Bedchamber to the Young Pretender [i.e., Bonnie Prince Charlie]): arrested by a nervous government, EH spends some weeks in custody; *The History of Cornelia*

1751  *The History of Miss Betsy Thoughtless*

1752  *The History of Jemmy and Jenny Jessamy*

1753  *Modern Characters*

# LOVE IN EXCESS;

## OR

# THE FATAL ENQUIRY:

## A NOVEL

————— *In vain from Fate we fly,*
*For first or last, as all must die,*
*So 'tis as much decreed above,*
*That first or last, we all must love.*

—————Lansdown.[1]

---

1   George Granville, Baron Lansdown (1667-1735), poet and playwright as well as
    courtier, statesman, and patron.

Frontispiece to the 1722 edition of *Love in Excess* (engraved by Elisha Kirkall).

# TO

## MRS. OLDFIELD[1]

Madam,

*There is not any thing can excuse this presumption, but my intention in doing it. If you please to call to mind your late goodness to me, you'll find it requires my utmost acknowledgment.*

*But good actions from you are like ill ones from others, no sooner done, than forgot. I might expatiate on the many beauties of your mind and person, but it would be like telling the world 'twere broad day at noon.*

*The author of the following lines is a young lady, whose greatest pride is in the patroness I have chose her; but she's fearful in not pleasing one who I am well assured is a real critick without their ill nature.[2]*

*I shan't here mention the many authors that have been obliged to you by the amendments[3] in your inimitable performances. I would only advise 'em for the future to give you but the plan of what they would have said, and leave the rest to you.*

*I shall think my self very happy if I could have it to say the reading these following lines had filled up the casma[4] of one of your vacant hours. But I must not offend, in endeavouring to excuse my self; I only beg you'll accept this, from your*

Most Faithful, Obedient
Humble Servant,
W. Chetwood[5]

---

1 London's most popular and successful actress from the first decade of the eighteenth century until her death, Anne Oldfield (c. 1683-1730) moved in aristocratic circles as mistress of Brigadier General Charles Churchill (natural son of the Duke of Marlborough's brother); a potentially valuable patron she helped support Richard Savage.

2 Increasingly professionalised, critics were often satirised for their rudeness.

3 Plays were usually altered for performance, and Oldfield improves the original; that is, she is qualified to be a good writer as well as a good-natured critic.

4 Chasm, vacancy; only in a moment of ladylike boredom, the compliment suggests, would so august a figure seek amusement in so humble a work.

5 Haywood's bookseller (i.e., publisher).

# LOVE IN EXCESS;

## OR,

## THE FATAL ENQUIRY.

*Part the First.*

In the late war between the French and the confederate armies,[1] there were two brothers, who had acquired a more than ordinary reputation under the command of the great and intrepid Luxembourgh. But the conclusion of the peace taking away any further occasions of shewing their valour, the eldest of 'em, whose name was Count D'elmont, returned to Paris, from whence he had been absent two years, leaving his brother at St. Omer's, 'till the cure of some slight wounds were perfected.

The fame of the Count's brave actions arrived before him, and he had the satisfaction of being received by the King and Court, after a manner that might gratifie the ambition of the proudest. The beauty of his person, the gaity of his air, and the unequalled charms of his conversation, made him the admiration of both sexes; and whilst those of his own strove which should gain the largest share of his friendship; the other, vented fruitless wishes, and in secret, cursed that custom which forbids women to make a declaration of their thoughts.[2] Amongst the number of these, was Alovisa,[3] a lady descended (by the father's side) from the noble family of D'La Tours formerly Lord of

---

1  The War of the Spanish Succession, which lasted from 1701 until the Treaty of Utrecht in 1713; France, with Bavaria and Spain, opposed a confederation of Britain, Austria, Prussia, Denmark, the Netherlands, and Savoy.
2  Though society expected a woman to attract and marry an eligible man, it forbade her to show interest in a man before he formally declared his wish to marry her; this constraint is an important theme in eighteenth-century novels by women.
3  A version of Eloisa or Eloise, English forms of Héloïse, the name of the medieval woman famous for her tragic love for and separation from her teacher Abelard; the poet Alexander Pope had recently explored her story in a verse epistle, "Eloisa to Abelard" (1717).

Beujey, and (by her mother's) from the equally illustrious house of Montmorency. The late death of her parents had left her co-heiress (with her sister,) of a vast estate.[1]

Aloisa, if her passion was not greater than the rest, her pride, and the good opinion she had of her self, made her the less able to support it; she sighed, she burned, she raged, when she perceived the charming D'elmont behaved himself toward her with no mark of a distinguishing affection. "What," said she, "have I beheld without concern a thousand lovers at my feet, and shall the only man I ever endeavoured or wished to charm, regard me with indifference? Wherefore has the agreeing world joyned with my deceitful glass to flatter me into a vain belief I had invincible attractions? D'elmont sees 'em not, D'elmont is insensible." Then would she fall into ravings, sometimes cursing her own want of power, sometimes the coldness of D'elmont. Many days she passed in these inquietudes, and every time she saw him (which was very frequently either at Court, at church, or publick meetings,) she found fresh matter for her troubled thoughts to work upon. When on any occasion he happened to speak to her, it was with that softness in his eyes, and that engaging tenderness in his voice, as would half persuade her that, that god had touched his heart, which so powerfully had influenced hers;[2] but if a glimmering of such a hope gave her a pleasure inconceivable, how great were the ensuing torments, when she observed, those looks and accents were but the effects of his natural complaisance,[3] and that to whom soever he addressed, he carried an equality in his behaviour, which sufficiently evinced his hour was not yet come to feel those pains he gave; and if the afflicted fair ones found any consolation, it was in the reflection that no triumphant rival could boast a conquest, each now despaired of gaining. But the impatient Alovisa disdaining to be ranked with those, whom her vanity

1   Women were usually under the authority of a father, guardian, or husband; Alovisa and her sister Ansellina combine their wealth and high rank with an atypical freedom to choose for themselves.
2   That the god of love had touched his heart too; in novelists of this period, as in earlier romance, Cupid is a tyrant who enjoys subduing those who resist his power.
3   Not complacency but "civility; desire of pleasing" (Johnson).

made her consider as infinitely her inferiors, suffered her self to be agitated almost to madness between the two extreams of love and indignation; a thousand *chimeras*[1] came into her head, and sometimes prompted her to discover the sentiments she had in his favour. But these resolutions were rejected, almost as soon as formed, and she could not fix on any for a long time; 'till at last, love (ingenious in invention,) inspired her with one, which probably might let her into the secrets of his heart, without the shame of revealing her own.

The celebration of Madam the Dutchess of Burgundy's birth-day being to be solemnized with great magnificence, she writ this *billet* to him on the night before.

To Count D'elmont.

*Resistless as you are in war, you are much more so in love. Here you conquer without making an attack, and we surrender before you summons;*[2] *the law of arms obliges you to show mercy to an yielding enemy, and sure the Court cannot inspire less generous sentiments than the field. The little god lays down his arrows at your feet, confesses your superior power, and begs a friendly treatment; he will appear to you to morrow night at the ball, in the eyes of the most passionate of all his voteresses; search therefore for him in her, in whom (amongst that bright assembly) you would most desire to find him; I am confident you have too much penetration to miss of him, if not byassed by a former inclination, and in that hope, I shall (as patiently as my expectations will let me) support till then, the tedious hours.*

Farewell.

This she sent by a trusty servant, and so disguised, that it was impossible for him to be known, with a strict charge to deliver it to the Count's own hands, and come away before he had read it; the fellow performed her orders exactly, and when the

---

1   Mythological monsters with a lion's head, a goat's body, and a dragon's tail; commonly used (as here) for wild fancies.
2   "To summons" is to summon; Alovisa employs the formal language of legal and military command.

Count who was not a little surprized at the first opening it, asked for the messenger, and commanded he should be stayed; his gentleman[1] (who then was waiting in his chamber,) told him he ran down stairs with all the speed imaginable, immediately on his lordship's receiving it. D'elmont having never experienced the force of love, could not presently comprehend the truth of this adventure; at first he imagined some of his companions had caused this letter to be writ, either to sound his inclinations, or upbraid his little disposition to gallantry; but these cogitations soon gave place to others; and tho' he was not very vain, yet he found it no difficulty to persuade himself to an opinion that it was possible for a lady to distinguish him from other men. Nor did he find any thing so displeasing in that thought as might make him endeavour to repell it; the more he considered his own perfections, the more he was confirmed in his belief, but who to fix it on, he was at a loss as much as ever; he then began to reflect on all the discourses and little railleries that had passed between him and the ladies whom he had conversed with since his arrival, but could find nothing in any of 'em of consequence enough to make him guess at the person. He spent great part of the night in thoughts very different from those he was accustomed to, the joy which naturally rises from the knowledge 'tis in ones power to give it, gave him notions which till then he was a stranger to; he began to consider a mistress as an agreeable, as well as fashionable amusement, and resolved not to be cruel.

In the mean time poor Alovisa was in all the anxiety imaginable, she counted every hour, and thought 'em ages, and at the first dawn of day she rose, and calling up her women,[2] who were amazed to find her so uneasie, she employed 'em in placing her jewels on her cloaths to the best advantage, while she consulted her glass after what manner she should dress, her eyes, the gay, the languishing, the sedate, the commanding, the beseeching air were put on, a thousand times, and, as often rejected; and she had scarce determined which to make use of,

---

1   "The servant who waits about the person of a man of rank" (Johnson).
2   Her personal attendants.

when her page brought her word, some ladies who were going to Court desired her to accompany them; she was too impatient not to be willing to be one of the first, so went immediately, armed with all her lightnings,[1] but full of unsettled reflections. She had not been long in the drawing room, before it grew very full of company, but D'elmont not being amongst 'em, she had her eyes fixed toward the door, expecting every moment to see him enter; but how impossible is it to represent her confusion, when he appeared, leading the young Amena,[2] daughter to Monsieur Sanseverin, a gentleman, who tho' he had a very small estate, and many children, had by a partial indulgence, too common among parents, neglecting the rest, maintained this darling of his heart in all the pomp of quality[3] – The beauty and sweetness of this lady was present death to Alovisa's hopes; she saw, or fancied she saw an unusual joy in her eyes, and dying love in his; disdain, despair, and jealousie at once crowded into her heart, and swelled her almost to bursting; and 'twas no wonder that the violence of such terrible emotions kept her from regarding the discourses of those stood by her, or the devoirs that D'elmont made as he passed by, and at length threw her into a swoon; the ladies ran to her assistance, and her charming rival, being one of her particular acquaintance, shewed an extraordinary assiduity in applying means for her relief; they made what hast they could to get her into another room, and unfasten her robe,[4] but were a great while before they could bring her to her self; and when they did, the shame of having been so disordered in such an assembly, and the fears of their suspecting the occasion, added to her former agonies, and racked her with most terrible revulsions, every one now despairing of her being able to assist at[5] that

---

1 Her charms, compared in the language of gallantry to the lightning of the mythological sky god, Jove.
2 *Amoena* is Latin for "pleasant" or "charming"; the lushly described *amoena* (*loca amoena*, singular *locus amoenus* — "delightful place") of pastoral romance are idealized places of amorous dalliance.
3 The ceremony and display appropriate to high rank.
4 Loosen the ties and stays of her clothing so that she can breathe more freely.
5 To be present at, to attend (French *assister à*).

night's entertainment, she was put into her chair,[1] in order to be carried home; Amena who little thought how unwelcome she was grown, would needs have one called, and accompanyd her thither, in spight of the intreaties of D'elmont, who had before engaged her for his partner in dancing; not that he was in love with her, or at that time believed he could be touched with a passion which he esteemed a trifle in it self, and below the dignity of a man of sense; but Fortune (to whom this lady, no less enamoured than Alovisa, had made a thousand invocations) seemed to have allotted her the glory of his first addresses; she was getting out of her chariot just as he alighted from his, and offering her his hand, he perceived hers trembled, which engaging him to look upon her more earnestly than he was wont, he immediately fancied he saw something of that languishment in her eyes, which the obliging mandate[2] had described. Amena was too lovely to make that belief disagreeable, and he resolved on the beginnings of an amour, without giving himself the trouble of considering the consequences; the evening being extreamly pleasant, he asked if she would not favour him so far as to take a turn or two with him in the palace-garden. She who desired nothing more than such a particular conversation, was not at all backward of complying; he talked to her there for some time in a manner as could leave her no room to doubt he was intirely charmed, and 'twas the air such an entertainment had left on both their faces, as produced those sad effects in the jealous Alovisa. She was no sooner led to her apartment, but she desired to be put to bed, and the good natured Amena, who really had a very great kindness for her, offered to quit the diversions of the ball, and stay with her all night; but unfortunate Alovisa was not in a condition to endure the presence of any, especially her, so put her off as civilly as her anxiety would give her leave, chusing rather to suffer her return to the ball, than retain so hateful an object (as she was now become) in her sight; and 'tis likely the other was

---

1   Her sedan chair, an enclosed chair carried through the streets on poles by two chairmen.
2   The love letter that obliges D'elmont to seek out his admirer.

not much troubled at her refusal. But how, (when left alone, and abandoned to the whirlwinds of her passion,) the desperate Alovisa behaved, none but those, who like her, have burned in hopeless fires can guess, the most lively description would come far short of what she felt; she raved, she tore her hair and face, and in the extremity of her anguish was ready to lay violent hands on her own life. In this tempest of mind, she continued for some time, 'till at length rage beginning to dissipate it self in tears, made way for cooler considerations; and her natural vanity resuming its empire in her soul, was of no little service to her on this occasion. "Why am I thus disturbed? mean spirited as I am!" said she, "D'elmont is ignorant of the sentiments I am possessed with in his favour; and perhaps 'tis only want of incouragement that has so long deprived me of my lover; my letter bore no certain mark by which he might distinguish me, and who knows what arts that creature might make use of to allure him. I will therefore," pursued she, with a more cheerful countenance, "direct his erring search." As she was in this thought, (happily[1] for her, who else might have relapsed,) her women who were waiting in the next room, came in to know if she wanted any thing; "yes," answered she, with a voice and eyes wholly changed; "I'll rise, one of you help me on with my cloaths, and let the other send Charlo to me, I have instant business with him." 'Twas in vain for 'em to represent to her the prejudice it might be to her health to get out of her bed at so unseasonable an hour, it being then just midnight. They knew her too absolute[2] a mistress not to be obeyed, and executed her commands, without disputing the reason. She was no sooner ready, than Charlo was introduced, who being the same person that carried the letter to D'elmont, guessed what affair he was to be concerned in, and shut the door after him. "I commend your caution," said his lady, "for what I now am going to trust you with is of more concernment than my life." The fellow bowed, and made a thousand protestations of an eternal fidelity. "I doubt it not," resumed

---

1  Fortunately, luckily.
2  Tyrannical, like an absolute monarch who tolerates no hesitation or opposition.

she, "go then immediately to the Court, 'tis not impossible but in this hurry you may get into the drawing room; but if not, make some pretence to stay as near it as you can 'till the ball be over; listen carefully to all discourses where you hear Count D'elmont[1] mentioned, enquire who he dances with, and above all watch what company he comes out with, and bring me an exact account. Go," continued she hastily, "these are all the orders I have for you to night, but to morrow I shall employ you farther." Then turning to her *escritore*,[2] she sat down, and began to prepare a second letter, which she hoped would be more lucky than the former. She was not long writing, love, and wit, suggested a world of passionate and agreeable expressions to her in a moment; but when she had finished this so full a discovery[3] of her heart, and was about to sign her name to it, not all that passion which had inspired her with a resolution to scruple nothing that might advance the compassing her wishes, nor the vanity which assured her of success, were forcible enough to withstand the shock it gave her pride; "No, let me rather die!" said she, starting up, and frighted at her own designs, "then be guilty of a meanness which would render me unworthy of life; Oh! heavens, to offer love, and poorly sue for pity! 'tis insupportable! What bewitched me to harbour such a thought as even the vilest of my sex would blush at? To pieces then," added she tearing the paper, "to pieces, with this shameful witness of my folly, my furious desires may be the destruction of my peace, but never of my honour, that shall still attend my name when love and life are fled." She continued in this temper (without being able to compose her self to rest,) till day began to appear, and Charlo returned with news which confirmed her most dreaded suspicions. He told her that he had gained admittance to the drawing room several times, under pretence of delivering messages to some of the ladies; that the whole talk among 'em was, that D'elmont was no longer insensible of beauty; that he observed that gentleman in very partic-

---

1    4th ed.; 1st ed. reads "D'elmont's".
2    Escritoire, a writing desk or table.
3    Revelation. "*Dis*cover" usually means "*un*cover"; discovering a secret is not learning it but revealing it to a third party.

ular conference with Amena, and that he waited on her home in his chariot, her own not being in the way. "I know it," said Alovisa (walking about in a disordered motion) "I did not doubt but that I was undone, and to my other miseries, have that of being aiding to my rival's happiness. Whatever his desires were, he carefully concealed 'em, 'till my cursed letter prompted a discovery; tenacious as I was, and too, too confident of this little beauty!" Here she stopped, and wiping away some tears which in spight of her ran down her cheeks, gave Charlo leave to ask if she had any more commands for him. "Yes," answered she, "I will write once more to this undiscerning man, and let him know, 'tis not Amena that is worthy of him; that I may do without prejudicing my fame, and 'twill be at least some easement to my mind to undeceive the opinion he may have conceived of her wit, for I am almost confident she passes for the authoress of those lines which have been so fatal to me"; in speaking this, without any further thought, she once more took her pen and wrote these words.

To Count D'elmont.

*If ambition[1] be a fault, 'tis only in those who have not a sufficent stock of merit[2] to support it; too much humility is a greater in you, whose person and qualities are too admirable; not to render any attempt you shall make justifiable, as well as successful. Heaven when it distinguished you in so particular a manner from the rest of mankind, designed you not for vulgar conquests, and you cannot without a manifest contradiction to its will, and an irreparable injury to your self, make a present of that heart to Amena, when one, of at least an equal beauty, and far superior in every other consideration, would sacrifice all to purchase the glorious trophy. Continue then no longer in a willful ignorance,*

---

1  The desire for social distinction can dictate marriage to someone of superior rank and fortune; hence the Count's loveless marriage to Alovisa. In Frances Burney's *Evelina* (1778), the heroine's guardian interprets as ambition her desire to visit London (and so to be seen in public places).

2  The individual quality that deserves reward by a social superior — "excellence deserving honour or reward" (Johnson).

*aim at a more exalted flight, and you will find it no difficulty to discover who she is that languishes, and almost dies for an opportunity of confessing (without too great a breach of modesty) that her soul, and all the faculties of it, are, and must be*

Eternally Yours,

This she gave to Charlo, to deliver with the same caution as the former; but he was scarce got out of the house before a new fear assaulted her, and she repented her uncircumspection. "What have I done!" cried she, "who knows but D'elmont may shew these letters to Amena, she is perfectly acquainted with my hand, and I shall be the most exposed and wretched woman, in the world." Thus industrious was she in forming notions to torment her self; nor indeed was there any thing of improbability in this conjecture. There are too many ungenerous enough to boast such an adventure; but D'elmont tho' he would have given good part of his estate to satisfie his curiosity, yet chose rather to remain in a perpetual ignorance, than make use of any means that might be disadvantageous to the ladies reputation. He now perceived his mistake, and that it was not Amena who had taken that method to engage him, and possibly was not disgusted to find she had a rival of such merit, as the letter intimated. However he had said too many fine things to her to be lost, and thought it as inconsistent with his honours inclination to desist a pursuit in which he had all the reason in the world to assure himself of victory; for the young Amena (little versed in the art of dissimulation, so necessary to her sex,) could not conceal the pleasure she took in his addresses and without even a seeming reluctancy had given him a promise of meeting him the next day in the Tuilleries;[1] nor could all his unknown mistress had writ, perswade him to miss this assignation, nor let that be succeeded with another, and that by a third, and so on, 'till by making a shew of tenderness he began to fancy himself really touched with a passion he only designed to represent.[2] 'Tis certain this way of fooling raised

---

1   The Tuileries, a fashionable royal garden in Paris.
2   To imitate.

desires in him little different from what is commonly called love; and made him redouble his attacks in such a manner, as Amena stood in need of all her vertue to resist; but as much as she thought her self obliged to resent such attempts, yet he knew so well how to excuse himself, and lay the blame on the violence of his passion, that he was still too charming, and too dear to her not to be forgiven. Thus was Amena (by her too generous and open temper) brought to the very brink of ruin, and D'elmont was possibly contriving means to compleat it, when her page brought him this letter.

### To Count D'elmont.

*Some malicious persons have endeavoured to make the little con-*
*versation I have had with you, appear as criminal; therefore to*
*put a stop to all such aspersions, I must for the future deny my*
*self the honour of your visits, unless commanded to receive 'em*
*by my father, who only has the power of disposing of*
                                                        Amena.[1]

The consternation he was in at the reading of these lines, so very different from her former behaviour, is more easily imagined than expressed, 'till casting his eyes on the ground, he saw a small note, which in the opening of this, had fallen out of it, which he hastily took up, and found it contained these words.

*I guess the surprize my lovely friend is in, but have not time*
*now to unriddle the mystery; I beg you will be at your lodgings*
*towards the evening, and I will invent a way to send to you.*

'Twas now that D'elmont began to find there were embarrasments[2] in an intriegue of this nature, which he had not foreseen, and stayed at home all day, impatiently expecting the clearing of an affair which at present seemed so ambiguous.

---

1   Only Amena's father can give her away in marriage; to prevent seduction (and disgrace), M. Sanseverin tries to force D'elmont to declare an honorable intention to marry his daughter before he sees her again.
2   "Perplexit[ies]; entanglement[s]" (Johnson).

When it grew a little duskish, his gentleman brought in a young woman, whom he immediately knew to be Anaret, an attendant on Amena; and when he had made her sit down, told her he hoped she was come to make an *eclaircisment*,[1] which would be very obliging to him, and therefore desired she would not defer it.

"My lord," said she, "'tis with an unspeakable trouble I discharge that trust my lady has reposed in me, in giving you a relation of her misfortunes; but not to keep you longer in a suspence, which I perceive is very uneasie to you; I shall acquaint you, that soon after you were gone, my lady came up into her chamber, where as I was preparing to undress her, we heard Monsieur Sanseverin in an angry tone ask where his daughter was? and being told she was above, we immediately saw him enter, with a countenance so enflamed, as put us both in a mortal apprehension. 'An ill use,' said he to her, 'have you made of my indulgence, and the liberty I have allowed you! Could neither the considerations of the honour of your family, your own reputation, nor my eternal repose, deter you from such imprudent actions, as you cannot be ignorant must be the inevitable ruin of 'em all.' My poor lady was too much surprized at these cruel words, to be able to make any answer to 'em, and stood trembling, and almost fainting, while he went on with his discourse. 'Was it consistent with the niceties[2] of your sex,' said he, 'or with the duty you owe me, to receive the addresses of a person whose pretensions I was a stranger to? If the Count D'elmont has any that are honourable, wherefore are they concealed?' 'The Count D'elmont!' cried my lady, more frighted than before, 'never made any declarations to me worthy of your knowledge, nor did I ever entertain him otherwise, than might become your daughter.' ''Tis false,' interrupted he furiously, 'I am but too well informed of the contrary; nor has the most private of your shameful meetings escaped my ears!' Judge, sir, in what a confusion my lady was in at this discourse; 'twas in vain, she mustered all her courage to perswade him

---

1  Clarification, explanation (French *éclaircissement*).
2  Fastidious delicacy.

from giving credit to an intelligence so injurious to her, he grew the more enraged, and after a thousand reproaches, flung out of the room with all the marks of a most violent indignation. But though your lordship is too well acquainted with the mildness of Amena's disposition, not[1] to believe she could bear the displeasure of a father[2] (who had always most tenderly loved her,) with indifference; yet 'tis impossible for you to imagine in what an excess of sorrow she was plunged, she found every passage of her ill conduct (as she was pleased to call it) was betrayed, and did not doubt but whoever had done her that ill office to her father, would take care the discovery should not be confined to him alone. Grief, fear, remorse, and shame by turns assaulted her, and made her incapable of consolation; even the soft pleas of love were silenced by their tumultuous clamours, and for a time she considered your lordship in no other view than that of her undoer." "How!" cried D'elmont (interrupting her) "could my Amena, who I thought all sweetness judge so harshly of me." "Oh! my lord," resumed Anaret, "you must forgive those first emotions, which as violent as they were, wanted but your presence to dissipate in a moment; and if your idea[3] had not presently that power, it lost no honour by having foes to struggle with, since at last it put 'em all to flight, and gained so entire a victory, that before morning, of all her troubles, scarce any but the fears of losing you remained. And I must take the liberty to assure your lordship, my endeavours were not wanting to establish a resolution in her to despise every thing for love and you. But to be as brief as I can in my relation; the night was no sooner gone, than Monsieur her father came into the chamber, with a countenance, tho' more composed than that with which he left us, yet with such an air of austerity, as made my timerous lady lose

---

1   Amena cannot easily bear such displeasure, so the sense seems to require deleting this "not" or adding a second one after "could"; a few complex negative constructions go astray in *Love in Excess*.
2   No matter how tyrannical their fathers, eighteenth-century heroines (and heroes) risk their displeasure reluctantly if at all. Since paternal authority is central to the ideology of a royalist society based on the transmission of land from fathers to eldest sons, defiance of a father's wishes is a shocking transgression.
3   Mental image.

most of the spirit she had assumed for this encounter. 'I come not now Amena,' said he, 'to upbraid or punish your disobedience, if you are not wholly abandoned by your reason, your own reflections will be sufficiently your tormentors. But to put you in a way (if not to clear your fame, yet to take away all occasion of future calumny,) you must write to Count D'elmont.

"'I will have no denials,' continued he (seeing her about to speak,) and leading her to her escritore, constrained her to write what he dictated, and you received; just as she was going to seal it, a servant brought word that a gentleman desired to speak with Monsieur Sansevarin, he was obliged to step into another room, and that absence gave her an opportunity of writing a note, which she dextrously slipped into the letter, unperceived by her father at his return, who little suspecting what she had done, sent it away immediately. 'Now,' said he, 'we shall be able to judge of the sincerity of the Count's affections, but till then I shall take care to prove my self a person not disinterested in the honour of my family.' As he spoke these words, he took her by the hand, and conducting her thro' his own into a little chamber (which he had ordered to be made ready for that purpose) shut her into it; I followed to the door, and seconded my lady in her desires, that I might be permitted to attend her there; but all in vain, he told me, he doubted not but that I had been her confident in this affair, and ordered me to quit his house in a few days. As soon as he was gone out, I went into the garden, and sauntered up and down a good while, hoping to get an opportunity of speaking to my lady thro' the window, for I knew there was one that looked into it; but not seeing her, I bethought me of getting a little stick, with which I knocked gently against the glass, and engaged her to open it. As soon as she perceived me, a beam of joy brightened in her eyes, and glistened thro' her tears. 'Dear Anaret,' said she, 'how kindly do I take this proof of thy affection, 'tis only in thy power to alleviate my misfortunes, and thou I know art come to offer thy assistance.' Then after I had assured her of my willingness to serve her in any command, she desired me to wait on you with an account of all had happened, and to give you her vows of an eternal love. 'My eyes,' said she weeping, 'perhaps may ne'er behold him more, but imagination shall supply that want, and from my heart he never shall be absent.'" "Oh! do not talk thus," cried the Count, extreamly touched at this discourse, "I must, I will see her, nothing shall hold her from me." "You may," answered Anaret, "but then it must be with the approbation of Monsieur Sansevarin, he will be proud to receive you in quality of a suitor to his daughter, and 'tis only to oblige you to a publick declaration that he takes these measures." D'elmont was not perfectly pleased with these words; he was too quick sighted not to perceive immediately what Monsieur Sanseverin drove at, but as well as he liked Amena, found no inclination in himself to marry her, and therefore was not desirous of an explanation of what he resolved not to seem to understand. He walked two or three turns about the room, endeavouring to conceal his disgust,[1] and when he had so well overcome the shock, as to banish all visible tokens of it, "I would willingly," said he coldly, "come into any proper method for the obtaining the person[2] of Amena, as well as her heart; but there are certain reasons for which I cannot make a discovery of my designs to her father, 'till I have first spoken with her." "My lord," replied the subtle Anaret (easily guessing at his meaning) "I wish to heaven there were a possibility of your meeting; there is nothing I would not risque to forward it, and if your lordship can think of any way in which I may be serviceable to you, in this short time I am allowed to stay in the family, I beg you would command me." She spoke this with an air as made the Count believe she really had it in her power to serve him in this occasion, and presently hit on the surest means to bind her to his interest. "You are very obliging," said he, "and I doubt not but your ingenuity is equal to your good nature, therefore will leave the contrivance of my happiness entirely to you; and that you may not think your care bestowed on an ungrateful per-

---

1   "Aversion of the palate from anything" (Johnson). Amena is poor and D'elmont, Alovisa says later, wants to restore his family's depleted fortunes by marrying an heiress.
2   Frequently, as here, the body, "Human Being; considered with respect to mere corporal existence" (Johnson).

son, be pleased," continued he, giving her a purse of Lewis-dor's,[1] "to accept this small earnest of my future friendship." Anaret like most of her function,[2] was too mercinary to resist such a temptation, tho' it had been given her to betray the hon-our of her whole sex; and after a little pause, replied, "Your lordship is too generous to be refused, tho' in a matter of the greatest difficulty, as indeed this is; for in the strict confinement my lady is, I know no way but one, and that extreamly haz-ardous to her; however, I do not fear but my perswasions, joyned with her own desires, will influence her to attempt it. Your lordship knows we have a little door at the farther end of the garden, that opens into the Tuillerys." "I do," cried D'elmont interrupting her, "I have several times parted from my charmer there, when my entreaties have prevailed with her to stay longer with me than she would have the family to take notice of." "I hope to order the matter so," resumed Anaret, "that it shall be the scene this night of a most happy meeting. My lady unknown to her father has the key of it, she can throw it to me from her window, and I can open it to you, who must be walking near it, about twelve or one a clock, for by that time every body will be in bed." "But what will that avail," cried D'elmont hastily; "since she lies within her father's chamber, where 'tis impossible to pass without alarming him." "You lovers are so impatient," rejoyned Anaret smiling, "I never designed you should have entrance there, tho' the window is so low, that a person of your lordship's stature and agility might mount it with a galliard step, but I suppose it will turn to as good an account if your mistress by my assistance gets out of it." "But can she," interrupted he, "will she, dost thou think?" "Fear it not, my lord," replied she, "be but punctual to the hour, Amena shall be yours, if love, wit and opportunity have power to make her so." D'elmont was transported with this promise, and the thoughts of what he expected to possess by her means,

---

1   *Louis d'ors*, French gold coins; as gold rather than the more common copper or sil-ver, they represent a considerable sum.
2   Like most servants. By romance convention and aristocratic prejudice, servants are mercenary beings incapable of the "nobler" or "gentler" feelings typical of the upper classses — nobles, gentlemen and gentlewomen.

raised his imagination to so high a pitch, as he could not forbear kissing and embracing her with such raptures as might not have been very pleasing to Amena, had she been witness of 'em. But Anaret who had other things in her head than gallantry, disengaged her self from him as soon as she could, taking more satisfaction in forwarding an affair in which she proposed so much advantage, than in the caresses of the most accomplished gentleman in the world.

When she came home she found every thing as she could wish, Monsieur abroad, and his daughter at the window, impatiently watching her return; she told her as much of the discourse she had with the Count as she thought proper, extolling his love and constancy, and carefully concealing all she thought might give an umbrage to her vertue. But in spight of all the artifice she made use of, she found it no easie matter to perswade her to get out of the window; the fears she had of being discovered, and more exposed to her father's indignation, and the censure of the world, damped her inclinations, and made her deaf to the eager solicitations of this unfaithful woman. As they were disputing, some of the servants hap'ning to come into the garden, obliged 'em to break off, and Anaret retired not totally despairing of compassing her designs, when the appointed hour should arrive, and Amena should know the darling object of her wishes was so near. Nor did her hopes deceive her, the resolutions of a lover, when made against the interest of the person beloved, are but of a short duration; and this unhappy fair was no sooner left alone, and had leisure to contemplate on the graces of the charming D'elmont, but love plaid his part with such success, as made her repent she had chid Anaret for her proposal, and wished for nothing more than an opportunity to tell her so. She passed several hours in disquietudes she had never known before, till at last she heard her father come into the next room to go to bed, and soon after somebody knocked softly at the window, she immediately opened it, and perceived by the light of the moon which then shone very bright, that it was Anaret, she had not patience to listen to the long speech the other had prepared to perswade her, but putting her head as far as she could to prevent being heard by her father, "Well Anaret," said she, "where is this adventrous lover, what is it he requires of me?" "Oh! madam," replied she, overjoyed at the compliable humour she found her in, "he is now at the garden door, there's nothing wanting but your key to give him entrance; what farther he requests himself shall tell you," "Oh heavens!" cried Amena searching her pockets, and finding she had it not; "I am undone, I have left it in my cabinet in the chamber where I used to lie." These words made Anaret at her wits end, she knew there was no possibility of fetching it, there being so many rooms to go thro'; she ran to the door, and endeavoured to push back the lock, but had not strength; she then knew not what to do, she was sure D'elmont was on the other side, and feared he would resent this usage to the disappointment of all her mercenary hopes, and durst not call to acquaint him with this misfortune for fear of being heard. As for Amena, she now was more sensible than ever of the violence of her inclinations, by the extream vexation this disappointment gave her. Never did people pass a night in greater uneasiness, than these three; the Count who was naturally impatient could not bear a balk of this nature without the utmost chagrin.[1] Amena languished, and Anaret fretted to death, tho' she resolved to leave no stone unturned to set all right again. Early in the morning she went to his lodgings, and found him in a very ill humour, but she easily pacified him, by representing with a great deal of real grief, the accident that retarded his happiness, and assuring him there was nothing could hinder the fulfilling it the next night.[2] When she had gained this point, she came home, and got the key into her possession, but could not get an opportunity all day of speaking to her lady, Monsieur Sanseverin did not stir out of doors, and spent most of it with his daughter; in his discourse to her, he set the passion the Count had for her in so true a light, that it made a very great alteration in her sentiments, and she began to reflect on the condescensions she had given a man who had

---

1    "Ill humour; vexation; fretfulness; peevishness" (Johnson); also spelled *chagreen* and pronounced to rhyme with *machine*.
2    4th ed.; 1st ed. reads "... fulfilling it. The next night, when ...."

never so much as mentioned marriage to her with so much shame, as almost overwhelmed her love, and she was now determined never to see him, till he should declare himself to her father in such a manner as would be for her honour.

In the mean time Anaret waited with a great deal of impatience for the family going to bed; and as soon as all was hush, ran to give the Count admittance; and leaving him in an alley on the farther side of the garden, made the accustomed sign at the window. Amena presently opened it, but instead of staying to hear what she would say, threw a letter out, "Carry that," said she, "to Count D'elmont, let him know the contents of it are wholly the result of my own reason. And as for your part, I charge you trouble me no further on this subject"; then shutting the casement hastily, left Anaret in a strange consternation at this suddain change of her humour; however she made no delay, but running to the place where the Count waited her return, delivered him the letter, but advised him (who was ready enough of himself) not to obey any commands might be given him to the hindrance of his designs. The moon was then at the full, and gave so clear a light, that he easily found it contained these words.

To Count D'elmont.

*Too many proofs have I given you of my weakness, not to make you think me incapable of forming or keeping any resolution to the prejudice of that passion you have inspired me with. But know, thou undoer of my quiet, tho' I have loved and still do love you with a tenderness, which I fear will be unvanquishable; yet I will rather suffer my life, than my virtue to become its prey. Press me then no more I conjure you to such dangerous interviews, in which I dare neither trust my self, nor you; if you believe me worthy your real regard, the way thro' honour is open to receive you; religion, reason, modesty, and obedience forbid the rest.*

Farewel.

D'elmont knew the power he had over her too well, to be

much discouraged at what he read, and after a little consultation with Anaret, they concluded he should go to speak to her, as being the best sollicitor in his own cause. As he came down the walk Amena saw him thro' the glass, and the sight of that beloved object, bringing a thousand past endearments to her memory, made her incapable of retiring from the window, and she remained in a languishing and immoveable posture, leaning her head against the shutter, 'till he drew near enough to discern she saw him. He took this for no ill omen, and instead of falling on his knees at an humble distance, as some romantick lovers would have done, redoubled his pace, and love and fortune which on this occasion were resolved to befriend him, presented to his view a large rolling-stone[1] which the gard'ner had accidentally left there; the iron-work that held it was very high, and strong enough to bear a much greater weight than his, so he made no more to do, but getting on the top of it, was almost to the waste above the bottom of the casement. This was a strange trial, for had she been less in love, good manners would have obliged her to open it; however she retained so much of her former resolution as to conjure him to be gone, and not expose her to such hazards; that if her father should come to know she held any clandestine correspondence with him, after the commands he had given her, she were utterly undone, and that he never must expect any condescensions[2] from her, without being first allowed by him. D'elmont, tho' he was a little startled to find her so much more mistress of her temper than he believed she could be, yet resolved to make all possible use of this opportunity, which probably might be the last he should ever have, looked on her as she spoke, with eyes so piercing, so sparkling with desire accompanied with so bewitching softness, as might have thawed the most frozen reservedness, and on the melting soul stamped love's impression. 'Tis certain they were too irresistible to be long with-

---

1  A garden roller, a "heavy stone used to level walks" (Johnson, "roller").

2  In Haywood's rank-conscious society, condescension was often attractive, a superior's willingness to dispense with the forms due to her or his rank. But Amena has only the superiority of the courted mistress, not D'elmont's real social power, and her freedom encourages a dangerous intimacy.

stood, and putting an end to Amena's grave remonstrances, gave him leave to reply to 'em in this manner. "Why my life, my angel," said he, "my everlasting treasure of my soul, should these objections now be raised? how can you say you have given me your heart; nay, own you think me worthy that inestimable jewel, yet dare not trust your person with me a few hours. What have you to fear from your adoring slave, I want but to convince you how much I am so, by a thousand yet uninvented vows." "They may be spared," cried Amena, hastily interrupting him, "one declaration to my father, is all the proof that he or I demands of your sincerity." "Oh! thou inhuman and tyrannick charmer," answered he (seizing her hand, and eagerly kissing it) "I doubt not but your faithful Anaret has told you, that I could not without the highest imprudence presently discover the passion I have for you to the world." "I have, my lord," said that cunning wench who stood near him, "and that 'twas only to acquaint her with the reasons why for some time you would have it a secret, that you so much desired to speak with her." "Besides," rejoyned the Count, "consider my angel how much more hazardous it is for you to hold discourse with me here, than at a farther distance from your father; your denying to go with me is the only way to make your fears prove true; his jealousie of you may possibly make him more wakeful than ordinary, and we are not sure but that this minute he may tear you from my arms; whereas if you suffer me to bear you hence, if he should happen to come even to your door, and hear no noise, he will believe you sleeping, and return to his bed well satisfied." With these and the like arguments she was at last overcome, and with the assistance of Anaret, he easily lifted her down. But this rash action, so contrary to the resolution she thought her self a few moments before[1] so fixed in, made such a confusion in her mind, as rendered her insensible for some time of all he said to her. They made what hast they could into the Tuilleries; and D'elmont having placed her on one of the most pleasant seats, was resolved to loose no time, and having given her some reasons for his not addressing to her father;

---

1    4th ed.; 1st ed. reads "before a few moments before."

which tho' weak in themselves, were easily believed by a heart so willing to be deceived as hers, he began to press for a greater confirmation of her affection than words; and 'twas now this inconsiderate[1] lady found her self in the greatest strait she had ever yet been in; all nature seemed to favour his design, the pleasantness of the place, the silence of the night, the sweetness of the air, perfumed with a thousand various odours wafted by gentle breezes from adjacent gardens compleated the most delightful scene that ever was, to offer up a sacrifice to love; not a breath but flew winged with desire, and sent soft thrilling wishes to the soul; Cynthia[2] her self, cold as she is reported, assisted in the inspiration, and sometimes shone with all her brightness, as it were to feast their ravished eyes with gazing on each others beauty; then veiled her beams in clouds, to give the lover boldness, and hide the virgins blushes. What now could poor Amena do, surrounded with so many powers, attacked by such a charming force without, betrayed by tenderness within? Vertue and pride, the guardians of her honour fled from her breast, and left her to her foe, only a modest bashfulness remained, which for a time made some defence, but with such weakness as a lover less impatient than D'elmont would have little regarded. The heat of the weather, and her confinement having hindred her from dressing that day, she had only a thin silk night gown on, which flying open as he caught her in his arms, he found her panting heart beat measures of consent, her heaving breast swell to be pressed by his, and every pulse confess a wish to yield; her spirits all dissolved sunk in a lethargy of love, her snowy arms unknowing grasped his neck, her lips met his half way, and trembled at the touch; in fine, there was but a moment betwixt her and ruine; when the tread of some body coming hastily down the walk, obliged the half-blessed pair to put a stop to farther endearments. It was Anaret who having been left centinel in the garden, in order to open the door when her lady should return, had seen lights in every room in

---

1  "Careless; thoughtless; negligent; inattentive; inadvertent" (Johnson).
2  The moon, from a classical name for the moon goddess; "cold" because the moon goddess was traditionally a virgin.

the house, and heard great confusion, so ran immediately to give 'em notice of this misfortune. These dreadful tidings soon roused Amena from her dream of happiness, she accused the influence of her amorous stars, upbraided Anaret, and blamed the Count in terms little differing from distraction, and 'twas as much as both of 'em could do to perswade her to be calm. However, 'twas concluded that Anaret should go back to the house, and return to 'em again, as soon as she had learned what accident had occasioned this disturbance. The lovers had now a second opportunity, if either of 'em had been inclined to make use of it, but their sentiments were entirely changed with this alarm; Amena's thoughts were wholly taken up with her approaching shame, and vowed she would rather die than ever come into her father's presence, if it were true that she was missed; the Count who wanted not good nature, seriously reflecting on the misfortunes he was likely to bring on a young lady who tenderly loved him, gave him a great deal of real remorse, and the consideration that he should be necessitated, either to own an injurious design, or come into measures for the clearing of it, which would in no way agree with his ambition, made him extreamly pensive, and wish Amena again in her chamber, more earnestly than ever he had done to get her out of it, they both remained in a profound silence, impatiently waiting the approach of Anaret; but she not coming as they expected, and the night wearing away apace, very much encreased the trouble they were in; at length the Count after revolving a thousand inventions in his mind advised to walk toward the garden and see whether the door was yet open. "'Tis beter for you, madam," said he, "whatsoever has happened, to be found in your own garden, than in any place with me." Amena complied, and suffered her self to be led thither, trembling and ready to sink with fear and grief at every step; but when they found all fast, and that there was no hopes of getting entrance, she fell quite senseless, and without any signs of life at her lover's feet; he was strangely at a loss what to do with her, and made a thousand vows, if he got clear of this adventure, never to embark in another of this nature; he was little skilled in proper means to recover her, and 'twas more to her youth and the goodness of her constitution that she owed the return of her[1] senses, than his aukward endeavours; when she revived, the piteous lamentations she made, and the perplexity he was in how to dispose of her, was very near reducing him to as bad a condition as she had been in; his never 'till now having had occasion for a confident, rendered him so unhappy[2] as not to know any one person at whose house he could with any convenience trust her and to carry her to that where he had lodgings was the way to be made the talk of all Paris. He asked her several times if she would not command him to wait on her to some place where she might remain free from censure till she heard from her father, but could get no answer but upbraidings from her. So making a virtue of necessity, he was obliged to take her in his arms, with a design to bring her (tho' much against his inclinations) to his own apartment. As he was going thro' a very fair street which led to that in which he lived, Amena cried out with a sort of joy, "loose me my lord, I see a light in yonder house, the lady of it is my dearest friend, she has power with my father, and if I beg her protection, I doubt not but she will afford it me, and perhaps find some way to mitigate my misfortunes"; the Count was overjoyed to be eased of his fair burthen, and setting her down at the gate was preparing to take his leave with an indifference, which was but too visible to the afflicted lady. "I see, my lord" said she, "the pleasure you take in getting rid of me, exceeds the trouble for the ruine you have brought upon me; but go, I hope I shall resent this usage as I ought, and that I may be the better enabled to do so, I desire you to return the letter I writ this fatal night; the resolution it contained will serve me to remind me of my shameful breach of it."

"Madam," answered he coldly, but with great complaisance, "you have said enough to make a lover less obedient refuse; but because I am sensible of the accidents that happen to letters, and to shew that I can never be repugnant even to the most rigorous of your commands, I shall make no scruple in fulfilling

---

1    4th ed.; 1st ed. reads "his."
2    Unfortunate.

this, and trust to your goodness for the re-settling me in your esteem, when next you make me so happy as to see you." The formality of this compliment touched her to the quick, and the thought of what she was like to suffer on his account, filled her with so just an anger, that as soon as she got the letter, she knocked hastily at the gate, which being immediately opened, broke off any farther discourse, she went in, and he departed to his lodging, ruminating on every circumstance of this affair, and consulting with himself how he should proceed. Alovisa (for it was her house which Amena by a whimsical effect of chance had made choice of for her sanctuary) was no sooner told her rival was come to speak with her, but she fell into all the raptures that successful malice could inspire, she was already informed of part of this night's adventur for the cunning Charlo who by her orders had been a diligent spy on Count D'elmont's actions, and as constant an attendant on him as his shadow, had watched him to Monsieur Sanseverin's garden, seen him enter, and afterwards come with Amena into the Tuillerys, where perceiving 'em seated, ran home and brought his lady an account; rage, jealousie and envy working their usual effects in her, at this news, made her promise the fellow infinite rewards if he would invent some stratagem to seperate 'em, which he undertaking to do, occasioned her being up so late, impatiently waiting his return; she went down to receive her with great civility, mixed with a feigned surprize to see her at such an hour, and in such a dishabilee,[1] which the other answering ingeniously, and freely letting her into the whole secret, not only of her amour, but the coldness she observed in D'elmont's behaviour at parting, filled this cruel woman with so exquisite a joy as she was hardly capable of dissembling; therefore to get liberty to indulge it, and to learn the rest of the particulars of Charlo, who she heard was come in, she told Amena she would have her go to bed, and endeavour to compose her self, and that she would send for Monsieur Sanseverin in the morning, and endeavour to reconcile him to her. "I will also," added she with a deceitful smile, "see the Count D'el-

---

1   Dishabille (French *déshabillé*), "Undress; loose dress" (Johnson).

mont, and talk to him in a manner as shall make him truly sensible of his happiness; nay, so far my friendship shall extend, that if there be any real cause for making your amour a secret, he shall see you at my house, and pass for a visitor of mine; I have no body to whom I need to be accountable for my actions, and am above the censures of the world." Amena thanked her in terms full of gratitude, and went with the maid, whom Alovisa had ordered to conduct her to a chamber prepared for her; as soon as she had got rid of her, she called for Charlo, impatient to hear by what contrivance this lucky chance had befallen her. "Madam," said he, "tho' I formed a thousand inventions, I found not any so plausible, as to alarm Monsieur Sanseverin's family, with an outcry of fire. Therefore I rang the bell at the fore-gate of the house, and bellowed in the most terrible accent I could possible turn my voice to, 'Fire, fire, rise or you will all be burnt in your beds.' I had not repeated this many times, before I found the effect I wished; the noises I heard, and the lights I saw in the rooms, assured me there were no sleepers left; then I ran to the Tuilliers, designing to observe the lover's proceedings, but I found they were apprized of the danger they were in of being discovered, and were coming to endeavour an entrance into the garden." "I know the rest," interrupted Alovisa, "the event has answered even beyond my wishes, and thy reward for this good service shall be greater than thy expectations." As she said these words she retired to her chamber, more satisfied than she had been for many months. Quite different did poor Amena pass the night, for besides the grief of having disobliged her father, banished her self his house, and exposed her reputation to the unavoidable censures of the unpitying world; for an ungrateful, or at best an indifferent lover. She received a vast addition of afflictions, when taking out the letter which D'elmont had given her at parting, possible to weep over it; and accuse her self for so inconsiderately breaking the noble resolution it contained. She found it was Alovisa's hand, for the Count by mistake had given her the second he received from that lady, instead of that she desired him to return. Never was surprize, confusion, and dispair, at such a height, as in Amena's soul at this discovery; she was now assured by what she read, that she had fled for protection to the very person she ought most to have avoided; that she had made a confident of her greatest enemy, a rival dangerous to her hopes in every circumstance. She considered the high birth and vast possessions that Alovisa was mistress of, in opposition to her father's scanted power of making her a fortune. Her wit and subtilty against her innocence and simplicity; her pride, and the respect her grandeur commanded from the world, against her own deplored and wretched state, and looked upon her self as wholly lost. The violence of her sorrow is more easily imagined than expressed; but of all her melancholy reflections, none racked her equal to the belief she had that D'elmont was not unsensible by this time whom the letter came from, and had only made a court to her to amuse himself a while, and then suffer her to fall a sacrifice to his ambition, and feed the vanity of her rival; a just indignation now opened the eyes of her understanding, and considering all the passages of the Count's behaviour, she saw a thousand things which told her, his designs on her were far unworthy of the name of love. None that were ever touched with the least of those passions which agitated the soul of Amena, can believe they would permit sleep to enter her eyes. But if grief and distraction kept her from repose; Alovisa had too much business on her hands to enjoy much more. She had promised Amena to send for her father, and the Count, and found there were not too many moments before morning, to contrive so many different forms of behaviour, as should deceive 'em all three, compleat the ruin of her rival, and engage the addresses of her lover; as soon as she thought it a proper hour, she dispatched a messenger to Count D'elmont, and another to Monsieur Sanseverin, who full of sorrow as he was, immediately obeyed her summons. She received him in her dressing-room, and with a great deal of feigned trouble in her countenance, accosted him in this manner. "How hard is it," said she, "to dissemble grief, and in spite of all the care which I doubt not you have taken to conceal it, in consideration of your own and daughter's honour. I too plainly perceive it in your face to imagine that my own is hid." "How, madam," cried the impatient father, (then giving a loose to his tears) "are you acquainted then with my misfortune?" "Alas," answered she, "I fear by the consequences you have been the last to whom it has been revealed. I hoped that my advice, and the daily proofs the Count gave your daughter of the little regard he had for her, might have fired her to a generous disdain, and have a thousand pardons to ask of you for breach of friendship, in concealing an affair so requisite you should have known." "Oh! madam," resumed he, interrupting her, "I conjure you make no apologies for what is past, I know too well the greatness of your goodness, and the favour you have always been pleased to honour her with, not to be assured she was happy[1] in your esteem, and only beg I may no longer be kept in ignorance of the fatal secret." "You shall be informed of all," said she, "but then you must promise me to act by my advice"; which he having promised, she told him after what manner Amena came to her house, the coldness the Count expressed to her, and the violence of her passion for him. "Now," said she, "if you should suffer your rage to break out in any publick manner against the Count, it will only serve to make your daughters dishonour the table-talk of all Paris. He is too great at Court, and has too many friends to be compelled to any terms for your satisfaction; besides, the least noise might make him discover by what means he first became acquainted with her, and her excessive, I will not say troublesom fondness of him, since which should he do, the shame would be wholly her's, for few would condemn him for accepting the offered caresses of a lady so young and beautiful as Amena." "But is it possible," cried he (quite confounded at these words) "that she should stoop so low to offer love. Oh heavens! is this the effect of all my prayers, my care, and my indulgence." "Doubt not," resumed Alovisa, "of the truth of what I say, I have it from her self, and to convince you it is so, I shall inform you of something I had forgot before." Then she told him of the note she had slipped into the letter he had forced her to write, and of sending Anaret to his lodgings, which she heightned with all the aggravating circumstances her wit and malice could sug-

---

1   "Lucky; successful; fortunate" (Johnson).

gest; till the old man believing all she said as an oracle, was almost senseless between grief and anger; but the latter growing rather the most predominant, he vowed to punish her in such a manner as should deter all children from disobedience. "Now," said Alovisa, "it is, that I expect the performance of your promise; these threats avail but little to the retrieving your daughter's reputation,[1] or your quiet; be therefore perswaded to make no words of it, compose your countenance as much as possible to serenity, and think if you have no friend in any monastry where you could send her till this discourse, and her own foolish folly be blown over. If you have not, I can recommend you to one at St. Dennis where the abbess is my near relation, and on my letter will use her with all imaginable tenderness." Monsieur was extreamly pleased at this proposal, and gave her those thanks the seeming kindness of her offer deserved. "I would not," resumed she, "have you take her home, or see her before she goes; or if you do, not till all things are ready for her departure, for I know she will be prodigal of her promises of amendment, 'till she has prevailed with your fatherly indulgence to permit her stay at Paris, and know as well she will not have the power to keep 'em in the same town with the Count. She shall if you please, remain concealed in my house, 'till you have provided for her journey, and it will be a great means to put a stop to any farther reflections the malicious may make on her; if you give out she is already gone to some relations in the country." As she was speaking, Charlo came to acquaint her, one was come to visit her. She made no doubt but 'twas D'elmont, therefore hastned away Monsieur Sanseverin, after having fixed him in a resolution to do every thing as she advised. It was indeed Count D'elmont that was come, which as soon as she was assured of, she threw off her dejected and mournful air, and assumed one all gaity and good humour, dimpled her mouth with smiles, and called the laughing cupids to her eyes.

"My lord," said she, "you do well by this early visit to

---

1  Amena has compromised her public character or reputation by meeting a man privately and openly professing her love.

retrieve your sexes drooping fame of constancy, and prove the nicety of Amena's discernment in conferring favours on a person, who to his other excellent qualifications, has that of assiduity to deserve them"; as he was about to reply, the rush of somebody coming hastily down the stairs which faced the room they were in, obliged 'em to turn that way. It was the unfortunate Amena, who not being able to endure the thoughts of staying in her rivals house, distracted with her griefs, and not regarding what should become of her, as soon as she heard the doors were open, was preparing to fly from that detested place. Alovisa was vexed to the heart at sight of her, hoping to have had some discourse with the Count before they met; but she dissembled it, and catching hold of her as she was endeavouring to pass, asked where she was going, and what occasioned the disorder she observed in her. "I go," answered Amena, "from a false lover, and a falser friend, but why should I upbraid you," continued she looking wildly sometimes on the Count, and sometimes on Alovisa, "Treacherous pair, you know too well each others baseness, and my wrongs, no longer then, detain a wretch whose presence, had you the least sense of honour, gratitude, or even common humanity, would fill your consciences with remorse and shame; and who has now no other wish, than that of shunning you for ever." As she spoke this, she strugled to get loose from Alovisa's arms, who, in spite of the amazement she was in, still held her. D'elmont was no less confounded, and intirely ignorant of the meaning of what he heard, was at a loss how to reply, 'till she resumed her reproaches in this manner. "Why ye monsters of barbarity," said she, "do you delight in beholding the ruins you have made? Is not the knowledge of my miseries, my everlasting miseries sufficient to content you? And must I be debarred that only remedy for woes like mine? Death! Oh cruel return for all my love, my friendship! and the confidence I reposed in you. Oh! to what am I reduced by my too soft and easie nature, hard fate of tenderness, which healing others, only wounds it's self. – Just heavens! – " here such stopped the violence of her resentment endeavouring to vent it self in sighs, rose in her breast with such an impetuosity as choaked the passage of her words, and she fell in a swoon, tho' the Count, and Alovisa were both in the greatest consternation imaginable, yet neither of 'em were negligent in trying to recover her; as they were busied about her, that fatal letter which had been the cause of this disturbance, fell out of her bosom, and both being eager to take it up (believing it might make some discovery) had their hands on it at the same time; it was but slightly folded, and immediately shewed 'em from what sourse Amena's dispair proceeded. Her upbraidings of Alovisa, and the blushes and confusion which he observed in that ladies face, as soon as ever she saw it opened, put an end to the mistery, and one less quick of apprehension then D'elmont, would have made no difficulty in finding his unknown admirer in the person of Alovisa. She to conceal the disorder she was in at this adventure, as much as possible, called her women, and ordered 'em to convey Amena into an other chamber where there was more air; as she was preparing to follow turning a little towards the Count, but still extreamly confused, "you'l pardon, me, my lord," said she, "if my concern for my friend obliges me to leave you." "Ah madam," replied he, "forbear to make any apologies to me, rather summon all your goodness to forgive a wretch so blind to happiness as I have been." She either could not, or would not make any answer to these words, but seeming as tho' she heard 'em not went hastily into the room where Amena was, leaving the Count full of various, and confused reflections; the sweetness of his disposition made him regret his being the author of Amena's misfortunes, but how miserable is that womans condition, who by her mismanagement is reduced to so poor a comfort as the pity of her lover; that sex is generally too gay, to continue long uneasie, and there was little likelihood he could be capable of lamenting ills which his small acquaintance with the passion from which they sprang, made him not comprehend. The pleasure the discovery gave him of a secret, he had so long desired to find out, kept him from being too much concerned at the adventure that occasioned it, but he could not forbear accusing himself of intollerable stupidity, when he considered the passages of Alovisa's behaviour, her swooning at the ball, her constant glances, her frequent blushes when he talked to her, and all his cogitations whether on Alovisa or Amena, were mingled with a wonder that love should have such power. The diversity of his thoughts would have entertained him much longer, if they had not been interrupted by his page, who came in a great hurry, to acquaint him, that his brother the young Chevalier Brillian was just come to town, and waited with impatience for his coming home; as much a stranger as D'elmont was to the affairs of love, he was none to those of friendship, and making no doubt but that the former ought to yield to the latter in every respect, contented himself with telling one of Alovisa's servants, as he went out, that he would wait on her in the evening, and made what hast he could to give his beloved brother the welcome he expected after so long an absence, and indeed the manner of their meeting expressed a most intire and sincere affection on both sides; the Chevalier was but a year younger than the Count, they had been bred together from their infancy, and there was such a simpathy in their souls, and so great a resemblance in their persons, as very much contributed to endear 'em to each other with a tenderness far beyond that which is ordinarily found among relations. After the first testimonies of it were over, D'elmont began to question him how he had past his time since their separation, and to give him some little reproaches for not writing so often as he might have expected. "Alas! my dearest brother," replied the Chevalier, "such various adventures have hap'ned to me since we parted, as when I relate 'em will I hope excuse my seeming negligence"; these words were accompanied with sighs, and a melancholly air immediately overspreading his face, and taking away great part of the vivacity, which lately sparkled in his eyes, raised an impatient desire in the Count to know the reason of it, which, when he had exprest, the other, (after having engaged him that whatever causes he might find to ridicule his folly, he would suspend all appearance of it, 'till the end of his narration) began to satisfie in this manner.

## The Story of the Chevalier Brillian.

"At St. Omers where you left me, I hapned to make an acquaintance with one Monsieur Bellpine a gentleman, who was there on some business; we being both pretty much strangers in the place occasioned an intimacy between us, which the disparity of our tempers, would have prevented our commencing at Paris, but you know I was never a lover of solitude, and for want of company more agreeable, was willing to encourage his. He was indeed so obliging as to stay longer at St. Omers then his affairs required, purposely to engage me to make Amiens in my way to Paris. He was very vain, and fancying himself happy in the esteem of the fair sex, was desirous I should be witness to the favours they bestowed on him. Among the number of those he used to talk of, was Madamoiselle Ansellina De La Tour, a Parisian lady, and heiress of a great estate, but had been some time at Amiens, with Madam the Baroness de Beronville her god-mother. The wonders he told me of this young ladies wit, and beauty, inclined me to a desire of seeing her, and as soon as I was in a condition to travel, we took our way towards Amiens; he used me with all the friendship he was capable of expressing, and soon after we arrived, carried me to the Baronesses. But oh heavens! how great was my astonishment when I found Ansellina as far beyond his faint description, as the sun beams the imitation of art; besides the regularity of her features, the delicacy of her complexion, and the just simmetry of her whole composition, she has an undiscribable sweetness that plays about her eyes, and mouth, and softens all her air. But all her charms dazling as they are would have lost their captivating force on me if I had believed her capable of that weakness for Bellpine that his vanity would have made me think. She is very young and gay, and I easily perceived she suffered his addresses more out of diversion then any real regard she had for him; he held a constant correspondence at Paris, and was continually furnished with every thing that was *novel*, and by that means introduced himself into many companies who else would not have endured him; but when at any time I was so happy as to entertain the lovely Ansellina alone, and we had opportunity for serious discourse, (which was impossible in his company) I found that she was mistress of a wit, poynant enough to be satyrical, yet it was accompanied with a discretion as very much heightened her charms, and compleated the conquest that her eyes begun. I will confess to you brother that I became so devoted to my passion that I had no leisure for any other sentiments. Fears, hopes, anxieties, jealous pains, uneasie pleasures, all the artillery of love, were garrisoned in my heart, and a thousand various half formed resolutions filled my head. Ansellina's insensibility among a crowd of admirers, and the disparity of our fortunes would have given me just causes of dispair, if the generosity of her temper had not disipated the one, and her youth, and the hope her hour was not yet come, the other. I was often about letting her know the power she had over me, but something of an awe which none but those who truly love can guess at, still prevented my being able to utter it, and I believe should have languished 'till this moment in an unavailing silence, if an accident had not hap'ned to embolden me. I went one day to visit my adorable, and being told she was in the garden, went thither in hopes to see her, but being deceived in my expectation, believed the servant who gave me that information was mistaken, and fancying she might be retired to her closet[1] as she very often did in the afternoon, and the pleasantness of the place inducing me to stay there till she was willing to admit me, I sat down at the foot of a Diana,[2] curiously carved in marble, and full of melancholly reflections without knowing what I did, took a black lead pen[3] out of my pocket, and writ on the pedestal these two lines.

> Hopeless, and silent, I must still adore,
> Her heart's more hard than stone whom I'd implore.

---

1   "A small room of privacy and retirement" (Johnson).
2   A statue of Diana, the virgin moon goddess of classical mythology in her most familiar — and formidable — guise as a wilderness hunter.
3   A pencil; a slip of graphite, it would be wrapped or carried in a "port-craion," a four- or five-inch wooden case with a spring and button for holding and moving the graphite. (In Haywood's day, the word "pencil" described a fine brush.)

"I had scarce finished 'em, when I perceived Ansellina at a good distance from me, coming out of a little close arbor; the respect I had for her, made me fear she should know I was the author of 'em, and guess what I found I had not gained courage enough to tell her. I went out of the alley as I imagined unseen, and designed to come up another, and meet her, before she could get into the house. But tho' I walked prety fast, she had left the place before I could attain it; and in her stead, (casting my eyes toward the statue with an intention to rub out what I had writ) I found this addition to it.

> You wrong your love, while you conceal your pain,
> Stones will dissolve with constant drops of rain.

"But, my dear brother, if you are yet insensible of the wonderful effects of love, you will not be able to imagine what I felt at this view; I was satisfied it could be writ by no body but Anselina, there being no other person in the garden, and knew as well she could not design that encouragement for any other man, because on many occasions she had seen my hand; and the day before had written a song for her, which she desired to learn, with that very pen I now had made use of; and going hastily away at the sight of her, had forgot to take with me. I gazed upon the dear obliging characters, and kissed the marble which contained 'em a thousand times before I could find in my heart to efface 'em; as I was in this agreeable amazement, I heard Belpine's voice calling to me as he came up the walk, which obliged me to put an end to it, and the object which occasioned it. He had been told as well as I, that Ansellina was in the garden, and expressing some wonder to see me alone, asked where she was. I answered him with a great deal of real truth, that I knew not, and that I had been there for some time, but had not been so happy as to entertain her. He seemed not to give credit to what I said, and began to use me after a fashion as would have much more astonished me from any other person. 'I would not have you,' said he, 'be concerned at what I am about to say, because you are one of those for whom I am willing to preserve a friendship; and to convince you of my sincerity, give you leave to address after what manner you please to any of the ladies with whom I have brought you acquainted, excepting Ansellina. But I take this opportunity to let you know I have already made choice of her, with a design of marriage, and from this time forward, shall look on any visits you shall make to her, as injurious to my pretensions.' Tho' I was no stranger to the vanity and insolence of Bellpine's humour, yet not being accustomed to such arbitrary kind of treatment, had certainly resented it, (if we had been in any other place) in a very different manner than I did, but[1] the consideration that to make a noise there, would be a reflection rather than a vindication on Ansellina's fame; I contented my self with telling him, he might be perfectly easie, that whatever qualifications the lady might have that should encourage his addresses, I should never give her any reason to boast a conquest over me. These words might have born two interpretations, if the disdainful air with which I spoke 'em, and which I could not dissemble, and my going immediately away, had not made him take 'em as they were really designed, to affront him. He was full of indignation and jealousie, (if it is possible for a person to be touched with that passion, who is not capable of the other, which generally occasions it) but however having taken it into his head to imagine I was better received by Ansellina than he desired, envy, and a sort of womanish spleen, transported him so far as to go to Ansellina's apartment, and rail at me most profusely (as I have since been told) and threaten how much he'd be revenged, if he heard I ever should have the assurance to visit there again. Ansellina at first laughed at his folly, but finding he persisted, and began to assume more liberty than she ever meant to afford him; instead of listning to his entreaties, to forbid me the privilege I had enjoyed of her conversation, she passed that very sentence on him, and when next I waited of her, received me with more respect than ever; and when at last I took the boldness to acquaint her with my passion, I had the

---

1   Brillian's concern for Ansellina is clearer than his syntax: "had ... resented it ... but [for] the consideration that ...;" or "but [upon] the consideration that ..., I contented my self ...."

satisfaction to observe from the frankness of her disposition that I was not indifferent to her; nor indeed did she, even in publick affect any reservedness more than the decencies of her sex and quality required; for after my pretensions to her were commonly talked of, and those who were intimate with her, would railly her about me, she passed it off with a spirit of gaity and good humour peculiar to her self, and 'bated nothing of her usual freedom to me; she permitted me to read to her, to walk and dance with her, and I had all the opportunities of endeavouring an encrease of her esteem that I could wish, which so incensed Bellpine, that he made no scruple of reviling both her and me in all companies wherever he came; saying I was a little worthless fellow, who had nothing but my sword to depend upon;[1] and that Ansellina having no hopes of marrying him, was glad to take up with the first that asked her. These scandalous reports on my first hearing of 'em had assuredly been fatal to one of us, if Ansellina had not commanded me by all the passion I professed, and by the friendship she freely acknowledged to have for me, not to take any notice of 'em. I set too high a value on the favours she allowed me, to be capable of disobedience; and she was too nice[2] a judge of the punctillio's of our sexes honour, not to take this sacrifice of so just a resentment, as a very great proof how much I submitted to her will, and suffered not a day to pass without giving me some new mark how nearly she was touched with it. I was the most contented and happy person in the world, still hoping that in a little time, she having no relations that had power to contradict her inclinations, I should be able to obtain every thing from her that an honourable passion could require; 'till one evening coming home pretty late from her, my servant gave me a letter which he told me was left for me by one of Bellpine's servants; I presently suspected the contents, and found I was not mistaken; it was really a challenge to meet him the next morning, and must confess, tho' I longed for an opportunity to chastize his

---

1  The sword was a sign of gentle birth; Bellpine suggests that Brillian is a penniless fortune hunter using his appearance of gentlemanliness to attract a rich bride.
2  Scrupulous, fastidious.

insolence, was a little troubled how to excuse my self to Anselline, but there was no possibility of evading it, without rendring my self unworthy of her, and hoped that circumstance would be sufficient to clear me to her. I will not trouble you brother with the particulars of our duel, since there was nothing material, but that at the third pass (I know not whether I may call it the effect of my good or evil fortune) he received my sword a good depth in his body, and fell with all the symptoms of a dying-man. I made all possible hast to send a surgeon to him. In my way I met two gentlemen, who it seems he had made acquainted with his design (probably with an intention to be prevented). They asked me what success, and when I had informed 'em, advised me to be gone from Amiens before the news should reach the ears of Bellpine's relations, who were not inconsiderable in that place. I made 'em those retributions their civilities deserved; but how eminent soever the danger appeared that threatned me, could not think of leaving Amiens, without having first seen Anselline. I went to the Baronesses, and found my charmer at her toylet, and either it was my fancy, or else she really did look more amiable in that undress than ever I had seen her, tho' adorned with the utmost illustrations. She seemed surprized at seeing me so early, and with her wonted good humor asking me the reason of it, put me into a mortal agony how to answer her, for I must assure you brother, that the fears of her displeasure were a thousand times more dreadful to me, than any other apprehensions; she repeated the question three or four times before I had courage to reply, and I believe she was pretty near guessing the truth by my silence, and the disorder in my countenance before I spoke; and when I did, she received the account of the whole adventure with a vast deal of trouble, but no anger; she knew too well what I owed to my reputation, and the post his majesty had honoured me with,[1] to believe I could, or ought to dispence with submit-

---

1    As both a man of honour and an army officer, Brillian feels that he must preserve the reputation for courage that he would lose if he declined a challenge to a duel. Though duelling was practiced, it was increasingly subject to fashionable critique, notably in a series of periodical essays by Sir Richard Steele in *The Tatler*. It was illegal and could lead to a trial for murder.

ting to the reflections which must have fallen on me, had I acted otherwise than I did. Her concern and tears, which she had not power to contain at the thoughts of my departure, joyned with her earnest conjurations to me to be gone, let me more than ever into the secrets of her heart, and gave me a pleasure as inconceivable as the necessity of parting did the contrary. Nothing could be more moving than our taking leave, and when she tore her self half willing and half unwilling from my arms, had sent me away inconsolable, if her promises of coming to Paris as soon as she could without being taken notice of, and frequent writing to me in the mean time, had not given me a hope, tho' a distant one of happiness. Thus brother, have I given you, in as few words as I could, a recital of every thing that has hapned to me of consequence since our separation, in which I dare believe you will find more to pity than condemn." The afflicted Chevalier could not conclude without letting fall some tears; which the Count perceiveing, ran to him, and tenderly embracing him, said all that could be expected from a most affectionate friend to mitigate his sorrows, nor suffered him to remove from his arms 'till he had accomplished his design; and then believing the hearing of the adventures of another, (especially one he was so deeply interested in) would be the surest means to give a truce to the more melancholy reflections on his own, related every thing that had befallen him since his coming to Paris. The letters he received from a lady *incognito*, his little gallantries with Amena, and the accident that presented to his view, the unknown lady in the person of one of the greatest fortunes in all France. Nothing could be a greater cordial to the Chevalier, than to find his brother was beloved by the sister of Ansellina, he did not doubt but that by this means there might be a possibility of seeing her sooner than else he could have hoped, and the two brothers began to enter into a serious consultation of this affair, which ended with a resolution to fix their fortunes there. The Count had never yet seen a beauty formidable enough to give him an hours uneasiness (purely for the sake of love) and would often say, Cupid's quiver never held an arrow of force to reach his heart; those little delicacies, those trembling aking transports, which every sight of the beloved object occasions, and so visibly distinguishes a real passion from a counterfeit, he looked on as the chimera's of an idle brain, formed to inspire notions of an imaginary bliss, and make fools lose themselves in seeking; or if they had a being, it was only in weak souls, a kind of a disease with which he assured himself he should never be infected. Ambition was certainly the reigning passion in his soul, and Alovisa's quality and vast possessions, promising a full gratification of that, he ne'er so much as wished to know, a farther happiness in marriage.

But while the Count and Chevalier were thus employed, the rival ladies past the hours in a very different entertainment, the dispair and bitter lamentations that the unfortunate Amena made, when she came out of her swooning, were such as moved even Alovisa to compassion, and if any thing but resigning D'elmont could have given her consolation, she would willingly have applied it. There was now no need of further dissimulation, and she confessed to Amena, that she had loved the charming Count with a kind of madness from the first moment she beheld him; that to favour her designs on him, she had made use of every stratagem she could invent; that by her means, the amour was first discovered to Monsieur Sanseverin, and his family alarmed the night before; and lastly, that by her persuasions, he had resolved to send her to a monastry, to which she must prepare her self to go in a few days without taking any leave even of her father; "have you," cried Amena hastily interrupting her, "have you prevailed with my father to send me from this hated place, without the punishment of hearing his upbraidings?" Which the other answering in the affirmative, "I thank you," resumed Amena, "that favour has cancelled all your score of cruelty, for after the follies I have been guilty of, nothing is so dreadful as the sight of him, and who would, oh heavens!" continued she bursting into a flood of tears, "wish to stay in a world so full of falshood." She was able to utter no more for some moments, but at last, raising her self on the bed where she was laid, and endeavouring to seem a little more composed, "I have two favours, madam, yet to ask of you," rejoined she, "neither of 'em will I believe seem difficult to you to grant: that you will make use of the power you have with my father, to let my departure be as sudden as possible, and that while I am here, I may never see Count D'elmont." It was not likely that Alovisa should deny requests so suitable to her own inclinations, and believing with a great deal of reason that her presence was not very grateful, left her to the care of her women, whom she ordered to attend her with the same diligence, as her self. It was evening before the Count came, and Alovisa spent the remainder of the day in very uneasie reflections, she knew not as yet, whether she had cause to rejoice in, or blame her fortune in so unexpectedly discovering her passion, and an incessant vicissitude of hope and fears, racked her with most intollerable inquietude, 'till the darling object of her wishes appeared, and tho' the first sight of him, added to her other passions, that of shame, yet he managed his address so well, and so modestly and artfully hinted the knowledge of his happiness, that every sentiment gave place to a new admiration of the wonders of his wit, and if before she loved, she now adored, and began to think it a kind of merit in her self to be sensible of his. He soon put it in her power to oblige him, by giving her the history of his brothers passion for her sister, and she was not at all backward in assuring him how much she approved of it, and that she would write to Ansellina by the first post, to engage her coming to Paris with all imaginable speed. In fine, there was nothing he[1] could ask refused, and indeed it would have been rediculous for her to have affected coiness, after the testimonies she had long since given him of one of the most violent passions that ever was; this foreknowledge saved abundance of dissimulation on both sides, and she took care that if he should be wanting in his kind expressions after marriage, he should not have it in his power to pretend (as some husbands have done) that his stock was exhausted in a tedious courtship. Every thing was presently agreed upon, and the wedding-day appointed, which was to be as soon as every thing could be got ready to make it magnificent; tho' the Counts good nature made him desirous to learn something of

---

1    4th ed.; 1st ed. reads "she."

Amena, yet he durst not enquire for fear of giving an umbrage to his intended bride, but she, imagining the reason of his silence, very frankly told him, how she was to be disposed of; this knowledge made no small addition to his contentment, for had she stayed in Paris, he could expect nothing but continual jealousies from Alovisa, besides as he really wished her happy, tho' he could not make her so, he thought absence might banish a hopeless passion from her heart, and time and other objects efface an idea, which could not but be distructive to her peace. He stayed at Alovisa's house 'till it was pretty late, and perhaps they had not parted in some hours longer, if his impatience to inform his brother, his success, had not carried him away. The young Chevalier was infinitely more transported at the bare hopes of being something nearer the aim of all his wishes then D'elmont was at the assurance of loseing his,[1] and could not forbear rallying him for placing the ultimate of his wishes on such a toy, as he argued woman was, which the Chavalier endeavouring to confute, there began a very warm dispute, in which neither of 'em being able to convince the other, sleep at last, interposed as moderator. The next day they went together to visit Alovisa, and from that time were seldom asunder, but in compassion to Amena, they took what care they could to conceal the design they had in hand, and that unhappy lady was in a few days according to her rivals contrivance hurried away without seeing any of her friends. When she was gone, and there was no further need of keeping it a secret, the news of this great wedding was immediately spread over the whole town, and every one talked of it, as their particular interests or affections dictated. All D'elmonts friends were full of joy, and he met no inconsiderable augmentation of it himself, when his brother recieved a letter from Ansellina, with an account that Bellpine's wound was found not dangerous, and

---

1  Apparently contrasting the loving Chevalier's hope of gaining the aim of his desire with the ambitious Count's relief at losing Amena, the now inconvenient aim of his desire. But 4th ed. solves the problem differently: "The young Chevalier was infinitely more transported at the bare hopes of being something nearer the aim of all his *hopes*, than D'elmont was at the assurance of losing his *in possession*, ..." (emphasis added).

that he was in a very fair way of recovery. And it was concluded that as soon as the wedding was over, the young Chevalier
should go in person to Amiens to fetch his beloved Ansellina,
in order for a second, and as desired nuptial. There was no
gloom now left to cloud the gaity of the happy day, nothing
could be more grand then the celebration of it; and Alovisa
now thought her self at the end of her cares, but the sequel of
this glorious beginning, and what effect the dispair and imprecations of Amena (when she heard of it) produced, shall with
the continuance of the Chevalier Brillian's adventures be faithfully related in the next part.

*Finis.*

# LOVE IN EXCESS;

## OR,

## THE FATAL ENQUIRY:

## A NOVEL.

*Part the Second.*

*Each day we break the bond of humane laws*
*For love, and vindicate the common cause.*
*Laws for defence of civil rights are placed,*
*Love throws the fences down, and makes a gen'ral waste.*
*Maids, widows, wives, without distinction fall,*
*The sweeping deluge love comes on and covers all.*[1]

*By Mrs. Haywood*

---

1   "Palamon and Arcite; or, The Knight's Tale, from Chaucer" I.331-36; Dryden's
translation of Chaucer's ironic tale of chivalry appeared in *Fables, Ancient and Mod-*
*ern* (1700).

To
Mrs. Eliz. Haywood,
on Her Novel Called
Love in Excess, &c.[1]


Fain would I here my vast ideas raise,
To paint the wonders of Eliza's praise;
But like young artists where their stroaks decay,
I shade those glories which I can't display.
Thy prose in sweeter harmony refines,
Than numbers flowing thro' the Muse's lines;
What beauty ne'er could melt, thy touches fire,
And raise a musick that can love inspire;
Soul-thrilling accents all our senses wound,
And strike with softness, whilst they charm with sound!
When thy Count pleads, what fair his suit can flye?
Or when thy nymph laments, what eyes are dry?
Ev'n Nature's self in sympathy appears,
Yields sigh for sigh, and melts in equal tears;
For such descriptions thus at once can prove
The force of language, and the sweets of love.
The myrtle's leaves[2] with those of fame[3] entwine,
And all the glories of that wreath are thine!
As eagles can undazzled view the force
Of scorching Phœbus in his noon-day course,[4]
Thy genius to the god its lustre plays,
Meets his fierce beams, and darts him rays for rays!
Oh glorious strength! Let each succeeding page

---

1  Prefatory poems and letters of praise – called puffs because they puffed up the fame
   of the book – were a standard feature of eighteenth-century publishing. Later editions of *Love in Excess* gathered all three parts together, moving these poems to the
   front and adding others.
2  Sacred to Venus, goddess of love.
3  Laurel leaves (bays) conventionally crown the successful poet.
4  The sun, for Phoebus Apollo, the god of poetry and music, was a sun god. Eagles
   were conventionally keen-sighted birds that could look unblinking into the sun.

*Still boast those charms and luminate the age;*
*So shall thy beamful fires with light divine*
*Rise to the spheres, and there triumphant shine.*[1]

*Richard Savage.*[2]

By an Unknown Hand,
To the most Ingenious Mrs. Haywood,
on her Novel, Entitled, *Love in Excess.*


*A stranger muse, an unbeliever too,*
*That womens souls such strength of vigour knew!*
*Nor less an atheist to love's pow'r declared,*
*Till* YOU *a champion for the sex appeared!*
*A convert now, to both, I feel that fire*
YOUR *words alone can paint!* YOUR *looks inspire!*
*Resistless now, loves shafts, new pointed fly*
*Winged with* YOUR *flame, and blazing in* YOUR *eye*
*With sweet, but pow'rful force the charm-shot heart*
*Receives th' impression of the conquering dart,*
*And ev'ry art'ry huggs the joy-tipt smart!*
*No more of Phœbus rising vainly boast.*
*Ye tawny sons of a luxuriant coast!*
*While our blest isle is with such rays replete,*
*Britain shall glow with more than Eastern heat!*

---

1  Immortalized by fame, Haywood will shine among the stars in heaven (which according to Ptolemaic cosmology rest on earth-centred spheres).

2  An aspiring poet and playwright in Haywood's circle, and for a time her lover, Richard Savage (c.1697-1743) also wrote a prefatory poem for Haywood's *The Rash Resolve* (1723, the year before they quarrelled).

# LOVE IN EXCESS;

## OR, THE FATAL ENQUIRY.

### Part the Second.

THE contentment that appeared in the faces of the new married pair, added so much to the impatience of the Chevalier Brillian to see his beloved Ansellina, that in a few days after the wedding, he took leave of them, and departed for Amiens. But as human happiness is seldom of long continuance, and Alovisa placing the ultimate of her's in the possession of her charming husband, secure of that, despised all future events, 'twas time for Fortune, who long enough had smiled, now to turn her wheel, and punish the presumption that defied her power.

As they were one day at dinner, a messenger came to acquaint Count D'elmont that Monsieur Frankville was taken suddenly so violently ill, that his physicians dispaired of his life, and that he begged to speak with him immediately. This gentleman had been guardian to the Count during his minority,[1] and the care and faithfulness with which that trust had been discharged made him with reason regret the danger of losing so good a friend. He delayed the visit not a moment, and found him as the servant had told him, in a condition as could cherish no hopes of recovery; as soon as he perceived the Count come into the chamber, he desired to be left alone with him, which order being presently obeyed, "My dear charge," said he taking him by the hand and pressing it to his trembling bosom, "you see me at the point of death, but the knowledge of your many virtues, and the confidence I have that you will not deny me the request I am about to ask, makes me support the thoughts of it with moderation." The other assuring him of his readiness to serve him in any command, encouraged the old gentleman to prosecute his discourse in this manner: "You are not ignorant

---

1 A guardian was legally responsible for, and controlled the estate of, a minor between the father's death and the minor's coming of age or marriage.

my lord," rejoined he, "that my son (the only one I have) is on his travels, gone by my approbation, and his own desires to make the tour of Europe;[1] but I have a daughter, whose protection I would entreat you to undertake; her education in a monastery has hitherto kept her intirely unacquainted with the gayeties of a court, or the conversation of the beau monde,[2] and I have sent for her to Paris purposely to introduce her into company, proper for a young lady, who I never designed for a recluse; I know not whether she will be here time enough to close my eyes, but if you will promise to receive her into your house, and not suffer her artless and unexperienced youth to fall into those snares which are daily laid for innocence, and take so far a care, that neither she, not the fortune I leave her, be thrown away upon a man unworthy of her, I shall dye well satisfied." D'elmont answered this request, with repeated assurances of fulfilling it, and frankly offered , if he had no other person in whom he rather would confide, to take the management of the whole estate he left behind him, 'till young Frankville should return – The anxious father was transported at this favour, and thanked him in terms full of gratitude and affection; they spent some hours in settling this affair, and perhaps had not ended it so soon, if word had not been brought that the young lady his daughter was allighted at the gate; 'tis impossible to express the joy which filled the old gentleman's heart at this news, and he began afresh to put the Count in mind of what he had promised concerning her. As they were in this endearing, tho' mournful entertainment, the matchless Melliora[3] entered, the surprize and grief for her father's indisposition (having heard of it but since she came into the house) hindred her from regarding any thing but him, and throwing herself on her knees by the bed-side, washed the hand which he stretched out to raise her with, in a flood of tears, accompanied with expressions, which unstudied, and incoherent as they were, had a delicacy in 'em, that showed her wit not inferior to

---

1   A tour of European cities (the grand tour) completed the education of noblemen and gentlemen.
2   Fashionable society.
3   *Melior* is Latin for "better."

her tenderness, and that no circumstance could render her otherwise than the most lovely person in the world; when the first transports of her sorrow were over, and that with much ado she was persuaded to rise from the posture she was in, "The affliction I see thee in my dear child," said her father, "would be a vast addition to the agonies I feel, were I not so happy as to be provided with means for a mitigation of it; think not in losing me thou wilt be left wholly an orphan, this worthy lord will dry thy tears. Therefore, my last commands to thee shall be to oblige thee to endeavour to deserve the favours he is pleased to do us in accepting thee for –" He would have proceeded, but his physicians (who had been in consultation in the next room) coming in prevented him, and Count D'elmont taking the charming Melliora by the hand, led her to the window, and beginning to speak some words of consolation to her, the softness of his voice, and graceful manner with which he delivered himself (always the inseparable companions of his discourse, but now more particularly so) made her cast her eyes upon him; but alass, he was not an object to be safely gazed at, and in spight of the grief she was in, she found something in his form which dissipated it; a kind of painful pleasure, a mixture of surprize, and joy, and doubt ran thro' her in an instant; her fathers words suggested to her imagination, that she was in a possibility of calling the charming person that stood before her, by a name more tender than that of guardian, and all the actions, looks, and address of D'elmont served but to confirm her in that belief. For now it was that this insensible began to feel the power of beauty, and that heart which had so long been impregnable surrendered in a moment, the first sight of Melliora gave him a discomposure he had never felt before, he sympathized in all her sorrows, and was ready to joyn his tears with hers, but when her eyes met his, the god of love seemed there to have united all his lightnings for one effectual blaze; their admiration of each others perfections was mutual, and tho' he had got the start in love, as being touched with that almighty dart, before her affliction had given her leave to regard him, yet the softness of her soul, made up for that little loss of time, and it was hard to say whose passion was the strongest; she listned to his condolements, and assurances of everlasting friendship with a pleasure which was but too visible in her countenance, and more enflamed the Count. As they were exchanging glances, as if each vyed with the other who should dart the fiercest rays, they heard a sort of ominous whispering about the bed, and presently one of those who stood near it beckoned them to come thither; the physicians had found Monsieur Frankville in a much worse condition than they left him in, and soon after perceived evident symptoms in him of approaching death, and indeed there were but a very few moments between him and that other unfathomable world; the use of speech had left him, and he could take no other leave of his dear daughter than with his eyes; which sometimes were cast tenderly on her, sometimes on the Count, with a beseeching look as it were to conjure him to be careful to his charge, then up to Heaven, as witness of the trust he reposed in him. There could not be a scene more melancholly than this dumb farewell, and Melliora, whose soft disposition had never before been shocked, had not courage to support so dreadful a one as this, but fell upon the bed just as her father breathed his last, as motionless as he. It is impossible to represent the agony's which filled the heart of D'elmont at this view, he took her in his arms, and assisted those who were endeavouring to recover her, with a wildness in his countenance, a trembling horror shaking all his fabrick in such a manner, as might have easily discovered to the spectators (if they had not been too busily employed to take notice of it) that he was actuated by a motive far more powerful than that of compassion. As soon as she came to herself, they forced her from the dead body of her father (to which she clung) and carried her into another room, and it being judged convenient that she should be removed from that house, where every thing would serve but to remind her of her loss; the Count desired the servants of Monsieur Frankville should be called, and then in the presence of 'em all, declared their master's last request, and ordered an account of all affairs should be brought to his house, where he would immediately conduct their young lady as he had promised her father. If Melliora had been without any other cause of grief, this eclaircissment had been sufficient to have made her miserable. She had already entertained a most tender affection for the Count, and had not so little discernment as not to be sensible she had made the like impression on him; but now she waked as from a dream of promised joys, to certain woes, and the same hour which gave birth to her passion, commenced an adequate dispair, and killed her hopes just budding.

Indeed there never was any condition so truly deplorable as that of this unfortunate lady; she had just lost a dear and tender father, whose care was ever watchful for her, her brother was far off, and she had no other relation in the world to apply her self to for comfort, or advice; not even an acquaintance at Paris, or friend, but him who but newly was become so, and whom she found it dangerous to make use of, whom she knew it was a crime to love, yet could not help loving; the more she thought, the more she grew distracted, and the less able to resolve on any thing; a thousand times she called on death to give her ease, but that pale tyrant flys from the pursuer, she had not been yet long enough acquainted with the ills of life, and must endure (how unwilling soever) her part of sufferings in common with the rest of human kind.

As soon as D'elmont had given some necessary directions to the servants, he came to the couch, where she was sitting in a fixed and silent sorrow (tho' inwardly tossed with various and violent agitations) and offering her his hand entreated her to permit him to wait on her from that house of woe. "Alass!" said she, "to what purpose should I remove, who bear my miseries about me? Wretch that I am!" – a flood of tears, here interposed, and hindred her from proceeding, which falling from such lovely eyes, had a magnetick influence to draw the same from every beholder; but D'elmont who knew that was not the way to comfort her, dried his as soon as possible, and one more begged she would depart; "suffer my return then," answered she, "to the monastery, for what have I to do in Paris since I have lost my father?" "By no means madam," resumed the Count hastily, "that were to disappoint your fathers designs, and contradict his last desires; believe, most lovely Melliora," continued he taking her by the hand and letting fall some tears which he could not restrain, upon it, "that I bear at least an equal share in your affliction, and lament for you, and for my self. Such a regard my grateful soul paid Monsieur Frankville for all his wondrous care and goodness to me, that in his death methinks I am twice an orphan. But tears are fruitless to reinspire his now cold clay, therefore must transmit the love and duty I owed him living, to his memory dead, and an exact performance of his will; and since he thought me worthy of so vast a trust as Melliora, I hope she will be guided by her fathers sentiments, and believe that D'elmont (tho' a stranger to her) has a soul not uncapable of friendship. Friendship! did I say?" rejoyned he softning his voice, "that term is too mean to express a zeal like mine, the care, the tenderness, the faith, the fond affection of parents, – brothers, – husbands, – lovers, all comprized in one! one great unutterable! comprehensive meaning, is mine! is mine for Melliora!" She returned no answer but sighs, to all he said to her; but he renewing his entreaties, and urging her father's commands, she was at last prevailed upon to go into his chariot, which had waited at the door all the time of his being there.

As they went, he left nothing unsaid that he believed might tend to her consolation, but she had griefs which at present he was a stranger to, and his conversation, in which she found a thousand charms, rather encreased, than diminished the trouble she was in. Every word, every look of his, was a fresh dagger to her heart, and in spight of the love she bore her father, and the unfeigned concern his sudden death had given her, she was now convinced that Count D'elmont's perfections were her severest wounds.

When they came to his house, he presented her to Alovysa, and giving her a brief account of what had happened, engaged that lady to receive her with all immaginable demonstrations of civility and kindness.

He soon left the two ladies together, pretending business, but indeed to satisfie his impatience, which longed for an opportunity to meditate on this adventure. But his reflections were now grown far less pleasing than they used to be; real sighs flew from his breast uncalled. And Melliora's image in dazling brightness! in terrible array of killing charms! fired him with (impossible to be attained) desires; he found by sad experience what it was to love, and to dispair. He admired! adored! and wished, even to madness! yet had too much honour, too much gratitude for the memory of Monsieur Franckville, and too sincere an awe for the lovely cause of his uneasiness, than to form a thought that could encourage his new passion. What would he not have given to have been unmarried? How often did he curse the hour in which Alovysa's fondness was discovered? and how much more, his own ambition which prompted him to take advantage of it? and hurried him precipitatly to a hymen,[1] where love (the noblest guest) was wanting. It was in these racks of thought, that the unfortunate Amena was remembered, and he could not forbear acknowledging the justice of that doom, which inflicted on him, these very torments he had given her. A severe repentance seized on his soul, and Alovysa for whom he never had any thing more than an indifferency, now began to seem distastful to his fancy, he looked on her, as indeed she was, the chief author of Amena's misfortunes, and abhorred her for that infidelity. But when he considered her, as the bar 'twixt him and Melliora she appeared like his ill genius to him, and he could not support the thoughts of being obliged to love her (or at least to seem as if he did) with moderation. In the midst of these reflections, his servant came in and delivered this letter to him which had been just left by the post. The Count immediately knew the hand to be Amena's, and was covered with the utmost confusion and remorse when he read these lines.

To the too charming and perfidious D'elmont

*Now hopes, and fears, and jealousies are over! doubt is no more!*
*you are for ever lost! and my unfaithful, happy rival! triumphs in*
*your arms, and my undoing! – I need not wish you joy, the hast*
*you made to enter into Hymen's bonds, and the more than ordi-*
*nary pomp with which that ceremony was celebrated, assures me*

---

1 The classical god of marriage, whose name was a synonym for "wedding" or "marriage"; Haywood also spells it Himen.

you are highly satisifed with your condition; and that any future testimonies of the friendship of so wretched a creature as *Amena*, would be received by you, with the same disregard, as those she has given you of a more tender passion. – Shameful remembrance! Oh that I could blot it out! – Erace from the book of time those fond deluded hours! Forget I ever saw the lovely false *D'elmont*! Ever listned to his soft persuasive accents! And thought his love a mighty price for ruin! – My father writes that you are married, commands my return to *Paris*, and assume an air as gay, and chearful as that with which I used to appear. – Alass! how little does he know his daughters heart? And how impossible is it, for me to obey him, can I look on you as the husband of *Alovysa*, without remembring you were once the lover of *Amena*? Can love like mine so fierce, so passionately tender, e're sink to a calm, cold indifference? Can I behold the fond endearments of your bridal joys (which you'd not be able to restrain, even before me) and not burst with envy? No, the sight would turn me quite distracted, and I should commit some desperate violence that would undoe us all. – Therefore, I hide my self for ever from it, bid an everlasting adieu to all the gay delights and pleasures of my youth. – To all the pomp and splendour of the Court. – To all that the mistaken world calls happiness. – To father, friends, relations, all that's dear.– But your idea, and that, not even these consecrated walls, nor iron gates keep out, sleeping, or waking you are ever with me, you mingle with my most solemn devotions; and while I pray to Heaven that I may think on you no more, a guilty pleasure rises in my soul, and contradicts my vows! All my confessions are so many sins, and the same breath which tells my ghostly father I abjure your memory, speaks your dear name with transport. Yes – cruel! ungrateful! – faithless as you are, I still do love you – love you to that infinite degree, that now, methinks fired with thy charms (repenting all I've said) I could wish even to renew those moments of my ruin! – Pity me *D'elmont*, if thou hast humanity. – Judge what the rackings of my soul must be, when I resolve, with all this love, this languishment about me; never to see you more.

Every thing is preparing for my reception into holy orders, (how unfit I am Heaven knows) and in a few days I shall put on the vail

*which excludes me from the world for ever; therefore, if these distract-*
*ed lines are worth an answer, it must be speedy, or it will not come to*
*my hands. Perhaps not find me living. — I can no more —Farewel*
*(thou dear distroyer of my soul.)*

Eternally Farewel, Amena.

P.S. *I do not urge you to write, Alovysa (I wish I could not say*
*your wife) will perhaps think it too great a condescention, and not*
*suffer you so long from her embraces. — Yet if you can get loose. —*
*But you know best what's proper to be done — Forgive the restless-*
*ness of a dispairing wretch, who cannot cease to love, tho' from this*
*moment she must cease to tell you so. —*

Once more, and for ever. Adieu.

Had this letter come a day sooner, 'tis probable it would have
had but little effect on the soul of D'elmont, but his sentiments
of love were now so wholly changed, that what before he
would but have laughed at, and perhaps dispised, now filled him
with remorse and serious anguish. He read it over several times,
and found so many proofs in it of a sincere and constant affection, that he began to pity her, with a tenderness like that of a
relation, but no more. The charming Melliora had engrossed all
his fonder wishes; else it is not impossible but that Alovysa
might have had more reason to fear her rivalship after marriage
than before. That lady having been without the presence of her
dear husband some hours, had not patience to remain any
longer without seeing him, and making an excuse to Melliora
for leaving her alone, came running to the closet where he was;
how unwelcome she was grown, the reader may imagine; he
received her, not as he was wont; the gaity which used to
sparkle in his eyes, (at once declaring and creating amorous
desires) now gave place to a sullen gloominess, he looked not
on her, or if by chance he did, 'twas more with anger than with
love; in spite of his endeavours to conceal it, she was too quick
sighted (as all are that truly love) not to be sensible of[1] this
alteration. However she took no notice of it, but kissing and

---

1   To perceive through the senses.

embracing him (according to her custom whenever they were alone) begged him to leave his solitary amusement, and help her to comfort the afflicted lady he brought there. Her endearments served but to encrease his peevishness and heighten her surprize at his behaviour; and indeed, the moment that she entered the closet was the last of her tranquility.

When with much perswasions she had prevailed with him to go with her into the room where Melliora was, he appeared so disordred at the second sight of that charmer, as would certainly have let Alovysa into the secret of his passion, had she not been retired to a window to recover her self from the confusion, her husbands coldness had thrown her in, and by that fortunate disregard of his looks at that critical instant, given him (who never wanted presence of mind) leave to form both his countenance and manner of address, so as to give no suspicion of the truth.

This little company was far from being entertaining to one another; every one had their particular cogitations, and were not displeased not to be interrupted in them. It growing late, Alovysa conducted Melliora to a chamber which she had ordered to be prepared for her, and then retired to her own, hoping that when the Count should come to bed, she might be able to make some discovery of the cause of his uneasiness. But she was deceived, he spoke not to her, and when by a thousand little inventions she urged him to reply to what she said, it was in such a fashion as only let her see, that he was extreamly troubled at something, but could not guess at what. As soon as day broke, he rose, and shutting himself into his closet, left her in the greatest consternation immaginable; she could not think it possible that the death of Monsieur Frankville should work this transformation, and knew of no other misfortune that had happened. At last she rememb'red she had heard one of the servants say, a letter was brought to their master by the post, and began to reflect on every thing (in the power of fortune to determine) that could threaten a disturbance, yet was still as ignorant as ever. She lay not long in bed, but putting on her cloths with more expedition than usual, went to the closet, resolving to speak to him in a manner as should oblige him to put an end to the uncertainty she was in, but finding the door locked, her curiosity made her look thro' the key-hole, and she saw him sometimes very intentively[1] reading a letter, and sometimes writing, as tho' it were an answer to it. A sudden thought came into her head, and she immediately went softly from the place where she was, without knocking at the door, and stayed in a little chamber adjacent to it, where none could pass either to, or from the closet, without being perceived by her; she had not waited long, before she heard the Count ring, and presently saw a servant enter, and soon after return with a letter in his hand; she would not speak to him then, for fear of being over heard by her husband, but followed him down stairs, and when he came towards the bottom, called to him in a low voice to tarry 'till she came to him; the fellow durst not but obey, and there being no body near 'em, commanded him to deliver her the letter. But he either afraid or unwilling to betray his trust, excused himself from it as well as he could, but she was resolved to have it; and when threats would not avail, condiscended to entreaties, to which she added bribes, which last article joined to the promise she made of never revealing it, won him to her purpose. She had scarce patience to forbear opening it before she got to her chamber. The superscription (which she saw was for Amena) fired her with disdain and jealousie, and it is hardly possible to immagine, much less to discribe the torrent of her indignation, when she found that it contained these words.

To the lovely Amena.

*You accuse me of cruelty, when at the same time you kill me with yours. How vile! How despicable, must I be grown in your opinion, when you believe I can be happy, when you are miserable. – Can I enjoy the pleasures of a court, while you are shut within a cloyster? – Shall I suffer the world to be deprived of such a treasure as Amena? for the crime of worthless D'elmont – No, no fair, injured softness, return, and bless the eyes of every beholder! Shine out again in your native lustre, uneclipsed by grief. The*

---

1  Intentive means "busily attentive" (Johnson).

*star of beauty and the guide of love. – And, if my unlucky pres-*
*ence will be a damp to the brightness of your fires, I will for ever*
*quit the place. – Tho' I could wish you'd give me leave some-*
*times to gaze upon you, and draw some hoped presages of future*
*fortune from the benignity of your influence. – Yes Amena, I*
*would sigh out my repentance at your feet, and try at least to*
*obtain a pardon for my infidelity. – For, 'tis true, what you have*
*heard, – I am married – But oh Amena! Happiness is not*
*always an attendant on Himen. – However, I yet may call you*
*friend – I yet may love you, tho' in a different way from what I*
*once pretended to; and believe me, that the love of souls, as it is*
*the most uncommon, especially in our sex, so 'tis the most refined*
*and noble of all passions, and such a love shall be for ever yours.*
*Even Alovysa (who has robbed you of the rest) cannot justly*
*resent my giving you that part, – You'll wonder at this alteration*
*in my temper, but 'tis sincere, I am no more the gay, the roving*
*D'elmont, and when you come to Paris, perhaps you will find*
*me in a condition more lyable to your pity than indignation.*
*What shall I say Amena? My crime is my punishment, I have*
*offended against love, and against thee, and am, if possible, as*
*miserable, as guilty. Torn with remorse, and tortured with – I*
*cannot – I must not name it – but 'tis something which can be*
*termed no other than the utmost severity of my fate. – Hast then*
*to pity me, to comfort, to advise me, if (as you say) you yet retain*
*any remains of your former tenderness for this ungrateful man.*

D'elmont.

"Ungrateful indeed!" cried Alovysa, transported with excess
of rage and jealousie, " Oh the villain! – What miseries? What
misfortunes are these thou talk'st of? What unhappiness has
waited on thy himen? 'Tis I alone am wretched! base deceiv-
er!"

Then, as if she wanted to discover something farther to
heighten the indignation she was in, she began to read it over
again, and indeed the more she considered the meaning of
what she read, the more her passions swelled, 'till they got at
last the entire dominion of her reason. She tore the letter in a

thousand pieces, and was not much less unmerciful to her hair and garments. 'Tis possible that in the violence of her fury, she might have forgot her promise to the servant, to vent some part of it on her husband, if her woman coming into the room to know if she was ready to dress had not prevented her, by telling her the Count was gone abroad, and had left word, that he should not return 'till the evening. Alovysa had thrown herself on the bed, and the curtains being drawn discovered not the disorder she was in, and which her pride made her willing should be still a secret, therefore dismist her with saying, she would call her when she wanted any thing; tho' Alovysa was too apt to give a loose to her passions on every occasion, to the destruction of her own peace; yet she knew well enough how to disguise 'em, when ever she found the concealing of them would be an advantage to her designs. And when the transports of her rage was so far over, as to give her liberty of reflection, and she began to examine the state of her affection to the Count, she soon perceived it had so much the better of all other considerations, that in spite of the injustice she thought him guilty of to her, she could not perswade her self to do any thing that might give him a pretence to quarrel with her. She thought she had done enough in intercepting this letter, and did not doubt but that Amena would take his not writing to her so much to heart, as to prevent her ever returning to Paris, and resolved to omit nothing of her former endearments, or make a shew of being in the least disobliged; this sort of carriage she immagined would not only lay him more open and unguarded to the diligent watch she designed to make on all his words and actions, but likewise awaken him to a just sense of her goodness, and his own ingratitude. – She rightly judged that when people are married, jealousie was not the proper method to revive a decayed passion, and that after possession it must be only tenderness, and constant assiduity to please, that can keep up desire, fresh and gay. Man is too arbitrary a creature to bear the least contradiction, where he pretends an absolute authority, and that wife who thinks by ill humour and perpetual taunts, to make him weary of what she would reclaim him from, only renders her self more hateful, and makes that justifiable which before was blameable in him. These, and the like considerations made Alovysa put on a countenance of serenity, and she so well acted the part of an unsuspecting wife, that D'elmont was far from immagining what she had done. However he still behaved with the same caution as before to Melliora; and certainly never did people disguise the sentiments of their souls more artfully than did these three – Melliora vailed her secret languishments, under the covert of her grief for her father, the Count his burning anguish, in a gloomy melancholy for the loss of his friend; but Alovysa's task was much the hardest, who had no pretence for grief (raging, and bleeding with neglected love, and stifled pride) to frame her temper to a seeming tranquility – All made it their whole study to deceive each other, yet none but Alovysa was intirely in the dark; for the Count and Melliora had but too true a guess at one anothers meaning, every look of his, for he had eyes that need no interpreter, gave her intelligence of his heart, and the confusion which the understanding those looks gave her, sufficiently told him how sensible she was of 'em. – Several days they lived in this manner, in which time Monsieur Frankville was interred. Which solemnity, the Count took care should be performed with a magnificence suitable to the friendship he publickly profest to have born him, and the secret adoration his soul paid to his remains.[1]

Nothing hapned of moment, 'till a day or two after the funeral, a gentleman newly arrived at Paris, came to visit the Count, and gave him an account of Amena's having taken the habit; "How," said D'elmont interrupting him, "is it possible? – Has she then profest?" "Yes," answered the gentleman, "having a sister whom I always tenderly loved at the monastery at St. Dennis, my affection obliged me to make it in my way to visit her. Amena was with her at the grate, when she received me; I know not how among other discourses we hapned to talk of the fine gentlemen of Paris, which it was impossible to do, without mentioning Count D'elmont"; the Count answered not this complement as he would have done at another time,

---

1   Since both are public figures, the occasion calls for a public display of affection.

but only bowing with an humble air, gave him liberty to prosecute his discourse; "the moment," resumed he, "that Amena heard your name, the tears run from her fair eyes, in such abundance, and she seemed opprest with so violent a grief, that she was not able to stay any longer with us. When she was gone, my sister whom she had made her confident, gave me the history of her misfortunes, and withal, told me, that the next day she was to be initiated into holy orders. My curiosity engaged me to stay at St. Dennis, to see the ceremony performed, which was solemn; but not with that magnificence which I expected; it seems it was Amena's desire that it should be as private as possible, and for that reason, none of her relations were there, and several of the formalities of entrance omitted. After it was over, my sister beckoned me to come to the grate, where I saw her before, and conjured me in the name of her new sister, to give this to your hands; in speaking these words, he took a letter out of his pocket, which the Count immediately opening to his great surprize found it contained as follows.

To the Inhuman D'elmont.

*To be pitied by you, and that you should tell me so, was all the recompence I asked for loss of father, friends, reputation, and eternal peace; but now, too late, I find that the fond maid who scorns the world for love, is sure to meet for her reward the scorn of him she loves – Ungrateful man! Could you not spare one moment from that long date of happiness, to give a last farewel to her you have undone? What would not his barbarous contempt have drawn upon you, were I of Alovysa's temper? Sure I am, all that disdain, and rage, could inspire malice with, had been inflicted on you, but you well know my soul is of another stamp. – Fool that I was, and little versed in the base arts of man, believed I might by tenderness, and faithful friendship gain esteem; tho' wit and beauty the two great provocatives to create love were wanting. But do not think that I am yet so mean as to desire to hear from you; no, I have put all future correspondence with you out of my power, and hope to drive it even from my wish. Whether your disdain, or the holy banner I am lifted under, has wrought this*

*effect, I know not, but methinks I breath another air, think on*
*you with more tranquility and bid you without dying,*

Eternally Adieu Amena.

P.S. *Let Alovysa know I am no more her rival, Heaven has my*
*soul, and I forgive you both.*

D'elmont was strangely fired at the reading these lines
which left him no room to doubt that his letter had miscarried,
he could not presently immagine by what means, but was
resolved if possible to find it out. However, he dissembled his
thoughts 'till the gentleman had taken his leave; then calling for
the servant, whom he had entrusted with the carrying it, he
took him by the throat and holding his drawn sword directly to
his breast, swore that moment should be his last, if he did not
immediately confess the truth; the poor fellow frighted almost
to death, trembling, and falling on his knees, implored forgiveness, and discovered all. Alovysa who was in the next chamber,
hearing her husband call for that servant, with a tone somewhat more imperious than what he was accustomed to, and a
great noise soon after, immagined some accident had hapned to
betray her, and ran in to know the certainty, just as the Count
had discharged the servant at once from his service and his
presence. "You have done well madam," said D'elmont looking
on her with eyes sparkling with indignation, "you have done
well, by your impertinent curiosity and imprudence, to rouze
me from my dream of happiness, and remind me that I am that
wretched thing a husband!" "'Tis well indeed," answered
Alovysa, who saw now that there was no need of farther dissimulation, "that any thing can make you remember both what
you are, and what I am." "You," resumed he, hastily interrupting
her, "have taken an effectual method to prove your self a wife!
– a very wife! – insolent – jealous – and censorious! – But
madam," continued he frowning, "since you are pleased to
assert your priveledge, be assured, I too shall take my turn, and
will exert the – husband!" In saying this, he flung out of the
room in spite of her endeavours to hinder him, and going
hastily through a gallery which had a large window that looked

into the garden, he perceived Melliora lying on a green bank, in a melancholy but a charming posture, directly opposite to the place where he was; her beauties appeared if possible more to advantage than ever he had seen them, or at least he had more opportunity thus unseen by her, to gaze upon 'em; he in a moment lost all the rage of temper he had been in, and his whole soul was taken up with softness; he stood for some moments fixed in silent admiration, but love has small dominion in a heart, that can content it self with a distant prospect, and there being a pair of back stairs at the farther end of the gallery, which led to the garden, he either forgot or not regarded what construction Alovysa might make on this private interview, if by chance from any of the windows she should be witness of it.

Melliora was so intent on a book she had in her hand, that she saw not the Count 'till he was close enough to her to discern what was the subject of her entertainment, and finding it the works of Monsieur L'fontenelle,[1] "Phylosophy madam at your age," said he to her with an air which exprest surprize, "is as wondrous as your other excellencies, but I am confident, had this author ever seen Melliora, his sentiments had been otherwise than now they seem to be, and he would have been able to write of nothing else but love and her." Melliora blushed exremely at his unexpected presence, and the complement he made her; but recollecting her self as soon as she could, "I have a better opinion of Monsieur L'fontenelle," answered she, "but if I were really mistress of as many charms as you would make me believe, I should think my self little beholding to nature, for bestowing them on me, if by their means I were deprived of so choice an improvement as this book has given me." "Thank Heaven then madam," resumed he, "that you were born in an age successive to that which has produced so many fine treatises of this kind for your entertainment; since (I am very confident) this, and a long space of future time will have no other

---

1   The French writer, Bernard le Bovier, Sieur de Fontenelle (1657-1757). Melliora seeks solace for her emotional distress in the cosmic scale of his popular *Discourse concerning the Plurality of Worlds* (1686), which presented modern astronomy in a series of dialogues with a noblewoman.

theme, but that which at present you seem so much averse to."
Melliora found so much difficulty in endeavouring to conceal
the disorder she was in at this discourse, that it rendred her
unable to reply; and he, (who possibly guest the occasion of her
silence) taking one of her hands and tenderly pressing it
between his, looked so full in her eyes, as heightened her confusion, and discovered to his ravished view, what most he
wished to find. Ambition, envy, hate, fear, or anger, every other
passion that finds entrance in the soul, art and discretion may
disguise, but love, tho' it may be feigned, can never be concealed; not only the eyes (those true and most perfect intelli-
gencers of the heart) but every feature, every faculty betrays it!
It fills the whole air of the person possest with it; it wanders
round the mouth! plays in the voice! trembles in the accent!
and shows it self a thousand different, nameless ways! Even
Melliora's care to hide it, made it more aparent, and the transported D'elmont not considering where he was, or who might
be a witness of his rapture, could not forbear catching her in his
arms, and grasping her with an extasie, which plainly told her
what his thoughts were, tho' at the time he had not power to
put 'em into words; and indeed there is not greater proof of a
vast and elegant passion, than the being uncapable of expressing
it. – He had perhaps held her in this strict embrace, 'till some
accident had discovered and separated him from her; if the
alarm this manner of proceeding gave her modesty, had not
made her force her self from him. – They both stood in a silent
consternation, nor was he much less disordered at the temerity,
the violence of his ungovernable passion had made him guilty
of, than she was at the liberty he had taken; he knew not how
to excuse, nor she, to reproach; respect (the constant attendant
on a sincere affection) had tyed his tongue, and shame mixed
with the uncertainty after what manner she should resent it,
hers. At last, the natural confidence of his sex encouraged him
to break this mute entertainment. – "There are times madam,"
said he, "in which the wisest have not power over their own
actions – If therefore I have offended, impute not the crime to
me, but that unavoidable impulse which for a moment hurried
me from my self; for be assured while D'elmont can command

his thoughts they shall be most obedient to your wishes." – As Melliora was about to reply, she saw a servant coming hastily to speak to the Count, and was not a little glad of so favourable an opportunity to retire without being obliged to continue a discourse in which she must either lay a severe punishment on her inclinations by making a quarrel with him, or by forgiving him too easily trespass against the strict precepts of virtue she had always professed. She made what haste she could into her chamber, and carried with her a world of troubled meditations; she now no longer doubted the Count's passion, and trembled with the apprehension of what he might in time be prompted to; but when she reflected how dear that person she had so much cause to fear, was to her, she thought her self, at once the most unfortunate and most guilty of her sex.

The servant who gave 'em this seasonable interruption delivered a letter to his master, which he opening hastily, knowing that it came from his brother by the seal, found the contents as follows.

*I hoped (my dearest friend, and brother) by this day to have embraced you, but Fortune takes delight to disappoint our wishes, when highest raised and nearest to their aim. – The letter I carried from her, whom I think it my happiness to call sister joyned with my own faith, love, and assiduity; at length truimphed over all the little niceties and objections my charmer made against our journey, and she condescended to order every thing requisite for our departure from Amiens should be got ready. – But how shall I express the grief, the horrour, the distraction of my soul, when the very evening before the day we should have set out, as I was sitting with her, a sudden, but terrible illness, like the hand of death seized on her, she fell (oh! my brother) cold, and speechless in my arms – Guess, what I endured at that afflicting moment, all that I had of man, or reason left me; and sure had not the care of the Baroness and some other ladies (whom my cries drew in to her assistance) in a little time recovered her, I had not now survived to give you this account. Again, I saw the beauties of her eyes, again I heard her voice, but her disorder was yet so great that it was thought convenient she should be put to bed; the Barroness seeing my dispair, desired me not to quit her house, and by that means I had news every hour, how her feavor encreased, or abated, for the physicians being desired to deal freely, assured us, that was her distemper. For several days she continued in a condition that could give us no hopes of her recovery; in which time as you may imagine, I was little capable of writing. – The wildness of my unruly grief, made me not be permitted to come into her chamber; but they could not without they had made use of force, hinder me from lying at her door. I counted all her groans, heard every sigh the violence of her pain drew from her, and watched the countenance of every person who came out of her chamber, as men who would form a judgment of future consequences, do the signs in Heaven. – But I trouble you with this tedious recital, she is now, if there is any dependance on the doctors skill, past danger, tho' not fit to travel at least this month, which gives no small alleviation to the greatness of my joys (which otherwise would be unbounded) for her recovery, since it occasions so long a separation from the best of brothers, and of friends. Farewel, may all your wishes meet success, and an eternal round of happiness attend you; to add to mine, I beg you'll write by the first post, which next to seeing you, is the greatest I can taste. I am my lord with all imaginable tenderness and respect your most affectionate brother and humble servant.*

Brillian.

The Count judged it proper that Alovysa should see this letter, because it so much concerned her sister, and was ordering the servant to carry it to her, (not being willing himself to speak to her) just as she was coming towards him. She had received a letter from the Barroness De Beronvill, at the same time that the Chevalier Brillian's was brought and was glad to take the opportunity of communicating the contents of it, in hopes by this conversation to be reconciled to her husband. But the gloomy sullenness of the humour he had left her with, returned at sight of her, and after some little discourse of family affairs, which he could not avoid answering, walked carelessly away. She followed him at a distance 'till he was got up to the gallery, and perceiving he went toward his closet, mended her pace and was close to him when he was going in. "My lord," said she, with a voice but half assured and which would not have given her leave to utter more, if he had not interrupted her, by telling her he would be alone, and shutting the door hastily upon her; but she prevented his locking of it by pushing against it with all her force, and he, not exerting his, for fear of hurting her, suffered her entrance but looked on her with a countenance so forbidding, as in spite of the natural haughtiness of her temper, and the resolution she had made to speak to him, rendered her unable for some moments to bring forth a word; but the silent grief, which appeared in her face, pleaded more with the good nature of the Count, than any thing she could have said. He began to pity the unhappiness of her too violent affection, and to wish himself in a capacity of returning it; however, he (like most husbands) thought it best to keep up his resentments, and take this opportunity of quelling all the woman in her soul, and humbling all the little remains of pride that love had left her. "Madam," resumed he, with an accent, which tho' something more softened, was still imperious enough, "if you have anything of consequence to impart to me, I desire you will be as brief as you can, for I would be left to the freedom of my thoughts." – Alovysa could not yet answer, but letting fall a shower of tears, and throwing her self on the ground, embraced his knees with so passionate a tenderness, as sufficiently exprest her repentance for having been guilty of any thing to disoblige him. D'elmont was most sensibly[1] touched at this behaviour, so vastly different from what he could have expected from the greatness[2] of her spirit, and raising her with an obliging air, "I am sorry," said he, "that any thing should happen to occasion this submission, but since what's past, is out of either of our powers to recal, I shall endeavour to think of it no more, provided you'l promise me, never for the future to be guilty of any thing which may give me an uneasiness by the sight of yours." – 'Tis impossible to represent the transport of Alovysa at this kind expression, she hung upon his neck, kissed the dear mouth which had pronounced her pardon with

---

1   Noticeably, "perceptibly to the senses" (Johnson).
2   4th ed.; 1st ed. reads "greatest."

raptures of unspeakable delight, she sighed with pleasure, as before she had done with pain, she wept, she even died with joy! – "No, no my lord, my life, my angel," cried she, assoon as she had power to speak, "I never will offend you more, no more be jealous; no more be doubtful of my happiness! You are, and will be only mine, I know you will – your kind forgiveness of my folly, assures me that you are mine, not more by duty, than by love! a tye far more valuable than that of marriage." The Count conscious of her mistake had much ado to conceal his disorder at these words, and being unwilling she should proceed, as soon as he could (without seeming unkind or rude) disingage himself from her arms, took a pen in his hand, which he told her he was about to employ in answering Chevalier Brillian's letter. Alovysa who now resolved an entire obedience to his will, and remembring he had desired to be alone, withdrew, full of the idea, of an immagined felicity – Her heart was now at ease, she believed, that if her husband had any remains of passion for Amena, the impossibility of ever seeing her again, would soon extinguish them, and since she was so happily reconciled, was far from repenting her intercepting of his letter. But poor lady, she did not long enjoy this peace of mind, and this intervall of tranquility served but to heighten her ensuing miseries.

The Count's secret passion for Melliora grew stronger by his endeavouring to suppress it, and perceiving that she carefully avoided all opportunities of being alone with him one moment, since his behaviour to her in the garden, he grew almost distracted, with the continual restraint he was forced to put on all his words and actions. He durst not sigh, nor send an amorous glance for fear of offending her, and alarming his wives jealousie, so lately lulled to sleep. He had no person in whom he had confidence enough to trust with his misfortune, and had certainly sunk under the pressure of it, if Alovysa who observing an alteration in his countenance and humour, and fearing he was really indisposed (which was the excuse he made for his melancholy) had not perswaded him to go into the country, hoping that change of air might do him good. He had a very fine seat near Anjerville in the province of Le

Beausse, which he had not been at in some years, and he was very willing to comply with Alovysa's desires of passing the remainder of the summer in a solitude, which was now become agreeable to him; the greatest difficulty was in perswading Melliora to accompany them thither; he guessed by her reserved behaviour, that she only waited an opportunity to leave the place where he was, and was not mistaken in his conjecture. One day as they were talking of it, she told them that she was resolved to return to the monastery where she had been educated, that the world was too noisy a place for one of her taste, who had no relish for any of the diversions of it. Every word she spoke, was like a dagger to D'elmont's heart; yet he so artfully managed his endeavours, between the authority of a guardian, and the entreaties of a friend, that she was at last overcome. 'Tis hard for the severest virtue to deny themselves the sight of the person beloved, and whatever resolutions we make, there are but few, who like Melliora might not by such a lover, be prevailed upon to break them.

As soon as their coming into the country was spread abroad, they were visited by all the neighbouring people of quality, but there was none so welcome to D'elmont as the Baron D'espernay; they had before the Count's going into the army been very intimate acquaintance, and were equally glad of this opportunity to renew a friendship, which time and absence had not entirely eraced. The Baron had a sister young, and very agreeable, but gay even to coquetry; they lived together, being both single, and he brought her with him, hearing the Count was married, to visit his lady. There were several other young noble men, and ladies there at the same time, and the conversation grew so delightfully entertaining that it was impossible for persons less preposest than the Count and Melliora to retain their *chagrin*, but, tho' there were scarce any in the company that might not have list'ned with a pleased attention, to what those two admirable persons were capable of saying, yet their secret sorrows kept them both in silence, 'till Melantha, for that was the name of the Barons sister took upon her, to divert the company with some verses on love; which she took out of her pocket-book and read to 'em. Every body extolled the softness of the stile, and the subject they were upon. But Melliora who was willing to take all opportunities of condemning that passion, as well to conceal it in her self, as to check what ever hopes the Count might have, now discovered the force of her reason, the delicacy of her wit, and the penetration of her judgment, in a manner so sweetly surprizing to all that were strangers to her, that they presently found, that it was not want of noble, and truly agreeable thoughts or words to express 'em, that had so long deprived them of the pleasure of hearing her; she urged the arguments she brought against giving way to love, and the danger of all softning amusements, with such a becoming fierceness, as made every body of the opinion that she was born only to create desire, not be susceptible of it her self. The Count as he was most concerned, took the most particular notice of all she said, and was not a little alarmed to see her appear so much in earnest, but durst not answer, or endeavour to confute her, because of Alovysa's presence. But it was not long before he had an opportunity; a few days after he met with one, as full as he could wish. Returning one evening from the Baron D'espernay's whom he had now made the confident of his passion, and who had encouraged him in it, he was told that Alovysa was gone out to take the air, and hearing no mention of Melliora's being with her, he stayed not to enquire, but running directly to her chamber, made his eyes his best informers. He found her lying on a couch in a most charming dissabillee; she had but newly come from bathing, and her hair unbraided, hung down upon her shoulders with a negligence more beautiful than all the aids of art could form in the most exact *decorum* of dress, part of it fell upon her neck and breast, and with it's lovely shadyness, being of a delicate dark brown, set off to vast advantage, the matchless whiteness of her skin. Her gown and the rest of her garments were white, and all ungirt, and loosely flowing, discovered a thousand beauties, which modish[1] formalities conceal. A book lay open by her on which she had reclined her head, as if been tired with reading; she blushed at sight of the Count, and rose from off the couch

---

1  Fashionable.

with a confusion which gave new lustre to her charms, but he not permitting her to stir from the place she was in, sat down by her, and casting his eyes on the book which lay there, found it to be Ovid's *Epistles*.[1] "How madam," cried he, not a little pleased with the discovery, "dare you, who the other day so warmly inveighed against writings of this nature, trust your self with so dangerous an amusement? How happens it, that you are so suddenly come over to our party?" "Indeed my lord," answered she, growing more disordered, "it was chance rather than choice, that directed this book to my hands, I am yet far from approving subjects of this kind, and believe I shall be ever so. Not that I can perceive any danger in it, as to my self; the retirement I have always lived in, and the little propensity I find to entertain a thought of that uneasie passion, has hitherto secured me from any prepossession, without which, Ovid's art is vain." "Nay, madam," replied the Count, "now you contradict your former argument, which was that these sort of books were, as it were, preparatives to love, and by their softning influence melted the soul, and made it fit for amorous impressions, and so far, you certainly were in the right, for when once the fancy is fixed on a real object, there will be no need of auxillary forces, the dear idea will spread it self thro' every faculty of the soul, and in a moment inform us better, than all the writings of the most experienced poets, could do in an age." "Well, my lord," said she endeavouring to compose her self, "I am utterly unambitious of any learning this way, and shall endeavour to retain in memory, more of the misfortunes that attended the passion of Sappho,[2] than the tender, tho' never so elegant expressions it produced. And if all readers of romances took this method, the votaries of Cupid would be fewer, and the dominion of reason more extensive." "You speak," answered D'elmont, "as tho' love and reason were incompatible"; "there

---

1 Also called *Heroides*, they contained verse letters from legendary heroines to their absent husbands or lovers. The most popular work in this period by the Latin poet Ovid, they were translated in 1680 by a group that included John Dryden.
2 The most famous woman poet of classical antiquity, the Greek love poet Sappho figures in Ovid's *Epistles*, which Melliora has been reading, through the legend that she loved and was spurned by Phaon.

is no rule," said she, "my lord, without exception, they are indeed sometimes united; but how often they are at variance, where may we not find proofs? History is full of them, and daily examples of the many hair-brained matches, and slips much less excusable, sufficiently evince how little reason has to do in the affairs of love; I mean," continued she, with a very serious air, "that sort of love, for there are two, which hurries people on to an immediate gratification of their desires, tho' never so prejudicial to themselves, or the person they pretend to love." "Pray madam," said the Count a little netled at this discourse, "what love is that which seems at least to merit the approbation of a lady so extremely nice?" "It has many branches," replied she; "in the first place that which we owe to heaven; in the next to our king, our country, parents, kindred, friends; and lastly, that which fancy inclines, and reason guides us to, in a partner for life; but here every circumstance must agree, parity of age, of quality, of fortune, and of humour, consent of friends, and equal affection in each other, for if any one of these particulars fail, it renders all the rest of no effect." "Ah, madam," cried the Count not able to suffer her to proceed, "What share of pity then can you afford to a man who loves where almost all these circumstances are wanting, and what advice would you give a wretch so curst?" "I would have him think," said she more gravely then before. "How madam," resumed he, "'think' did you say? Alas! 'Tis thought that has undone him"; "that's very possible," answered she, "but yet 'tis want of thinking justly, for in a lovers mind illusions seem realities, and what at an other time would be looked on as impossible, appears easie then. They indulge, and feed their new-born folly with a prospect of hope, tho' ne're so distant a one, and in the vain pursuit of it, fly consideration, 'till dispair starts up in the midway, and bar's their promised view; whereas if they gave way to due reflection, the vanity of the attempt would presently be shown, and the same cause that bid 'em cease to hope, would bid 'em cease to wish." "Ah madam," said he, "how little do you know of that passion, and how easily could I disprove you by the example of my friend; dispair and love are of an equal age in him, and from the first moment he beheld his adorable charmer, he has languished without the least mixture of a flattering hope. I grant the flames with which our modern gallants are ordinarily animated, cannot long subsist without fewel, but where love is kindled in a generous heart by a just admiration of the real merits of the object beloved, reason goes hand in hand with it, and makes it lasting as our life." "In my mind," answered Melliora coldly, "an esteem so grounded may more properly be ascribed to friendship"; "then be it so madam," rejoyned the Count briskly, "friendship and love, where either are sincere, vary but little in their meaning; there may indeed be some distinctions in their ceremonies, but their essentials are still the same. And if the gentleman I speak of were so happy as to hope his friendship would be acceptable, I dare promise that he never would complain his love were not so." "You have a strange way," said she, "to confound idea's, which in my opinion are so vastly different, that I should make no difficulty in granting my friendship to as many of my acquaintance, as had merit to deserve it; but if I were to love in that general manner, 'twould be a crime would justly render me contemptible to mankind." "Madam," replied the Count, "when I spoke of the congruity of love and friendship, I did not mean that sort, which to me, seems unworthy of the name of either, but that exalted one, which made Orestes and Pilades, Theseus and Perithous[1] so famous; that, which has no reserve, no separate interest, or divided thoughts, that which fills all, – gives all the soul, and esteems even life a trifle, to prove it self sincere – What can love do more then yeild every thing to the object beloved? And friendship must do so too, or is not friendship! Therefore take heed fair angel," continued he taking her hand, and kissing it, "how you promise freindship, where you ne're mean to love." And observing she was silent, "Your hand," said he, "your lip, your neck, your breast, your all – all this whole heaven of beauty must be no longer in your own disposal – All is the prize of friendship!" As much confused as Melliora was, at these words which gave her sufficient reason to fear he would now declare himself more fully than she desired, she had

---

1   Pairs of classical male heroes famous for their devoted friendship.

spirit and resolution enough to withdraw her hand from his, and with a look, that spoke her meaning but too plainly for the repose of the enamoured D'elmont, "I shall take care my lord," said she, "how I commence a friendship with any person who shall make use of it to my prejudice."

The Count was now sensible of his error in going so far, and fearing he had undone himself in her esteem by his rash proceeding, thought it was best at once to throw off a disguise which in spite of his endeavours would fall off, of it's self, and by making a bold and free confession of his real sentiments, oblige her to a discovery of hers. – "I do not doubt your caution madam," answered he, "in this point. Your reserved behaviour, even to me, convinces me, but too fully, how little you are disposed to give, or receive any proofs of friendship. But perhaps," continued he with a deep sigh, "my too presuming eyes have rendred me a suspected person, and while you find in me the wretch I have discribed, you find nothing in me worthy of a happier fortune." "You are worthy of every thing my lord," said Melliora quite beside her self at these words, "nor are you less happy than you deserve to be; and I would rather that these eyes should lose their sight than view you otherwise than now I see you, blest in every circumstance, the darling of the world, the idol of the Court, and favourite of heaven!" "Oh stop!" cried D'elmont hastily interrupting her, "forbear to curse me farther, rather command my death, than wish the continuance of my present miseries. Cruel Melliora, too well, alass, you know what I have endured from the first fatal moment I beheld you and only feign an ignorance to distract me more. A thousand times you have read my rising wishes, sparkling in my eyes, and glowing on my cheeks, as often seen my virtue strugling in silent tremblings, and life-wasting anguish to suppress desire. Nay, madam," said he catching fast hold of both her hands, seeing her about to rise, "by all my sleepless nights, and restless days, by all my countless burning agonies ; by all the torments of my galled, bleeding heart, swear, that you shall hear me." "I have heard too much," cried Melliora not able to contain her self, "and tho' I am unwilling to believe you have any farther aim in this discourse than your diversion, yet I must tell your lordship there are themes more proper for it, than the daughter of your friend, who was entrusted to your care with a far different opinion of your behaviour to her." "What have I done," resumed the almost distracted Count, falling at her feet, and grasping her knees, "what have I done, inhumane Melliora! to deserve this rigour? My honour has hitherto prevailed above desire, fierce, and raging as it is, nor had I any other hopes by making this declaration than to meet that pity my misfortunes merit, and you cannot without ingratitude deny. Pity, even to criminals is allowed, and sure, where the offence is unvoluntary, like mine, 'tis due. 'Tis impossible to guess the conflict in Melliora's breast at this instant; she had heard a most passionate declaration of love from a married man, and by consequence, whatever his pretences were, could look on his designs no otherwise than aimed at the destruction of her honour, and was fired with a virtuous indignation. But then she saw in this married man, the only person in the world, who was capable of inspiring her with a tender thought; she saw him reduced to the last extremity of dispair for her sake. She heard his sighs, she felt his tremblings as he held her, and could not refrain shedding some tears, both for him and for her self, who indeed suffered little less; but the Count was not so happy as to be witness of this testimony of her compassion. He had reclined his head on her lap, possibly to hide those that forced their way thro' his eyes, at the same time; and Alovisa's voice which they heard below, giving them both an alarm, they had no further opportunity for speech, and the Count was but just gone out of the room, and Melliora laid on the couch in the same careless posture which he had found her in, when Alovysa entered the chamber, and after having a little pleasantly reproached her for being so lazy as not to accompany her in the walk she had been takeing, asked her if she had not seen the Count who she had been told was come home. Poor Melliora had much ado to conceal the disorder she was in at this question, but recovering her self as well as she could, answered in the affirmative; but that he had not stayed there longer than to enquire where she was gone, and that she knew not but he might be gone in search of her. This was enough to make Alovysa take her leave, impatient for the sight of her dear lord, a happiness she had not enjoyed since morning, but she was disappointed of her hope. The Count as late as it was in the evening, went into his chaise, which had not been set up, since he came from the Baron D'espernay's, and drove thither again with all the speed he could.

The Baron was extremely surprized at his sudden return, and with so much confusion and melancholy in his countenance. But much more so, when he had given him an account of what had passed between him and Melliora, and could not forbear rallying him excessively on the occasion. "What," said he, "a man of wit, and pleasure like Count D'elmont, a man who knows the sex so well, could he let slip so favourable an opportunity with the finest woman in the world; one for whose enjoyment he would die, – Could a frown, or a little angry coiness (which ten to one was but affected) have power to freeze such fierce desires." The Count was not at present in a humour to relish this merriment, he was too seriously in love to bear that any thing relating to it should be turned into ridicule, and was far from repenting he had done no more, since what he had done, had occasioned her displeasure. But the Baron, who had designs in his head, which he knew could not by any means be brought to succeed, but by keeping the Count's passion warm, made use of all the artifice he was master of, to embolden this respective[1] lover, to the gratification of his wishes. And growing more grave than he had been, "my lord," said he, "you do not only injure the dignity of our sex in general, but your own merits in particular, and perhaps even Melliora's secret inclinations, by this unavailing distant carriage, and causeless dispair. – Have you not confest that she has[2] looked on you with a tenderness, like that of love, that she has blushed at your sight, and trembled at your touch? – What would you more that she should do, or what indeed can she do more, in modesty to prove her heart is yours? A little resolution on your side would make her all yours – Women are taught by custom to deny what most they covet, and to seem angry when

---

1    Not respectful but "accurate; nice; careful; cautious" (Johnson).
2    4th ed.; 1st ed. reads "has she."

they are best pleased; believe me, D'elmont that the most rigid virtue of 'em all, never yet hated a man for those faults which love occasions." "All this," answered the Count, "is what I readily agree to, – but O her father's memory! My obligations to him! Her youth and innocence are daggers to my cool reflections — Would it not be pity Espernay," continued he with a deep sigh, "even if she should consent, to ruin so much sweetness?" The Baron could not forbear laughing at these words, and the Count who had started these objections, only with the hope of having them removed, easily suffered himself to be perswaded to follow his inclinations; and it was soon concluded betwixt them, that on the first opportunity, Melliora should fall a sacrifice to love.

The Count came not home until the next morning, and brought the Baron with him, for they were now become inseparable friends. At his return, he found Alovysa in a very ill humour for his being abroad all night, and in spite of the resolution she had made of shewing a perfect resignation to her husbands will, could not forbear giving him some hints, how unkindly she took it, which he but little regarded; all his thoughts were now bent on the gaining Melliora. But that lady alarmed at his late behaviour, and with reason doubting her own power of resenting it as she ought, or indeed resisting any future attempts he might make, feigned the necessity of performing some private rules of devotion enjoyned her as a pennance, and kept her chamber that she might not see him.

The disquietudes of D'elmont for being forced to live but for three or four days without the happiness of beholding her, convinced him how impossible it was for him to overcome his passion, tho' he should never so vigorously endeavour it, and that whatever method he should make use of to satisfie it, might be excused by the necessity.

What is it that a lover cannot accomplish when resolution is on his side? D'elmont after having formed a thousand fruitless inventions, at last pitched on one, which promised him, an assurance of success. In Melliora's chamber there was a little door that opened to a pair of back stairs, for the convenience of the servants coming to clean the room, and at the bottom of that discent, a gate into the garden. The Count set his wits to work to get the keys of those two doors, that of the garden stood always in it, nor could he keep it, without it's being mist at night, when they should come to fasten the gate, therefore, he carefully took the impression in wax, and had one made exactly like it. The other he could by no means compass without making some excuse to go to Melliora's chamber, and she had desired that none might visit her. But he overcome this bar to his design at last; there was a cabinet in it, where he told Alovysa he had put some papers of great concern which he now wanted to look over, and desired she would make an apology for his coming in, to fetch them. Melliora imagined this was only a pretence to see her, but his wife being with him, and he saying nothing to her, or taking any farther notice, than what common civility required, was not much troubled at it. While Alovysa was paying a complement, to the recluse, he was dextrous enough to slip the key out of the door, unperceived by either of them.

As soon as he had got the passport to his expected joys in his possession, he ordered a couple of saddle horses to be made ready, and only attended by one servant, rid out, as if to take the air; but when they were got about two or three miles from his house, commanded him to return, and tell his lady, that he should lye that night at the Baron D'espernay's; the fellow obeyed, and clapping spurs to his horse, was immediately lost in a cloud of dust.

D'elmont had sent this message to prevent any of the family sitting up expecting him, and instead of going to the Baron's, turned short, and went to Angerville, where meeting with some gentlemen of his acquaintance, he passed the hours 'till between twelve and one, as pleasantly as his impatience to be with Melliora, would give him leave. He had not much above a furlong to ride, and his desires made him not spare his horse, which he tyed by the bridle, hot and foaming as he was, to a huge oak which grew pretty near his garden; it was incompassed only with a hedge, and that so low, that he got over it without any difficulty. He looked carefully about him, and found no tell-tale lights in any of the rooms, and concluding all was as hushed as he could wish, opened the first door, but the encreasing transports of his soul, as he came up stairs, to be so near the end of all his wishes, are more easily imagined than exprest, but as violent as they were, they presently received a vast addition, when he came into the happy chamber, and by a most delightful gloom, a friend to lovers, for it was neither dark nor light, he beheld the lovely Melliora in her bed, and fast asleep; her head was reclined on one of her arms, a pillow softer and whiter far than that it leaned on; the other was stretched out, and with it's extention had thrust down the bed-cloths so far, that all the beauties of her neck and breast appeared to view. He took an inexpressible pleasure, in gazing on her as she lay, and in this silent contemplation of her thousand charms, his mind was agitated with various emotions, and the resistless posture he beheld her in, rouzed all that was honourable in him; he thought it pity even to wake her, but more to wrong such innocence, and he was sometimes prompted to return and leave her as he found her.

But whatever dominion, honour and virtue may have over our waking thoughts, 'tis certain that they fly from the closed eyes; our passions then exert their forceful power, and that which is most predominant in the soul, agitates the fancy, and brings even things impossible to pass. Desire, with watchful diligence repelled, returns with greater violence in unguarded sleep, and overthrows the vain efforts of day. Melliora in spite of her self, was often happy in idea, and possest a blessing, which shame and guilt, deterred her from in reality. Imagination at this time was active, and brought the charming Count much nearer than indeed he was, and he, stooping to the bed, and gently laying his face close to her's, (possibly designing no more than to steal a kiss from her, unperceived) that action, concurring at that instant, with her dream, made her throw her arm (still slumbering) about his neck, and in a soft and languishing voice, cry out, "Oh D'elmont, cease, cease to charm, to such a height – Life cannot bear these raptures. – And then again, embracing him yet closer, – O! too, too lovely Count – extatick ruiner!"

Where was now the resolution he was forming some moments before? If he had now left her, some might have applauded an honour so uncommon; but more would have condemned his stupidity, for I believe there are very few men, how stoical soever they pretend to be, that in such a tempting circumstance would not have lost all thoughts, but those, which the present opportunity inspired. That he did, is most certain, for he tore open his wastcoat, and joyned his panting breast to her's, with such a tumultuous eagerness! seized her with such a rapidity of transported hope-crowned passion, as immediately waked her from an imaginary felicity, to the approaches of a solid one. "Where have I been?" said she, just opening her eyes, "where am I?" – And then coming more perfectly to her self, "Heaven! What is this?" – "I am D'elmont," cried the orejoyed Count, "the happy D'elmont! Melliora's, the charming Melliora's D'elmont." "Oh, all ye saints," resumed the surprized, trembling fair, "ye ministring angels! whose business 'tis to guard the innocent! protect, and shield my virtue! O! say, how came you here, my lord?" "Love," said he, "love that does all, that wonder-working power has sent me here, to charm thee, sweet resister, into yielding." "O! hold," cried she, finding he was proceeding to liberties, which her modesty could not allow of, "forbear, I do conjure you, even by that love you plead, before my honour, I'll resign my life! Therefore, unless you wish to see me dead, a victim to your cruel, fatal passion, I beg you to desist, and leave me." – "I cannot – must not," answered he, growing still more bold, "what, when I have thee thus! thus, naked in my arms, trembling, defenceless, yeilding, panting with equal wishes, thy love confest, and every thought, desire! What could'st thou think if I should leave thee? How justly would'st thou scorn my easie tameness; my dulness, unworthy of the name of lover, or even of man! – Come, come no more reluctance," continued he, gathering kisses from her soft snowy breast at every word, "damp not the fires thou hast raised with seeming coiness! I know thou art mine! All mine! And thus I –" "Yet think," said she interrupting him, and struling in his arms, "think what 'tis that you would do, nor for a moments joy, hazard your peace for ever." "By Heaven," cried he, "I will this night be master of my wishes, no matter what to morrow may bring forth." As soon as he had spoke these words, he put it out of her power either to deny, or to reproach him, by stopping her mouth with kisses, and was just on the point of making good what he had vowed, when a loud knocking at the chamber door, put a stop to his beginning exstacy, and changed the sweet confusion Melliora had been in, to all the horrors of a shame and guilt distracted apprehension. They made no doubt but that it was Alovysa, and that they were betrayed; the Count's greatest concern was for Melliora, and the knocking still continuing and growing louder, all he could do in this exigence, was to make his escape, the way he came; there was no time for taking leave, and he could only say, perceiving she was ready to faint with her fears, "Be comforted, my angel, and resolute in your denials, to whatever questions the natural insolence of a jealous wife, may provoke mine to ask you; and we shall meet again (if D'elmont survives this disappointment without danger of so quick, so curst a separation)." Melliora was in too much distraction to make any answer to what he said, and he had left the room some moments before she could get spirit enough to ask who was at the door; but when she did, was as much surprized to find it was Melantha, who desired to be let in, as before she was frighted at the belief it was Alovysa; however, she immediately slipt on her night-gown, and slippers, and opened the door.

"You are a sound sleeper indeed," cried Melantha laughing, "that all the noise I have made could not wake you." "I have not been all this time asleep," answered Melliora, "but not knowing you were in the house, could not imagine who it was that gave me this disturbance." "I heartily ask your pardon," said Melantha, "and I know, my dear, you are too good natured to refuse it me, especially when you know the occasion, which is so very whimsical, that, as grave as you are, you cannot help being diverted with it – But come," continued she, "get on your cloths, for you must go along with me." "Where?" said Melliora, "Nay, nay, ask no questions," resumed Melantha, "but make hast, every minute that we idle away here, loses us the diversion of an age." As she spoke these words, she fell into such an excessive laughter, that Melliora thought her mad, but being far from sympathizing in her gayety, "it has always," said she, "been hitherto my custom to have some reason for what I do, tho' in never so trifling an affair, and you must excuse me, if I do not break it now." "Pish," cried Melantha, "you are of the oddest temper, – but I will give you your way for once, – provided you'll get your self ready in the mean time." "I shall certainly put on my cloaths," said Melliora, "lest I should take cold, for I expect you'll not permit me to sleep any more this night." "You may be sure of it," rejoyned Melantha. "But to the purpose, – you must know, having an hour or two on my hands, I came this evening to visit Alovysa, and found her in the strangest humour! Good God! What unaccountable creatures these married women are! – Her husband it seems had sent her word that he would lye at my brothers, and the poor loving soul could not bear to live a night without him. I stayed to condole with her, (tho' on my life, I could scarce forbear laughing in her face) 'till it was too late to go home. – About twelve a clock she yawned, stretched, and grew most horridly out of temper; railed at mankind prodigiously, and cursed matrimony as heartily as one of fourscore could do, that had been twice a widow, and was left a maid! – With much ado, I made her women thrust her into bed, and retired to a chamber which they showed me, but I had no inclination to sleep, I remembered my self of five or six *billet-doux*[1] I had to answer, – A lover, that growing foolishly troublesome, I have some thoughts of discharging to morrow – Another that I design to countenance, to pique a third – A new suit of cloaths, and trimmings for the next ball – Half a hundred new songs – and – a thousand other affairs of the utmost consequence to a young lady, came into my head in a moment; and the night being extreamly pleasant, I set the candle in the chimney, opened the window, and fell to considering – But I had not been able to come to a conclusion what I should do in any one thing I was thinking of, before I was interrupted in my cogitations with a noise of something rushing hastily thro' the mirtles under my window, and presently after, saw it was a man going hastily along toward the great alley of the garden. – At first I was going to cry out and alarm the family, taking it for a thief; but, dear Melliora, how glad am I that I did not! – For who do you think when I looked more heedfully, I perceived it was?" "Nay, how should I know?" cried Melliora peevishly, fearing

---

1    Love letters; such fashionable French phrases (see *beau-monde* below) place Melantha in the artificial world of gallantry and flirtation.

the Count's inadvertency had exposed himself and her to this foolish woman's curiosity. "It was Count D'elmont," resumed Melantha, "I'll lay my life, that he has been on some intreague to night. And met with a disappointment in it, by his quick return. – But prithee make hast, for I long to rally him about it." "What would you do madam?" said Melliora, "you would not sure go to him?" "Yes," answered Melantha, "I will go down into the garden, and so shall you. – I know you have a back way from your chamber – therefore lay aside this unbecoming demureness, and let us go, and talk him to death." "You may do as you please," said Melliora, "but for my part, I am for no such frolicks." "Was there every any thing so young, so formal as you are!" rejoyned Melantha, "but I am resolved to teaze you out of a humour so directly opposite to the *beau-monde*, and, if you will not consent to go down with me, I will fetch him up to your chamber." – "Hold! Hold," cried Melliora perceiving she was going, "what do you mean, for Heavens sake stay, what will Alovysa think?" – "I care not," replied the other, "I have set my heart on an hours diversion with him, and will not be baulked, if the repose of the world, much less that of a jealous, silly wife, depended on it."

Melliora saw into the temper of this capricious young lady too well not to believe she would do, as she had said, and perhaps, was not over willing to venture her with the Count alone, at that time of night, and in the humour she knew he was; therefore putting on an air more chearful than that she was accustomed to wear, "well," said she, "I will accompany you into the garden, since it will so much oblige you; but if the Count be wise, he will, by quitting the place, as soon as he see's us, disappoint you worse than I should have done, if I had kept you here." With these words she took her by the hand, and they went down the stairs, where the Count was but just past before them.

He had not power to go away, without knowing who it was, that had given him that interruption, and had stood all this time, on the upper step behind the inner door. His vexation, and disdain when he heard it was Melantha gave him as much pain, as his concern while he believed it Alovysa, and he could not forbear muttering a thousand curses on her impertinence. He always dispised, but now abhorred her. She had behaved her self to him in a fashion, as made him sufficiently sensible she was desirous of engaging him, and he resolved to mortifie by the bitterest slights, both her pride, and love, if 'tis proper to call that sort of liking which agitates the soul of *coquet*,[1] by that name.

The ladies walked in the garden for some time, and Melantha searched every bush, before she found the Count, who stood concealed in the porch, which being covered with *jessamin* and *fillaree*,[2] was dark enough to hide him from their view, tho' they had passed close to him as they came out. He had certainly remained there 'till morning, and disappointed Melantha's search in part of the revenge he owed her, if his desires to be with Melliora, on any terms, had not prevailed, even above his anger to the other. But he could not see that charmer of his soul, and imagine there might be yet an opportunity that night of stealing a kiss from her (now he believed resistless) lips, of touching her hand! her breast! And repeating some farther freedoms which his late advantage over her had given him, without being filled with wishes too fiery and too impatient to be restrained. He watched their turning, and when he saw they were near an alley which had another that led to it, he went round and met them.

Melantha was overjoyed at sight of him, and Melliora tho' equally pleased, was covered with such a confusion, at the remembrance of what had passed, that it was happy for her that her companions volubility gave her no room for speech. There is nothing more certain than that love, tho' it fills the mind with a thousand charming ideas, which those untouched by that passion, are not capable of conceiving, yet it entirely takes away the power of utterance, and the deeper impression it had[3] made on the soul, the less we are able to express it, when will-

---

1 Coquette – "a gay, airy girl; a girl who endeavours to attract notice" (Johnson). Note the widespread cultural assumption that girls should not seek notice; i.e. express ambition.
2 Jasmine, a climbing shrub, and (apparently) Phillyrea, a family of evergreen shrubs.
3 *Sic*, though the sense requires "has."

ing to indulge and give a loose to thought; what language can furnish us with words sufficient, all are too poor, all wanting both in sublimity, and softness, and only fancy! a lovers fancy! can reach the exalted soaring of a lovers meaning! But, if so impossible to be described, if of so vast, so wonderful a nature as nothing but it's self can comprehend, how much more impossible must it be entirely to conceal it! What strength of boasted reason? What force of resolution? What modest fears, or cunning artifice can correct the fierceness of it's fiery flashes in the eyes, keep down the strugling sighs, command the pulse, and bid the trembling, cease? Honour, and virtue may distance bodies, but there is no power in either of those names, to stop the spring that with a rapid whirl transports us from our selves, and darts our souls into the bosom of the darling object. This may seem strange to many, even of those who call, and perhaps believe that they are lovers, but the few who have delicacy enough to feel what I but imperfectly attempt to speak, will acknowledge it for truth, and pity the distress of Melliora.

As they were passing thro' a walk with trees on each side, whose intermingling boughs made a friendly darkness, and every thing undistinguishable, the amorous D'elmont throwing his eager arms round the wast of his (no less transported) Melliora, and printing burning kisses on her neck, reaped painful pleasure, and created in her, a racking kind of extasie, which might perhaps, had they been now alone, proved her desires were little different from his.

After Melantha had vented part of the raillery, she was so big with, on the Count, which he but little regarded, being wholly taken up with other thoughts, she proposed, going into the wilderness,[1] which was at the farther end of the garden, and they readily agreeing to it, "Come my lord," said she to the Count, "you are melancholy, I have thought of a way which will either indulge the humour you are in, or divert it, as you shall chuse. There are several little paths in this wilderness, let us take each a separate one, and when we meet, which shall be

---

1  Part of a garden cultivated to be less formal and regular than the rest, it has obvious symbolic value for a novelist presenting sexual pursuit in a formal society. The wilderness at Sotherton serves a similar purpose in Jane Austen's *Mansfield Park* (1814).

here, where we part, agree to tell an entertaining story, which whoever fails in, shall be doomed to the punishment of being left here all night." The Count at these words, forgot all his animosity, and was ready to hug her for this proposal. Melliora did a little oppose it; but the others were too powerful, and she was forced to submit. "Thou art the dullest creature, I lay my life my lord," cried Melantha, taking hold of the Count in a gay manner, "that it falls to her lot to stay in the wilderness." "Oh madam," replied the Count, "you are too severe, we ought always to suspend our judgment 'till after the tryal, which I confess my self so pleased with, that I am impatient for it's coming on." "Well then," said she laughing, "farewel for half an hour." "Agreed," cried the Count, and walked away. Melantha saw which way he went and took another path, leaving Melliora to go forward in that, in which they were, but I believe the reader will easily imagine that she was not long to enjoy the priviledge of her meditations.

After the Count had gone some few paces, he planted himself behind a thicket, which while it hid him, gave him the opportunity of observing them, and when he found the coast clear, rushed out, and with unhurting gripe, seized once more on the unguarded prey. "Blest turn of Fortune," said he in a rapture, "happy, happy moment!" – "Lost, lost Melliora," said she, "most unhappy maid! – Oh why, why my lord, this quick return?" "This is no place to answer thee," resumed he taking her in his arms, and bearing her behind that thicket, where himself had stood; 'twas in vain for her to resist, if she had had the power over her inclinations, 'till he setting her softly down, and beginning to caress her, in the manner he had done, when she was in bed, she assumed strength enough to raise her self a little, and catching hold of his transgressing hands, laid her face on 'em, and bathed 'em in a shower of tears. "O! D'elmont," said she, "cruel D'elmont! Will you then take advantage of my weakness? I confess I feel for you, a passion far beyond all, that yet, ever bore the name of love, that I no longer can withstand the too powerful magick of your eyes, nor deny any thing that charming tongue can ask, but now's the time to prove your self the heroe, subdue your self, as you have conquered me, be satisfied with vanquishing my soul, fix there your throne, but leave my honour free!" "Life of my life," cried he, "wound me no more by such untimely sorrows. I cannot bear thy tears, by Heaven they sink in to my soul, and quite unman me, but tell me," continued he tenderly kissing her, "could'st thou, will all this love, this charming – something more then softness – could'st thou I say, consent to see me pale and dead, stretched at thy feet, consumed with inward burnings, rather than blest, than raised by love, and thee, to all a deity in thy embraces. For O! Believe me when I swear, that 'tis impossible to live without thee." "No more, no more," said she letting her head fall gently on his breast, "too easily I guess thy sufferings by my own. But yet, D'elmont, 'tis better to die in innocence, than to live in guilt." "O! why," resumed he, sighing as if his heart would burst, "should what we can't avoid, be called a crime? Be witness for me Heaven! How much I have strugled with this rising passion, even to madness struggled! – But in vain, the mounting flame blazes the more, the more I would suppress it – My very soul's on fire – I cannot bear it – Oh Melliora! Did'st thou but know the thousandth part, of what this moment I endure, the strong convulsions of my warring thoughts, thy heart steeled as it is, and frosted round with virtue, would burst it's icy shield and melt in tears of blood to pity me." "Unkind and cruel!" answered she, "do I not pertake them then? – Do I not bear, at least, an equal share in all your agonies? – Hast thou no charms – Or have not I a heart? – A most susceptible, and tender heart? – Yes, you may feel it throb, it beats against my breast, like an imprisoned bird, and fain would burst it's cage! To fly to you, the aim of all it's wishes! – Oh D'elmont –" With these words she sunk wholly into his arms unable to speak more. Nor was he less disolved in rapture, both their souls seemed to take wing together, and left their bodies motionless, as unworthy to bear a part in their more elevated bliss.

But D'elmont at his returning sense, repenting the effects of the violent transport he had been in, now was preparing to take from the resistless Melliora, the last, and only remaining proof that she was all his own,[1] when Melantha (who had contrived

---

1   Logic might prefer "[not] all his own," but D'elmont may see Melliora's virginity as a trophy or waver between her virginity (proof she's not his) and the imminent consummation (proof she is).

this separation only with a design to be alone with the Count, and had carefully observed which way he took) was coming towards them. The rustling of her cloths among the bushes, gave the disappointed couple leave to rise from the posture they were in, and Melliora to abscond behind a tree, before she could come near enough to discern who was there.

Melantha, as soon as she saw the Count, put on an air of surprize, as if it were but by chance, that she was come into his walk, and laughing with a visible affection;[1] "bless me! You here, my lord!" said she, "I vow this has the look of assignation, but I hope you will not be so vain as to believe I came on purpose to seek you." "No madam," answered he coldly, "I have not the least thought of being so happy." "Lord! You are strangely grave," rejoyned she, "but suppose I really had come with a design to meet you, what kind of a reception might I have expected?" "I know no reason madam," said he, "that can oblige me to entertain a supposition so unlikely." "Well then," resumed she, "I'll put it past a supposition, and tell you plainly, that I did walk this way on purpose to divert your spleen." "I am sorry," replied he, tired to death with her impertinence, "that you are disappointed; for I am not in a humour at present, of receiving any diversion." "Fie," said she, "is this an answer for the gay, gallant, engaging Count D'elmont, to give a lady who makes a declaration of admiring him – who thinks it not too much to make the first advances, and who would believe her self fully recompenced for breaking thro' the nice decorums[2] of her sex, if he received it kindly." – "Madam," said he, not a little amazed at her imprudence, "I know of no such person, or if I did, I must confess, should be very much puzled how to behave in an adventure so uncommon." "Pish," answered she, growing vext at his coldness, "I know that such adventures are not uncommon with you. I'm not to learn the story of Alovysa, and if you had not been first addressed perhaps might have been 'till now unmarried." "Well madam," said he, more out of humour, "put the case that what you say were

---

1    The sense seems to require "affectation," the reading of the 4th ed.
2    This flirtatious reference to the precise conventions of female modesty again types Melantha as a coquet; Lady Wishfort, the carnal widow in William Congreve's comedy, *The Way of the World*, also affects nervousness about decorums.

true, I am married"; "and therefore," interrupted she, "you ought to be better acquainted with the temper of our sex, and know that a woman, where she says she loves, expects a thousand fine things in return." "But there is more than a possibility," answered he, "of her being disappointed, and methinks madam, a lady of your gaity should be conversant enough with poetry, to remember these too lines of a famous English poet.

*All naturally fly, what does pursue*
*'Tis fit men should be coy, when women woe.*"[1]

Melantha was fretted to the heart to find him so insensible, but not being one of those who are apt to repent any thing they have done, she only pretended to fall into a violent fit of laughter, and when she came out of it, "I confess," said she, "that I have lost my aim, which was, to make you believe I was dying for love of you, raise you to the highest degree of expectation, and then have the pleasure of baulking you at once, by letting you know the jest. – But your lordship is too hard for me, even at my own weapon, ridicule!" "I am mightily obliged to you madam," answered he, more briskly than before, "for your intention; however, but 'tis probable, if I could have been drawn into a belief that you were in earnest, I might at such a time, and such a place as this, have taken some measures which would have sufficiently revenged me on you – But come madam," continued he, "the morning begins to break, if you please we will find out Melliora, and go into the house." As he spoke these words, they perceived her coming towards them, who had only taken a little round to meet 'em, and they all three made what hast they could in; Count D'elmont asked a formal leave of Melliora to go thro' her chamber, none of the servants being yet stirring, to let him into the house any other way; which being granted, he could not help sighing as he passed by the bed, where he had been lately so cruelly disappointed, but had no opportunity to speak his thoughts at that time to Melliora.

---

1  Not identified; "too lines," of course is two lines, "woe" is *woo* (to rhyme with "pursue").

The Count rung for his gentleman to rise to undress him, and ordered him to send somebody to take care of his horse, and went to bed; Alovysa was very much surprized at his return from the Baron's at so unseasonable an hour, but much more so, when in the morning, Melantha came laughing into the chamber, and told her, all that she knew of the adventure of the night before; her old fit of jealousie now resumed it's dominion in her soul, she could not forbear thinking, that there was something more in it, than Melantha had discovered, and presently imagined that her husband stayed not at the Baron's, because she was abroad, but she was more confirmed in this opinion, when Melantha calling for her coach to go home, the Count told her that he would accompany her thither, having urgent business with her brother. 'Tis almost impossible to guess the rage Alovysa was in, but she dissembled it 'till they were gone, then going to Melliora's chamber, she vented part of it there, and began to question her about their behaviour in the wilderness. Tho' Melliora was glad to find, since she was jealous, that she was jealous of any body rather than her self, yet she said all that she could, to perswade her, that she had no reason to be uneasie.

But Alovysa was always of too fiery a nature to listen patiently to any thing could be offered, to alter the opinion she had taken up, tho' it were with never so little an appearance of reason, but much more now, when she thought her self, in a manner confirmed. "Forbear," said she, "dear Melliora to take the part of perfidy. I know he hates me, I read it in his eyes, and feel it on his lips; all day he shuns my converse, and at night, colder than ice he receives my warm embraces, and when (oh that I could tear the tender folly from my heart) with words as soft as love can form, I urge him to disclose the cause of his disquiet, he answers but in sighs, and turns away." "Perhaps," replied Melliora, "his temper naturally is gloomy, and love it self, has scarce the power to alter nature." "Oh no," interrupted Alovysa, "far from it. Had I ne'er known him otherwise, I could forgive what now I know, but he was once as kind as tender mothers to their new born babes, and fond as the first wishes of desiring youth. Oh! With what eagerness has he approached me, when absent but an hour – Hadst thou e're seen him in those days of joy, even thou, cold, colystered maid, must have adored him! What majesty, then sat upon his brow! – What matchless glories shone around him! – Miriads of Cupids, shot resistless darts in every glance, – his voice when softned in amorous accents, boasted more musick than the poets Orpheus![1] When e're he spoke, methought the air seemed charmed, the winds forgot to blow, all nature listned, and like Alovysa melted into transport – But he is changed in all – the heroe, and the lover are extinct, and all that's left, of the once gay D'elmont, is a dull, senceless picture." Melliora was too sensibly touched with this discourse, to be able presently to make any answer to it, and she could not forbear accompanying her in tears, while Alovysa renewed her complaints in this manner, "His heart," said she, "his heart is lost, for ever ravished from me, that bosom, where I had treasured all my joys, my hopes, my wishes, now burns and pants, with longings for a rival, curst, curst Melantha; by heaven they are even impudent in guilt, they toy, they kiss, and make assignations before my face, and this tyrant husband braves me with his falsehood, and thinks to awe me into calmness. But, if I endure it – No," continued she stamping, and walking about the room in a disordered motion, "I'll be no longer the tame easie wretch I have been – All France shall eccho with my wrongs – The ungrateful monster! – Villain, whose well nigh wasted stream of wealth had dried, but for my kind of supply, shall he enslave me – Oh Melliora shun the marriage bed, as thou would'st a serpent's den; more ruinous, more poysonous far, is man."

'Twas in vain that Melliora endeavoured to pacifie her, she continued in this humour all day, and in the evening received a considerable addition to her former disquiet. The Count sent a servant of the Barons (having not taken any of his own with him) to acquaint her, that he should not be at home that night. "'Tis well," said she ready to burst with rage, "let the Count know that I can change as well as he, and shall excuse his absence tho' it lasts to all eternity. Go," continued she, seeing

---

1   The mythical poet whose music charmed even wild animals.

him surprized, "deliver this message, and withal, assure him, that what I say, I mean." She had scarce made an end of these words, when she flung out of the room, unable to utter more, and locked her self into her chamber, leaving Melliora no less distracted, tho' for different reasons, to retire to her's.

She had not 'till now, had a moments time for reflection, since her adventure in the wilderness, and the remembrance of it, joyned with the dispair, and grief of Alovysa, which she knew her self the sole occasion of, threw her into most terrible agonies. She was ready to die with shame, when she considered how much the secret of her soul was laid open to him, who of all the world she ought most to have concealed it from, and with remorse, for the miseries her fatal beauty was like to bring on a family for whom she had the greatest friendship.

But these thoughts soon gave way to another, equally as shocking; she was present when the servant brought word the Count would lie abroad, and had all the reason imaginable to believe that message was only a feint, that he might have an opportunity to come unobserved to her chamber, as he had done the night before. She could not presently guess by what means he had got in, and therefore was at a loss how to prevent him, 'till recollecting all the circumstances of that tender interview, she remembred that when Melantha had surprized them, he made his escape by the back stairs into the garden, and that when they went down, the door was locked; therefore concluded it must be by a key, that he had gained admittance, and began to set her invention to work, how to keep this dangerous enemy to her honour, from coming in, a second time. She had no keys that were large enough to fill the wards,[1] and if she had put one in, on the inside, it would have fallen out immediately on the least touch, but at last, after trying several ways, she tore her hankerchief into small pieces, and thrust it into the hole with her busk,[2] so hard that it was impossible for any key to enter.

---

1   "The part of a lock which, corresponding to the proper key, hinders any other form opening it" (Johnson); Melliora is blocking the key-hole of an old-fashioned lock that can be opened from either side.

2   "A piece of steel or whalebone, worn by women to strengthen their stays" (Johnson); women's clothes (here the bodice) were reinforced by whalebone.

Melliora thought she had done a very heroick action, and sat her self down on the bed-side in a pleased contemplation of the conquest, she believed her virtue had gained over her passion. But alas! How little did she know the true state of her own heart? She no sooner heard a little noise at the door, as presently after she did, but she thought it was the Count, and began to tremble, not with fear, but desire.

It was indeed Count D'elmont who had borrowed horses and a servant of the Baron, and got into the garden as before, but with a much greater assurance now of making himself entirely happy in the gratification of his utmost wishes. But 'tis impossible to represent the greatness of his vexation and surprize, when all his efforts to open the door, were in vain. He found something had been done to the lock but could not discover what, nor by any means remove the obstacle which Melliora had put there. She, on the other hand was in all the confusion imaginable. Sometimes prompted by the violence of her passion, she would run to the door, resolving to open it, and then, frighted with apprehension of what would be the consequence, as hastily fly from it. If he had stayed much longer, 'tis possible love would have got the better of all other considerations, but a light appearing on the other side of the garden, obliged the thrice disappointed[1] lover to quit his post. He had sent away the horses by the servant who came with him, and had no opportunity of going to the Barons that night, so came to his own fore-gate, and thundered with a force, suitable to the fury that he was possest with; it was presently opened, most of the family being up. Alovysa had raved her self into fits, and her disorder created full employment for the servants, who busily running about the house with candles fetching things for her occasioned that reflection which he had seen.

The Count was told of his ladies indisposition, but he thought he had sufficient pretence not to come where she was, after the message she had sent him by the Baron's servant, and ordered a bed to be made ready for him in another chamber.

Alovysa soon heard he was come in, and it was with much ado, that her women prevailed on her not to rise and go to him

---

1  4th ed.; 1st ed. reads "thrice disappointment."

that moment, so little did she remember what she had said. She passed the night in most terrible inquietudes, and early in the morning went to his chamber, but finding it shut, she was obliged to wait, tho' with a world of impatience, 'till she heard he was stirring, which not being 'till towards noon, she spent all that time in considering how she should accost him.

As soon as the servant who she had ordered to watch, brought her word that his lord was dressing, she went into the room; there was no body with him but his gentleman, and he withdrawing out of respect, imagining by both their countenances there might something be said, not proper for him to hear, "I see," said she, "my presence is unwished, but I have learned from you to scorn constraint, and as you openly avow your falshood, I shall my indignation, and my just disdain!" "Madam," answered he, sullenly, "if you have any thing to reproach me with, you could not have chose a more unlucky time for it, than this, nor was I ever less disposed to give you satisfaction." "No, barbarous cold insulter," resumed she, "I had not the least hope you would, I find that I am grown so low in your esteem, I am not worth pains of an invention. – By Heaven, this damned indifference is worse than the most vile abuse! – 'Tis plain contempt! – O that I could resent it as I ought – then sword, or poison should revenge me – Why, why am I so curst to love you still? – O that those fiends," continued she, bursting into tears, "that have deformed thy soul, would change thy person too, turn every charm to horrid blackness, grim as thy cruelty, and foul as thy ingratitude, to free that heart, thy perjury has ruined." "I thought madam," said he, with an accent maliciously ironical, "that you had thrown off, even the appearances of love for me, by the message you sent me yesterday." – "O thou tormentor," interrupted she, "hast thou not wronged me in the tenderest point, driven me to the last degree of misery! To madness! – to dispair? And dost thou – can'st thou reproach me for complaining? – Your coldness, your unkindness stung me to the soul, and then I said, I know not what – But I remember well, that I would have seemed careless, and indifferent like you." "You need not," replied he, "give your self the trouble of an apology, I have no design to make a quarrel of it, and wish, for both our peace, you could as easily moderate your passions, as I can mine, and that you may the better do so, I leave you to reflect on what I have said, and the little reason I have ever given you, for such intemperance." He left the chamber with these words, which instead of quelling, more enflamed Alovysa's rage. She threw her self down into an elbow chair[1] that stood there, and gave a loose to the tempest of her soul. Sometimes she curst, and vowed the bitterest revenge. Sometimes she wept, and at others, was resolved to fly to death, the only remedy for neglected love. In the midst of these confused meditations, casting her eye on a table by her, she saw paper and something written on it, which hastily taking up, found it the Count's character, and read (to her inexpressible torment) these lines.

The Dispairing D'elmont to his Repenting Charmer.

*What cruel star last night, had influence over my inhumane dear? Say, to what cause must I ascribe, my fatal disappointment? For I would fain believe I owe it not to thee! – Such an action, after what thou hast confest, I could expect from nothing but a creature of Melantha's temper – No 'tis too much of the vain coquet, and indeed, too much of the jilt, for my adorable to be guilty of – And yet – Oh how shall I excuse thee? – When every thing was hushed, darkness my friend, and all my wishes raised, when every nerve trembled with fierce desires, and my pulse beat a call to love, or death, – (for if I not enjoy thee, that will soon arrive) then, then what, but thy self, forgetting all thy vows, thy tender vows of the most ardent passion, could have destroyed my hopes? – Oh where was then that love which lately flattered my fond doating soul, when sinking, dying in my arms, my charmer lay! And suffered me to reap each prologue favour to the greatest bliss. – But they are past, and rigid honour stands to guard those joys which –*

There was no more written, but there needed no more to make Alovysa, before half distracted, now quite so. She was

---

1  "A chair with arms to support the elbows" (Johnson).

now convinced that she had a much more dangerous rival than Melantha, and her curiosity who it might be, was not much less troublesome to her than her other passions.

She was going to seek her husband with this testimony of his infidelity in her hand, when he, remembring he had left it there, was coming hastily back to fetch it. The excess of fury which she met him with, is hardly to be imagined, she upbraid-ed him in such a fashion as might be called reviling, and had so little regard to good manners, or even decency in what she said, that it dissipated all the confusion he was in at first, to see so plain a proof against him in her hands, and rouzed him to a rage not much inferior to her's. She endeavoured (tho' she took a wrong method) to bring him to a confession, he had done amiss, and he, to lay the tempest of her tongue by storm-ing louder; but neither succeeded in their wish. And he, stung with the bitterness of her reproaches, and tired with clamour, at last flung from her with a solemn vow never to eat, or sleep with her more.

A wife if equally haughty and jealous, if less fond than Alovysa will scarce be able to comprehend the greatness of her sufferings. And it is not to be wondered at, that she, so violent in all her passions, and agitated by so many, at once, committed a thousand extravagancies, which those who know the force but of one, by the aid of reason may avoid. She tore down the Count's picture which hung in the room, and stamped on it, then the letter, her own cloths, and hair, and whoever had seen her in that posture would have thought she appeared more like what the Furies[1] are represented to be, than a woman.

The Count when he took leave the night before of the Baron D'espernay, had promised to return to him in the morn-ing, and give him an account of his adventure with Melliora, but the vexation of his disappointment, and quarrel with his wife, having hindred him all this time, the Baron came to his house, impatient to know the success of an affair on which his own hopes depended. He was told by the servants that their lord was above, and running hastily up without ceremony,

---

1   The classical female deities of revenge, usually three in number, who were often represented with snaky hair.

the first person he saw was Alovysa, in the condition I have discribed.

The Baron had passionately loved this lady from the first moment he had seen her, but it was with that sort of love, which considers more it's own gratification than the interest, or quiet of the object beloved. He imagined by the wildness of Alovysa's countenance and behaviour that the Count had given her some extraordinary occasion of distast, and was so far from being troubled at the sorrow he beheld her in, that he rejoyced in it, as the advancement of his designs. But he wanted not cunning to disguise his sentiments, and approaching her with a tender, and submissive air, entreated her to tell him the cause of her disorder. Alovysa had always considered him as a person of worth, and one who was entitled to her esteem by the vast respect he always paid her, and the admiration, which on every opportunity, he exprest for her wit and beauty. She was not perhaps far from guessing the extent of his desires, by some looks, and private glances he had given her, and notwithstanding her passion for the Count, was too vain to be offended at it. On the contrary, it pleased her pride, and confirmed her in the good opinion she had of her self, to think a man of his sense should be compelled by the force of her irresistable attractions to adore, and to dispair, and therefore made no difficulty of dis-burthening all the anguish of her soul, in the bosom of this, as she believed, so faithful friend.

The Baron seemed to receive this declaration of her wrongs, with all imaginable concern, and accused the Count of stupidi-ty in so little knowing the value of a jewel he was master of, and gave her some hints, that he was not unsensible who the lady was, that had been the cause of it, which Alovysa presently taking hold on, "O speak her name," said she; "quick, let me know her, or own thy friendship was but feigned to undo me, and that thou hat'st the wretched Alovysa." "O far," resumed he, "far be such thought, first let me die, to prove my zeal – my faith, sincere to you, who only next to Heaven, are worthy ado-ration –But forgive me if I say, in this, you must not be obeyed." "O why?" said she; "perhaps," answered he, "I am a trusted per-son – a confident, and if I should reveal the secret of my friend,

I know, tho' you approved the treachery, you would detest the traytor." "O! never," rejoyned she impatiently, "'twould be a service, more than the whole study of my life can pay. – Am I not racked, – stabbed – and mangled in idea? by some dark hand shaded with night and ignorance, and should I not be grateful for a friendly clue to guide me from this labyrinth of doubt, to a full day of certainty, where all the feind may stand exposed before me, and I have scope to execute my vengeance. Besides," continued she, finding he was silent and seemingly extreamly moved at what she said, "'tis joyning in the cause of guilt to hide her from me – Come, you must tell me – Your honour suffers else – Both that, and pity, plead the injured's cause." "Alas," said he, "honour can ne'er consent to a discovery of what, with solemn vows I have promised to conceal, but Oh – there is something in my soul, more powerful, which says, that Alovysa must not be denied." "Why then," cried she, "do you delay? Why keep me on the rack, when one short word would ease me of my torment?" "I have considered," answered he after a pause; "madam, you shall be satisfied, depend on it you shall, tho' not this moment, you shall have greater proofs than words can give you – occular demonstration[1] shall strike denial dumb." "What mean you?" interrupted she; "you shall behold," said he, "the guilty pair, linked in each others arms." "Oh Espernay," rejoyned she, "coud'st thou do that?" – "'Tis easie," answered he, "as I can order matters – But longer conference may render me suspected – I'll go seek the Count, for he must be my engine to betray himself – In a day or two, at farthest you shall enjoy all the revenge detection can bestow."

Alovysa would fain have perswaded him to have told her the name of her rival, in part of that full conviction he had promised her, but in vain, and she was obliged to leave the issue of this affair entirely to his management.

The Baron was extreamly pleased with the progress he had

---

1   Visible proof. Shakespeare's Othello jealously demands "ocular proof" of his wife's alleged infidelity (Othello III.iii.360). An actress, Haywood may also recall "ocular Proof" and "demonstrative Proof" from The Double Dealer (Complete Plays of William Congreve, ed. Herbert Davis [Chicago: U of Chicago P, 1967], 182), a comedy that features a sexually interested false friend and a jealous woman.

made, and did not doubt but for the purchase of this secret he should obtain every thing he desired of Alovysa. He found Count D'elmont full of troubled and perplexed thoughts, and when he had heard the history of his disappointment, "I am sorry to hear," said he, "that the foolish girl does not know her own mind – But come, my lord," continued he, after a little pause, "do not suffer your self to sink beneath a caprice, which all those who converse much with that sex must frequently meet with – I have a contrivance in my head, that cannot fail to render all her peevish virtue frustrate and make her happy in her own dispite." "Oh Espernay!" replied the Count, "thou talkest as friendship prompts thee, I know thou wishest my success, but alas! so many, and such unforseen accidents have happened hitherto to prevent me, that I begin to think the hand of fate has set me down for lost." "For shame my lord," interrupted the Baron, "be not so poor in spirit – Once more I tell you that she shall be yours – A day or two shall make her so – And because I know you lovers are unbelieving, and impatient – I will communicate the means. A ball, and entertainment shall be provided at my house, to which all the neighbouring people of condition shall be envited, amongst the number your self, your lady, and Melliora; it will be late before 'tis done, and I must perswade your family, and some others who live farthest off (to countenance the design)[1] to stay all night; all that you have to do, is to keep up your resentment to Alovysa that you may have a pretence to sleep from her. I shall take care to have Melliora placed where no impediment may bar your entrance." "Impossible suggestion!" cried D'elmont shaking his head, "Alovysa is in too much rage of temper to listen to such an invitation, and without her, we must not hope for Melliora." "How industrious are you," resumed the Baron, "to create difficulties where there is none, tho' I confess this may have, to you, a reasonable appearance of one. But know, my friendship builds it's hopes to serve you on a sure foundation – this jealous, furious wife, makes me the confident of her imagined injuries, conjures me to use all my interest with you for a reconcilement, and believes

---

1   To give a face (a plausible appearance) to the scheme.

I am now pleading for her – I must for a while rail at your ingratitude, and condemn your want of taste, to keep my credit with her, and now and then sweeten her with a doubtful hope that it may be possible at last to bring you to acknowledge that you have been in an error; this, at once confirms her, that I am wholly on her side, and engages her to follow my advice."

Tho' nothing palls desire so much as too easie an assurance of means to gratifie it, yet a little hope is absolutely necessary to preserve it. The fiery wishes of D'elmont's soul, before chilled by dispair, and half supprest with clouding griefs, blazed now, as fierce, and vigorous as ever, and he found so much probability in what the Baron said, that he was ready to adore him for the contrivance.

Thus all parties but Melliora remained in a sort of pleased expectation. The Count doubted not of being happy, nor Alovysa of having her curiosity satisfied by the Baron's assistance, nor himself of the reward he designed to demand of her for that good service, and each longed impatiently for the day, or rather night, which was to bring this great affair to a period. Poor Melliora was the only person, who had no interval of comfort. Restrained by honour, and enflamed by love, her very soul was torn. And when she found that Count D'elmont made no attempt to get into her chamber again, as she imagined he would, she fell into a dispair more terrible than all her former inquietudes, she presently fancied that the disappointment he had met with the night before, had driven the hopeless passion from his heart, and the thoughts of being no longer beloved by him were unsuppportable. She saw him not all that day, nor the next, the quarrel between him and Alovysa having caused separate tables, she was obliged in decency, to eat at that where she was, and have the mortification of hearing her self cursed every hour, by the enraged wife, in the name of her unknown rival, without daring to speak a word in her own vindication.

In the mean time the Baron diligent to make good the promises he had given the Count and Alovysa, for his own ends, got every thing ready, and came himself to D'elmont's house, to entreat their company at his. "Now madam," said he to Alovysa, "the time is come to prove your servants faith. This night shall put an end to your uncertainty." They had no opportunity for further speech; Melliora came that moment into the room, who being asked to go to the ball, and seeming a little unwilling to appear at any publick diversion by reason of the late death of her father, put the Baron in a mortal apprehension for the success of his undertaking. But Alovysa joyning in his entreaties she was at last prevailed upon. The Count went along with the Baron in his chariot. And the lady soon followed in an other.

There was a vast deal of company there, and the Count danced with several of the ladies, and was extreamly gay amongst them. Alovysa watched his behaviour, and regarded every one of them, in their turn, with jealousie, but was far from having the least suspicion of her whom only she had cause.

Tho' Melliora's greatest motive to go was, because she might have the happiness of seeing her admired Count, a blessing, she had not enjoyed these two days, yet she took but little satisfaction in that view, without an opportunity of being spoke to by him. But that uneasiness was removed, when the serious dances being over, and they all joyning in a grand ballet, he every now and then got means to say a thousand tender things to her, and would sometimes when at distance from Alovysa pretend to be out, on purpose to stand still and talk to her. This kind of behaviour banished part of her sufferings, for tho' she could consider both his, and her own passion in no other view, than that of a very great misfortune to them both, yet there are so many pleasures even in the pains of love. Such tender thrillings, such soul-ravishing amusements attend some happy moments of contemplation, that those who most endeavour, can wish but faintly to be freed from.

When it grew pretty late, the Baron made a sign to the Count to follow him into a little room joyning to that where they were, and when he had, "Now my lord," said he, "I doubt not but this night will make you entirely possessor of your wishes. I have prolonged the entertainment on purpose to detain those who 'tis necessary for our design, and have ordered a chamber for Melliora which has no impediment to bar your entrance." "O! Thou best of friends," answered D'elmont, "how shall I requite thy goodness?" "In making," resumed the Baron, "a right use of the opportunity I give you, for if you do not, you render fruitless all the labours of my brain, and make me wretched while my friend is so." "Oh! fear me not," cried D'elmont in a rapture, "I will not be denied, each faculty of my soul is bent upon enjoyment, tho' death in all it's various horrors glared upon me, I'd scorn 'em all in Melliora's arms – O! the very name transports me – new fires my blood, and tingles in my vains – Imagination points out all her charms – Methinks I see her lie in sweet confusion – fearing – wishing – melting – her glowing cheeks – her closing dying eyes – her every kindling – Oh 'tis too vast for thought! Even fancy flags, and cannot reach her wonders!" As he was speaking, Melantha who had taken notice of his going out of the room, and had followed him with a design of talking to him, came time enough to hear the latter part of what he said, but seeing her brother with him withdrew with as much hast as she came, and infinitely more uneasiness of mind; she was now but too well assured that she had a greater difficulty than the Count's matrimonial engagement to get over, before she could reach his heart, and was ready to burst with vexation to think she was supplanted. Full of a thousand tormenting reflections she returned to the ball room, and was so out of humour all the night that she could hardly be commonly civil to any body that spoke to her.

At last the hour so much desired by the Count, the Baron, and Alovysa (tho' for various reasons) was arrived. The company broke up, those who lived near, which were the greatest part went home, the others, being entreated by the Baron stayed. When they were to be conducted to their chambers, he called Melantha and desired she would take care of the ladies as he should direct, but above all charged to place Alovysa and Melliora in two chambers which he showed her.

Melantha was now let into the secret she so much desired to know, the name of her rival, which she had not come time enough to hear, when she did the Count's rapturous description of her. She had before found out, that her brother was in love with Alovysa, and did not doubt but that there was a double intrigue to be carried on that night, and was the more confirmed in that opinion, when she remembred that the Baron had ordered the lock that day to be taken off the door of that chamber where Melliora was to be lodged. It presently came into her head, to betray all she knew to Alovysa, but she soon rejected that resolution for another, which she thought would give her a more pleasing revenge. She conducted all the ladies to such chambers as she thought fit, and Alovysa to that her brother had desired, having no design of disappointing him, but Melliora she led to one where she always lay her self, resolving to supply her place in the other, where the Count was to come. "Yes," said she to her self, "I will receive his vows in Melliora's room, and when I find him raised to the highest pitch of expectation, declare who I am, and awe him into tameness; 'twill be a charming piece of vengeance, besides if he be not the most ungrateful man on earth, he must adore my generosity in not exposing him to his wife, when I have him in my power, after the coldness, he has used me with. She found something so pleasing in this contrivance, that no considerations whatever could have power to deter her from pursuing it.

When the Baron found every thing was silent, and ready for his purpose, he went softly to Count D'elmont's chamber, where he was impatiently expected; and taking him by the hand, led him to that, where he had ordered Melliora to be lodged; when they were at the door, "You see my lord," said he, "I have kept my promise. There lies the idol of your soul, go in, be bold, and all the happiness you wish attend you." The Count was in too great a hurry of disordered thoughts to make him any other answer than a passionate embrace, and gently pushing open the door, which had no fastning to it, left the Baron to prosecute the remaining part of his treacherous design.

Alovysa had all the time of her being at the Baron's, endured most grievous racks of mind; her husband appeared to her, that night, more gay, and more lovely if possible than ever, but that contentment which sat upon his face, and added to his graces, stung her to the soul, when she reflected how little simpathy their was between them; "scarce a month," said she to her self, "was I blessed[1] with those looks of joy, a pensive sullenness has dwelt upon his brow e're since, 'till now, 'tis from my ruin that his pleasure flows, he hates me, and rejoyces in a pretence, tho' ne'er so poor a one, to be absent from me." She was inwardly tossed with a multitude of these, and the like perturbations, tho' the assurance the Baron had given her of revenge, made her conceal them tollerably well, while she was in company, but when she was left alone in the chamber, and perceived the Baron did not come so soon as she expected, her rage broke out in all the violence imaginable. She gave a loose to every furious passion, and when she saw him enter, "Cruel Espernay," said she, "where have you been! – Is this the friendship which you vowed? To leave me here distracted with my griefs, while my perfidious husband, and the cursed she, that robs me of him, are perhaps, as happy, as their guilty love can make them?" "Madam," answered he, "'tis but a moment since they are met"; "a moment!" interrupted she, "a moment is too much; the smallest particle of undivided time, may make my rival blest, and vastly recompence for all that my revenge can do." "Ah madam," resumed the Baron, "how dearly, do you still love, that most ungrateful man. I had hopes that the full knowledge of his falshood might have made you scorn the scorner"; "I shall be able by to morrow," replied the cunning Alovysa who knew his drift well enough, "to give you a better account of my sentiments than now I can. – But why do we delay," continued she impatiently, "are they not together?" – The Baron saw this was no time to press her farther, and therefore taking a wax-candle which stood on the table, in one hand, and offering the other to lead her, "I am ready madam," said he, "to make good my promise, and shall esteem no other hours of my life happy but those which may be serviceable to you." They had only a small part of a gallery to go thro', and Alovysa had no time to answer to these last words, if she had been composed enough to have done it, before they were at the door, which as soon as the Baron had brought her to, he withdrew will all possible speed.

---

1  4th ed.; 1st ed. reads "bless."

Tho' the Count had been but a very little time in the arms of his supposed Melliora, yet he had made so good use of it, and had taken so much advantage of her complying humour, that all his fears were at an end, he now thought himself the most fortunate of all mankind; and Melantha was far from repenting the breach of the resolution she had made of discovering her self to him. His behaviour to her was all rapture, all killing extacy, and she flattered herself with a belief, that when he should come to know to whom he owed that bliss he had possessed, he would not be ungrateful for it.

What a confused consternation must this pair be in, when Alovysa rushed into the room; – 'tis hard to say, which was the greatest, the Count's concern for his imagined Melliora's honour, or Melantha's for her own; but if one may form a judgment from the levity of the one's temper, and the generosity of the other's, one may believe that his had the preheminence. But neither of them were so lost in thought, as not to take what measures the place and time would permit, to baffle the fury of this incensed wife. Melantha slunk under the cloaths, and the Count started up in the bed at the first appearance of the light, which Alovysa had in her hand, and in the most angry accent he could turn his voice to, asked her the reason of her coming there; rage, at this sight (prepared and armed for it as she was) took away all power of utterance from her; but she flew to the bed, and began to tear the cloaths (which Melantha held fast over her head) in so violent a manner that the Count found the only way to tame her, was to meet force with force; so jumping out, he seized on her, and throwing her into a chair, and holding her down in it, "Madam, madam," said he, "you are mad, and I as such shall use you, unless you promise to return quietly and leave me." She could yet bring forth no other words, than "villain," – "monster!" and such like names, which her passion, and injury suggested, which he but little regarding but for the noise she made, "for shame," resumed he, "expose not thus your self and me; if you cannot command your temper, at least confine your clamours" – "I will not stir," said she, raving and struggling to get loose, 'till I have seen the face that has undone me, I'll tear out her bewitching eyes – the curst adultress! and

leave her mistress of fewer charms than thou canst find in me."
She spoke this with so elevated a voice, that the Count endeavoured to stop her mouth, that she might not alarm the company that were in the house, but he could not do it time enough
to prevent her from schrikeing[1] out, "Murder. – Help! or the
barbarous man will kill me!" At these words the Baron came
running in immediately, full of surprize and rage at something
he had met with in the mean time. "How came this woman
here," cried the Count to him. "Ask me not my lord," said he,
"for I can answer nothing, but every thing this cursed night, I
think, has happened by enchantment"; he was going to say
something more, but several of his guests hearing a noise, and
cry of murder, and directed by the lights they saw in that room,
came in, and presently after a great many of the servants, that
the chamber was as full as it could hold. The Count let go his
wife on the sight of the first stranger that entered; and indeed,
there was no need of his confining her in that place (tho' he
knew not so much) for the violence of so many contrary passions warring in her breast at once, had thrown her into a
swoon, and she fell back when he let go his hold of her,
motionless, and in all appearance dead. The Count said little,
but began to put on his cloaths, ashamed of the posture he had
been seen in; but the Baron endeavoured to perswade the company, that it was only a family quarrel of no consequence, told
them he was sorry for the disturbance it had given them, and
desired them to return to their rest, and when the room was
pretty clear, ordered two or three of the maids to carry Alovysa
to her chamber, and apply things proper for her recovery; as
they were bearing her out, Melliora who had been frighted as
well as the rest with the noise she heard, was running along the
gallery to see what had happened, and met them; her trouble to
find Alovysa in that condition was unfeigned, and she assisted
those that were employed about her, and accompanied them
where they carried her.

The Count was going to the bed-side to comfort the concealed fair, that lay still under the cloaths, when he saw Mel-

---

1   "Shrieking" in an odd but expressive spelling; 4th ed. reads "schrieking."

liora at the door. What surprize was ever equal to his, at this view – He stood like one transfixed with thunder, he knew not what to think, or rather could not think at all, confounded with a seeming impossibility. He beheld the person, whom he thought had lain in his arms, whom he had enjoyed, whose bulk and proportion he still saw in the bed, whom he was just going to address to, and for whom he had been in all the agonies of soul imaginable, come from a distant chamber, and unconcerned, ask cooly how Alovysa came to be taken ill. He looked confusedly about, sometimes on Melliora, sometimes toward the bed and sometimes on the Baron; "am I awake," said he, "or is every thing I see and hear illusion?" The Baron could not presently resolve after what manner he should answer, tho' he perfectly knew the truth of this adventure, and who was in the bed; for, when he had conducted Alovysa to that room, in order to make the discovery he had promised, he went to his sister's chamber, designing to abscond there, in case the Count should fly out on his wife's entrance, and seeing him there, imagine who it was that betrayed him; and finding the door shut, knocked and called to have it opened; Melliora, who began to think she should lye in quiet no where, asked who was there, and what he would have; "I would speak with my sister," replied he, as much astonished then, to hear who it was that answered him, as the Count was now to see her, and Melliora having assured him that she was not with her, left him no room to doubt, by what means the exchange had been made. Few men, how amorous soever themselves, care that the female part of their family should be so, and he was most sencibly mortified with it, but reflecting that it could not be kept a secret, at least from the Count, "My lord," said he, pointing to the bed, "there lyes the cause of your amazement, that wicked woman has betrayed the trust I reposed in her, and deceived both you and me; rise," continued he, throwing open the curtains, "thou shame of thy sex, and everlasting blot and scandal of the noble house thou art descended from, rise, I say, or I will stabb thee here in this scene of guilt"; in speaking these words, he drew out his sword, and appeared in such a real fury, that the Count tho' more and more amazed with every thing he saw and heard, made no doubt but he would do as he said, and run to hold his arm.

As no woman that is mistress of a great share of wit *will* be a coquet, so no woman that has not a little *can* be one. Melantha, tho' frighted to death with these unexpected occurrences, feigned a courage, which she had not in reality, and thrusting her head a little above the cloaths, "Bless me brother," said she, "I vow I do not know what you mean by all this bustle, neither am I guilty of any crime. I was vext indeed to be made a property of, and changed beds with Melliora for a little innocent revenge; for I always designed to discover my self to the Count time enough to prevent mischief." The Baron was not so silly as to believe what she said, tho' the Count as much as he hated her, had too much generosity to contradict her, and keeping still hold of the Baron, "Come Espernay," said he, "I believe your sister's stars and mine have from our birth been at variance, for this is the third disappointment she has given me; once in Melliora's chamber, then in the wilderness, and now here; but I forgive her, therefore let us retire and leave her to her repose. The Baron was sensible that all the rage in the world could not recal what had been done, and only giving her a furious look, went with the Count out of the room, without saying any thing more to her at that time.

The Baron with much entreating, at last prevailed on Count D'elmont to go into his bed, where he accompanied him; but they were both of them too full of troubled meditations to sleep. His sister's indiscretion vext the Baron to the heart, and took away great part of the joy, for the fresh occasion the Count had given Alovysa to withdraw her affection from him. But with what words can the various passions that agitated the soul of D'elmont be described? The transports he had enjoyed in an imaginary felicity, were now turned to so many real horrors; he saw himself exposed to all the world, for it would have been vanity to the last degree, to believe this adventure would be kept a secret; but what gave him the most bitter reflection was, that Melliora, when she should know it, as he could not doubt but she immediately would be told it by Alovysa, would judge of it by the appearance, and believe him, at once, the most vicious, and most false of men. As for his wife he thought not of her, with any compassion for his[1] sufferings, but with rage and hate, for that jealous curiosity, which he supposed had led her to watch his actions that night, (for he had not the least suspicion of the Baron). Melantha he always dispised, but now detested, for the trick she had put upon him, yet thought it would be not only unmanly, but barbarous to let her know he did so. It was in vain for him to endeavour to come to a determination after what manner he should behave himself to any of them, and when the night was past in forming a thousand several resolutions, the morning found him as much to seek as before. He took his leave early of the Baron, not being willing to see any of the company after what had happened, 'till he was more composed.

He was not deceived in his conjectures concerning Melliora, for Alovysa was no sooner recovered from her swoon, than she with bitter exclamations told her what had been the occasion, and put that astonished fair one into such a visible disorder, as had she not been too full of misery to take notice of it, had made her easily perceive that she was deeply interested in the story. But whatever she said against the Count, as she could not forbear something, calling him ungrateful, perjured, deceitful, and inconstant, Alovysa took only, as a proof of friendship to her self, and the effects of that just indignation all women ought to feel for him, that takes a pride in injuring any one of them.

When the Count was gone, the Baron sent to Alovysa to enquire of her health, and if he might have leave to visit her in her chamber, and being told she desired he should, resolved now to make his demand. Melliora had but just parted from her, in order to get herself ready to go home, and she was alone when he came in. As soon as the first civilities were over, she began afresh to conjure him to let her know the name of her rival, which he artfully evading, tho' not absolutely denying, made her almost distracted; the Baron carefully observed her every look and motion, and when he found her impatience was

---

1   *Sic*, though the sense seems to require "her."

raised to the highest degree; "Madam," said he, taking her by the hand and looking tenderly on her, "you cannot blame a wretch, who had lavished all he had away to one poor jewel, to make the most he can of that, to supply his future wants. I have already forfeited all pretence to honour, and even common hospitality, by betraying the trust that was reposed in me, and exposing under my own roof, the man who takes me for his dearest friend, and what else I have suffered from that unavoidable impulse which compelled me to do all this, your self may judge, who too well know the pangs, and tortures of neglected love – Therefore" continued he with a deep sigh, "since the last reserve is all my hopes dependance, do not, oh charming Alovysa think me mercinary, if I presume to set a price upon it, which I confess too high, yet nothing less can purchase." "No price," replied Alovysa, who thought a little condescention was necessary to win him to her purpose, "can be too dear to buy my peace, nor recompence too great for such a service." "What, not your love?" said the Baron eagerly kissing her hand. "No," resumed she, forcing herself to look kindly on him, "not even that, when such a proof of your's engages it; but do not keep me longer on the rack, give me the name and then" – She spoke these last words with such an air of languishment, that the Baron thought his work was done, and growing bolder, from her hand he proceeded to her lips, and answered her only in kisses, which distastful as they were to her, she suffered him to take without resistance, but that was not all he wanted, and believing this the critical minute, he threw his arms round her waste, and began to draw her by little and little toward the bed; which she affected to permit with a kind of an unwilling willingness, saying, "well if you would have me be able to deny you nothing you can ask, tell me the name I so much wish to know." But the Baron was as cunning as she, and seeing thro' her artifice, was resolved to make sure of his reward first; "yes, yes, my adorable Alovysa," answered he, having brought her now very near the bed, "you shall immediately know all; thy charms will force the secret from my breast, close as its lodged within my utmost soul. – Dying with rapture, I will tell thee all. – If that a thought of this injurious husband can interpose amidst extatick joys." What will not some women venture to satisfy a jealous curiosity? Alovysa had feigned to consent to his desires (in hopes to engage him to a discovery) so far, and had given him so many liberties, that now, it was as much as she could do to save herself, from the utmost violence, and perceiving she had been outwitted, and that nothing but the really yielding up her honour could oblige him to reveal what she desired. "Villain," said she, struggling to get loose from his embrace, "dare thy base soul believe so vilely of me? Release me from thy detested hold, or my cries shall force thee to it, and proclaim thee for what thou art, a monster!" The Baron was not enough deluded by her pretence of kindness to be much surprized at this sudden turn of her behaviour, and only cooly answered, "Madam, I have no design of using violence, but perceive if I had depended on your gratitude, I had been miserably deceived." "Yes," said she looking contemptibly on him, "I own thou woud'st; for whatsoever I might say, or thou coud'st hope, I love my husband still, with an unbated fondness doat upon him! Faithless and cruel as he is, he still is lovely! His eyes loose nothing of their brightness, nor his tongue its softness! His very frowns have more attraction in them, than any others smiles! And canst thou think? thou, so different in all from him, that thou seem'st not the same species of humanity, nor ought'st to stile thy self a man, since he is no more. Can'st thou, I say, believe a woman, blest as Alovysa has been, can e're blot out the dear remembrance and quit her hopes of regained paradise in his embrace, for certain hell in thine?" She spoke these words with so much scorn, that the Baron skilled as he was in every art to tempt, could not conceal the spite he conceived at them, and letting go her hand (which perforce he had held), "I leave you, madam," said he, "to the pleasure of enjoying your own humour; neither that, nor your circumstances are to by envied, but I would have you to remember that you are your own tormentor, while you refuse the only means can bring you ease." "I will have ease another way," said she, incensed at the indignity she imagined he treated her with, "and if you still persist in refusing to discover to me the person who has injured me, I shall make no difficulty of letting the

Count know how much of his secrets you have imparted, and for what reason you conceal the other." "You may do so," answered he, "and I doubt not but you will – Mischief is the darling favourite of woman! Blood, is the satisfaction perhaps, that you require, and if I fall by him, or he by me, your revenge will have its aim, either on the unloving, or the unloved; for me, I set my life at nought, without your love, 'tis Hell; but do not think that even dying, to purchase absolution I'd reveal one letter of that name, you so much wish to hear; the secret shall be buryed with me. – Yes, madam," continued he with a malicious air, "that happy fair unknown, whose charms have made you wretched, shall undiscovered, and unguessed at, triumph in those joys, you think none but your Count can give." Alovysa had not an oppportunity to make any answer to what he said; Melliora came that moment into the room, and asked if she was ready to go, and Alovysa saying that she was, they both departed from the Baron's house, without much ceremony on either side.

Alovysa had not been long home before a messenger came to acquaint her, that her sister having mist of her at Paris, was now on her journey to Le Beausse, and would be with her in a few hours. She rejoyced as much at this news, as it was possible for one so full of disquiet to do, and ordered her chariot and six to be made ready again, and went to meet her.

D'elmont heard of Ansellina's coming almost as soon as Alovysa, and his complaisance for ladies, joyned with the extream desire he had of seeing his brother, whom he believed was with her, would certainly have given him wings to have flown to them with all imaginable speed, had not the late quarrel between him and his wife, made him think it was improper, to join company with her on any account whatever. He was sitting in his dressing-room window in a melancholly and disturbed meditation, ruminating on every circumstance of his last nights adventure, when he perceived a couple of horsemen come galloping over the plain, and make directly toward his house. The dust they made, kept him from distinguishing who they were, and they were very near the gate before he discovered them to be the Chevalier Brillian, and his servant. The surprize he was in to see him without Ansellina was very great, but much more so, when running down, as soon as he saw he was alighted, and opening his arms eagerly to embrace him; the other drawing back, "No, my lord," said he, "since you are pleased to forget I am your brother, I pretend no other way to merit your embraces. Nor can think it any happyness to hold him in my arms, who keeps me distant from his heart." "What mean you," cried D'elmont, extreamly astonished at his behaviour; "you know so little," resumed the Chevalier, "of the power of love, your self, that perhaps, you think I ought not to resent what you have done to ruin me in mine. But, however sir, ambition is a passion which you are not a stranger to, and having settled your own fortune according to your wish, methinks you should not wonder that I take it ill, when you endeavour to prevent my doing so too." The Count was perfectly confounded at these words, and looking earnestly on him; "Brother," said he, "you seem to lay a heavy accusation on me, but if you still retain so much of that former affection which was between us, as to desire I should be cleared in your esteem, you must be more plain in your charge, for tho' I easily perceive that I am wronged, I cannot see by what means I am so." "My lord, you are not wronged," cried the Chevalier hastily, "you know you are not. If my tongue were silent, the dispair that sits upon my brow, my altered looks, and grief-sunk eyes, would proclaim your barbarous — most unnatural usage of me." "Ungrateful Brillian," said the Count, at once inflamed with tenderness and anger, "is this the consolation I expected from your presence? I know not for what cause I am upbraided, being innocent of any, nor what your troubles are, but I am sure my own are such, as needed not this weight to overwhelm me." He spoke this so feelingly, and concluded with so deep a sigh as most sencibly touched the heart of Brillian. "If I could believe that you had any," replied he, "it were enough to sink me quite, and rid me of a life which Ansellina's loss has made me hate." "What said you," interrupted the Count, "Ansellina's loss? If that be true, I pardon all the wildness of your unjust reproaches, for well I know, dispair has small regard to reason, but quickly speak the cause of your misfortune. — I was about to enquire the reason that I saw you not together, when your unkind behaviour drove it from my thoughts." "That question," answered the Chevalier, "asked by you, some moments since, would have put me past all the remains of patience, but I begin to hope I am not so unhappy as I thought, but still am blest in friendship, tho' undone in love – But I'll not keep you longer in suspence, my tale of grief is short in the repeating, tho' everlasting in its consequence." In saying this, he sat down, and the Count doing the like, and assuring him of attention, he began his relation in this manner.

"Your lordship may remember that I gave you an account by letter of Ansellina's indisposition, and the fears I was in for her; but by the time I received your answer, I thought my self the happyest of mankind. She was perfectly recovered, and every day I received new proofs of her affection. We began to talk now of coming to Paris, and she seemed no less impatient for that journey than my self; and one evening, the last I ever had the honour of her conversation, she told me that in spite of the physicians caution she would leave Amiens in three or four days. You may be sure I did not disswade her from that resolution; but, how great was my astonishment, when going the next morning to the Baronesses, to give the ladies the *bon jour*, as I constantly did every morning, I perceived an unusual coldness in the face of every one in the family; the Baroness herself spoke not to me, but to tell me that Ansellina would see no company. 'How, madam,' said I, 'am I not excepted from those general orders, what can this sudden alteration in my fortune mean?' 'I suppose,' replied she, 'that Ansellina has her reasons for what she does.' I said all that dispair could suggest to oblige her to give me some light into this mistery, but all was in vain, she either made me no answers, or such as were not satisfactory, and growing weary with being importuned, she abruptly went out of the room, and left me in a confusion not to be expressed. I renewed my visit the next day, and was then denied admittance by the porter. The same the following one, and as servants commonly form their behaviour, according to that of those they serve, it was easy for me to observe I was far from being a welcome guest. I writ to Ansellina, but had my letter returned unopened. And that scorn so unjustly thrown upon me, tho' it did not absolutely cure my passion, yet it stirred up so much just resentment in me, that it abated very much of its tenderness. About a fortnight I remained in this perplexity, and at the end of it was plunged into a greater, when I received a little *billet* from Ansellina, which as I remember contained these words.

"Ansellina to the Chevalier Brillian.

*"I sent your letter back without perusing, believing it might contain something of a subject which I am resolved to encourage no farther. I do not think it proper at present to acquaint you with my reasons for it; but if I see you at Paris, you shall know them. I set out for thence to morrow, but desire you not to pretend to accompany me thither, if you would preserve the esteem of,*

Ansellina.

"I cannot but say, I thought this manner of proceeding very odd, and vastly different from that openness of nature, I always admired in her, but as I had been always a most obsequious lover, I resolved not to forfeit that character, and give a proof of an implicite obedience to her will, tho' with what anxiety of mind you may imagine. I stood at a distance, and saw her take coach, and as soon as her attendants were out of sight, I got on horseback, and followed; I several times lay at the same inn where she did, but took care not to appear before her. Never was any sight more pleasing to me, than that of Paris, because I there hoped to have my destiny unravelled; but your being out of town, preventing her making any stay, I was reduced to another tryal of patience; about some seven furlongs from hence, hapning to bait[1] at the same *cabaret*[2] with her, I saw her woman, who had been always perfectly obliging to me, walking alone in the garden; I took the liberty to show my self to her, and ask her some questions concerning my future fate, to

---

1   "To give meat [food] to one's self, or horses, on the road" (Johnson).
2   "A tavern" (Johnson).

which she answered with all the freedom I could desire, and observing the melancholly which was but too apparent in my countenance, 'Sir,' said she, 'tho' I think nothing can be more blame-worthy then to betray the secrets of our superiors, yet I hope I shall stand excused for declaring so much of my lady's, as the condition you are in, seems to require; I would not therefore have you believe that in this separation, you are the only sufferer, I can assure you, my lady bears her part of sorrow to.' – 'How can that be possible,' cried I, 'when my misfortune is brought upon me, only by the change in her inclination?' 'Far from it,' answered she, 'you have a brother – he only is to blame, she has received letters from Madam D'elmont which have –' As she was speaking, she was called hastily away, without being able to finish what she was about to say, and I was so impatient to hear. Her naming you in such a manner, planted ten thousand daggers in my soul! – What could I imagine by those words, 'You have a brother, he only is to blame,' and her mentioning letters from that brother's wife, but that it was thro' you I was made wretched; I repeated several times over to my self, what she had said, but could wrest no other meaning from it, than that you being already possessed of the elder sister's fortune, were willing to engross the other's too, by preventing her from marrying. Pardon me, my lord, if I have injured you, since I protest, the thoughts of your designing my undoing, was, if possible more dreadful to me than the ill it self."

"You will," replied the Count, "be soon convinced, how little hand I had in those letters, whatever they contained, when you have been here a few days." He then told him of the disagreement between himself and Alovysa, her perpetual jealousy, her pride, her rage, and the little probability there was of their being ever reconciled, so as to live together as they ought, omitting nothing of the story, but his love for Melliora, and the cause he had given to create this uneasiness. They both concluded, that Ansellina's alteration of behaviour was entirely owing to something her sister had written, and that she would use her utmost endeavour to break off the match wholly, in revenge to her husband. As they were discoursing on means to prevent it, the ladies came to the gate; they saw them thro' the window, and ran to receive them immediately. The Count handed Ansellina out of the coach, with great complaisance, while the Chevalier would have done the same by Alovysa, but she would not permit him, which the Count observing, when he had paid those complements to her sister, which he thought civility required, "Madam," said he, turning to her frowning, "is it not enough, you make me wretched by your continual clamours, and upbraidings, but that your ill nature must extend to all, whom you believe I love?" She answered him only with a disdainful look, and haughty toss, which spoke the pleasure she took in having it in her power to give him pain, and went out of the room with Ansellina.

D'elmont's family was now become a most distracted one, every body was in confusion, and it was hard for a disinterested person, to know how to behave among them. The Count was ready to dye with vexation, when he reflected on the adventure at the Baron's with Melantha, and how hard it would be to clear his conduct in that point with Melliora. She, on the other hand, was as much tormented at his not attempting it. The Chevalier was in the height of dispair, when he found that Ansellina continued her humour, and still avoided letting him know the occasion of it. And Alovysa tho' she contented herself for some hours with relating to her sister, all the passages of her husband's unkind usage of her, yet when that was over, her curiosity returned, and she grew so madly zealous to find out, who her rival was, that she repented her behaviour to the Baron, and sent him the next day privately, a *billet*, wherein she assured him, that she had acquainted the Count with nothing that had passed between them, and that she desired to speak with him. 'Tis easy to believe he needed not a second invitation; he came immediately, and Alovysa renewed her entreaties in the most pressing manner she was capable of, but in vain, he told her plainly, that if he could not have her heart, nothing but the full possession of her person[1] should extort the secret from him. 'Twould swell this discourse beyond what I design, to recount her various starts of passions, and different turns of

---

1   The conventional contrast between having her love and merely possessing her body sexually.

behaviour, sometimes louder than the winds she raved! commanded! threatened! then, still as April showers, or summer dews she wept, and only whispered her complaints now dissembling kindness, then declaring unfeigned hate; 'till at last, finding it impossible to prevail by any other means, she promised to admit him at midnight into her chamber. But as it was only the force of her too passionate affection for her husband, which had worked her to this pitch of raging jealousie, so she had no sooner made the assignation, and the Baron had left her (to seek the Count to prevent any suspicion of their long conversation) but all D'elmont's charms came fresh into her mind, and made the thoughts of what she had promised odious and insupportable; she opened her mouth more than once to call back the Baron, and recant all that she had said; but her ill genius, or that devil curiosity, which too much haunts the minds of women, still prevented her. "What will become of me," said she to her self, "what is it I am about to do? Shall I forgoe my honour – quit my virtue, – sully my yet unspotted name with endless infamy – and yield my soul to sin, to shame, and horror, only to know what I can ne'er redress? If D'elmont hates me now, will he not do so still? – What will this cursed discovery bring me but added tortures, and fresh weight of woe." Happy had it been for her if these considerations could have lasted, but when she had been a minute or two in this temper, she would relapse and cry, "What must I tamely bear it then? – Endure the flouts of the malicious world, and the contempt of every saucy girl, who while she pitys, scorns my want of charms – Shall I neglected tell my tale of wrongs, (O, Hell is in that thought) 'till my dispair shall reach my rival's ears, and crown her adulterous joys with double pleasure. – Wretch that I am! – Fool that I am, to hesitate, my misery is already past addition, my everlasting peace is broke! Lost even to hope, what can I more endure? – No, since I must be ruined, I'll have the satisfaction of dragging with me to perdition, the vile, the cursed she that has undone me. I'll be revenged on her, than dye my self, and free me from pollution. As she was in this last thought, she perceived at a good distance from her the Chevalier Brillian and Ansellina in discourse; the sight of him immediately put a new contrivance into her head, and she composed her self as well as she could, and went to meet them.

Ansellina having been left alone, while her sister was entertaining the Baron, had walked down into the garden to divert herself, where the Chevalier, who was on the watch for such an opportunity, had followed her; he could not forbear, tho' in terms full of respect, taxing her with some little unjustice for her late usage of him, and breach of promise, in not letting him know her reasons for it. She, who by nature was extreamly averse to the disguising her sentiments, suffered him not long to press her for an *eclaircisment,* and with her usual freedom, told him what she had done, was purely in complyance with her sister's request, that she could not help having the same opinion of him as ever, but that she had promised Alovysa to defer any thoughts of marrying him, till his brother should confess his error. The obliging things she said to him, tho' she persisted in her resolution, disipated great part of his chagreen, and he was beginning to excuse D'elmont, and perswade her that her sister's temper was the first occasion of their quarrel when Alovysa interrupted them. Ansellina was a little out of countenance at her sister's presence, immagining she would be insenced at finding her with the Chevalier; but that distressed lady was full of other thoughts, and desiring him to follow her to her chamber, as soon as they were set down, confessed to him, how, fired with his brother's falshood, she had endeavoured to revenge it upon him, that she had been his enemy, but was willing to enter into any measures for his satisfaction, provided he would comply with one, which she should propose, which he faithfully promising, after she had sworn him to secrecy, discovered to him every circumstance, from her first cause of jealousy, to the assignation she had made with the Baron; "Now," said she, "it is in your power to preserve both your brother's honour, and my life (which I sooner will resign than my virtue) if you stand concealed in a little closet, which I shall convey you to, and the moment he has satisfied my curiosity by telling me her name that has undone me, rush out and be my protector." The Chevalier was infinitely surprized at what he heard, for his brother had not given him the least hint of his passion, but thought the request she made, too reasonable to be denied.

While they were in this discourse, Melliora, who had been sitting indulging her melancholly in that closet which Alovysa spoke of, and which did not immediately belong to that chamber, but was a sort of an entry or passage into another, and tired with reflection was fallen asleep, but on the noise which Alovysa and the Chevalier made in coming in, waked, and heard to her inexpressible trouble, the discourse that passed between them. She knew that unknown rival was herself, and condemned the Count of the highest imprudence, in making a confidant, as she found he had of the Baron; she saw her fate, at least that of her reputation was now upon the crisis, that, that very night she was exposed to all the fury of an enraged wife, and was so shook with apprehension, that she was scarce able to go out of the closet time enough to prevent their discovering she was there; what could she do in this exigence, the thoughts of being betrayed, was worse to her than a thousand deaths, and it was to be wondred at, as she has since confest, that in that height of desparation, she had not put an end to the tortures of reflection, by laying violent hands on her own life. As she was going from the closet hastily to her own apartment, the Count and Baron passed her, and that sight heightening the distraction she was in, she stept to the Count, and in a faultring, scarce intelligible accent, whispered, "for Heaven's sake let me speak with you before night, make some pretence to come to my chamber, where I'll wait for you." And as soon as she had spoke these words darted from him so swift, that he had no opportunity of replying, if he had not been too much overwhelmed with joy at this seeming change of his fortune to have done it; he misunderstood part of what was said, and instead of her desiring to speak with him "before night," he imagined, she said "at night." He presently communicated it to the Baron, who congratulated him upon it; and never was any night more impatiently longed for, than this was by them both. They had indeed not many hours of expectation, but Melliora thought them ages, all her hopes were, that if she could have an opportunity of discovering to Count D'elmont what she had heard between his wife and brother, he might find some means to prevent the Baron's treachery from taking effect. But when night grew on, and she perceived he came not, and she considered how near she was to inevitable ruin, what words can sufficiently express her agonies? So I shall only say, they were too violent to have long kept company with life; guilt horour, fear, remorse, and shame at once oppressed her, and she was very near sinking beneath their weight, when somebody knocked softly at the door; she made no doubt but it was the Count, and opened it immediately, and he catching her in his arms with all the eagerness of transported love, she was about to clear his mistake, and let him know it was not an amourous entertainment she expected from him; when a sudden cry of murder, and the noise of clashing swords made him let go his hold, and draw his own, and run along the gallery to find out the occasion, where being in the dark, and only directed by the noise he heard in his wife's chamber, something met the point, and a great shriek following it, he cried for lights, but none coming immediately, he stepping farther stumbled at the body which had fallen; he then redoubled his outcrys, and Melliora frightened as she was, brought one from her chamber, and at the same instant that they discovered it was Alovysa, who coming to alarm the family, had by accident run on her husband's sword, they saw the Chevalier pursuing the Baron, who mortally wounded, dropt down by Alovysa's side; what a dreadful view was this? The Count, Melliora, and the servants, who by this time were most of them rowzed, seemed without sence or motion, only the Chevalier had spirit enough to speak, or think, so stupified was every one with what they saw. But he ordering the servants to take up the bodies, sent one of 'em immediately for a surgeon, but they were both of them past his art to cure. Alovysa spoke no more, and the Baron lived but two days, in which time the whole account, as it was gathered from the mouths of those chiefly concerned, was set down, and the tragical part of it being laid before the King, there appeared so much of justice in the Baron's death, and accident in Alovysa's, that the Count and Chevalier found it no difficult matter to obtain their pardon. The Chevalier was soon after married to his beloved Ansellina; but Melliora looked on herself as the most guilty person upon earth, as being the primary cause of all the misfortunes that had happened, and retired immediately to a monastery, from whence, not all the entreaties of her friends, nor the implorations of the amorous D'elmont could bring her; she was now resolved to punish by a voluntary banishment from all she ever did, or could love, the guilt of indulging that passion, while it was a crime. He, not able to live without her, at least in the same climate, committed the care of his estate to his brother, and went to travel, without an inclination ever to return. Melantha who was not of a humour to take any thing to heart, was married in a short time, and had the good fortune not to be suspected by her husband, though she brought him a child in seven months after her wedding.

*Finis.*

# LOVE IN EXCESS;

# OR,

# THE 'FATAL ENQUIRY.

## A NOVEL

*The Third and Last Part.*

*Success can then alone your vows attend,*
*When worth's the motive, constancy the end.*

— Epilogue to *The Spartan Dame.*[1]

*By Mrs. Haywood.*

---

1   A play by Thomas Southerne (1660-1746), best known for his popular dramatic
adaptation of Aphra Behn's novel *Oroonoko*; the epilogue is by Major Richardson
Pack.

# LOVE IN EXCESS;

## OR, THE FATAL ENQUIRY

### *The Third and Last Part.*

THO' Count D'elmont never had any great tenderness for Alovysa, and her extravagance of rage and jealousy, joyned to his passion for Melliora had every day abated it, yet the manner of her death was too great a shock to the sweetness of his disposition to be easily worn off; he could not remember her uneasiness, without reflecting that it sprung only from her too violent affection for him; and tho' there was no possibility of living happily with her, when he considered that she died, not only for him, but by his hand, his compassion for the cause, and horror for the unwished, as well as undesigned event, drew lamentations from him, more sincere, perhaps, then some of those husbands, who call themselves very loving ones, would make.

To alleviate the troubles of his mind, he had endeavoured all he could, to perswade Melliora to continue in his house; but that afflicted lady was not to be prevailed upon, she looked on her self, as, in a manner, accessary to Alovysa's death, and thought the least she owed to her reputation was to see the Count no more, and tho' in the forming this resolution, she felt torments unconceivable, yet the strength of her virtue enabled her to keep it, and she returned to the monastery, where she had been educated, carrying with her nothing of that peace of mind with which she left it.

Not many days passed between her departure, and the Count's; he took his way towards Italy, by the perswasions of his brother, who, since he found him bent to travel, hoped that garden of the world might produce something to divert his sorrows; he took but two servants with him, and those rather for conveniency than state.[1] *Ambition*, once his darling passion, was now wholly extinguished in him by these misfortunes, and he

---

1   The number of servants signalled wealth and social importance, so this is a symptom that the Count has abandoned ambition.

no longer thought of making a figure in the world; but his *love* nothing could abate, and 'tis to be believed that the violence of that would have driven him to the use of some fatal remedy, if the Chevalier Brillian, to whom he left the care of Melliora's and her brother's fortune as well as his own, had not, tho' with much difficulty, obtained a promise from her of conversing with him by letters.

This was all he had to keep hope alive, and indeed it was no inconsiderable consolation, for she that allows a correspondence of that kind with a man that has any interest in her heart, can never persuade herself, while she does so, to make him become indifferent to her. When we give our selves the liberty of even talking of the person we have once loved, and find the least pleasure in that discourse, 'tis ridiculous to imagine we are free from that passion, without which, the mention of it would be but insipid to our ears, and the remembrance to our minds; tho' our words are never so cold, they are the effects of a secret fire, which burns not with less strength for not being dilated. The Count had too much experience of all the walks and turns of passion to be ignorant of this, if Melliora had endeavoured to disguise her sentiments, but she went not so far, she thought it a sufficient vindication of her virtue to withhold the rewarding of his love, without feigning a coldness to which she was a stranger, and he had the satisfaction to observe a tenderness in her stile, which assured him that her *heart* was unalterably his, and very much strengthed his hopes that one day her *person* might be so too, when time had a little effaced the memory of those circumstances, which had obliged her to put this constraint on her inclinations!

He wrote to her from every post-town, and waited till he received her answer; by this means his journey was extreamly tedious, but no adventures of any moment, falling in his way 'till he came to Rome, I shall not trouble my readers with a recital of particulars which could be no way entertaining.

But, how strangely do they deceive themselves, who fancy that they are lovers, yet on every little turn of Fortune, or change of circumstance, are agitated, with any vehemence, by cares of a far different nature? *Love* is too jealous, too arbitrary a monarch to suffer any other passion to equalize himself in that heart where he has fixed his throne. When once entered, he becomes the whole business of our lives, we think – we dream of nothing else, nor have a wish not inspired by him. Those who have the power to apply themselves so seriously to any other consideration as to forget him, tho' but for a moment, are but lovers in conceit, and have entertained desire but as an agreeable amusement, which when attended with any inconvenience, they may without much difficulty shake off. Such a sort of passion may be properly enough called *liking*, but falls widely short of *love*. *Love*, is what we can neither resist, expel, nor even alleviate, if we should never so vigorously attempt it; and tho' some have boasted, "Thus far will I yield and no farther," they have been convinced of the vanity of forming such resolutions by the impossibility of keeping them. *Liking* is a flashy flame, which is to be kept alive only by ease and delight. *Love*, needs not this fewel to maintain its fire, it survives in absence, and disappointments, it endures, unchilled, the wintry blasts of cold indifference and neglect, and continues its blaze, even in a storm of hatred and ingratitude, and reason, pride, or a just sensibility of conscious worth, in vain oppose it. *Liking*, plays gayly round, feeds on the sweets in gross, but is wholly insensible of the thorns which guard the nicer, and more refined delicacies of desire, and can consequently give neither pain, nor pleasure in any superlative degree. *Love* creates intollerable torments! unspeakable joys! raises us to the highest heaven of happiness, or sinks us to the lowest hell of misery.

Count D'elmont experienced the truth of this assertion; for neither his just concern for the manner of Alovysa's death could curb the exuberance of his joy, when he considered himself beloved by Melliora; nor any diversion, of which Rome afforded great variety, be able to make him support being absent from her with moderation. There are I believe, but few modern lovers, how passionate and constant soever they pretend to be, who would not in the Count's circumstances have found some matter of consolation; but he seemed wholly dead to gaiety. In vain, all the Roman nobility courted his acquaintance; in vain the ladies made use of their utmost artifice to engage him. He preferred a solitary walk, a lonely shade, or the bank of some purling stream, where he undisturbed might contemplate on his beloved Melliora, to all the noisy pleasures of the Court, or the endearments of the inviting fair. In fine, he shunned as much as possible all conversation with the men, or correspondence with the women; returning all their *billet-deux*, of which scarce a day past, without his receiving some, unanswered.

This manner of behaviour in a little time delivered him from the persecutions of the discreet; but having received one letter which he had used as he had done the rest, it was immediately seconded by another; both which contained as follows:

Letter I.

To The Never Enough Admired Count D'elmont.

*In your country, where women are allowed the previledge of being seen and addressed to, it would be a crime unpardonable to modesty, to make the first advances. But here, where rigid rules are bar's, as well to reason, as to nature, it would be as great a one, to feign an insensibility of your merit. I say, feign, for I look on it, as an impossibility really to behold you with indifferency. But, if I could believe that any of my sex were in good earnest so dull, I must confess, I should envy that happy stupidity, which would secure me from the pains such a passion as you create must inflict; unless, from the millions whom your charms have reached, you have yet a corner of your heart unprepossessed, and an inclination willing to receive the impression of,*

Your most Passionate and Tender,
(but 'till she receives a favourable
Answer) Your unknown Adorer.

## Letter II.

### To the Ungrateful D'elmont.

*Unworthy of the happiness designed you! Is it thus, that you return the condescention of a lady? How fabulous is report, which speaks those of your country, warm and full of amorous desires? — Thou, sure, ar't colder than the bleak northern islanders — Dull, stupid wretch! insensible of every passion which give lustre to the soul, and differ man, from brute! — Without gratitude — Without love — Without desire — Dead, even to curiosity! — How I could dispise thee for this narrowness of mind, were there not something in thy eyes and mein which assure me, that this negligent behaviour is but affected; and that there are within thy breast, some seeds of hidden fire, which want but the influence of charms, more potent perhaps, then you have yet beheld, to kindle into blaze. Make hast then to be enlivened, for I flatter my self 'tis in my power to work this wonder, and long to inspire so love-ly a form with sentiments only worthy of it. – The bearer of this, is a person who I dare confide in — Delay not to come with him, for when once you are taught what 'tis to love; you'll not be igno-rant that doubtful expectation is the worst of racks, and from your own experience. Pity what I feel, thus chilled with doubt, yet burning with desire.*

Yours, Impatiently.

The Count was pretty much surprized at the odd turn of this billet; but being willing to put an end to the ladies trouble, as well as his own, sat down, and without giving himself much time to think, writ these lines in answer to hers.

### To the Fair Incognita.

Madam,
*If you have no other design in writing to me, than your diver-sion, methinks my mourning habit, to which my countenance and behaviour are no way unconformable, might inform you, I*

*am little disposed for raillery. If in earnest you can find any thing*
*in me which pleases you, I must confess my self entirely unwor-*
*thy of the honour, not only by my personal demerits, but by the*
*resolution I have made of conversing with none of your sex while*
*I continue in Italy. I should be sorry however to incurr the asper-*
*sion of an unmannerly contemner of favours, which tho' I do not*
*desire, I pretend not to deserve. I therefore beg you will believe*
*that I return this, as I did your former, only to let you see, that*
*since I decline making any use of your condescentions to my*
*advantage, I am not ungenerous enough to do so to your preju-*
*dice, and to all ladies deserving the regard of a disinterested well-*
*wisher shall be an,*

Humble Servant, D'Elmont.

The Count ordered one of his servants to deliver this letter
to the person who brought the other; but he returned immediately with it in his hand, and told his lordship that he could not
prevail on the fellow to take it; that he said he had business
with the Count, and must needs see him, and was so importu-
nate, that he seemed rather to demand than entreat a grant of
his request. D'elmont was astonished, as well he might, but
commanded he should be admitted.

Nothing could be more comical than the appearance of this
fellow; he seemed to be about threescore years of age, but time
had not been the greatest enemy to his face, for the number of
scars, was far exceeding that of wrincles; he was tall above common stature, but so lean, that, till he spoke, he might have been
taken for one of those wretches who have passed the hands of
the anatomists,[1] nor would his walk have disipated that opinion, for all his motions, as he entered the chamber, had more of
the air of clockwork, than of nature; his dress was not less particular, he had on a suit of cloaths, which might perhaps have
been good in the days of his great grand-father, but the person
who they fitted must have been five times larger about the
body than him who wore them; a large broad buff belt how-

---

1   A skeleton, perhaps a criminal's, for executed criminals' bodies were used for med-
    ical dissection.

ever remedied that inconvenience, and girt them close about his waste, in which hung a fauchion,[1] two daggers, and a sword of a more than ordinary extent; the rest of his equipage was a cloak, which buttoning round his neck fell not so low as his hips, a hat, which in rainy weather kept his shoulders dry much better than an Indian umberrello, one glove, and a formidable pair of whiskers. As soon as he saw the Count, "My lord," said he, with a very impudent air, "my orders were to bring your self, not a letter from you, nor do I use to be employed in affairs of this nature, but to serve one of the richest, and most beautiful ladys in Rome, who I assure you, it will be dangerous to disoblige." D'elmont eyed him intentively all the time he spoke, and could scarce, notwithstanding his chagreen, forbear laughing at the figure he made, and the manner of his salutation. "I know not," answered he, ironically, "what employments you have been used to, but certainly you appear to me, one of the most unfit persons in the world for what you now undertake, and if the contents of the paper you brought me had not informed me of your abilities this way, I should never have suspected you for one of Cupid's agents." "You are merry my lord," replied the other, "but I must tell you I am a man of family and honour, and shall not put up an affront; but," continued he, shaking the few hairs which frequent skirmishes had left upon his head, "I shall deferr my own satisfaction 'till I have procured the ladies; therefore, if your lordship will prepare to follow, I shall walk before, at a perceivable distance, and without St. Peter's key open the gate of heaven." "I should be apt," said the Count, not able to keep his countenance at these words, "rather to take it for the other place; but be it as it will, I have not the least inclination to make the experiment; therefore, you may walk as soon as you please without expecting me to accompany you." "Then you absolutely refuse to go," cried the fellow, clapping his hand on his forehead, and staring at him, as if he meant to scare him into complyance! "Yes," answered the Count laughing more and more, "I shall neither go, nor waste any farther time or words with you, so would

---

1   A falchion, a broad curved sword.

advise you not to be saucy, or tarry till my anger gets the better of my mirth, but take the letter and be gone, and trouble me no more." The other, at these words laid his hand on his sword, and was about to make some very impudent reply, when D'elmont, growing weary of his impertinence, made a sign to his servants, that they should turn him out, which he perceiving, took up the letter without being bid a second time, and muttering some unintelligible curses between his teeth, marched out, in the same affected strutt, with which he entered.

This adventure, tho' surprizing enough to a person so entirely unacquainted with the character and behaviour of these *bravo's*[1] as D'elmont was, gave him but very little matter of reflection, and it being the time for evening service at St. Peter's, he went, according to his custom to hear vesper's there.

Nothing is more common than for the nobility and gentry of Rome to divert themselves with walking, and talking to one another in the *collonade* after mass, and the Count tho' averse to all other publick assemblies, would sometimes spend an hour or two there.

As he was walking there this evening, a lady of a very gallant mein passed swiftly by him, and flurting[2] out her handkerchief with a careless air, as it were by chance, dropped an *Agnus Dei*[3] set round with diamonds at his feet; he had too much complaisance to neglect endeavouring to overtake the lady, and prevent the pain he imagined she would be in, when she should miss so rich a jewel. But she, who knew well enough what she had done, left the walk where the company were, and crossed over to the fountain, which being more retired was the most proper for her design. She stood looking on the water, in a thoughtful posture, when the Count came up to her, and bowing, with an air peculiar to himself, and which all his chagreen could not

---

1 Hired murderers; the English viewed Italy as a place of fanatical pride of rank, duels, and elaborate corruption.
2 To flirt in this sense is "to throw anything with a quick elastick motion" (Johnson).
3 An image of Christ as the lamb of God (see John 1.29), carrying a cross or flag; here an ostentatious jewel but traditionally a wax medallion bearing this image and blessed by the Pope.

deprive of an irresistable power of attraction, presented the *Agnus Dei* to her. "I think my self, madam," said he, "highly indebted to Fortune, for making me the means of your recovering a jewel, the loss of which would certainly have given you some disquiet." "Oh Heavens!" cried she, receiving it with an affected air of surprize, "could a trifle like this which I knew not that I had let fall, nor perhaps should have thought on more, could this, and belonging to a woman too, meet the regard of him, who prides in his insensibility? Him! who has no eyes for beauty, nor no heart for love!" As she spoke these words she contrived to let her vail fall back as if by accident, and discovered a face, beautiful even to perfection! eyes black and sparkling, a mouth formed to invite, a skin dazling white, thro' which a most delightful bloom diffused a chearful warmth, and glowed in amorous blushes on her cheeks. The Count could not forbear gazing on her with admiration, and perhaps, was, for a moment, pretty near receeding from that insensibility she had reproached him with; but the image of Melliora, yet unenjoyed, all ravishingly kind and tender, rose presently in his soul, filled all his faculties, and left no passage free for rival charms. "Madam," said he after a little pause, "the Italian ladies take care to skreen their too dazling lustre behind a cloud, and, if I durst take that liberty, have certainly reason to tax your accusation of injustice; he, on whom the sun has never vouchsafed to shine, ought not to be condemned for not acknowledging its brightness; yours is the first female face I have beheld, since my arrival here, and it would have been as ridiculous to have feigned my self susceptible of charms which I had never seen, as it would be stupidity, not to confess those I now do, worthy adoration." "Well," resumed she smiling, "if not the *lover's*, I find, you know to act the *courtier's* part; but," continued she, looking languishingly on him, "all you can say, will scarce make me believe, that there requires not a much brighter sun than mine, to thaw a certain frozen *resolution*, you pretend to have made." There needed no more to confirm the Count in the opinion he had before conceived, that this was the lady from whom he had received the two letters that day, and thought he had now the fairest opportunity in the world to put an end to her passion, by assuring her how impossible it was for him ever to return it, and was forming an answer to that purpose; when a pretty deal of company coming toward them, she drew her vail over her face, and turning hastily from him, mingled with some ladies, who seemed to be of her acquaintance.

The Count knew by experience, the unutterable perturbations of suspence, and what agonizing tortures rend an amorous soul, divided betwixt hope and fear. Dispair itself is not so cruel as uncertainty, and in all ills, especially in those of love, it is less misery to *know*, than *dread* the worst. The remembrance of what he had suffered thus agitated, in the beginning of his passion for Melliora, made him extreamly pity the unknown lady, and regret her sudden departure; because it had prevented him from letting her into so much of his circumstances, as he believed were necessary to induce her to recall her heart. But when he considered how much he had struggled, and how far he had been from being able to repell desire, he began to wonder that it could ever enter into his thoughts that there was even a possibility for *woman*, so much stronger in her fancy, and weaker in her judgment, to suppress the influence of that powerful passion; against which, no laws, no rules, no force of reason, or philosophy, are sufficient guards.

These reflections gave no small addition to his melancholy; Amena's retirement from the world; Alovysa's jealousy and death; Melliora's peace of mind and reputation, and the despair of several, whom he was sensible, the love of him, had rendred miserable, came fresh into his memory, and he looked on himself as most unhappy, in being the occasion of making others so.

The night which succeeded this day of adventures, chancing to be abroad pretty late, as he was passing thro' a street, he heard a clashing of swords, and going nearer to the place where the noise was, he perceived by some lights which glimmered from a distant door, a gentleman defending himself with much bravery against three, who seemed eager for his death. D'Elmont was moved to the highest indignation at the sight of such baseness; and drawing his sword, flew furiously on the assassins, just as one of them was about to run his sword into the breast of the gentleman; who, by the breaking of his own blade, was left unarmed. "Turn villain," cried D'Elmont, "or while you are acting that inhumanity, receive the just reward of it from me." The ruffian faced about immediately, and made a pass at him, while one of his comrades did the same on the other side; and the third was going to execute on the gentleman, what his fellows surprize had made him leave undone. But he had now gained time to pull a pistol out of his pocket, with which he[1] shot him in a moment dead; and snatching his sword from him as he fell, ran to assist the Count, who 'tis likely would have stood in need of it, being engaged with two, and those the most desparate sort of *bravo's*, villains that make a trade of death. But the noise of the pistol made them apprehensive there was a farther rescue, and put 'em to flight. The gentleman seemed agitated with a more than ordinary fury; and instead of staying to thank the Count, or enquire how he had escaped, ran in pursuit of those who had assaulted him, so swiftly, that it was in vain for the Count, not being well acquainted with the turnings of the streets, to attempt to follow him, if he had a mind to it. But seeing there was a man killed, and not knowing either the persons who fought, or the occasion of their quarrel, he rightly judged, that being a stranger in the place, his word would not be very readily taken in his own vindication; therefore thought his wisest course would be to make off, with what speed he could, to his lodging. While he was considering, he saw something on the ground which glittered extreamly; and taking it up, found that it was part of the sword which the assaulted gentleman had the misfortune to have broke. The hilt was of a fine piece of agat, set round on the top with diamonds, which made him believe the person whom he had preserved, was of considerable quality, as well as bravery.

He had not gone many paces from the place where the skirmish hapned, before a cry of murder met his ears, and a great concourse of people his eyes. He had received two or three slight wounds, which, tho' not much more than skin-deep, had made his linnen bloody, and he knew would be sufficient to make him be apprehended, if he were seen, which it was very

---

1 4th ed.; 1st ed. reads "she."

difficult to avoid. He was in a narrow street, which had no turning, and the crowd was very near him; when looking round him with a good deal of vexation in his thoughts, he discerned a wall, which in one part of it seemed pretty low. He presently resolved to climb it, and trust to fortune for what might befall him on the other side, rather than stay to be exposed to the insults of the outrageous mob; who, ignorant of his quality, and looking no farther than the outside of things, would doubtless have considered him, no otherwise, than a midnight *rioter*.

When he was got over the wall, he found himself in a very fine garden, adorned with fountains, statues, groves, and every ornament, that art, or nature, could produce for the delight of the owner. At the upper end there was a summer-house, into which he went, designing to stay there 'till the search was over.

But he had not been many moments in his concealment before he saw a door open from the house, and two women come out; they walked directly up to the place where he was; he made no doubt but that they designed to enter, and retired into the farthest corner of it. As they came pretty near, he found they were earnest in discourse, but could understand nothing of what they said, 'till she, who seemed to be the chief, raising her voice a little higher than she had done, "Talk no more, Brione," said she, "if e're thy eyes are blest to see this charmer of my soul, thou wil't cease to wonder at my passion; great as it is, 'tis wanting of his merit. – Oh! He is more than raptured poets feign, or fancy can invent!" "Suppose him so," cried the other, "yet still he wants that charm which should endear the others to you – softness – Heavens! to return your letters! to insult your messenger! to slight such favours as any man of soul would dye to obtain! Methinks such usage should make him odious to you, – even I should scorn so spiritless a wretch." "Peace, thou prophaner," said the lady in an angry tone, "such blasphemy deserves a stab – But thou hast never heard his voice, nor seen his eyes, and I forgive thee." "Have you then spoke to him?" interrupted the confident. "Yes," answered the lady, "and by that conversation, am more undone than ever; it was to tell thee this adventure, I came to night into this agreeable solitude." With these words, they came into the summer-house, and the lady seating her self on a bench, "Thou know'st," resumed she, "I went this evening to Saint Peter's, there I saw the glorious man; saw him in all his charms; and while I bowed my knee, in show to heaven, my soul was prostrate only to him. When the ceremony was over, perceiving he stayed in the *collonade*, I had no power to leave it, but stood, regardless who observed me, gazing on him with transports, which only those who love like me, can guess! – God! With what an air he walked! What new attractions dwelt in every motion – And when he returned the salutes of any that passed by him, how graceful was his bow! How lofty his mein, and yet, how affable! – A sort of an inexpressible awful grandeur, blended with tender languishments, strikes the amazed beholder at once with fear and joy! – Something beyond humanity shines round him! Such looks descending angels wear, when sent on heavenly embassies to some favorite mortal! Such is their form! Such radient beams they dart; and with such smiles they temper their divinity with softness! – Oh! with what pain did I restrain my self from flying to him! from rushing into his arms! from hanging on his neck, and wildly[1] uttering all the furious wishes of my burning soul! – I trembled – panted – raged with inward agonies. Nor was all the reason I could muster up, sufficient to bear me from his sight, without having first spoke to him. To that end I ventured to pass by him, and dropped an *Agnus Dei* at his feet, believing that would give him an occasion of following me, which he did immediately, and returning it to me, discovered a new hoard of unimagined charms – All my fond soul confessed before of his perfections were mean, to what I now beheld! Had'st thou but seen how he approached me – with what an awful reverence – with what a soft beseeching, yet commanding air, he kissed the happy trifle, as he gave it me, thou would'st have envied it as well as I! At last he spoke, and with an accent so divine, that if the sweetest musick were compared to the more celestial harmony of his voice, it would only serve to prove how vastly *nature* do's excell

---

1    4th ed.; 1st ed. reads "wilding."

all *art*." "But, madam," cried the other, "I am impatient to know the end of this affair; for I presume you discovered to him both what, and who you were?" "My face only," replied the lady, "for e're I had opportunity to do more, that malicious trifler, Violetta, perhaps envious of my happiness, came toward us with a crowd of impertinents at her heels, curse on the interruption, and broke off our conversation; just at that blest, but irrecoverable moment, when I perceived in my charming conqueror's eyes, a growing tenderness, sufficient to encourage me to reveal my own. Yes, Brione, those lovely eyes, while fixed on mine, shone, with a lustre, uncommon, even to themselves – A livelier warmth o'respread his cheeks – Pleasure sat smiling on his lips – those lips, my girl, which even when they are silent, speak; but when unclosed, and the sweet gales of balmy breath blow on you, he kills you in a sigh; each hurried sence is ravished, and your soul glows with wonder and delight. Oh! to be forced to leave him in this crisis, when new desire began to dawn; when love in its most lively symptoms was apparent, and seemed to promise all my wishes covet, what separation ever was so cruel?" "Compose your self, dear madam," said Brione, "if he be really in love; as who so senseless as not to be so, that once has seen your charms? That *love* will teach him speedily to find out an opportunity as favourable as that which you have lately missed; or if he should want contrivance to procure his own happiness, 'tis but your writing to appoint a meeting." "He must – he shall be mine!" cried the lady in a rapture, "my love, fierce as it was before, from hope receives addition to its fury; I rave – I burn – I am mad with wild desires – I dye, Brione, if I not possess him." In speaking these words, she threw her self down on a carpet which was spread upon the floor; and after sighing two or three times, continued to discover the violence of her impatient passion in this manner: "Oh that this night," said she, "were past – the blissful expectation of to-morrows joys, and the distracting doubts of disappointment, swell my unequal beating heart by turns, and rack me with vicissitudes of pain – I cannot live and bear it – Soon as the morning breaks, I'll know my doom – I'll send to him – But 'tis an age till then – Oh that I could sleep – Sleep might perhaps anticipate the blessing, and bring him in idea to my arms – But 'tis in vain to hope one moment's cool serenity in love like mine – My anxious thoughts hurry my sences in eternal watchings! – Oh D'Elmont! D'Elmont! Tranquill, cold, and calm D'Elmont! Little doest thou guess the tempest thou hast raised within my soul, nor know'st to pity these consuming fires!"

The Count list'ned to all this discourse with a world of uneasiness and impatience; and tho' at first he fancied he remembered the voice, and had reason enough from the beginning, especially when the *Agnus Dei* was mentioned, to believe it could be no other than himself, who the lady had so passionately described; yet he had not confidence to appear till she had named him; but then, no consideration was of force to make him neglect this opportunity of undeceiving her; his good sence, as well as good nature, kept him from that vanity, too many of his sex imitate the weaker in, of being pleased that it was in his power to create pains, which it was not in his power, so devoted as he was, to ease.

He stept from his retirement as softly as he could, because he was loath to alarm them with any noise, 'till they should discover who it was that made it, which they might easily do, in his advancing toward them never so little, that part of the bower being much lighter than that where he had stood; but with his over-caution in sliding his feet along, to prevent being heard, one of them tangled in the corner of the carpet, which hapned not to lie very smooth, and not being sensible presently what it was that embarrassed him, he fell with part of his body cross the lady, and his head in Brione's lap, who was sitting on the ground by her. The manner of his fall was lucky enough, for it hindered either of them from rising, and running to alarm the family, as certainly in such a fright they would have done, if his weight had not detained them; they both gave a great shriek, but the house being at a good distance, they could not easily be heard; and he immediately recovering himself, begged pardon for the terror he had occasioned them; and addressing to the lady, who at first was dying with her fears, and now with consternation, "D'Elmont madam," said he, "could not have had the assurance to appear before you, after hearing those undeserved praises your excess of goodness has been pleased to bestow upon him, but that his soul would have reproached him of the highest ingratitude, in permitting you to continue longer in an error, which may involve you in the greatest of misfortunes, at least I am —" As he was speaking, three or four servants with lights came running from the house; and the lady, tho' in more confusion than can be well exprest, had yet presence of mind enough to bid the Count retire to the place where he had stood before, while she and Brione went out of the summer-house to learn the cause of this interruption. "Madam," cried one of the servants, as soon as he saw her, "the officers of justice are within; who being raised by an alarm of murther, come to beg your ladyships permission to search your garden, being, as they say, informed that the offender made his escape over this wall." "'Tis very improbable," replied the lady, "for I have been here a considerable time, and have neither heard the least noise, nor seen any body. However, they may search, and satisfy themselves – go you, and tell them so." Then turning to the Count, when she had dismissed her servants; "My lord," said she trembling, "I know not what strange adventure brought you here to night, or whether you are the person for whom the search is made; but am sensible, if you are found here, it will be equally injurious to your safety, and my reputation; I have a back-door, thro' which you may pass in security. But, if you have honour," continued she sighing, "gratitude, or good nature, you will let me see you to-morrow night." "Madam," replied he, "assure yourself that there are not many things I more earnestly desire than an opportunity to convince you, how sensibly I am touched with your favours, and how much I regret my want of power to —" "You," interrupted she, "can want nothing but the *will* to make me the happiest of my sex – But this is no time for you to *give*, or me to *receive* any proofs of that return which I expect – Once more I conjure you to be here to-morrow night at twelve, where the faithful Brione shall attend to admit you. Farewell – be punctual and sincere – 'Tis all I ask." – "When I am not," answered he, "may all my hopes forsake me." By this time they were come to the door, which Brione opening softly, let him out, and shut it again immediately.

The Count took care to remark the place that he might

know it again, resolving nothing more than to make good his promise at the appointed hour, but could not help being extreamly troubled, when he considered how unwelcome his sincerity would be, and the confusion he must give the lady, when instead of those raptures the violence of her mistaking passion made her hope, she should meet with only cold civility, and the killing history of the pre-engagement of his heart. In these and the like melancholy reflections he spent the night; and when morning came, received the severest augmentation of them, which fate could load him with.

It was scarce full day when a servant came into his chamber to acquaint him, that a young gentleman, a stranger, desired to be admitted, and seemed so impatient till he was that, said the fellow, "not knowing of what consequence his business may be, I thought it better to risque your lordship's displeasure for this early disturbance, than by dismissing him, fill you with an unsatisfied curiosity." The Count was far from being angry, and commanded that the gentleman should be brought up, which order being immediately obeyed, and the servant with-drawn out of respect, putting his head out of the bed, he was surprized with the appearance of one of the most beautiful chevaliers he had ever beheld, and in whose face, he imagined he traced some features not unknown to him. "Pardon me, sir," said he, throwing the curtains more back than they were before, "that I receive the honour you do me, in this manner – But being ignorant of your name, quality, the reason of your desire to see me, or any thing but your impatience to do so, in gratifying that, I fear, I have injured the respect, which, I believe, is due; and which, I am sure, my heart is inclinable to pay to you." "Visits, like mine," replied the stranger, "require but little ceremony, and I shall easily remit that respect you talk of, while I am unknown to you, provided you will give me one mark of it, that I shall ask of you, when you do." "There are very few," replied D'Elmont, "that I could refuse to one, whose aspect promises to deserve so many." "First then," cried the other pretty warmly, "I demand a sister of you, and not only her, but a reparation of her honour, which can be done no otherwise than by your blood." It is impossible to represent the Count's astonishment at these words, but conscious of his innocence in any such affair, "I should be sorry Signior," said he cooly, "that precipatation should hurry you to do any action, you would afterwards repent; you must certainly be mistaken in the person to whom you are talking – Yet, if I were rash like you, what fatal consequences might ensue; but there is something in your countenance which engages me to wish a more friendly interview than what you speak of; therefore would persuade you to consider calmly, and you will soon find, and acknowledge your mistake; and, to further that reflection, I assure you, that I am so far from conversing with any lady, in the manner you seem to hint, that I scarcely know the name, or face of any one. – Nay, more, I give you my word, to which I joyn my honour, that, as I never *have*, I never *will* make the least pretensions of that kind to any woman during the time of my residence here." "This poor evasion," replied the stranger with a countenance all inflamed, "ill suits a man of honour. – This is no Roman, no Italian *bono-roba*,[1] who I mean – but French like you – like both of us. – And if your ingratitude had not made it necessary for your peace, to erace all memory of Monsieur Frankville, you would before now, by the near resemblance I bear to him, have known me for his son, and that 'tis Melliora's – the fond – the lost – the ruined Melliora's cause which calls for vengeance from her brother's arm!" Never was any soul agitated with more violent emotions, than that of Count D'Elmont at these words. Doubt, grief, resentment, and amazement, made such a confusion in his thoughts, that he was unable for some moments to answer this cruel accusation; and when he did, "the brother of Melliora," said he with a deep sigh, "would certainly have been, next to her self, the most welcome person upon earth to me; and my joy to have embraced him as the dearest of my friends, at least have equalled the surprize I am in, to find him without cause my enemy. – But, sir, if such a favour may be granted to an unwilling foe, I would desire to know, why you joyn *ruin* to your sisters name?" "Oh! give me patience heaven," cried young Frankville more enraged; "Is this

---

1   *Bona-roba*, "a whore" (Johnson).

a question fit for you to ask, or me to answer? Is not her honour tainted − fame betrayed − her self a vagabond, and her house abused, and all by you; the unfaithful guardian of her injured innocence? − And can you ask the cause? − No, rather rise this moment, and if you are a man, who dare maintain the ill you have done, defend it with your sword; not with vain words and womanish excuses." All the other passions which had warred within D'Elmont's breast, now gave way to indignation. "Rash young man," said he, jumping hastily out of the bed, and beginning to put his cloths on. "Your father would not thus have used me; nor, did he live, could blame me, for vindicating as I ought my wounded honour − That I do love your sister is as true, as that you have wronged me − basely wronged me. But that her virtue suffers by that love, is false! − And I must write the man that speaks it, 'lyar,' tho' in her brothers heart." Many other violent expressions to the same effect, passed between them, while the Count was dressing himself, for he would suffer no servant to come in, to be witness of his disorder. But the steddy resolution with which he had attested his innocence, and the inexpressible sweetness of deportment, equally charming to both sexes, and which not even *anger* could render less graceful, extreamly cooled the heat Frankville had been in a little before, and he in secret, began to receed very much from the ill opinion he had conceived, tho' the greatness of his spirit kept him from acknowledging he had been in an error; 'till chancing to cast his eyes on a table which stood in the chamber, he saw the hilt of the broken sword which D'Elmont had brought home the night before, lying on it; he took it up, and having first looked on it with some confusion in his countenance, "My lord," said he, turning to the Count, "I conjure you, before we proceed further, to acquaint me truely, how this came into your possession." Tho' D'Elmont had as great a courage, when any laudable occasion appeared to call it forth, as any man that ever lived; yet his natural disposition had such an uncommon sweetness in it, as no provocation could sowre; it was always a much greater pleasure to him to *forgive* than *punish* injuries; and if at any time he was *angry*, he was never *rude*, or *unjust*. The little starts of passion, Frankvilles rash behaviour had occasioned, all dissolved in his more accustomary softness, when he perceived the other growing calm. And answering to his question, with the most obliging accent in the world, "It was my good fortune," said he, "to be instrumental last night, in the rescue of a gentleman who appeared to have much bravery, and being attacked by odds, behaved himself in such a manner, as would have made him stand but little in need of my assistance, if his sword had been equal to the arm which held it; but the breaking of that, gave me the glory of not being unserviceable to him. After the skirmish was over, I took it up, hoping it might be the means sometime or other of my discovering who the person was, who wore it; not out of vanity of receiving thanks for the little I had done, but that I should be glad of the friendship of a person, who seems so worthy my esteem." "Oh far!" cried Frankville, with a tone and gesture quite altered, "infinitely far from it – It was my self whom you preserved; that very man whose life you but last night so generously redeemed, with the hazard of your own, comes now prepared to make the first use of it against you – Is it possible that you can be so heavenly good to pardon my wild passions heat?" "Let this be witness, with what joy I do," answered the Count, tenderly embracing him, which the other eagerly returning; they continued locked in each others arms for a considerable time, neither of them being able to say more, than – "And was it Frankville I preserved!" – "And was it to D'Elmont I owe my life!"

After this mutual demonstration of a perfect reconcilement was over, "See here, my lord," said Frankville, giving a paper to the Count, "the occasion of my rashness, and let my just concern for a sisters honour, be at least some little mitigation of my temerity, in accosting your lordship in so rude a manner." D'Elmont made no answer, but looking hastily over the paper found it contained these words.

To Monsieur Frankville.

*While your sisters dishonour was known but to few, and the injurious destroyer of it, out of the reach of your revenge, I thought it would ill become the friendship I have always professed to your family, to disquiet you with the knowledge of a misfortune, which it was no way in your power to redress.*

*But Count D'Elmont, having, by the sollicitations of his friends, and the remembrances of some slight services, obtained a pardon from the King, for the murder of his wife; has since taken but little care to conceal the reasons which induced him to that barbarous action; and all Paris is now sensible that he made that unhappy lady's life a sacrifice to the more attractive beauties of Melliora in bloody recompence for the sacrifice she had before made him of her virtue.*

*In short, the noble family of the Frankvilles is for ever dishonoured by this unfaithful guardian; and all who wish you well, rejoice to hear that his ill genius has led him to a place which, if he knew you were at, certainly prudence would make him of all others most avoid; for none believes you will so far degenerate from the spirit of your ancestors, as to permit him to go unpunished.*

*In finding the Count, you may probably find your sister too; for tho', after the death of Alovysa, shame made her retire to a monastry, she has since privately left it without acquainting the abbess, or any of the sisterhood, with her departure; nor is it known to any one, where, or for what cause she absconds; but most people imagine, as indeed it is highly reasonable, that the violence of her guilty passion for D'Elmont has engaged her to follow him.*

*I am not unsensible how much I shock your temper by this relation, but have too much real concern for your honour to endure you should, thro' ignorance of your wrongs, remain passive in such a cause, and perhaps hug the treacherous friend in your most strict embrace. Nor can I forbear, tho' I love not blood, urging you to take that just revenge, which next to heaven you have the greatest claim to.*

I am, Sir, with all due Respect
Yours, Sanseverin.


The Count swelled with indignation at every paragraph of this letter; but when he came to that which mentioned Melliora's having withdrawn her self from the monastry, he seemed to be wholly abandoned by his reason; all endeavours to represent his agonies would be vain, and none but those who have felt the same, can have any notion of what he suffered. He read the fatal scroll again and again, and every time grew wilder than before; he stamped, bit his lips, looked furiously about him, then, starting from the place where he had stood, measured the room in strange, disordered, and unequal paces; all his motions, all his looks, all his air were nothing but distraction. He spoke not for some time, one word, either prevented by the rising passions in his soul, or because it was not in the power of language to express the greatness of his meaning; and when, at last, he opened his mouth, it was but to utter half sentences, and broken complainings. "Is it possible," he cried, "– gone, – left the monastry unknown – and then again – false – false woman? – Wretched – wretched man! There's no such thing on earth as faith – Is this the effect of all her tender passion? – So soon forgot – What can be her reason? – This action suits not with her words, or letters." In this manner he raved with a thousand such-like breathings of a tormented spirit, tossed and confounded between various sentiments.

Monsieur Frankville stood for a good while silently observing him; and if before, he were not perfectly assured of his innocence, the agonies he now saw him in, which were too natural to be suspected for counterfeit, entirely convinced him he was so. When the first gust of passion was blown over, and he perceived any likelyhood of being heard, he said a thousand tender and obliging things to perswade him to moderation, but to very little effect, 'till finding that, that which gave him the most stinging reflection was, the belief that Melliora had forsook the monastry, either because she thought of him no more, and was willing to divert her enfranchaised inclination with the gaieties of the town, or that some happier man had supplanted him in her esteem, "Judge not, my lord," said he, "so rashly of my sister's fidelity, nor know so little of your own unmatched perfections, as to suspect that she, who is blest with your affection, can consider any other object as worthy her regard. For my part, since your lordship knows, and I firmly believe, that this letter contains a great many untruths, I see no reason why we should not imagine it all of a piece. I declare I think it much more improbable that she should leave the monastry, unless sollicited thereto by you, than that she had the power to deny you any thing your passion might request." The Count's disorder visibly abated at this remonstrance; and stepping hastily to his cabinet, he took out the last letter he received from Melliora, and found it was dated but two days before that from Monsieur Sanseverin; he knew she had not art, nor was accustomed to endeavour to disguise her sentiments; and she had written so many tender things in that, as, when he gave himself leave to consider, he could not, without believing her to be either the most dissembling, or most fickle of her sex, continue in the opinion which had made him, a few moments before, so uneasy, that she was no longer, what she always subscribed her self, entirely his.

The tempest of rage and grief being hushed to a little more tranquillity, Count D'Elmont, to remove all scruples which might be yet remaining in the breast of Monsieur Frankville, entertained him with the whole history of his adventures, from the time of his gallantry with Amena, to the misfortunes which had induced him to travel, disguising nothing of the truth, but some part of the discourses which had passed between him and Melliora that night when he surprized her in her bed, and in the wilderness. For tho' he freely confessed the violence of his own unbounded passion, had hurried him beyond all considerations but those of gratifying it; yet he was too tender of Melliora's honour, to relate any thing of her, which modesty might not acknowledge, without the expence of a blush.

Frankville listned with abundance of attention to the relation he made him, and could find very little in his conduct to accuse. He was himself too much susceptible of the power of love, not to have compassion for those that suffered by it, and had too great a share of good sense not to know that, that passion is not to be circumscribed; and being not only, not subservient, but absolutely *controller* of the *will*, it would be meer madness, as well as ill nature, to say a person was blame-worthy for what was unavoidable.

When love once becomes in our power, it ceases to be worthy of that name; no man really possest with it, *can* be master of his actions; and whatever effects it may enforce, are no more to be condemned, than poverty, sickness, deformity, or any other misfortune incident to humane nature. Methinks there is nothing more absurd than the notions of some people, who in other things are wise enough too; but wanting elegance of thought, delicacy, or tenderness of soul, to receive the impression of that harmonious passion, look on those to be mad, who have any sentiments elevated above their own, and either censure, or laugh, at what they are not refined enough to comprehend. These *insipids*, who know nothing of the matter, tell us very gravely, that we *ought* to love with moderation and discretion, – and take care that it is for our interest, – that we should never place our affections, but where duty leads, or at least, where neither religion, reputation, or law, may be a hindrance to our wishes. – Wretches! We know all this, as well as they; we know too, that we both do, and leave undone many other things, which we ought not; but perfection is not to be expected on this side the grave. And since 'tis impossible for humanity to avoid frailties of some kind or other, those are certainly least blameable, which spring only from a too great affluence of the nobler spirits. *Covetousness, envy, pride, revenge*, are the effects of an earthy, base, and sordid nature, *ambition* and *love*, of an exalted one; and if they are failings, they are such as plead their own excuse, and can never want forgiveness from a generous heart, provided no indirect courses are taken to procure the ends of the *former*, nor inconstancy, or ingratitude, stain the beauty of the *latter*.

Notwithstanding all that Monsieur Frankville could say, the Count, tho' not in the rage of temper he had been in, was yet very melancholy; which the other perceiving, "Alass, my lord," said he sighing, "if you were sensible of the misfortunes of others, you would think your own more easy to be born. You love, and are beloved; no obstacle remains between you and your desires, but the formality of custom, which a little time will remove, and at your return to Paris you will doubtless be happy, if 'tis in my sister's power to make you so. You have a sure prospect of felicity to *come*, but mine is *past*, never, I fear, to be retrieved." "What mean you?" cried the Count pretty much surprized at his words, and the change which he observed in his countenance; "I am in love!" replied he, "beloved! Nay, have enjoyed – Ay, there's the source of my dispair – I know the heaven I have lost, and that's my hell." – The interest D'Elmont had in his concerns, as being son to the man who he had loved with a kind of filial affection, and brother to the woman who he adored above the world, made him extreamly desirous to know what the occasion of his disquiet was, and having exprest himself to that purpose; "I shall make no difficulty," replied Frankville, "to reveal the secret of my love, to him who is a lover, and knows so well, how to pity, and forgive, the errors which that passion will sometimes lead us into." The Count was too impatient to hear the relation he was about to give him, to make any other answer to these words than with a half smile; which the other perceiving, without any farther prelude, began to satisfy his curiosity in this manner.

### *The History of Monsieur Frankville.*

"You know, my lord," said he, "that I was bred at Rhiems with my uncle, the bishop of that place, and continued with him 'till after, prompted by glory, and hope of that renown you have since so gallantly acquired, you left the pleasures of the Court for the fatigues and dangers of the field. When I came home, I never ceased solliciting my father to permit me to travel, 'till wearied with my continual importunities, and perhaps, not much displeased with my thirst of improvement, he at last gave leave. I left Paris a little before the conclusion of the peace, and by that means remained wholly a stranger to your lordship's person, tho' perfectly acquainted with those admirable accomplishments which fame is every-where so full of.

"I have been in the courts of England, Spain and Portugal, but nothing very material hapning to me in any of those places, it would be rather impertinent, than diverting, to defer, for trifles, the main business of my life, that of my love, which had not a being 'till I came into this city.

"I had been here but a little time before I had a great many acquaintance; among the number of them, was Signior Jaques

Honorius Cittolini. He, of all the rest, I was most intimate with; and tho' to the generality of people he behaved himself with an air of imperiousness, he was to me, all free, and easy; he seemed as if he took a pleasure in obliging me; carried me every-where with him; introduced me to the best company. When I was absent he spoke of me, as of a person who he had the highest esteem for; and when I was present, if there were any in company whose rank obliged him to place them above me in the *room*; he took care to testify that I was not below them in his *respect*; in fine, he was never more happy than when he was giving me some proof how much he was my friend; and I was not a little satisfied that a man of almost twice my years should believe me qualified for his companion in such a manner as he made me.

"When the melancholly account of my fathers death came to my ears, he omitted nothing to persuade me to sell my estate in France, and settle in Rome; he told me he had a daughter, whose heart had been the aim of the chiefest nobility; but that he would buy my company at that price, and to keep me here, would give me her. This proposition was not altogether so pleasing to me, as perhaps, he imagined it would be. I had heard much talk of this ladies beauty, but I had never seen her; and at that time, love was little in my thoughts, especially that sort which was to end in marriage. However, I would not absolutely refuse his offer, but evaded it, which I had the better pretence for, because Violetta (so was his daughter called) was gone to Vitterbo to visit a sick relation, and I could not have the opportunity of seeing her. In the mean time, he made me acquainted with his deepest secrets; among many other things he told me, that tho' their family was one of the greatest in Rome, yet by the too great liberality of his father, himself and one sister was left with very little to support the grandeur of their birth; but that his sister who was acknowledged a woman of an uncommon beauty, had the good fortune to appear so, to Signior Marcarius Fialasco; he was the possessor of immense riches, but very old; but the young lady found charms enough in his wealth to ballance all other deficiencies; she married, and buried him in a month's time, and he died so full of fondness to his lovely bride, that he left her mistress of all he had in the world; giving only to a daughter he had by a former wife, the fortune which her mother had brought him, and that too, and herself to be disposed of, in marriage, as this triumphant widow should think fit; and she, like a kind sister, thought none worthy of that alliance, but her brother; and in a few days he said, he did not doubt but that I should see him a bridgegroom. I asked him if he was happy enough to have made an interest in the young lady's heart; and he very frankly answered, that he was not of a humour to give himself much uneasiness about it, since it was wholly in his sisters power to make him master of her person, and she resolved to do that, or confine her in a monastry for ever. I could not help feeling a compassionate concern for this lady, tho' she was a stranger to me, for I could not believe, so beautiful and accomplished a woman, as he had often described her to be, could find any thing in her designed husband which could make this match agreeable. Nothing can be more different from graceful, than the person of Cittolini; he is of a black swarthy complexion, hooked nosed, wall eyed, short of stature, and tho' he is very lean, the worst shaped man I ever saw; then for his temper, as friendly as he behaved to me, I discerned a great deal of treachery, and baseness in it to others; a perpetual peevishness and pride appeared in his deportment to all those who had any dependance on him. And I had been told by some who knew him perfectly well, that his cruel usage of his first lady had been the means of her death; but this was none of my business, and tho' I pitied the lady, yet my gratitude to him engaged me to wish him success in all his undertakings. 'Till one day, unluckily both for him and me, as it has since proved; he desired me to accompany him to the house of Ciamara, for so is his sister called, being, willing I suppose, that I should be a witness of the extraordinary state she lived in; and indeed, in all the courts I had been at, I never saw any thing more magnificent than her apartments; the vast quantity of plate, the richness of the furniture, and the number of servants attending on her, might have made her be taken rather for a princess, than a private woman. There was a very noble collation, and she sat at table with us, her self, a particular favour from an Italian lady. She is by many years younger than her brother, and extreamly handsome; but has I know not what of fierceness in her eyes, which renders her, at least to me, a beauty, without a charm. After the entertainment, Cittolini took me into the gardens, which were answerable to what I had seen within, full of curiosities; at one end there was a little building of marble, to which he led me, and entering into it; 'see here, monsieur,' said he, 'the place where my sister spends the greatest part of her hours, and tell me if 'tis in this kind of diversion that the French ladies take delight.' I presently saw it was full of books, and guessed those words were designed for satyr[1] on our ladies, whose disposition to gallantry seldom affords much time for reading; but to make as good a defence for their honour as I was able, 'Signior,' replied I, 'it must be confest, that there are very few ladies of any nation, who think the *acquisition* of knowledge, worth the pains it must cost them in the *search*, but that ours is not without some examples, that all are not of that mind, our famous D'anois and D'acier[2] may evince.' 'Well, well,' interrupted he laughing; 'the propensity which that sex bears to learning is so trifling, that I shall not pretend to hold any argument on its praise; nor did I bring you here so much to engage you to admire my sisters manner of amusement, as to give you an opportunity of diverting your self, while I go to pay a compliment to my mistress; who, tho' I have a very great confidence in you, I dare not trust with the sight of so accomplished a chevalier.' With these words he left me, and I, designing to do as he had desired, turned to the shelves to take down what book I could find most suitable to my humour; but good God! as I was tumbling them over, I saw thro' a window which looked into a garden behind the study, tho' both belonging to one person, a woman, or rather angel, coming down a walk directly opposite to where I was; never did I see in one person such various perfections blended, never did any woman

---

1    Satire.
2    Marie-Catherine La Mothe, baronne d'Aulnoy (c.1650-1705), influential writer of fictionalized court memoirs and travels; Anne Dacier (c.1654-1720), Hellenist and Latinist most famous for her translations of Homer's *Iliad* and *Odyssey*.

wear so much of her soul in her eyes, as did this charmer. I saw that moment in her looks, all I have since experienced of her genius, and her humour; wit, judgment, good nature and generosity are in her countenance, conspicuous as in her actions; but to go about to make a description were to wrong her; she has graces so peculiar, that none, without knowing her, can be able to conceive; and tho' nothing can be finer than her shape, or more regular than her features; yet those, our fancy or a *painters* art may copy. There is something so inexpressibly striking in her air, such a delightful mixture of awful and attractive in every little motion, that no immagination can come up to. But if language is too poor to paint her charms, how shall I make you sensible of the effects of them on me! the surprize – the love – the adoration which this fatal view involved me in, but by that which, you say, your self felt at the first sight of Melliora. I was, methought, all spirit, – I beheld her with raptures, such as we imagine souls enjoy when freed from earth, they meet each other in the realms of glory; 'twas heaven to gaze upon her. But Oh! the bliss was short, the envious trees obscured her lustre from me. – The moment I lost sight of her, I found my *passion* by my *pain*; the *joy* was vanished, but the *sting* remained – I was so buried in thought, that I never so much as stirred a step to endeavour to discover which way she went; tho' if I had considered the situation of the place, it would have been easy for me to have known there was a communication between the two gardens, and if I had gone but a few paces out of the study, must have met her; but love had for the present deprived me of my sences; and it but just entered into my head that there was a possibility of renewing my happiness when I perceived Cittolini returning. When he came pretty near, 'Dear Frankville,' said he, 'pardon my neglect of you; but I have been at Camilla's[1] apartment, and am told she is in the lower garden; I will but speak to her, snatch a kiss and be with you again.' He went hastily by me without staying for any answer, and it was well he did so, for the confusion I was in, had made me little able to reply. His words left me no room to

---

1   The name of a warrior famous for her speed in Virgil's *Aeneid*.

hope it was any other than Camilla I had seen, and the treachery I was guilty of to my friend, in but wishing to invade his right, gave me a remorse which I had never known before. But these reflections lasted not long; love generally exerts himself on these occasions, and is never at a loss for means to remove all the scruples that may be raised to oppose him. 'Why,' said I to my self, 'should I be thus tormented? She is not yet married, and 'tis almost impossible she can with satisfaction, ever yield to be so, to him. Could I but have opportunity to talk to her, – to let her know my passion, – to endeavour to deliver her from the captivity she is in, perhaps she would not condemn my temerity.' I found a great deal of pleasure in this thought, but I was not suffered to enjoy it long. *Honour* suggested to me, that Cittolini loved me, had obliged me, and that to supplant him would be base and treacherous. 'But would it not be more so,' cried the dictates of my *love*, 'to permit the divine Camilla to fall a sacrifice to one so every way undeserving of her; one who 'tis likely she abhors; one who despises her heart, so he may but possess her fortune to support his pride, and her person to gratify a passion far unworthy of the name of *love*; one, who 'tis probable, when master of the one, and satiated with the other, may treat her with the utmost inhumanity.' Thus, for a time, were my thoughts at strife; but love at length got the victory, and I had so well composed my self before Cittolini's return, that he saw nothing of the disorder I had been in; but it was not so with him, his countenance, at the best displeasing enough, was now the perfect representative of ill nature, malice, and discontent. Camilla had assured him, that nothing could be more her aversion, and that she was resolved, tho' a monastick life was what she had no inclination to, yet she would fly to that shelter, to avoid his bed. You may imagine, my lord, I was transported with an excess of joy, when he told me this; but love taught me to dissemble it, 'till I had taken leave of him, which I made an excuse to do, as soon as possible.

"Now all that troubled me was to find an opportunity to declare my passion; and I confess, I was so dull in contrivance, that tho' it took up all my thoughts, none of them were to any purpose. Three or four days I spent in fruitless projections, the last of which I met with a new embarrassment; Cittolini's daughter was returned, he renewed his desires of making me his son, and invited me the next evening to his house, where I was to be entertained with the sight of her; I could not well avoid giving him my promise to be there, but resolved in my mind to behave my self in such a manner as should make her disapprove of me. While I was thus busied in contriving how to avoid Violetta, and engage Camilla, a woman wrapt up very closely in her vail came to my lodgings, and brought me a note, in which I found these words.

### To Monsieur Frankville,

*My father is resolved to make me yours; and if he has your consent, mine will not be demanded; he has commanded me to receive you tomorrow, but I have a particular reason to desire to see you sooner; I am to pass the night with Camilla at my Aunt Ciamara's; there is a little wicket that opens from the garden, directly opposite to the convent of St. Francis;[1] if you will favour me so far as to come there at ten a clock to night, and give seven gentle knocks at the gate, you shall know the cause of my entreating this private interview, which is of more moment than the life of*

Violetta.

"Never had I been more pleasingly surprized, than at the reading these lines; I could not imagine the lady could have any other reason for seeing me in private, than to confess that her heart was pre-engaged, and disswade me from taking the advantage of her father's authority; a secret hope too, sprung within my soul that my adorable Camilla might be with her, and after I had dismissed the woman, with an assurance that I would attend her lady, I spent my time in vast idea's of approaching happiness 'till the appointed hour arrived.

"But how great was my disappointment, when being admit-

---

1   4th ed.; 1st ed. reads "Sir Francis" here but St. Francis elsewhere.

ted, I could distinguish, tho' the place was very dark, that I was received but by one and accosted by her, in a manner very different from what I expected. 'I know not, monsieur,' said she, 'how you interpret this freedom I have taken; but whatever we pretend, our sex, of all indignities, can the least support those done to our beauty; I am not vain enough of mine, to assure my self of making a conquest of your heart; and if the world should know you have seen, and *refused* me, my slighted charms would be the theme of *mirth* to those whose *envy* now they are. I therefore beg, that if I am disliked, none but my self may know it; when you have seen my face, which you shall do so immediately, give me your opinion freely; and if it is not to my advantage, make some pretence to my father to avoid coming to our house.' I protest to you, my lord, that I was so much surprized at this odd kind of proceeding, that I knew not presently how to reply, which she imagining by my silence, 'Come, come, monsieur,' said she, 'I am not yet on even terms with you, having often seen *your* face, and you wholly a stranger to *mine*. But when our knowledge of each other is mutual, I hope you will be as free in your declaration as I have been in my request.' These words I thought were as proper for my purpose as I could wish, and drawing back a little, as she was about to lead me, 'Madam,' said I, 'since you have that advantage, methinks it were but just, you should reveal what sort of sentiments the sight of me has inspired, for I have too much reason from the knowledge of my demerit, to fear, you have no other designs in exposing your charms, than to triumph in the captivating a heart you have already doomed to misery'; 'I will tell you nothing,' answered she, 'of my sentiments 'till I have a perfect knowledge of yours.' As she spoke this, she gave me her hand to conduct me out of that place of darkness; as we went, I had all the concern at the apprehension of being too much approved of by this young lady, as I should have had for the contrary, if I had imagined who it was I had been talking with, for as soon as we came out of the grotto, I saw by the light of the moon, which shone that night with an uncommon lustre, the face which in those gardens had before so charmed me, and which had never since been absent from my thoughts.

What joy, what a mixture of extacy and wonder, then filled my raptured soul at this second view; at first I could not trust my eyes, or think my happiness was real. I gazed, and gazed again in silent transport, for the big bliss surpassed the reach of words. 'What monsieur,' said she, observing my confusion, 'are you yet dumb, is there anything so dreadful in the form of Violetta, to deprive you of your speech.' 'No madam,' replied I, ''tis not Violetta has that power, but she, who unknowing that she did so, caught at first sight the victory o're my soul, she, for whom I have vented so many sighs; she for whom I languished and almost died for, while Violetta was at Vitterbo. She! the divine Camilla only could inspire a passion such as mine'; – 'Oh heavens!' cried she, and at that instant I perceived her lovely face all crimsoned o're with blushes; 'is it then possible that you know me, have seen me before, and that I have been able to make any impression on you?' I then told her of the visit I had made to Ciamara with Cittolini, and how by his leaving me in the marble-study, I was blest with the sight of her; and from his friend became his rival. I let her know the conflicts my honour and my obligations to Cittolini had engaged me in; the thousand various inventions love had suggested to me, to obtain that happiness I now enjoyed, the opportunity of declaring my self her slave; and in short, concealed not the least thought tending to my passion from her. She, in requital, acquainted me, that she had often seen me from her window, go into the convent of St. Francis, walking in the *collonade* at St. Peter's, and in several other places, and, prompted by an extravagance of good nature, and generosity, confessed, that her heart felt something at those views, very prejudicial to her repose; that Cittolini, always disagreeable, was now grown odious; that the discourse she had heard of my intended marriage with his daughter, had given her an alarm impossible to be expressed, and that, unable longer to support the pangs of undiscovered passion, she had writ to me in that ladies name, who she knew I had never seen, resolving, if I liked her as Violetta, to own her self Camilla, if not, to go the next day to a monastry, and devote to Heaven those charms which wanted force to make a conquest where alone she wished they should.

"I must leave it to your lordship's imagination to conceive the wild tumultuous hurry of disordered joy which filled my ravished soul at this condescention; for I am now as unable to discribe it, as I was then to thank the dear, the tender author of it, but what *words* had not power to do, *looks* and *actions* tesitfyed. I threw my self at her feet, embraced her knees, and kissed the hand she raised me with, with such a fervor, as no false love could feign; while she, all softness, all divinely kind, yielded to the pressure of my glowing lips, and suffered me to take all the freedom, which honour and modesty would permit. This interview was too felicitous to be easily broken off; it was almost broad day when we parted, and nothing but her promise, that I should be admitted the next night, could have enabled me to take leave of her.

"I went away highly satisfied, as I had good reason, with my condition, and after recollecting all the tender passages of our conversation, I began to consider after what manner I should proceed with Cittolini; to visit and address his daughter, I thought would be treacherous and deceitful to the last degree; and how to come off, after the promise I made of seeing her that evening, I could not tell; at last, since necessity obliged me to one, I resolved of the two evils to chuse the least, and rather to seem *rude*, then *base*, which I must have been, had I by counterfeiting a desire to engage Violetta, left room for a possibility of creating one in her. I therefore, writ to Cittolini an excuse for not waiting on him and his daughter, as I had promised, telling him that I, on more serious reflection found it wholly inconsistent, either with my circumstances, or inclinations, to think of passing all my life in Rome; that I thanked him for the honour he intended me, but that it was my misfortune, not to be capable of accepting it. Thus, with all the artifice I was master of, I endeavoured to sweeten the bitter pill of refusal, but in vain; for he was so much disgusted at it, that he visited me no more. I cannot say, I had gratitude enough to be much concerned at being compelled to use him in this fashion; for, since I had beheld, and adored Camilla, I could consider him no longer as a friend, but as the most dangerous enemy to my hopes and me. All this time I spent the best part of the nights with Camilla, and in one of them, after giving, and receiving a thousand vows of ever-lasting faith, I snatched a lucking[1] moment, and obtained from the dear melting charmer, all that my fondest, and most eager wishes could aspire to. Yes, my lord, the soft, the trembling fair, dissolved in love; yielded without reserve, and met my transports with an equal ardor; and I truely protest to your lordship, that what in others, palls desire, added fresh force to mine; the more I knew, the more I was inflamed, and in the highest raptures of enjoyment, the bliss was dashed with fears, which proved alass, but too prophetick, that some curst chance might drive me from my heaven. Therefore, to secure it mine for ever, I pressed the lovely partner of my joys, to give me leave to bring a priest with me the next night; who by giving a sanction to our love, might put it past the power of malice to disunite us. Here, I experienced the greatness of her soul, and her almost unexampled generosity; for in spite of all her love, her tenderness, and the unbounded condescentions she had made me, it was with all the difficulty in the world, that I persuaded her to think of marrying me without a fortune; which by her father's *will*, was wholly in the disposal of Ciamara, who it would have been madness to hope, would ever bestow it upon me. However, my arguments at last prevailed; I was to bring a fryar of the order of St. Francis, who was my intimate friend, the next night to join our hands; which done, she told me, she would advise to leave Rome with what speed we could, for she doubted not but Cittolini would make use of any means, tho' never so base or bloody, to revenge his disappointment. This proposal infinitely pleased me, and after I had taken leave of her, I spent the remainder of the night, in contriving the means of our escape. Early in the morning I secured post-horses, and then went to the convent of St. Francis, a purse of *Lewis d'ors* soon engaged the fryar to my interest, and I had every thing ready in wonderful order, considering the shortness of time, for our design; when returning home towards evening, as well to take a little rest after the fatigue I had had, as to give some other necessary directions concerning the affair to

---

1    Possibly an error – Haywood uses "lucky moment" below (288)– but "to luck" is
     dialect for "to be lucky, prosper, succeed" (*OED*).

my servants, when one of them gave me a letter, which had been just left for me."

Monsieur Frankville could not come to this part of his story, without some sighs, but suppressing them as well as he was able, he took some papers out of his pocket, and singling out one, read to the Count as follows.

To Monsieur Frankville.

*With what words can I represent the greatness of my misfortune, or exclaim against the perfidy of my woman? I was obliged to make her the confidant of my passion, because without her assistance, I could not have enjoyed the happiness of your conversation, and 'tis by her that I am now betrayed – undone, – lost to all hopes of ever seeing you more – What have I not endured this day, from the upbraidings of Ciamara and Cittolini, but that I should dispise, nay, my own ruin too, if you were safe – But Oh! their malice aims to wound me most, through you – Bravo's are hired, the price of your blood is paid, and they have sworn to take your life – Guard it I conjure you, if you would preserve that of Camilla's – Attempt not to come near this house, nor walk alone, when night may be an umbrage[1] to their designs. – I hear my cruel enemies returning to renew their persecutions, and I have time to inform you no more, than that 'tis to the generous Violetta you are indebted for this caution. She, in pity of my agonies, and to prevent her father from executing the crime he intends, conveys this to you, slight it not, if you would have me believe you love,*

*Camilla.*

"What a turn was here," continued he, sadly, "in my fortune? How on a sudden was my scene of happiness changed to the blackest dispair? – But not to tire your lordship, and spin out my narration, which is already too long with unavailing complainings. I every day expected a challenge from Cittolini,

---

1   A cover; literally, a shade.

believing he would, at least, take that method at first, but it seems he was for chusing the *surest*, not the *fairest* way. And I have since proved, that my dear Camilla had too much reason for the caution she gave me. Ten days I lingred out without being able to invent any means, either to see her, or write to her; at the end of which, I received another letter from her, which, if I were to tell you the substance of, would be to wrong her; since no words but her own are fit to express her meaning, and 'tis for that reason only, I shall read it.

To Monsieur Frankville.

*Of all the woes which wait on humane life, sure there is none equal to that a lover feels in absence; 'tis a kind of hell, an earnest of those pains, we are told, shall be the portion of the damned — Ten whole nights, and days, according to the vulgar reckoning, but in mine, as many ages, have rolled their tedious hours away since last I saw you, in all which time my eyes have never known one moments cessation from my tears, nor my sad heart from anguish; restless I wander thro' this hated house — kiss the closed wicket — stop, and look at every place which I remember thy dear steps have blest, then, with wild ravings, think of past joys, and curse my present woes — yet, you perhaps are calm, no sympathizing pang invades your soul, and tells you what mine suffers, else, you would — you must have found some means to ease your self and me — 'tis true, I bid you not attempt it — but Oh! if you had loved like me, you could not have obeyed — Desire has no regard to prudence, it dispises danger, and overlooks even impossibilities — but whether am I going? — I say, I know not what — Oh, mark not what distraction utters! Shun these detested walls! — 'Tis reason now commands! Fly from this house, where injured love's enslaved, and death and treachery reign — I charge thee come not near, nor prove thy faith so hazardous a way — Forgive the little fears, which ever dwell with love — I know thou art all sincerity! — all godlike truth, and can'st not change — yet, if thou shouldst, — tormenting thought! — Why*[1]

---

1   Preceding dash supplied from previous page's catch-word.

*then, there's not a heaven-abandoned wretch, so lost — so curst as I. — What shall I do to shake off apprehension? In spite of all thy vows — thy ardent vows, when I but think of any maid, by love and fond belief undone, a deadly cold runs thro' my veins, congeals my blood, and chills my very soul! — Gazing on the moon last night, her lustre brought fresh to my memory those transporting moments, when by that light I saw you first a lover; and, I think inspired me, who am not usually fond of versifying to make her this complaint.*

The unfortunate Camilla's Complaint to the Moon, for the Absence of her Dear Henricus Frankville.

*Mild queen of shades! Thou sweetly shining light!*
*Once, more then Phoebus, welcome to my sight:*
*'Twas by thy beams I first Henricus saw*
*Adorned with softness, and disarmed of awe!*
*Never did'st thou appear more fair! more bright!*
*Than on that dear, that cause-remembred night!*
*When the dull tyes of friendship he disclaimed,*
*And to inspire a tend'rer passion aimed.*
*Alas! he could not long, in vain, implore*
*For that, which tho' unknown, was his before;*
*Nor had I art the secret to disguise,*
*My soul spoke all her meaning thro' my eyes,*
*And every glance bright'ned with glad surprize!*
*Lost to all thought, but his transporting charms,*
*I sunk, unguarded! melting in his arms!*
*Blest at that lavish rate, my state, that hour*
*I'd not have changed for all in Fortune's pow'r;*
*Nay, had discending angel's from on high*
*Spread their bright wings, to waft me to the sky,*
*Thus clasped! coelestial charms had failed to move*
*And heav'n been slighted, for Henricus love.*
*How did I then thy happy influence bless?*
*How watch each joyful night, thy lights encrease?*
*But Oh! how altered since — Dispairing now,*
*I view thy lustre with contracted brow,*

*Pensive, and sullen from thy rays would hide,*
*And scarce the glimmering star's my griefs abide,*
*In death-like darkness would my fate deplore*
*And wish thee to go down, to rise no more!*

*Pity the extravagance of a passion which only charms like thine could create, nor too severely chide this soft impertinence, which I could not refrain sending you, when I can neither see you, nor hear from you, to write, gives some little respite to my pains, because I am sure of being in your thoughts, while you are reading my letters. The tender hearted Violetta prefering the tyes of friendship to those of duty, gives me this happy opportunity, but my ill-fortune deprives me too of her, she goes to morrow to her fathers villa, and heaven knows when I shall find means to send to you again.*

*Farewel, thou loveliest, dearest, and divine charmer – Think of me with a concern full of tenderness, but that is not enough, and you must pardon me, when I confess, that I cannot forbear wishing you might feel some of those pains, impatient longings bring. – All others be far away, as far, as joy is, when you are absent from*

Your Unfortunate
Camilla.

P.S. *Since I writ this, a fancy came into my head, that if you could find a friend trusty enough to confide in, and one unknown to our family, he might gain admittance to me in Cittolini's name, as sent by him, while he is at the villa. I flatter my self you will take as much pleasure in endeavouring to let me hear from you, as I do in the hope of it. Once more Adieu.*

"Your lordship may judge, by what I have told you of the sincerity of my passion, how glad I should have been to have complied with her request, but it was utterly impossible to find any body fit for such a business. I passed three or four days more, in disquietudes too great to be exprest; I sauntered up and down the street where she lived, in hopes to see her at some of the windows, but fortune never was so favourable to me; thus I spent my days, and left the sight of those dear walls at nights, but in obedience to the charge she had given me of preserving my life.

"Thus, my lord, has the business of my love engrossed my hours, ever since your lordships arrival, and tho' I heard that you were here, and extreamly wished to kiss your hands, yet I could never get one moment composed enough to wait on you in, 'till what my desires could not do, the rashness of my indignation effected. Last night, being at my bankers where all my bills and letters are directed, I found this, from Monsieur Sanseverin; the rage which the contents of it put me in, kept me from remembring that circumspection, which Camilla had enjoyned, and I thought of nothing but revenging the injury I imagined you had done me. As I was coming home I was attacked as you saw, when you so generously preserved me, the just indignation I conceived at this base procedure of Cittolini's transported me so far, as to make me forget what I owed to my deliverer, to run in pursuit of those who assaulted me, but soon lost sight of them, and returning, as gratitude and honour called me, to seek, and thank you for your timely assistance, I found a throng of people about the body of the villain I had killed, some of them were for examining me, but finding no wounds about me, nor any marks of the engagement I had been in, I was left at my liberty.

"Thus, my lord, have I given you, in as brief a manner as the changes of my fortune would permit, the account of my present melancholly circumstances, in which, if you find many things blameable, you must acknowlege there are more which require compassion."

"I see no reason," answered the Count, "either for the one or the other, you have done nothing but what any man, who is a lover, would gladly have it in his power to do, and as for your condition it certainly is more to be envied than pitied. The lady loves, is constant, and doubtless will some way or other, find means for her escape. —" "Impossible!" cried Frankville, interrupting him, "she is too strictly watched to suffer such a hope." "If you will prepare a letter," resumed D'Elmont, "my self will undertake to be the bearer of it; I am intirely a stranger to the people you have been speaking of, or if I should chance to be known to them, cannot be suspected to come from you, since our intimacy, so lately born, cannot yet be talked of, to the prejudice of our design; and how do you know, continued he smiling, but, if I have the good fortune to be introduced to this lady, that I shall not be able to assist her invention to form some scheme, for both your future happiness." This offer was too agreeable to be refused, Frankville accepted it with all the demonstrations of gratitude and joy imaginable, and setting himself down to the Count's scrutore, was not long writing the following billet which he gave him to read before he sealed it.

To the most Lovely and Adorable
Camilla.

*If to consume with inward burnings, to have no breath but sighs, to wish for death, or madness to relieve me, from the racks of thought, be misery consummate, such is mine! and yet my too unjust Camilla thinks I feel no pain, and chides my cold tranquility; could I be so, I were indeed a wretch deserving of my fate, but far unworthy of your pity or regard. No, no, thou loveliest, softest, most angelic creature that heaven, in lavish bounty, ever sent to charm the adoring world; he that could know one moments stupid calm in such an absence, ought never to be blest with those unbounded joys thy presence brings. What would I not give, what would I not hazard but once more to behold thee, to gaze upon thy eyes, those suns of kindling transports, to touch thy enlivening hand, to feed upon the ravishing sweetness of thy lips; Oh the immagination's extacy, life were too poor to set on such a cast, and you should long e're this have proved the little value I have for it, in competition with my love, if your commands had not restrained me. Cittolini's malice, however, had last night been gratified, if the noble Count D'Elmont had not been inspired for my preservation; it is to him I am indebted, not only for my life, but a much greater favour, that of conveying to you the assurance, how much my life, my soul, and all the faculties of it are eternally yours. Thank him, my Camilla, for your*

*Frankville, for words like thine are only fit to praise, as it deserves, such an exalted generosity; 'tis with an infinite deal of satisfaction I reflect how much thy charms will justify my conduct when he sees thee, all that excess of passion, which my fond souls too full of to conceal, that highth of adoration, which offered to any other woman would be sacriledge, the wonders of thy beauty and thy wit, claim as their due, and prove Camilla, like heaven, can never be too much reverenced! be too much loved! − But, Oh! how poor is language to express what 'tis I think, thus raptured with thy idea, thou best, thou brightest − thou most perfect − thou something more than excellence itself − thou far surpassing all that words can speak, or heart, unknowing thee, conceive; yet I could dwell for ever on the theme, and swell whole volumes with enervate, tho' well-meaning praises, if my impatience, to have what I have already writ, be with you, did not prevent my saying any more than, that but in you I live, nor could support this death-like absence, but for some little intervals of hope, which sometimes flatter me, that fortune will grow weary of persecuting me, and one day re-unite my body to my soul and make us both inseparably yours,*

Frankville.

These new made friends having a fellow-feeling of each others sufferings, as proceeding from one source, passed the time in little else but amorous discourses, till it was a proper hour for the Count to perform his promise, and taking a full direction from Frankville how to find the house, he left him at his lodgings to wait his return from Ciamara's, forming, all the way he went, a thousand projects to communicate to Camilla for her escape; he was still extreamly uneasy in his mind concerning Melliora, and longed to be in Paris to know the truth of that affair, but thought he could not in honour leave her brother in this embarrassment, and resolved to make use of all his wit and address to perswade Camilla to hazard every thing for love, and was not a little pleased with the imagination, that he should lay so considerable an obligation on Melliora, as this service to her brother would be. Full of these reflections he found himself in the portico of that magnificent house he was to enter, and seeing a crowd of servants about the door, desired to be brought to the presence of Donna Camilla Fialaso, one of them, immediately conducted him into a stately room, and leaving him there, told him, the lady should be made acquainted with his request; presently after came in a woman, who, tho' very young, seemed to be in the nature of a duenna;[1] the Count stood with his back toward her as she entered, but hearing somebody behind him, and turning hastily about, he observed she startled at sight of him, and appeared so confused that he knew not what to make of her behaviour, and when he asked if he might speak with Camilla, and said he had a message to deliver from Cittolini, she made no other answer than several times, with an amazed accent, ecchoing the names of Camilla and Cittolini, as if not able to comprehend his meaning; he was obliged to repeat his words over and over before she could recollect herself enough to tell him, that she would let him know her lady's pleasure instantly. She left him in a good deal of consternation, at the surprize he perceived the sight of him had put her into; he formed a thousand uncertain guesses what the occasion should be, but the mistery was too deep for all his penetration to fathom, and he waited with abundance of impatience for her return, or the appearance of her lady, either, of which, he hoped, might give a solution to this seeming riddle.

He attended a considerable time, and was beginning to grow excessive uneasy, at this delay, when a magnificent *anti-porta* being drawn up, he saw, thro' a glass door, which opened into a gallery, the *duenna* approaching. She had now entirely composed her countenance, and with an obliging smile told him, she would conduct him to her lady. She led him thro' several rooms, all richly furnished and adorned, but far inferior to the last he came into, and in which he was again left alone, after being assured that he should not long be so.

Count D'Elmont could not forbear giving truce to his more serious reflections, to admire the beauties of the place he was in, where e'er he turned his eyes, he saw nothing but what was

---

1   A chaperon, "an old woman kept to guard a younger" (Johnson).

splendidly luxurious, and all the ornaments contrived in such a manner, as might fitly be a pattern, to paint the palace of the Queen of Love by. The ceiling was vastly high and beautified with most curious paintings, the walls were covered with tapestry, in which, most artificially were woven, in various couloured silk, intermixed with gold and silver, a great number of amorous stories; in one place he beheld a naked Venus sporting with Adonis;[1] in another, the love-transformed Jupiter, just resuming his shape, and rushing to the arms of Leda;[2] there, the seeming chast Diana embracing her entranced Endimion;[3] here, the god of soft desires himself, wounded with an arrow of his own, and snatching kisses from the no less enamoured Psiche.[4] Betwixt every one of these pieces hung a large looking-glass, which reached to the top of the room, and out of each sprung several crystal branches, containing great wax-tapers, so that the number of lights vied with the sun, and made another, and more glorious day, than that which lately was withdrawn. At the upper end of this magnificent chamber, there was a canopy of crimson velvet, richly embossed, and trimmed with silver, the corners of which were supported by two golden Cupids, with stretched out wings, as if prepared to fly; two of their hands grasped the extremity of the valen,[5] and the other, those nearest to each other, joyned to hold a wreath of flowers, over a couch, which stood under the canopy. But tho' the Count was very much taken at first with what he saw, yet he was too true a lover to be long delighted with any thing in the absence of his mistress. "How heavenly," said he to himself sighing, "would be this place, if I expected Melliora here! But Oh! how preferable were a cottage blest with her, to all this

---

1 The goddess of love herself loved the mortal Adonis, who was later killed by a boar.

2 Jupiter, the amorous ruler of the gods, transformed himself into a swan to approach Leda, who later gave birth to Helen of Troy.

3 The moon goddess (usually called Selene in this story) loved Endymion, a mortal who was placed in a permanent sleep where she visited him nightly.

4 Cupid loves the mortal woman Psyche in an episode in Apuleius' late-classical satire *The Golden Ass*; her beauty provokes his mother Venus' jealousy, but after secret love, separation, and the ordeals Venus imposes on Psyche, the lovers are united in heaven.

5 The valence, a short curtain.

pomp and grandeur with any other"; this consideration threw him into a deep musing, which made him forget either where he was, or the business which brought him there, till roused from it by the dazling owner of this sumptuous apartment; nothing could be more glorious than her appearance; she was by nature, a woman of a most excellent shape, to which, her desire of pleasing, had made her add all the aids of art; she was drest in a gold and silver stuff petticoat, and a wastcoat of plain blue sattin, set round the neck and sleves, and down the seams with diamonds, and fastned on the breast, with jewels of a prodigious largeness and lustre; a girdle of the same encompassed her waste; her hair, of which she had great quantity, was black as jet, and with a studied negligence, fell part of it on her neck in careless ringlets, and the other was turned up, and fastened here and there with bodkins, which had pendant diamonds hanging to 'em, and as she moved, glittered with a quivering blaze, like stars darting their fires from out a sable sky; she had a vail on, but so thin, that it did not, in the least, obscure the shine of her garments; or her jewels, only she had contrived to double that part of it which hung over her face, in so many folds, that it served to conceal her as well as a *vizard* mask.

The Count made no doubt but this was the lady for whom he waited, and throwing off that melancholly air he had been in, assumed one, all gay and easy, and bowing low, as he advanced to meet her, "Madam," said he, "if you are that incomparable Camilla whose goodness, nothing but her beauty can equalize, you will forgive the intrusion of a stranger, who confesses himself no other way worthy of the honour of your conversation, but by his desires to serve him who is much more so." "A friend of Cittolini's," answered she, "can never want admittance here, and if you had no other plea, the name you come in, is a sufficient warrant for your kind reception." "I hope," resumed he, in a low voice, and looking round to see if there were no attendants in hearing, "I bring a letter from Frankville, madam, the adoring Frankville, I have these credentials to justify my visit"; in speaking this he delivered the letter to her, which she retiring a few paces from him to read, gave him an opportunity of admiring the majesty of her walk, and the agreeable loftiness of her mein, much more than he had time to do before.

She dwelt not long on the contents of the letter, but throwing it carelessly down on a table which stood near her, turned to the Count and with an accent which expressed not much satisfaction; "and was it to you, my lord," said she, "that Monsieur Frankville owed his preservation?" "I was so happy," replied he, "to have some little hand in it, but since I have known how dear he is to you, think my self doubly blest by Fortune for the means of acting any thing conducive to your peace." "If you imagine that this is so," resumed she hastily, "you are extreamly mistaken, as you will always be, when you believe, where Count D'Elmont appears, any other man seems worthy the regard of a discerning woman; but," continued she, perceiving he looked surprized, "to spare your suspence, and my self the trouble of repeating what you know already, behold who she is, you have been talking to, and tell me now, if Frankville has any interest in a heart to which this face belongs?" With these words she threw off her vail, and instead of lessening his amazement, very much encreased it, in discovering the features of the lady, with whom he had discoursed the night before in the garden. He knew not what to think, or how to reconcile to reason, that Camilla, who so lately loved, and had granted the highest favours to Frankville should on a sudden be willing, uncourted, to bestow them on another, nor could he comprehend how the same person should at once live in two several places, for he conceived the house he was in, was far distant from the garden which he had been in the night before.

They both remained for some moments in a profound silence, the lady expecting when the Count should speak, and he endeavouring to recollect himself enough to do so, 'till she, at last, probably guessing at his thoughts, resumed her discourse in this manner. "My lord," said she, "wonder not at the power of love, a form like yours might soften the most rugged heart, much more one, by nature so tender as is mine. – Think but what you are," continued she sighing, and making him sit down by her on the couch, "and you will easily excuse whatever my passion may enforce me to commit." "I must confess, madam," answered he very gravely, "I never in my life wanted presence of mind so much as at this juncture, to see before me here, the person, who, I believed, lived far from hence, who, by appointment, I was to wait on this night at a different place. – To find in the mistress of my friend, the very lady, who seems unworthily to have bestowed her heart on me, are circumstances so incoherent as I can neither account for, or make evident to *reason*, tho' they are too truly so to *sense*." "It will be easy," replied she, "to reconcile both of these seeming contradictions, when you shall know that the gardens belonging to this house, are of a very large extent, and not only that, but the turning of the streets are so ordered, as make the distance between the fore and back door appear much greater than realy it is; and for the other, as I have already told you, you ought to be better acquainted with your self, than to be surprized at consequences which must infallibly attend such charms"; in saying this, she turned her head a little on one side, and put her handkerchief before her face, affecting to seem confused at what she spoke; but the Count redned in good earnest, and with a countenance which expressed sentiments, far different from those she endeavoured to inspire. "Madam," said he, "tho' the good opinion you have of me is owing entirely to the *error* of your *fancy*, which too often, especially in your sex, blinds the *judgment*, yet, 'tis certain, that there are not many men, whom such praises, coming from a mouth like yours, would not make happy and vain; but if I was ever of a humour to be so, it is now wholly mortified in me, and 'tis but with the utmost regret, that I must receive the favours you confer on me to the prejudice of my friend." "And is that," interrupted she hastily, "is that the *only* cause? Does nothing but your friendship to Frankville prevent my wishes?" "That, of itself," answered he, "were a sufficient bar to sunder us for ever, but there's another, if not a greater, a more tender one, which, to restore you to the path, which honour, gratitude, and reason call you to, I must inform you of, yes, I must tell you, madam, all lovely as you are, that were there no such man as Frankville, in the world – Were you as free as air, I have a defence within, which all your charms can never pierce, nor softness melt – I am already bound, not with the weak tyes of vows or formal obligations, which confine no farther than the body, but inclination! – the fondest inclination! that ever swelled a *heart* with rapturous hopes." The lady had much ado to contain herself till he had done speaking; she was by nature extreamly haughty, insolent of her beauty, and impatient of any thing she thought looked like a slight of it, and this open defyance of *her* power, and acknowledging *anothers*, had she been less in love would have been insupportable to her; "ungrateful and uncourtly man," said she, looking on him with eyes that sparkled at once with indignation and desire, "you might have spared yourself the trouble of repeating, and me the confusion of hearing in what manner you stand engaged; it had been enough to have told me you never could be mine, without appearing transported at the ruin which you make; if my too happy rival possesses charms, I cannot boast, methinks your *good manners* might have taught you not to insult my wants, and your *good nature*, to have mingled *pity* with your *justice*"; with these words she fell a weeping, but whether they were tears of love or anger, is hard to determine, 'tis certain that both those passions raged this moment in her soul with equal violence, and if she had, had it in her power, would doubtless have been glad to have hated him, but he was, at all times, too lovely to suffer a possibility of that, and much more so at this; for in spite of the shock, that infidelity he believed her guilty of to Frankville, gave him, he was by nature so compassionate, he *felt* the woes he *saw*, or *heard* of, even of those who were most indifferent to him, and could not now behold a face, in which all the horrors of dispair were in the most lively manner represented, without displaying a tenderness in his, which in any other man, might have been taken for love; the dazling radience of his eyes, gave place to a more dangerous, more bewitching softness, and when he sighed, in pity of her anguish, a soul inchanting languishment diffused itself thro' all his air, and added to his graces; she presently perceived it, and forming new hopes, as well from that, as from his silence, took hold of his hand, and pressing it eagerly to her bosom, "Oh my lord!" resumed she, "you cannot be ungrateful tho' you would. – I see you cannot –" "Madam," interrupted he, shaking off as much as possible that show of tenderness, which he found had given her incouragement; "I wish not to convince you how nearly I am touched, with what you suffer, least it should *encrease* an esteem, which, since prejudicial to your repose, and the interest of my friend, I rather ought to endeavour to *lessen*. – But, as this is not the entertainment I expected from Camilla, I beg to know an answer to the business I came upon, and what you decree for the unfortunate Frankville." If the lady was agitated with an extremity of vexation at the Count's declaration of his passion for another, what was she now, at this disappointment of the hopes she was so lately flattered with; instead of making any direct reply to what he said, she raged, stamped, tore her hair, cursed Frankville, all mankind, the world, and in that height of fury, scarce spared heaven itself; but the violence of her pride and resentment being a little vented, love took his turn, again she wept, again she prest his hand, nay she even knelt, and hung upon his feet, as he would have broke from her, and begged him with words as eloquent as wit could form, and desperate dying love suggest, to pity and relieve her misery. But he had now learned to dissemble his concern, lest it should a second time beguile her, and after raising her, with as careless and unmoved an air, as he was capable of putting on. "My presence, madam," said he, "but augments your disorder, and 'tis only by seeing you no more, that I am qualified to conduce to the recovery of your peace." With these words he turned hastily from her, and was going out of the room, when she, quick as thought, sprung from the place where she had stood, and being got between him and the door, and throwing herself into his arms, before he had time to prevent her; "you must not, shall not go," she cried, "till you have left me dead." "Pardon me, madam," answered he fretfully, and struggling to get loose from her embrace, "to stay after the discovery you have made of your sentiments, were to be guilty of an injustice almost equal to your's, therefore I beg you'd give me liberty to pass." – "Hear me but speak," resumed she, grasping him yet harder; "return but for a moment, – lovely barbarian, – hell has no tortures like your cruelty." Here, the different passions working in her soul, with such uncommon vehemence, hurried her spirits beyond what nature could support; her voice faultered in the accent, her trembling hands by slow degrees relinquished what so eagerly they had held, every sense forgot its use, and she sunk, in all appearance, lifeless on the floor. The Count was, if possible, more glad to be released, than grieved at the occasion, and contented himself with calling her women to her assistance, without staying to see when she would recover.

He went out of that house with thoughts much more discomposed than those with which he had entered it, and when he came home, where Frankville impatiently waited his return, he was at the greatest loss in the world, how to discover his misfortune to him; the other observing the trouble of his mind, which was very visible in his countenance; "my lord," said he, in a melancholly tone, "I need not ask you what success, the gloom which appears on your brow, tells me, my ill fortune has denied you means of speaking to Camilla"; "accuse not fortune," answered D'Elmont, "but the influence of malicious stars which seldom, if ever, suits our dispositions to our circumstances; I have seen Camilla, have talked to her, and 'tis from that discourse that I cannot forbear reflecting on the miseries of humanity, which, while it mocks us with a show of *reason*, gives us no power to curb our *will*, and guide the erring appetites to peace." Monsieur Frankville at these words first felt a jealous pang, and as 'tis natural to believe every body admires what we do, he presently imagined Count D'Elmont had forgot Melliora in the presence of Camilla, and that it was from the consciousness of his own weakness and inconstancy, that he spoke so feelingly. "I wonder not my lord," said he coldly, "that the beauties of Camilla should inspire you with sentiments, which, perhaps for many reasons, you would desire to be free from, and I ought, in prudence, to have considered, that tho' you are the most excellent of your kind, you are still a *man*, and have the passions incident to *man*, and not have exposed you to those dangers the sight of Camilla must necessarily involve you in." "I wish to heaven," answered the Count, easily guessing what his thoughts were, "no greater threatned you, and that you could think on Camilla with the same indifference as I can, or she of me with more;" then, in as brief a manner as he could, he gave him the substance of what had happened. Frankville, whose only fault was rashness, grew almost wild at the recital of so unexpected a misfortune, he knew not for a good while what to believe, loath he was to suspect the Count, but loather to suspect Camilla, yet flew into extremities of rage against both, by turns. The Count pitied and forgave all that the violence of his passion made him utter, but offered not to argue with him, 'till he found him capable of admitting his reasons, and then, that open sincerity, that honest noble assurance which always accompanied his sweetness, and made it difficult to doubt the truth of any thing he said, won the disordered lover to an entire conviction; he now concludes his mistress false, repents the tenderness he has had for her, and tho' she still appears as lovely to his *fancy* as ever, she grows odious to his *judgment*, and resolves to use his utmost efforts to banish her idea from his heart.

In this humour he took leave of the Count, it growing late, and his last nights adventure taught him the danger of nocturnal walks, but how he spent his time till morning, those can only guess, who have loved like him, and like him, met so cruel a disappointment.

The Count passed not the night in much less inquietude than Frankville; he grieved the powerful influence of his own attractions, and had there not been a Melliora in the world, he would have wished himself deformed, rather than have been the cause of so much misery, as his loveliness produced.

The next morning the Count designed to visit Frankville, to strengthen him in his resolution of abandoning all thoughts of the unconstant Camilla, but before he could get drest, the other came into his chamber. "My lord," said he, assoon as they were alone, "my perfidious mistress, failing to make a conquest of your heart, is still willing to preserve that she had attained over mine, but all her charms and her delusions are but vain, and to prove to your lordship that they are so, I have brought the letter I received from her, scarce an hour past, and the true copy of my answer to it."

To Monsieur Frankville.

*Tho' nothing proves the value of our presence, so much as the pangs our absence occasions, and in my last I rashly wished you might be sensible of mine, yet on examining my heart, I present-ly recalled the hasty prayer, and found I loved with that extrava-gance of tenderness, that I had rather you returned it too little than too much, and methinks could better bear to represent you to my fancy, careless and calm as common lovers are, than think, I saw you, burning, − bleeding, − dying, like me, with hopeless wishes, and unavailing expectations; but Ah! I fear such appre-hensions are but too un-necessary − You think not of me, and, if in those happy days, when no cross accident interveened to part me from your sight, my fondness pleased, you now find nothing in Camilla worth a troubled thought, nor breath one tender sigh in memory of our transports past. − If I wrong your love, impute it to distraction, for Oh! 'tis sure I am not in my senses, nor know to form one regular desire. I act, and speak, and think, a thousand incoherent things, and tho' I cannot forbear writing to you, I write in such a manner, so wild, so different from what I would, that I repent me of the folly I am guilty of, even while I am committing it; but to make as good a defence as I am able for these, perhaps, unwelcome lines, I must inform you that they come not so much to let you know my sentiments, as to engage a discovery of yours. Ciamara has discharged one of her servants from her attendance, who no longer courting her favour, or regard-ing her frowns, I have prevailed upon, not only to bring this to you, but to convey an answer back to me, by the help of a string which I am to let down to him from my window; therefore, if you are but as kind, as he has promised to be faithful, we may often enjoy the blessing of this distant conversation; heaven only knows when we shall be permitted to enjoy a nearer. Cittolini is this evening returned from his villa, and nothing but a miracle can save me from the necessity of making my choice of him, or a monastery, either of which is worse than death, since it must leave me the power to wish, but take away the means, of being what I so oft have swore to be*

Eternally Yours, and
Yours alone,
Camilla.

The Count could not forbear lifting up his eyes and hands in token of amazement, at the unexampled falshood this woman appeared guilty of, but perceiving Monsieur Frankville was about to read the following answer, would not interrupt him, by asking any questions 'till he had done.

## To Donna Camilla.

*If vows are any constraint to an inclination so addicted to liberty as yours, I shall make no difficulty to release you, of all you ever made to me! Yes madam, you are free to dispose both of your heart and person wheresoever you think fit, nor do I desire you should give your self the pains of farther dissimulation. I pay too entire an obedience to your will, then to continue in a passion which is no longer pleasing, nor will by an ill timed and unmannerly constancy disturb the serenity of your future enjoyments with any happier man than*

Frankville.

"You see, my lord," said he with a sigh, "that I have put it out of her power to triumph over my weakness, for I confess my heart still wears her chains, but e'er my eyes or tongue betray to her the shameful bondage, these hands should tear them out; therefore I made no mention of her behaviour to you, nor of my sending any letter by you, not only because I knew not if your lordship would think it proper, but lest she should imagine my resentment proceeded from jealousy, and that I loved her still. – No, she shall ne'er have cause to guess the truth of what I suffer. – Her *real perfidy* shall be repaid with *seeming inconstancy* and scorn. – Oh! how 'twill sting her pride, – by heaven, I feel a gloomy kind of pleasure in the thought, and will indulge it, even to the highest insults of revenge."

"I rather wish," replied the Count, "you could in *earnest* be indifferent, than only *feign* to be so, her unexampled levity and deceit, renders her as unworthy of your anger as your love, and there is too much danger while you preserve the *one*, that you will not be able to throw off the *other*." – "Oh! I pretend not to it," cried Frankville, interrupting him, "she has too deep a root within my soul ever to be removed – I boast no more than a concealment of my passion, and when I dress the horrors of a bleeding, breaking heart, in all the calm of cold tranquility; methinks, you should applaud the *noble* conquest." "Time," said the Count, after a little pause, "and a just reflection how little she deserves your thoughts, will teach you to obtain a *nobler*; that of numbring your love, among things that *were*, but *are* no more, and make you, with me, acknowledge that 'tis as great an argument of *folly* and *meanness of spirit* to continue the same esteem when the object ceases to deserve, which we professed before the discovery of that unworthyness, as it would be of *villany* and *inconstancy of mind*, to change, without an efficient cause." A great deal of discourse passed between them to the same effect, and it was but in vain that Count D'Elmont endeavoured to perswade him to a real forgetfulness of the charmer, tho' he resolved to seem as if he did so.

While they were disputing, one of D'Elmont's servants gave him a letter, which, he told him, the person who brought it, desired he would answer immediately; he no sooner broke it open, and had cast his eye over it, than he cried out in a kind of transport, "Oh, Frankville, what has fate been doing! You are happy. – Camilla is innocent, and perhaps the most deserving of her sex; I only am guilty, who, by a fatal mistake have wronged her virtue, and tormented you; but read," continued he, giving him the letter, "read, and satisfy your self."

Monsieur Frankville was too much astonished at these words to be able to make any reply, but immediately found the interpretation of them in these lines.

To the dear cruel Destroyer of my Quiet,
the never too much Admired Count D'Elmont.

*'Tis no longer the mistress of your friend, a perjured and unjust Camilla, who languishes and dyes by your contempt, but one, whom all the darts of love had strove in vain to reach, 'till from your charms they gained a god-like influence, and un-erring force! One, who tho' a widow, brings you the offering of a virgin heart.*

*As I was sitting in my closet, watching the progress of the lazy hours, which flew not half so swift as my desires to bring on the appointed time in which you promised to be with me in the garden; my woman came running in, to acquaint me, that you were in the house, and waited to speak with Camilla. Surprize, and jealousy at once assaulted me, and I sunk beneath the apprehension that you might by some accident have seen her, and also loved her; to ease my self of those tormenting doubts I resolved to appear before you, in her stead, and kept my vail over my face, 'till I found that hers was unknown to you. — You are not ignorant what followed, the deceit passed upon you for truth, but I was sufficiently punished for it, by the severity of your usage. I was just going to discover who I was, when the violence of my love, my grief, and my dispair threw me into that swoon, in which, to compleat your cruelty, you left me; 'twould be endless to endeavour to represent the agonies of my soul, when I recovered, and heard you were gone, but all who truly love, as they fear much, so they hope much; my tortures at length abated, at least, permitted me to take some intervals of comfort, and I began to flatter my self that the passion you seemed transported with, for a nameless mistress, was but a feint to bring me back to him you thought I was obliged to love, and that there was a possibility, that my person and fortune might not appear despicable to you, when you should know, I have no tyes but those of inclination, which can be only yours while I am*

Ciamara.

P.S. *If you find nothing in me worthy of your love, my sufferings are such, as justly may deserve your pity; either relieve or put an end to them I conjure you — Free me from the ling'ring death of doubt, at once decree my fate, for, like a god, you rule my very will, nor dare I, without your leave, throw off this wretched being; Oh then, permit me once more to behold you, to try, at least, to warm you into kindness with my sighs, to melt you with my tears, — to sooth you into softness by a thousand yet undiscovered fondnesses — and, if all fail, to dye before your eyes.*

Those who have experienced the force of love, need not to be informed what joy, what transport swelled in the heart of Monsieur Frankville, at this unexpected eclaircissment of his dear Camilla's innocence; when every thing concurs to make our woes seem real, when hopes are dead, and even desire is hushed by the loud clamours of dispair and rage, then, – then, to be recalled to life, to light, to Heaven and love again, is such a torrent of o're powering happiness, – such a surcharge of extacy, as sence can hardly bear.

What now would Frankville not have given that it had been in his power to have recalled the last letter he sent to Camilla? His soul severely reproached him for so easily believing she could be false; tho' his experience of the sweetness of her disposition, made him not doubt of a pardon from her, when she should come to know what had been the reason of his jealousy; his impatience to see her, immediately put it into his head, that as Ciamara had been the occasion of the mis-understanding between them, Ciamara might likewise be made the property to set it all right again; to this end, he entreated the Count to write her an answer of complyance, and a promise to come to her the next day, in which visit, he would, in a disguise attend him, and being once got into the house, he thought it would be no difficulty to steal to Camilla's apartment.

But he found it not so easy a task as he imagined, to perswade Count D'Elmont to come into this design, his generous heart, averse to all deceit, thought it base and unmanly to abuse with dissimulation the real tenderness this lady had for him, and tho' pressed by the brother of Melliora, and conjured to it, even by the love he professed for her, it was with all the reluctance in the world, that he, at last, consented, and his servant came several times into the room to remind him that the person who brought the letter, waited impatiently for an answer, before he could bring himself into a humour to write in the manner Monsieur Frankville desired; and tho', scarce any man ever had so sparkling a fancy, such a readiness of thought, or aptitude of expression, when the dictates of his soul, were the employment of his tongue or pen, yet he now found himself at a loss for words, and he wasted more time in these few lines, than a thousand times as many on any other subject would have cost him.

To the Beautiful and Obliging
Ciamara.

Madam

*If I did not sin against truth when I assured you that I had a mistress to whom I was engaged by inclination, I certainly did, when I appeared guilty of a harshness which was never in my nature; the justice you do me in believing the interest of my friend was the greatest motive for my seeming unkindness, I have not the power sufficiently to acknowledge, but, could you look into my soul, you would there, find the effects of your inspiration, something so tender, and so grateful, as only favours, such as you confer, could merit or create.*

*I design to make my self happy in waiting on you to morrow-night about eleven, if you will order me admittance at that back-gate, which was the place of our first appointment, 'till then, I am the lovely Ciamara's*

Most Devoted Servant
D'Elmont

P.S. *There are some reasons why I think it not safe to come alone, therefore beg you'll permit me to bring a servant with me, on whose secrecy I dare rely.*

When the Count had sent away this little billet, Monsieur Frankville grew very gay on the hopes of his design suceeding; and laughing, "my lord," said he, "I question whether Melliora would forgive me, for engaging you in this affair; Ciamara is extreamly handsome, has wit, and where she attempts to charm, has doubtless a thousand artifices to obtain her wish"; the Count was not in a temper to relish his raillery, he had a great deal of compassion for Ciamara, and thought himself inexcusable for deceiving her, and all that Frankville could do to disipate the gloom that reflection spread about him, was but vain.

They spent the greatest part of this day together, as they had done the former; and when the time came that Frankville thought it proper to take leave, it was with a much more chearful heart, than he had the night before; but his happiness was not yet secure, and in a few hours he found a considerable alteration in his condition.

As soon as it was dark enough for Camilla to let down her string to the fellow whom she had ordered to wait for it, he received another letter fastened to it, and finding it was directed as the other, for Monsieur Frankville, he immediately brought it to him.

It was with a mixture of fear and joy, that the impatient lover broke it open, but both those passions gave place to an adequate dispair, when having un-sealed it, he read these lines.

To Monsieur Frankville.

*I have been already so much deceived, that I ought not to boast of any skill in the art of divination, yet, I fancy, 'tis in my power to form a juster guess than I have done, what the sentiments of your heart will be when you first open this — Methinks, I see you put on a scornful smile, resolving to be still unmoved, either at upbraidings or complaints, for to do one of these, I am satisfied, you imagine is the reason of my troubling you with a letter. But sir, I am not altogether silly enough to believe the tenderest supplications the most humble of my sex could make, has efficacy to restore desire, once dead, to life; or if it could, I am not so mean spirited as to accept a return thus caused; nor would it be less impertinent to reproach; to tell you that you are perjured — base — ungrateful, is what you know already, unless your memory is so complaisant as not to remind you of either vows or obligations. But, to assure you, that I reflect on this sudden change of your humour without being fired with rage, or stupified with grief, is perhaps, what you least expect. — Yet, strange as it may seem, it is most certain, that she, whom you have found the softest, fondest, tenderest of her kind, is in a moment grown the most indifferent, for in spight of your inconstancy, I never shall deny that I have loved you, — loved you even to dotage; my passion took birth long before I knew you had a thought of feigning one for* me, which frees me from that imputation women too frequently deserve, of loving for no other reason than because they are beloved, for if you ne'er had seemed to love, I should have continued to do so in reality. I found a thousand charms in your person and conversation, and believed your soul no less transcending all others in excellent qualities, than I still confess your form to be in beauty; I drest you up in vain imagination, adorned with all the ornaments of truth, honour, good nature, generosity, and every grace that raise mortal perfection to the highest pitch, and almost reach divinity, – but you have taken care to prove your self, meer man, to like, dislike, and wish you know not what, nor why! If I never had any merits, how came you to think me worthy the pains you have taken to engage me? and if I had, how am I so suddenly deprived of them? – No, I am still the same, and the only reason I appear not so to you, is, that you behold me now, no more, with lover's eyes; the few charms, I am mistress of, looked lovely at a distance, but lose their lustre, when approached too near; your fancy threw a glittering burnish o're me, which free possession has worn off, and now, the woman only stands exposed to view, and I confess I justly suffer for the guilty folly of believing that, in your sex, ardors could survive enjoyment, or if they could, that such a miracle was reserved for me; but thank Heaven my punishment is past, the pangs, the tortures of my bleeding heart, in tearing your idea thence, already are no more! The fiery tryal is over, and I am now arrived at the Elizium of perfect peace, entirely unmolested by any warring passion; the fears, the hopes, the jealousies, and all the endless train of cares which waited on my hours of love and fond delusion, serve but to endear re-gained tranquility; and I can cooly scorn, not hate your falshood; and tho' it is a maxim very much in use among the women of my country, that, not to revenge, were to deserve ill-usage, yet I am so far from having a wish that way, that I shall always esteem your virtues, and while I pardon, pity your infirmities; shall praise your flowing wit, without an indignant remembrance how oft it has been employed for my undoing; shall acknowledge the brightness of your eyes, and not in secret curse the borrowed softness of their glances, shall think on all your past endearments, your sighs, your vows, your melting kisses, and the warm fury of your fierce embraces, but as a *pleasing dream, while reason slept, and wish not to renew at such a price.*

*I desire no answer to this, nor to be thought of more; go on in the same course you have began, change 'till you are tired with roving, still let your eyes inchant, your tongue delude, and oaths betray, and all who look, who listen, and believe, be ruined and forsaken like*

Camilla.

The calm and resolute resentment which appeared in the stile of this letter, gave Frankville very just grounds to fear, it would be no small difficulty to obtain a pardon for what he had so rashly written; but when he reflected on the seeming reasons, which moved him to it, and that he should have an opportunity to let her know them, he was not altogether inconsolable; he passed the night however in a world of anxiety and as soon as morning came, hurried away, to communicate to the Count this fresh occasion of his trouble.

It was now D'Elmont's turn to railly, and he laughed as much at those fears, which he imagined causeless, as the other had done, at the assignation he had perswaded him to make with Ciamara, but, tho' as most of his sex are, he was pretty much of the Count's opinion, yet, the re-instating himself in Camilla's esteem, was a matter of too great importance to him, to suffer him to take one moment's ease, 'till he was perfectly assured of it.

At last, the wished for hour arrived, and he, disguised so as it was impossible for him to be known, attended the Count to that dear wicket, which had so often given him entrance to Camilla; they waited not long for admittance, Brione was ready there to receive them; the sight of her, inflamed the heart of Monsieur Frankville with all the indignation immaginable, for he knew her to be the woman, who, by her treachery to Camilla, had gained the confidence of Ciamara, and involved him in all the miseries he had endured; but he contained himself, 'till she taking the Count by the hand, in order to lead him to her lady, bad him wait her return, which she told him should be immediately, in an outer room which she pointed him to.

In the mean time she conducted the Count to the door of that magnificent chamber, where he had been received by the supposed Camilla, and where he now beheld the real Ciamara, drest, if possible, richer than she was the night before, but loose as wanton fancy could invent; she was lying on the couch when he entered, and affecting to seem as if she was not presently sensible of his being there, rose not to receive him till he was very near her; they both kept silence for some moments, she, waiting till he should speak, and he, possibly, prevented by uncertainty after what manner he should form his address, so as to keep an equal medium between the two extreams, of being cruel, or too kind, till at last the violence of her impatient expectation burst out in these words, – "Oh that this silence were the effect of love!" – and then perceiving he made no answer; "tell me," continued she, "am I forgiven for thus intruding on your *pity* for a grant, which *inclination* would not have allowed me?" "Cease madam," replied he, "to encrease that confusion which a just sence of your favours, and my own ingratitude has cast me in. How can you look with eyes so tender and so kind, on him who brings you nothing in return? Rather despise me, hate me, drive me from your sight, believe me as I am, unworthy of your love, nor squander on a bankrupt wretch the noble treasure." "Oh inhuman!" interrupted she, "has then that mistress of whose charms you boasted, engrossed all your stock of tenderness? and have you nothing, nothing to repay me for all this waste of fondness, – this lavish prodigality of passion, which forces me beyond my sexes pride, or my own natural modesty, to sue, to court, to kneel and weep for pity." "Pity," resumed the Count, "would be a poor reward for love like yours, and yet alass!" continued he sighing, "'tis all I have to give; I have already told you, I am tyed by vows, by honour, inclination, to another, who tho' far absent hence, I still preserve the dear remembrance of! My fate will soon recall me back to her, and Paris; yours fixes you at Rome, and since we are doomed to be for ever separated, it would be base to cheat you with a vain pretence, and lull you with hopes pleasing dreams a while, when you must quickly wake to added tortures, and redoubled woe." "Heavens," cried she, with an air full of resentment, "are then my charms so mean, my darts so weak, that near, they cannot intercept those, shot at such a distance? And are you that dull, cold Platonist, which can prefer the visionary pleasures of an *absent* mistress, to the warm transports of the substantial *present*?" The Count was pretty much surprized at these words, coming from the mouth of a woman of honour, and began now to perceive what her aim was, but willing to be more confirmed, "Madam," said he, "I dare not hope your virtue would permit." – "Is this a time," interrupted she, looking on him with eyes which sparkled with wild desires, and left no want of further explanation of her meaning, "Is this an hour to preach of virtue? – Married, – betrothed, – engaged by love or law, what hinders but this moment you may be mine, this moment, well improved, might give us joys to baffle a whole age of woe; make us, at once, forget our troubles past, and by its sweet remembrance, scorn those to come"; in speaking these words, she sunk supinely on D'Elmont's breast; but tho' he was not so ill-natured, and unmannerly as to repel her, this sort of treatment made him lose all the esteem, and great part of the pity he had conceived for her.

The woes of love are only worthy commiseration, according to their causes; and tho' all those kinds of desire, which the difference of sex creates, bear in general, the name of love, yet they are as vastly wide as heaven and hell; that passion which aims chiefly at enjoyment, in enjoyment ends, the fleeting pleasure is no more remembred, but all the stings of guilt and shame remain; but that, where the interiour beauties are consulted, and *souls* are devotees, is truly noble; love *there* is a divinity indeed, because he is immortal and unchangeable, and if our earthy part partake the bliss, and craving nature is in all obeyed, possession thus desired, and thus obtained, is far from satiating; *reason* is not here debased to *sense*, but *sense* elevates itself to *reason*, the different powers unite, and become pure alike.

It was plain that the passion with which Ciamara was animated, sprung not from this last source; she had seen the

charming Count, was taken with his beauty, and wished no farther than to possess his lovely *person*, his *mind* was the least of
her thoughts, for had she the least ambition to reign there, she
would not have so meanly sought to obtain the one, after he
had assured her, the other, far more noble part of him was disposed of. The grief he had been in, that it was not in his power
to return her passion, while he believed it meritorious, was
now changed to the utmost contempt, and her quality, and the
state she lived in, did not hinder him from regarding of her, in
as indifferent a manner, as he would have done a common *cour-
tizan.*

Lost to all sense of honour, pride or shame, and wild to gratify her furious wishes, she spoke, without reserve, all they suggested to her, and lying on his breast, beheld, without concern,
her robes fly open, and all the beauties of her own exposed, and
naked to his view. Mad at his insensibility, at last she grew more
bold, she kissed his eyes, – his lips, a thousand times, then
pressed him in her arms with strenuous embraces, – and snatching his hand and putting it to her heart, which fiercely bound-
ed at his touch, bid him to be witness of his mighty influence
there.

Tho' it was impossible for any soul to be capable of a greater,
or more constant passion than his felt for Melliora, tho' no man
that ever lived, was less addicted to loose desires, – in fine, tho'
he realy was, as Frankville had told him, the most excellent of
his kind, yet, he was still a *man*! and, 'tis not to be thought
strange, if to the force of such united temptations, nature and
modesty a little yielded; warmed with her fires, and, perhaps,
more moved by curiosity, her behaviour having extinguished all
his respect, he gave his hands and eyes a full enjoyment of
all those charms, which had they been answered by a mind
worthy of them, might justly have inspired the highest raptures,
while she, unshocked, and unresisting, suffered all he did, and
urged him with all the arts she was mistress of, to more, and it is
not altogether improbable, that he might not[1] entirely have
forgot himself, if a sudden interruption had not restored his

---

1   Another teasing negative; D'elmont might well have forgotten himself.

reason to the consideration of the business which had brought him here.

Monsieur Frankville had all this time been employed in a far different manner of entertainment; Brione came to him, according to her promise, assoon as she had introduced the Count to Ciamara, and having been commanded by that lady to discourse with the supposed servant, and get what she could out of him, of the Count's affairs, she sat down and began to talk to him with a great deal of freedom; but he, who was too impatient to lose much time, told her he had a secret to discover, if the place they were in was private enough to prevent his being over-heard, and she assuring him that it was, he immediately discovered who he was, and clapped a pistol to her breast, swearing that moment should be the last of her life, if she made the least noise, or attempted to intercept his passage to Camilla. The terror she was in, made her fall on her knees, and conjuring him to spare her life, begged a thousand pardons for her infidelity, which she told him was not occasioned by any particular malice to him; but not being willing to leave Rome herself, the fear of being exposed to the revenge of Ciamara and Cittolini, when they should find out that she had been the instrument of Camilla's escape, prevailed upon her timerous soul to that discovery, which was the only means to prevent what she so much dreaded. Frankville contented himself with venting his resentment in two or three hearty curses, and taking her roughly by the arm, bid her go with him to Camilla's apartment, and discover before her what she knew of Ciamara's entertaining Count D'Elmont in her name, which she trembling promised to obey, and they both went up a pair of back stairs which led a private way to Camilla's chamber; when they entered, she was sitting in her night dress on the bed-side, and the unexpected sight of Brione, who, till now, had never ventured to appear before her, since her infidelity, and a man with her whom she thought a stranger, filled her with such a surprize, that it deprived her of her speech, and gave Frankville time to throw off his disguise, and catch her in his arms with all the transports of unfeigned affection, before she could enough recover herself to make any resistance, but when she did, it was with all the violence imaginable, and indeavouring to tear herself away, "Villain," said she, "comest thou again to triumph o're my weakness, – again to cheat me into fond belief?" There needed no more to make this obsequious lover relinquish his hold, and falling at her feet, was beginning to speak something in his vindication, when she, quite lost in rage, prevented him, by renewing her reproaches in this manner; "have you not given me up my vows?" resumed she, "have you not abandoned me to ruin, – to death, – to infamy, – to all the stings of self-accusing conscience and remorse? And come you now, by your detested presence, to alarm remembrance, and new-point my tortures? – That woman's treachery," continued she, looking on Brione, "I freely pardon, since by that little absence it occasioned, I have discovered the wavering disposition of your soul, and learned to scorn what is below my anger." "Here me but speak," cried Frankville, "or if you doubt my truth, as I confess you have almighty cause, let her inform you, what seeming reasons, what provocations urged my hasty rage to write that fatal, – that accursed letter." "I will hear nothing," replied Camilla, "neither from you nor her, – I see the base design, and scorn to joyn in the deceit, – you have had no cause, – not even the least pretence for your incontinency but one, which, tho' you are guilty of, you all disown, and that is, being loved too well. – I lavished all the fondness of my soul, and you, unable to reward, despized it. – But think not that the rage, you now behold me in, proceeds from my dispair – No, your inconstancy is the fault of nature, a vice which all your sex are prone to, and 'tis we, the fond believers only are to blame; *that* I forgave, my letter told you that I did – But thus to come – thus insolent in imagination, to dare to hope I were that mean souled wretch, whose easy tameness, and whose doating love, with joy would welcome your return, clasp you again in my deluded arms, and swear you were as dear as ever, is such an afront to my understanding, as merits the whole fury of revenge"; as she spoke these words, she turned disdainfully from him with a resolution to leave the room, but she could not make such hast to go away as the dispairing, the distracted Frankville did to prevent her, and catching hold of her garments, "stay madam," said he wildly, "either permit me to clear my self of this barbarous accusation, or, if you are resolved, unhearing, to condemn me, behold me, satiate all your rage can wish, for by heaven," continued he, holding the pistol to his own breast, as he had done a little before to Brione's, "by all the joys I have possest, by all the hell I now endure, this moment I'll be received your *lover*, or expire your *martyr*." These words pronounced so passionately, and the action that acompanied them made a visible alteration in Camilla's countenance, but it lasted not long, and resuming her fierceness, "your death," cried she, "this way would give me little satisfaction, the world would judge more nobly of my resentment, if by my hand you fell – Yet," continued she, snatching the pistol from him, and throwing it out of the window, which happened to be open, "I will not – cannot be the executioner. – No, live! and let thy punishment be, in *reality* to endure what thou well *dissemblest*, the pangs, the racking pangs of hopeless, endless love! – May'st thou *indeed* love *me*, as thou a thousand times hast falsely sworn, – for ever *love*, and I, for ever *hate*!" In this last sentence, she flew like lightning to her closet, and shut her self in, leaving the amazed lover still on his knees, stupified with grief and wonder; all this while Brione had been casting about in her mind, how to make the best use of this adventure with Ciamara, and encouraged by Camilla's behaviour, and taking advantage of Frankville's confusion, made but one step to the chamber door, and running out into the gallery, and down the stairs, cried "Murder, – help, a rape – Help, or Donna Camilla will be carried away." – She had no occasion to call often, for the pistol which Camilla threw out of the window chanced to go off in the fall, and the report it made, had alarmed some of the servants who were in an out house adjoyning to the garden, and imagining there were thieves, were gathering to search, some armed with staffs, some with iron bars, or any thing they could get in the hurry they were in; as they were running confusedly about, they met Monsieur Frankville pursuing Brione, with a design to stop her mouth, either by threatnings or bribes, but she was too nimble for him, and knowing the ways of the house much better than he did, went directly to the room where Ciamara was, carressing the

Count in the manner already mentioned. "Oh madam," said she, "you are imposed on, the Count has deceived your expectations, and brought Monsieur Frankville in disguise to rob you of Camilla." These words made them both, tho' with very different sentiments, start from the posture they were in, and Ciamara changing her air of tenderness for one all fury, "Monster!" cried she to D'Elmont, "have you then betrayed me?" "This is no time," replied he, hearing a great bustle, and Frankville's voice pretty loud without, "for me to answer you, my honour calls me to my friend's assistance"; and drawing his sword, run as the noise directed him to the place where Frankville was defending himself against a little army of Ciamara's servants; she was not much behind him, and enraged to the highest degree, cried out, "Kill, kill them both!" but that was not a task for a much greater number of such as them to accomplish, and tho' their weapons might easily have beat down, or broke the gentlemens sword; yet their fears kept from coming too near, and Ciamara had the vexation to see them both retreat with safety, and her self disappointed as well in her revenge, as in her love.

Nothing could be more surprized, than Count D'Elmont was, when he got home, and heard from Frankville all that had passed between him and Camilla, nor was his trouble less, that he had it not in his power to give him any advice in any exigence so uncommon. He did all he could to comfort and divert his sorrows, but in vain, the wounds of bleeding love admit no ease, but from the hand which gave them; and he, who was naturally rash and fiery, now grew to that height of desparation and violence of temper, that the Count feared some fatal catastrophe, and would not suffer him to stir from him that night, nor the next day, till he had obliged him to make a vow, and bind it with the most solemn imprecations, not to offer any thing against his life.

But, tho' plunged into the lowest depth of misery, and lost, to all human probability, in an inextricable labyrinth of woe, Fortune will find, at last, some way to raise, and disentangle those, whom she is pleased to make her favorites, and that Monsieur Frankville was one, an unexpected adventure made him know.

The third day from that, in which he had seen Camilla, as he was sitting in his chamber, in a melancholly conversation with the Count, who was then come to visit him, his servant brought him a letter, which he said had been just left, by a woman of an extraordinary appearance, and who the moment she had given it into his hand, got from the door with so much speed, that she seemed rather to vanish than to walk.

While the servant was speaking, Frankville looked on the Count with a kind of a pleased expectations in his eyes, but then casting them on the direction of the letter, "Alas!" said he, "how vain was my imagination, this is not Camilla's, but a hand, to which I am utterly a stranger"; these words were closed with a sigh, and he opened it with a negligence which would have been unpardonable, could he have guessed at the contents, but assoon as he saw the name of Violetta at the bottom, a flash of hope re-kindled in his soul, and trembling with impatience he read.

### To Monsieur Frankville.

*I think it cannot be called treachery, if we betray the secrets of a friend, only when concealment were an injury; but however I may be able to answer this breach of trust, I am about to make, to my self, 'tis your behaviour alone, which can absolve me to Camilla and by your fidelity she must judge of mine.*

*Tho' daughter to the man she hates, she finds nothing in me unworthy of her love and confidence, and as I have been privy, ever since your mutual misfortunes, to the whole history of your amour, so I am now no stranger to the sentiments, your last conversation has inspired her with — She loves you still, monsieur — with an extremity of passion loves you — But, tho' she ceases to believe you unworthy of it, her indignation for your unjust suspicion of her will not be easily removed — She is resolved to act the heroine, tho' to purchase that character it should cost her life. She is determined for a cloyster, and has declared her intention, and a few days will take away all possibility of ever being yours; but I, who know the conflicts she endures, wish it may be in your power to prevent the execution of a design which cannot but be fatal to her. My father and Ciamara, I wish I could not call her aunt, were last night in private conferrence, but I over heard enough of their discourse, to know there has been some ungenerous contrivance carried on to make you, and Camilla appear guilty to each other, and 'tis from that knowledge I derive my hopes that you have honour enough to make a right use of this discovery; if you have any thing to say to farther the intercessions I am imployed in, to serve you, prepare a letter,[1] which I will either prevail on her to read, or oblige her, in spite of the resolution she has made, to hear. But take care, that, in the least, you hint not that you have received one from me, for I shall perswade her that the industry of your love has found means of conveying it to me without my knowledge. Bring it with you this evening to St. Peter's, and as soon as divine service is over, follow her who shall drop her handkerchief as she passes you, for by that mark you shall distinguish her whom you yet know, but by the name of*

Violetta.

P.S. *One thing, and indeed not the least which induced me to write, I had almost forgot, which is, that your friend the accomplished Count D'Elmont is as much endangered by the resentment of Ciamara, as your self by that of my father; bid him beware how he receives any letter, or present from a hand unknown, lest he should experience, what he has doubtless heard of, our Italian art of poysoning by the smell.[2]*

When Monsieur Frankville had given this letter to the Count to read, which he immediately did, they both of them broke into the highest encomiums on this young lady's generosity, who contrary to the custom of her sex, which seldom forgives an affront of that kind, made it her study to serve the man who had refused her, and make her rival blest.

These testimonies of a grateful acknowledgement being

---

1   1st ed. reads "discovery, if you ... Prepare ..."; 4th ed. reads "discovery if you... you; Prepare ...."

2   Witch-like treachery fits the English stereotype of Italy; *Tatler* No. 63 applies this image to Delarivier Manley's political satire.

over, Frankville told the Count he believed the most, and indeed the only effectual means to extinguish Camilla's resentment would be entirely, to remove the cause, which could be done no other way, than by giving her a full account of Ciamara's behaviour, while she passed for her. D'Elmont readily consented, and thought it not at all inconsistent with his honour to expose that of the woman who had shewn so little value for it her self. And when he saw that Frankville had finished his letter, which was very long, for lovers cannot easily come to a conclusion, he offered to writ a note to her, enclosed in the other, which should serve as an evidence of the truth of what he had alledged in his vindication. Frankville gladly embraced the kind proposal, and the other immediately made it good in these words.

To Donna Camilla.
Madam,

*If the severity of your justice requires a victim, I only am guilty, who being imposed upon my self, endeavoured, for I cannot say I could accomplish it, to involve the unfortunate Frankville in the same fatal error, and at last prevailed on him to write, what he could not be brought, by all my arguments to think.*

*Let the cause which led me to take this freedom, excuse the presumption of it, which, from one so much a stranger, would be else unpardonable. But when we are conscious of a crime, the first reparation we can make to innocence, is, to acknowledge we have offended; and, if the confession of my faults, may purchase an absolution for my friend, I shall account it in the noblest work of superogation.*

*Be assured, that as inexorable as you are, your utmost rigour would find it's satisfaction, if you could be sensible of what I suffer in a sad repentance for my sin of injuring so heavenly a virtue, and, perhaps, in time be moved by it to pity and forgive*

The Unhappily deceived
D'Elmont.

The time in which they had done writing, immediately brought on that of Violetta's appointment, and the Count would needs accompany Monsieur Frankville in this assignation, saying, he had an acknowledgment to pay to that lady, which he thought himself obliged, in good manners and gratitude, to take this opportunity to do; and the other being of the same opinion, they went together to St. Peter's.

When prayers were done, which, 'tis probable, *one* of these gentlemen, if not *both*, might think too tedious, they stood up, and looking round, impatiently expected when the promised signal should be given; but among the great number of ladies, which passed by them, there were very few, who did not stop a little to gaze on these two accomplished *chevaliers*, and they were several times tantalized with an *imaginary* Violetta, before the *real* one appeared. But when the crowd were almost dispersed, and they began to fear some accident had prevented her coming, the long expected token was let fall, and she who threw it, tripped hastily away to the farther end of the *collonade*, which hapned to be entirely void of company. The Count and his companion, were not long behind her, and Monsieur Frankville being the person chiefly concerned, addressed himself to her in this manner. "With what words madam," said he, "can a man so infinitely obliged, and so desirous to be grateful as Frankville, sufficiently make known his admiration of a generosity like yours? Such an unbounded goodness, shames all description! makes language vile since it affords no phrase to suit your worth, or speak the mighty sense my soul has of it." "I have no other aim," replied she, "in what I have done, than justice; and 'tis only in the proof of your sincerity to Camilla that I am to be thanked." Frankville was about to answer with some assurances of his faith, when the Count stepping forward, prevented him. "My friend, madam," said he bowing, "is most happy in having it in his power to obey a command, which is the utmost of his wishes; but how must I acquit my self of any part of that return which is due to you for that generous care you have been pleased to express for the preservation of my life?" "There needs no more," interrupted she, with a perceivable alteration in her voice, "than to have *seen* Count D'Elmont to be interested in his concerns." – She paused a little after speaking these words, and then, as if she thought she had said too much, turned hastily to Frankville, "the letter, monsieur," continued she, "the letter, – 'tis not impossible but we may be observed, – I tremble with the apprehension of a discovery." Frankville immediately delivered it to her, but saw so much disorder in her gesture, that it very much surprized him. She trembled indeed, but whether occasioned by any danger she perceived of being taken notice of, or some other secret agitation she felt within, was then unknown to any but herself, but whatever it was, it transported her so far, as to make her quit the place, without being able to take any other leave than a hasty *curtsy*, and bidding Frankville meet her the next morning at *mattins*.

Here was a new cause of disquiet to D'Elmont; the experience he had of the too fatal influence of his dangerous attractions, gave him sufficient reason to fear this young lady was not insensible of them, and that his presence was the sole cause of her disorder; however, he said nothing of it to Frankville 'till the other mentioning it to him, and repeating her words, they both joyned in the opinion that love had been too busy in her heart, and that it was the feeling the effects of it in herself, had inclined her to so much compassion for the miseries she saw it inflicted upon others. The Count very well knew that when desires of this kind are springing in the soul, every sight of the beloved object, encreases their growth, and therefore, tho' her generous manner of proceeding had created in him a very great esteem, and he would have been pleased with her conversation, yet he ceased to wish a farther acquaintance with her, lest it should render her more unhappy, and forbore going the next day to church with Frankville as else he would have done.

Violetta failed not to come as she had promised, but instead of dropping her handkerchief, as she had done the evening before, she knelt as close to him as she could, and pulling him gently by the sleeve, obliged him to regard her, who else, not knowing her, would not have suspected she was so near, and slipped a note into his hand, bidding him softly not take any father notice of her. He obeyed, but 'tis reasonable to believe, was too impatient to know what the contents were, to listen with much attention and devotion to the remainder of the ceremony; as soon as he was released, he got into a corner of the *cathedral*, where, unobserved he might satisfy a curiosity which none who love, will condemn him for, any more than they will for the thrilling extacy which filled his soul at the reading these lines.

To Monsieur Frankville.

*For fear I should not have an opportunity of speaking to you, in safety, I take this method to inform you, that I have been so successful in my negotiation, as to make Camilla repent the severity of her sentence, and wish for nothing more than to recall it; you are now entirely justified in her opinion, by the artifice which was made use of to deceive you, and she is, I believe, no less enraged at Ciamara for depriving her of that letter you sent by the Count, than she was at you for that unkind one, which came to her hands. She is now under less restraint, since Brione's report of her behaviour to you, and the everlasting resentment she vowed, and I have prevailed on her to accompany me in a visit I am to make, to-morrow in the evening, to Donna Clara Metteline, a nun, in the monastery of St. Augustine, and if you will meet us there, I believe it not impossible but she may be brought to a confession of all I have discovered to you of her thoughts.*

*The Count's letter was of no small service to you, for tho' without that evidence she would have been convinced of your constancy, yet she would hardly have acknowledged she was so; and if he will take the pains to come with you to-morrow, I believe his company will be acceptable; if you think it proper, you may let him know as much from*

Violetta.

P.S. *I beg a thousand pardons both of you and the Count for the abruptness of my departure last night; something happened to give me a confusion from which I could not at that time recover, but hope for the future to be more mistress of my self.*

Monsieur Frankville hasted to the Count's lodgings, to communicate his good fortune, but found him in a humour very unfit for congratulations; the post had just brought him a letter from his brother, the Chevalier Brillian, the contents whereof were these.

To Count D'Elmont.

My Lord,

*'Tis with an inexpressible grief that I obey the command you left me, for giving you from time to time an exact account of Melliora's affairs, since what I have now to acquaint you with, will make you stand in need of all your moderation to support it. But, not to keep your expectation on the rack, loth as I am, I must inform you, that Melliora is, by some unknown ravisher stolen from the monastery – The manner of it, (as I have since learned from those who were with her) was thus. As she was walking in the fields, behind the cloyster gardens, accompanied by some young lady's, pensioners there as well as her self, four men well mounted, but disguised and muffled, rode up to them, three of them jumped off their horses, and while one seized on the defenceless prey, and bore her to his arms, who was not alighted, the other two caught hold of her companions, and prevented the out-cryes they would have made, 'till she was carried out of sight, then mounting again their horses, immediately lost the amazed virgins all hopes of recovering her.*

*I conjure my dearest brother to believe there has been nothing omitted for the discovery of this villany, but in spite of all the pains and care we have taken in the search, none of us have yet been happy enough to hear the least account of her. That my next may bring you more welcome news, is the first wish of*

My Lord,
Your Lordship's most
Zealously Affectionate
Brother, and Humble Servant
Brillian

P.S. *There are some people here, malicious enough to report, that the design of carrying away Melliora, was contrived by you, and that it is in Rome she only can be found. It would be of great advantage to my peace, if I could be of the number of those who believe it, but I am too well acquainted with your principles to harbour such a thought. Once more, my dear lord, for this time, Adieu.*

After the Count had given this letter to Frankville to read, he told him, he was resolved to leave Rome the next day, that no body had so great an interest in her recovery as himself, that he would trust the search of her to no other, and swore with the most dreadful imprecations he could make, never to rest, but wander, *knight-errand* like, over the whole world 'till he had found her.

Tho' Monsieur Frankville was extreamly concerned at what had happened to his sister, yet he endeavoured to disswade the Count from leaving Rome till he knew the result of his own affair with Camilla; but all his arguments were for a long time ineffectual, 'till, at last, showing him Violetta's letter, he prevailed on him to defer his journey till they had first seen Camilla, on condition, that if she persisted in her rigour, he should give over any further fruitless solicitations, and accompany him to Paris. This Frankville promised to perform, and they passed the time in very uneasy and impatient cogitations, 'till the next day about five in the evening they prepared for the apointment.

Count D'Elmont and his longing companion were the first at the rendezvous, but in a very little while they perceived two women coming towards them. The idea of Camilla was always too much in Frankville's thoughts, not to make him know her, by that charming air (which he so much adored her for) tho' she was veiled never so closely, and the moment he had sight of them, "Oh heaven," cried he to D'Elmont, "yonder she comes, that, – that my lord, is the divine Camilla"; as they came pretty near she that indeed proved to be Camilla, was turning on one side, in order to go to the grate where she expected the *nun*. "Hold! hold Donna Camilla," cried Violetta, "I cannot suffer you should pass by your friends with an air so unconcerned; if Monsieur Frankville has done any thing to merit your displeasure, my lord the Count certainly deserves your notice, in the pains he has taken to undeceive you." "One so much a stranger as Count D'Elmont is," answered she, "may very well excuse my thanks for an explanation, which had he been acquainted with me, he would have spared." "Cruel Camilla!"[1] said Frankville, "is then the knowledge of my innocence unwelcome? – Am I become so hateful, or are you so changed, that you wish me guilty, for a justification of your rigour? If it be so, I have no remedy but death, which tho' you deprived me of, the last time I saw you, I now can find a thousand means to compass"; he pronounced these words in so tender, yet so resolved an accent, that Camilla could not conceal part of the impression they made on her, and putting her handkerchief to her eyes, which in spite of all she had done to prevent it, overflowed with tears; "talk not of death," said she, "I am not cruel to that degree; live Frankville, live! – But live, without Camilla!" "Oh, 'tis impossible!" resumed he, "the latter part of your command entirely destroys the first. – Life without your love, would be a hell, which I confess my soul's a coward, but to think of."

The Count and Violetta were silent all this time, and perceiving they were in a fair way of reconciliation, thought the best they could do to forward it, was to leave 'em to themselves, and walking a few paces from them, "You suffer my lord," said she, "for your generosity in accompanying your friend, since it condemns you to the conversation of a person who has neither *wit,* nor *gaiety* sufficient to make her self diverting." "Those," replied he, "who would make the excellent Violetta a subject of diversion, ought never to be blest with the company of any, but such women who merit not a serious regard. But you indeed, were your soul capable of descending to the follys of your sex, would be extreamly at a loss in conversation so little qualified as mine, to please the vanities of the fair; and you stand in need of all those more than *manly* virtues

---

1  4th ed.; 1st ed. reads "he would have spared the cruel Camilla! said Frankville, is ...."

you possess, to pardon a *chagreen*, which even your presence cannot dissipate." "If it could," interrupted she, "I assure your lordship, I should much more *rejoyce* in the happy effects of it on you, than *pride* my self in the power of such an influence — And yet," continued she with a sigh, "I am a very woman, and if free from the usual affectations and vanities of my sex, I am not so from faults, perhaps, less worthy of forgiveness." The Count could not presently resolve what reply to make to these words; he was unwilling she should believe he wanted complaisance, and affraid of saying any thing that might give room for a declaration of what he had no power of answering to her wish; but after the consideration of a moment or two, "Madam," said he, "tho' I dare not question your sincerity in any other point, yet you must give me leave to disbelieve you in this, not only, because, in my opinion, there is nothing so contemptibly rediculous as that self sufficiency, and vain desire of pleasing, commonly known by the name of *coquetry*, but also because she who escapes the contagion of this error, will not without much difficulty be led into any other." "Alas my lord," cried Violetta, "how vastly wide of truth is this assertion? That very foible, which is most pernicious to our sex, is chiefly by coquetry prevented. I need not tell you that 'tis love I mean, and as blameable as you think the *one*, I believe the *other* would find less favour from a person of your lordship's judgment." "How madam," interrupted the Count pretty warmly, "have I the character of a stoick? — Or do you immagine that my soul is composed of that course stuff, not to be capable of receiving, or approving a passion, which, all the brave, and generous think it their glory to profess, and which can only give refined delight, to minds enobled. — But I perceive," continued he growing more cool, "I am not happy enough in your esteem, to be thought worthy the influence of that god." "Still you mistake my meaning," said Violetta, "I doubt not of your sensibility, were there a possibility of finding a woman worthy of inspiring you with soft desires; and if that should ever happen, love would be so far from being a weakness, that it would serve rather as an embelishment to your other graces; it's only when we stoop to objects below our consideration, or vainly wing our wishes to those above our hopes that makes us appear rediculous or contemptible; but either of these is a folly which, —" "which the incomparable Violetta," interrupted D'Elmont, "never can be guilty of." "You have a very good opinion of my wit," resumed she, in a melancholly tone, "but I should be much happier than I am, if I were sure I could secure my self from doing any thing to forfeit it." "I believe," replied the Count, "there are not many things you have less reason to apprehend than such a change; and I am confident were I to stay in Rome as many *ages*, as I am determined to do but *hours*, I should, at last leave it, with the same esteem and admiration of your singular vertues, as I now shall do." Violetta could not prevent the disorder these words put her into, from discovering it self in the accent of her voice, when, "How! my lord," said she, "are we then to lose you? – Lose you in so short a time." As the Count was about to answer, Frankville and Camilla joyned them, and looking on Frankville, "if any credit," said he, "may be given to the language of the eyes, I am certain yours speak success, and I may congratulate a happiness you lately could not be persuaded to hope"; "had I a thousand eyes," cried the transported lover, "a thousand tongues, they all would be but insignificant to express the joy! – the unbounded extacy, my soul is full of, – but take the mighty meaning in one word, – Camilla's mine – for ever mine – the storm is past, and all the sunny heaven of love returns to bless my future days with ceaseless raptures. Now, my lord, I am ready to attend you in your journy, this bright! this beautious guardian angel will partake our flight! and we have nothing now to do, but to prepare with secrecy and speed fit means for our escape." As soon as Frankville had left off speaking, Count D'Elmont addressing himself to Camilla, made her abundance of retributions, for the happiness she gave his friend, which she receiving with a becoming chearfulness, and unaffected gayety, "I am afraid," said she, "your lordship will think a woman's resolution is, henceforth, little worth regarding; but," continued she, taking Violetta by the hand, "I see well, that this unfaithful creature has betrayed me, and to punish her infidelity, will, by leaving her, put it out of her power to deceive my confidence again."

Violetta either did not hear, or was not in a condition to return her *railery*, nor the praises which the Count and Monsieur Frankville concurred in of her generosity, but stood motionless and lost in thought, 'till Camilla seeing it grow towards night, told the gentlemen, she thought it best to part, not only to avoid any suspicion at home of their being out so long, but also that the others might order every thing proper for their departure, which it was agreed on between Frankville and her, should be the next night, to prevent the success of those mischievous designs she knew Ciamara and Cittolini were forming against both the Count and Monsieur Frankville.

Matters being thus adjusted to the entire satisfaction of the lovers, and not in a much less proportion to the Count, they all thought it best to avoid making any more appointments till they met to part no more, which was to be at the wicket at dead of night. When the Count took leave of Violetta, this being the last time he could expect to see her, she was hardly able to return his civilities, and much less to answer those which Frankville made her, after the Count had turned from her to give him way; both of them guessed the cause of her confusion, and D'Elmont felt a concern in observing it, which nothing but that for Melliora could surpass.

The next day found full employment for them all, but the Count as well as Frankville was too impatient to be gone, to neglect any thing requisite for their departure; there was not the least particular wanting, long before the time they were to wait at the wicket for Camilla's coming forth. The Count's lodging being the nearest, they stayed there, watching for the longed for hour; but a little before it arrived, a youth, who seemed to be about 13 or 14 years of age, desired to be admitted to the Count's presence, which being granted, pulling a letter out of his pocket, and blushing as he approached him, "I come, my lord," said he, "from Donna Violetta, the contents of this will inform you on what business; but lest the treachery of others, should render me suspected, permit me to break it open, and prove it carries no infection." The Count looked earnestly on him while he spoke, and was strangely taken with the uncommon beauty and modesty which he observed in him. "You need not give your self the trouble of that experiment," answered he, "Donna Violetta's name, and your own engaging aspect, are sufficient credentials, if I were liable to doubt"; in saying this, he took the letter and full of fears that some accident had happened to Camilla, which might retard their journey, hastily read over these lines.

To the Worthy Count D'Elmont.

My Lord,

*If any part of that esteem you professed to have for me, be real, you will not deny the request I make you to accept this youth, who is my relation, in quality of a page. He is inclined to travel, and of all places, France is that which he is most desirous of going to. If a diligent care, a faithful secrecy, and an unceasing watchfulness to please, can render him acceptable to your service, I doubt not but he will, by those, recommend himself, hereafter. In the mean time beg you will receive him on my word. And if that will be any inducement to prejudice you in his favour, I assure you, that tho' he is one degree nearer in blood[1] to my father, he is by many in humour and principles to*

Violetta.

P.S. *May health, safety, and prosperity attend you in your journey, and all the happiness you wish for, crown the end.*

The young Fidelio,[2] for so he was called, could not wish to be received with greater demonstrations of kindness than those the Count gave him. And perceiving that Violetta had trusted him with the whole affair of their leaving Rome in private, doubted not of his conduct, and consulted with him, who they found knew the place perfectly well, after what

---

1   A brother would be equally near in blood, not nearer; this riddling claim seems to mean that Fidelio is male like Violetta's father rather than female like Violetta. D'elmont fails to see through the riddle − or the disguise.

2   An Italianate (and operatic) name suggesting fidelity; Imogen, the wronged wife in Shakeseare's *Cymbelene*, adopts the similar name Fidele with her male disguise.

manner they should watch, with the least danger of being discovered, for Camilla's opening the wicket. Frankville was for going alone, lest if any of the servants should happen to be about, one person would be less liable to suspicion than if a company were seen; the Count thought it most proper to go all together, remembring Frankville of the danger he had lately scaped, and might again be brought into; but Fidelio told them, he would advise that they two should remain concealed in the *portico*, of the convent of St. Francis, while himself would watch alone at the wicket for Camilla, and lead her to them, and then afterwards they might go altogether to that place where the horses and servants should attend them; the page's counsel was approved by both of them, and the time being arrived, what they had contrived was immediately put in execution.

Every thing happened according to their desire, Camilla got safely to the arms of her impatient lover, and they all taking horse, rode with such speed, as some of them would have been little able to bear, if any thing less than life and love had been at stake.

Their eager wishes, and the goodness of their horses brought them, before day-break many miles from Rome; but tho' they avoided all high-roads, and travelled cross the country to prevent being met, or overtook by any that might know them, yet their desire of seeing themselves in a place of security was so great, that they refused to stop to take any refreshment 'till the next day was almost spent; but when they were come into the house where they were to lye that night, not all the fatigue they had endured, kept the lovers from giving and receiving all the testimonies imaginable of mutual affection.

The sight of their felicity added new wings to Count D'Elmont's impatience to recover Melliora, but when he considered the little probability of that hope, he grew inconsolable, and his new page Fidelio, who lay on a *pallet* in the same room with him, put all his wit, of which he had no small stock, upon the stretch to divert his sorrows; he talked to him, sung to him, told him a hundred pretty stories, and, in fine, made good the character Violetta had given him so well, that the Count looked on him as a blessing sent from heaven to lessen his misfortunes, and make his woes sit easy.

They continued travelling with the same expedition as when they first set out, for three or four days, but then, believing themselves secure from any pursuit, began to slacken their pace, and make the journey more delightful to Camilla and Fidelio, who, not being accustomed to ride in that manner, would never have been able to support it, if the strength of their *minds*, had not by far, exceeded that of their *bodies*.

They had gone so much about, in seeking the by-roads, that they made it three times as long before they arrived at Avigno, a small village on the borders of Italy, as any, that had come the direct way would have done; but the caution they had observed, was not altogether needless, as they presently found.

A gentleman who had been a particular acquaintance of Monsieur Frankville's, overtook them at this place, and after expressing some amazment to find 'em no farther on their journey told Monsieur Frankville he believed he could inform him of some things which had happened since his departure, and could not yet have reached his knowledge, which the other desiring him to do, the gentleman begun in this manner.

"It was no sooner day," said he, "than it was noised over all the city, that Donna Camilla, Count D'Elmont, and your self, had privately left Rome; every body spoke of it, according to their humour, but the friends of Ciamara and Cittolini were outragious, a complaint was immediately made to the *consistory*,[1] and all imaginable deligence used, to overtake, or stop you, but you were so happy as to escape, and the pursuers returned without doing any thing of what they went about. Tho' Cittolini's disappointment to all appearance, was the greatest, yet Ciamara bore it with the least patience, and having vainly raged, offered all the treasure she was mistress of, and perhaps spent the best part of it in fruitless means to bring you back; at last she swallowed poyson, and in the raving agonies of death, confessed, that it was not the loss of Camilla, but Count D'Elmont which was the cause of her dispair. Her death gave a

---

1    A court or Church court where Ciamara can obtain a legal warrant for the return of Camilla.

fresh occasion of grief to Cittolini, but the day in which she was interred, brought him yet a nearer; he had sent to his *villa* for his daughter Violetta to assist at the funeral, and the messenger returned with the surprizing account of her not having been there as she pretended she was; nothing was ever equal to the rage, the grief, and the amazement of this distracted father, when after the strictest enquiry, and search that could be made, she was no where to be found or heard of, it threw him into a fever, of which he lingered but a small time, and died the same day on which I left Rome."

The gentleman who made this recital, was entirely a stranger to any of the company but Monsieur Frankville, and they were retired into a private room during the time of their conversation, which lasted not long; Frankville was impatient to communicate to Camilla and D'Elmont what he had heard, and as soon as civility would permit, took leave of the gentleman.

The Count had too much compassion in his nature not to be extreamly troubled when he was told this melancholly catastrophe; but Camilla said little, the ill usage of Ciamara, and the impudent, and interested pretensions of Cittolini to her, kept her from being so much *concerned* at their misfortunes as she would have been at any other persons, and the generosity of her temper, or some other reason which the reader will not be ignorant of hereafter, from expressing any *satisfaction* in the punishment they had met. But when the Count, who most of all lamented Violetta, expressed his astonishment and affliction, at her elopement, she joyned with him in the praises of that young lady, with an eagerness which testified she had no part in the hatred she bore her father.

While they were discoursing Camilla observed that Fidelio who was all this while in the room, grew very pale, and at last saw him drop down on the ground, quite senseless; she run to him, as did his lord, and Monsieur Frankville, and after, by throwing water in his face, they brought him to himself again, he appeared in such an agony that they feared his fit would return, and ordered him to be laid on a bed, and carefully attended.

After they had taken a short repast, they began to think of setting forward on their journey, designing to reach Piedmont that night. The Count went himself to the chamber where his page was laid, and finding he was very ill, told him he thought it best for him to remain in that place, that he would order physicians to attend him, and that when he was fully recovered, he might follow them to Paris with safety. Fidelio was ready to faint a second time at the hearing these words, and with the most earnest conjurations accompanied with tears, begged that he might not be left behind. "I can but dye," said he, "if I go with you, but I am sure, that nothing if I stay, can *save* me." The Count seeing him so pressing, sent for a *litter*, but there was none to be got, and in spite of all Camilla or Frankville could say to disswade him, having his lord's leave, he ventured to attend him as he had done the former part of the journey.

They travelled at an easy rate, because of Fidelio's indisposition, and it being later than they imagined, night came upon 'em before they were aware of it, ushered in, by one of the most dreadful storms that ever was; the rain, the hail, the thunder, and the lightning, was so violent that it obliged 'em to mend their pace to get into some place of shelter, for there was no house near. But to make their misfortune the greater, they missed the road, and rode considerably out of their way, before they perceived that they were wrong; the darkness of the night, which had no illumination than now and then, a horrid flash of lightning, the wildness of the desart, which they had strayed into, and the little hopes they had of being able to get out of it, at least 'till day, were sufficient to have struck terror in the boldest heart. Camilla stood in need of all her love, to protect her from the fears which were beginning to assault her; but poor Fidelio felt an inward horror, which, by this dreadful scene encreased, made him appear wholly desparate. "Wretch that I am," cried he, "'tis for me the tempest rises! I justly have incurred the wrath of heaven, – and you who are innocent, by my accursed presence are drawn to share a punishment only due to crimes like mine!" In this manner he exclaimed, wringing his hands in bitter anguish, and rather *exposing* his lovely face to all the fury of the storm, than any way endeavouring to *defend* it. His lord, and the two generous lovers, tho' harassed almost to death themselves, said all they could to comfort him;

the Count and Monsieur Frankville considered his words rather as the effects of his indisposition, and the fatigue he endured than remorse for any crime he could have been guilty of, and the pity they had for one so young and innocent, made the cruelty of the weather more insuportable to them.

At last, after long wandring, and the tempest still encreasing, one of the servants, who was before,[1] was happy enough to explore a path, and cried out to his lord with a great deal of joy, of the discovery he had made; they were all of opinion that it must lead to some house, because the ground was beat down, as if with the feet of passengers, and intirely free from stubble, stones, and stumps of trees, as the other part of the desart they come thro' was encumbered with.

They had not rode very far before they discerned lights; the reader may imagine the joy this sight produced, and that they were not slow in making their approach encouraged by such a wished for signal of success. When they came pretty near, they saw by the number of lights, which were dispersed in several rooms distant from each other, that it was a very large and magnificent house, and made no doubt, but that it was the country-seat of some person of great quality. The wet condition they were in, made them almost ashamed of appearing, and they agreed not to discover who they were, if they found they were unknown.

They had no sooner knocked than the gate was immediately opened by a porter, who asking their business, the Count told him they were gentlemen, who had been so unfortunate to mistake the road to Piedmont, and desired the owners leave for refuge in his house, for that night; that is a curtesy, said the porter, which my lord never refuses; and in confidence of his assent, I may venture to desire you to a-light, and bid you welcome. They all accepted the invitation, and were conducted into a stately hall where they waited not long before the Marquess De Saguillier, having been informed they appeared like people of condition, came himself to confirm the character his servant had given of his hospitality. He was a man perfectly well

---

1 Who was ahead of the rest.

bred, and in spite of the disadvantages their fatigue had subjected them to, he saw something in the countenance of these travellers, which commanded his respect, and engaged him to receive them with a more than ordinary civility.

Almost the first thing the Count desired, was that his page might be taken care of; he was presently carried to bed, and Camilla (to whom the Marquess made a thousand apology's that being a batchellor, he could not accomodate her, as he could the gentlemen) was showed to a chamber, where some of the maid servants attended to put her on dry cloaths.

They were splendidly entertained that night, and when morning came, and they were preparing to take leave, the Marquess, who was strangely charmed with their conversation, entreated them to stay two or three days with him to recover themselves of the fatigue they had suffered. The Count's impatience to be at Paris, to enquire after his dear Melliora would never have permitted him to consent, if he had not been obliged to it, by being told that Fidelio was grown much worse, and not in a condition to travel. Frankville and Camilla had said nothing, because they would not oppose the Count's inclination, but were extreamly glad of an opportunity to rest a little longer, tho' sorry for the occasion.

The Marquess omitted nothing that might make their stay agreeable; but tho' he had a longing inclination to know the names, and quality of his guests, he forbore to ask, since he found they were not free to discover themselves. The conversation between these accomplished persons was extreamly entertaining, and Camilla, tho' an Italian, spoke French well enough to make no inconsiderable part of it; the themes of their discourse were various, but at last happning to mention love, the Marquess spoke of that passion so feelingly, and expressed himself so vigorously when he attempted to excuse any of those errors, it leads its votarys into, that is was easy to discover, he felt the influence he endeavoured to represent.

Night came on again; Fidelio's distemper encreased to that degree, that they all began to despair of his recovery, at least they could not hope it for a long time, if at all, and Count D'Elmont fretted beyond measure at this unavoidable delay of the progress of his journey to that place, where he thought there was only a possibility of hearing of Melliora. As he was in bed, forming a thousand various idea's, tho' all tending to one object, he heard the chamber door unlock, and opening his curtains, perceived somebody come in; a candle was burning in the next room, and gave light enough at the opening the door, to show it was a woman, but what sort of one he could not discern, nor did he give himself the trouble of asking who was there, believing it might be one of the servants come in to fetch something she wanted, 'till coming pretty near the bed, she cried twice in a low voice, "Are you a sleep"; "No," answered he, a little surprized at this disturbance, "What would you have?" "I come," said she, "to talk to you, and I hope you are more a chevalier than to prefer a little sleep, to the conversation of a lady, tho' she visits you at midnight." These words made D'Elmont believe he had met with a second Ciamara, and lest he should find the same trouble with this as he had done with the former, he resolved to put a stop to it at once, and with an accent as peevish as he could turn his voice to, "The conversation of lady's," replied he, "is a happiness I neither deserve, nor much desire at any time, especially at this; therefore whoever you are, to oblige me, you must leave me to the freedom of my thoughts, which at present afford me matter of entertainment more suitable to my humour than any thing I can find here!" "Oh heavens!" said the lady, "Is this the courtly, the accomplished Count D'Elmont? So famed for complaisance and sweetness? Can it be he, who thus rudely repels a lady, when she comes to make him a present of her heart?" The Count was very much amazed to find he was known in a place where he thought himself wholly a stranger; "I perceive," answered he, with more ill-humour if possible than before, "you are very well acquainted with my name, which I shall never deny (tho' for some reasons I concealed it) but not at all with my character, or you would know, I can esteem the love of a woman, only when 'tis *granted*, and think it little worth acceptance, *proffered*." "Oh unkind!" said she, "but perhaps the sight of me, may inspire you with sentiments less cruel." With these words she went hastily out of the room to fetch the candle she had left within; and the Count was so much surprized and vexed at the immodesty and imprudence he believed her guilty of, that he thought he could not put a greater affront upon her, than her behaviour deserved, and turned himself with his face the other way, designing to deny her the satisfaction even of a look; she returned immediately, and having set down the candle pretty near the bed, came close to it her self, and seeing how he was laid; "this is unkind indeed," said she, "'tis but one look I ask, and if you think me unworthy of another, I will for ever shun your eyes." The voice in which these words were delivered, for those she spoke before were in a feigned accent, made the heart-ravished D'Elmont turn to her indeed, with much more hast, than he had done to avoid her; those dear, those well-remembered sounds infused an extacy, which none but Melliora's could create; he heard, – he saw, – 'twas she, that very she, whose loss he had so much deplored, and began almost to despair of ever being able to retrieve! Forgetting all decorum, he flew out of the bed, catched her in his arms, and almost stifled her with kisses; which she returning with pretty near an equal eagerness, "you will not chide me from you now?" she cried; those who have ever experienced any part of that transport, D'Elmont now was in, will know it was impossible for him to give her any other answer, than repeating his caresses; words were too poor to express what 'twas he felt, nor had he time to spare for speech, employed in a far dearer, softer oratory, than all the force of language could come up to!

But, when at last, to gaze upon her with more freedom he released her from that strict embrace he had held her in, and she blushing, with down cast eyes began to reflect on the effects of her unbounded passion, a sudden pang seized on his soul, and trembling, and convulsed between extremity of *joy*, and extremity of *anguish*, "I find thee Melliora," cried he, "but oh, my angel! where is it thou art found? –in the house of the young amorous Marquese D'Saguillier!" "Cease, cease," interrupted she, "your causeless fears, – where ever I am found, I am, – I can be only yours. – And if you will return to bed, I will inform you, not only what accident brought me hither, but also every particular of my behaviour since I came."

These words first put the Count in mind of the indecency his transport had made him guilty of, in being seen in that manner, and was going hastily to throw on his night gown, when Melliora perceiving his intent, and fearing he would take cold, told him she would not stay a moment, unless he granted her request of returning to his bed, which he, after having made her sit down on the side of it, at last consented to. And contenting himself with taking one of her hands, and pressing it between his, close prisoner in his bosom, gave her liberty to begin in this manner the discovery she had promised.

"After the sad accident of Alovysa's death," said she, "at my return to the monastry I found a new *pensioner* there; it was the young Madamoiselle Charlotta D'Mezray, who being lately left an orphan, was entrusted to the care of our Abbess being her near relation, 'till her time of mourning was expired, and she should be married to this Marquess D'Sanguillier, at whose house we are; they were contracted by their parents in their infancy, and nothing but the sudden death of her mother had put a stop to the consummation of what *then*, they both wished with equal ardour. But alas! Heaven which decreed the little beauty I am mistress of, should be pernicious to my own repose, ordained it so, that this unfaithful lover, seeing me one day at the *grate* with Charlotta, should fancy he found something in *me* more worthy of creating a passion, than he had in her, and began to wish himself released from his engagement with her that he might have liberty to enter into an other, which he imagined would be more pleasing. Neither she, nor I had the least suspicion of his sentiments, and, we having commenced a very great friendship, she would for the most part desire me to partake in the visits he made her. He still continued to make the same protestations of affection to her as ever; but if on any occasion, she but turned her head, or cast her eyes another way, he would give me such looks, as, tho' I then but little regarded, I have since understood the meaning of, but too well; in this manner he proceeded for some weeks, 'till at last he came one day extreamly out of humour and told Charlotta the occasion of it was, that he had heard she gave encouragement to some other lover; she, amazed, as well she might, avowed her innocence, and endeavoured to undeceive him, but he who resolved not to be convinced, at least not to seem as if he was, pretended to be more enraged at what he called weak excuses, said he was satisfied she was more guilty, even than he would speak, –that he knew not if it were consistent with his honour, ever to see her more. – And in short, behaved himself in so unaccountable a manner, that there was no room to doubt that he was either the most *imposed* on, or most *base* of men. It would be endless for me to endeavour to represent poor Charlotta's afliction. So I shall only say, it was answerable to the tenderness she had for him, which could by nothing be exceeded, but by that, continued she sighing, and looking languishly on him, which, contrary to all the resolutions I had made brings *me* to seek the arms of my enchanting D'Elmont, to rouze remembrance of his former passion! to strengthen my idea in his heart! and influence him a new with love and softness!" This kind digression made the Count give truce to his *curiosity*, that he might indulge the raptures of his *love*, and raising himself in bed, and pressing her slender fine proportioned body close to his, would permit her no otherwise, than in this posture to continue her discourse.

"Several days," resumed Melliora, "were past, and we heard nothing of the Marquess, all which, as he has since told me, were spent in fruitless projections to steal me from the monastry; but at last, by the means of a *lay sister*, he found means to convey a letter to me; the contents of it, as near as I can remember were these.

To the Divine Melliora.

*'Tis not the falshood of Charlotta, but the charms of Melliora have produced this change in my behaviour; do not therefore, at the reading this, affect a surprize at effects, which I am sure cannot be uncommon to such excellence! Nor accuse an inconstancy, which I rather esteem a virtue than a vice. To change from you indeed would be the highest sin, as well as stupidity; but to change for you, is what all must, and ought to do, who boast a capacity of distinguishing. I love you, Oh divinest Melliora, I*

*burn, I languish for you in unceasing torments, and you would*
*find it impossible for you to condemn the boldness of this declara-*
*tion, if you could be sensible of the racks which force me to it, and*
*which must shortly end me, if not happy enough to be received*

Your Lover,
D'Sanguillier.

"'Tis impossible for me to express the grief, and vexation this letter gave me, but I forbore showing it to Charllotta, knowing how much it would encrease her anguish, and resolved when I next saw him, as I made no doubt but I should quickly do, to use him in such a fashion, as in spite of his vanity, should make him know I was not to be won in such a manner, for I confess, my dear D'Elmont, that his timerity gave no less a shock to my *pride*, then his infidelity to her I really loved did to my *friendship*. The next day I was told a gentleman enquired for me; I presently imagined it was he, and went to the grate, with a heart full of indignation; I was not deceived in my conjecture, it was indeed the Marquess who appeared on the other side, but with so much humility in his eyes, and awful fear, for what he saw in mine, as half disarmed my anger for what concerned my self, and had his passion not proceeded from his inconstancy, I might have been drawn to *pity* what was not in my power to reward; but his base usage of a woman so deserving as Charlotta made me express my self in terms full of disdain and detestation, and without allowing him to reply or make any excuses plucked the letter he had sent me out of my pocket, with a design to return it him just at that moment when a *nun* came hastily to call me from the grate. Some body had overheard the beginning of what I said, and had told the Abbess, who, tho' she was not displeased at what she heard of my behaviour to him, yet she thought it improper for me hold any discourse with a man, who declared himself my lover. I did not, however, let her know who the person was, fearing it might come to Charlotta's ears, and encrease an affliction, which was already too violent. I was vext to miss the opportunity of giving back his letter, but kept it still about me, not in the least questioning, but that boldness which had encouraged him to make a discovery of his desires, would again lead him to the prosecution of them in the same manner, but I was deceived, his passion prompted him to take other, as he believed, more effectual measures. One day, at least a fortnight after I had seen the Marquess, as I was walking in the garden with Charlotta, and another young *pensioner*, a fellow who was imployed in taking away rubbish, told us there were some statues carried by the gate, which opened into the fields, which were the greatest master-pieces of art that had ever been seen. "They are going," said he, "to be placed in the Seiur Valier's garden, if you step but out, you may get a sight of them." We, who little suspected any deceit, run without consideration to satisfie our curiosity, but instead of the statues we expected to see, four living men disguised, muffled, and well mounted came galloping up to us, and, as it were surrounded us, before we had time to get back to the gate we came out at. Three of them alighting, seized me, and my companions, and I, who was the destined prey, was in a moment thrown into the arms of him who was on horseback, and who no sooner received me, than as if we had been mounted on a Pegasus, we seemed rather to *fly* than *ride*; in vain I strugled, shrieked, and cried to heaven for help, my prayers were lost in air, as quickly was my speech; surprize, and rage, and dread, o'rewhelmed my sinking spirits, and unable to sustain the rapidity of such violent emotions I fell into a swoon, from which I recovered not, till I was at the door of some house, but where, I yet am ignorant; the first thing I saw, when I opened my eyes was one of those men who had been assistant in my carying away, and was now about to lift me from the horse. I had not yet the power to speak, but when I had, I vented all the passions of my soul in terms full of distraction and dispair. By what means the people of the house were gained to my ravishers interest, I know not, but they took little notice of the complaints I made, or my implorations for succour. I had now, not the least shadow of a hope, that any thing but death could save me from dishonour, and having vainly raged, I at last sat down meditating by what means, I should compass that only relief from the worse ruin which seemed to threaten me. While my thoughts were thus employed, he who appeared the chief of that insolent company, making a sign that the rest should withdraw, fell on his knees before me, and plucking off his vizard discovered to me the face of the Marquess D'Saguillier. Heavens! How did this sight inflame me? Mild as I am, by nature, I that moment was all fury! — 'Till now I had not the least apprehension who he was, and believed 'twas rather my fortune than my person, which had prompted some daring wretch to take this method to obtain it, but now, my woes appeared, if possible, with greater horror, and his quality and engagement with Charlotta made the act seem yet more base. 'I blame you not,' said he, 'Oh divinest Melliora! The presumption I am guilty of, is of so high a nature as justly may deserve your utmost rigour! — I know, and confess my crime. — Nay, hate my self for thus offending you. — But Oh! 'Tis unavoidable. — Be then, like Heaven, who when injured most, takes most delight to pardon.' 'Crimes unrepented,' answered I, 'can have no plea for mercy, still to persist, and still to ask forgiveness, is *mocking* of the power we seem to *implore* and but encreases sin. — Release me from this captivity, which you have betrayed me into, restore me to the monastry — And for the *future*, cease to shock my ears with tales of violated faith, detested passion! Then, I perhaps, *may* pardon what is *past*.' His reply to all this was very little to the purpose, only I perceived he was so far from complying with my request, or repenting what he had done, that he resolved to proceed yet further, and one of his associates coming in, to tell him that his chariot, which it seems he had ordered to meet him there, was ready, he offered to take me by the hand to lead me to it, which I refusing, with an air which testified the indignation of my soul, 'Madam,' said he, 'you are not here less in my power, than you will be in a place, where I can accommodate you in a manner more suitable to your quality, and the adoration I have for you. If I were capable of a base design on you, what hinders but I now might perpetrate it? But be assured your beauties are not of that kind, which inspire sentiments dishonourable; nor shall you ever find any other treatment from me, than what might become the humblest of your slaves; my love, fierce as it is, shall know it's limits, and never dare to breath an accent less chast than your own virgin dreams, and innocent as your desires.'

"Tho' the boldness he had been guilty of, and still persisted in, made me give but little credit to the latter part of his speech, yet the beginning of it awaked my consideration to a reflection, that I could not indeed be any where in a greater danger of the violence I feared, than where I was; but on the contrary it might so happen that in leaving that place I might possibly meet some persons who might know me, or at least be carried somewhere whence I might with more likelyhood, make my escape. In this last hope I went into the chariot, and indeed, to do him justice, neither in our journey, nor since I came into his house, has he ever violated the promise he made me; nothing can be with more humility than his addresses to me, never visiting me without first having obtained my leave! But to return to the particulars of my story, I had not been here many days, before a servant-maid of the house, being in my chamber doing something about me, asked me if it were possible I could forget her; the question surprized me, but I was much more so, when looking earnestly in her face, which I had never done before, I perfectly distinguished the features of Charlotta. 'Oh heavens!' cried I, 'Charlotta!' 'The very same,' said she, 'but I dare not stay now to unfold the mistery, lest any of the family take notice; at night when I undress you, you shall know the history of my transformation.'

"Never any day seemed so long to me as that, and I feigned my self indisposed, and rung my bell for some body to come up, several hours before time I used to go to bed, Charlotta guessing my impatience, took care to be in the way, and as soon as she was with me, not staying for my requesting it of her, begun the information she had promised, in this manner.

"'You see,' said she forcing her self to put on a half smile, 'your unhappy rival follows to interrupt the triumph of your conquest, but I protest to you, that if I thought you esteemed my perjured lover's heart an offering worthy your acceptance, I never would have disturbed your happiness, and 'tis as much the hopes of being able to be instrumental in serving you in your releasement, as the prevention of that blessing the injurious D'Saguillier aims at, which has brought me here. Of all the persons that bewailed your being carried away, I was the only one who had any guess at the ravisher, nor had I been so wise, but that the very day on which it happened, you dropped a letter, which I took up, and knowing it the Marquess's hand, made no scruple of reading it. I had no opportunity to upbraid you for the concealment of his falshood, but the manner of your being seized, convinced me you were innocent of favouring his passion, and his vizard slipping a little on one side, as he took you in his arms, discovered enough of that face, I have so much adored, for me to know who it was, that had took this method to gain you. I will not,' continued she, weeping, 'trouble you with any recital of what I endured from the knowledge of my misfortune, but you may judge it by my love; however, I bore up against the oppressive weight, and resolved to struggle with my fate, even to the last; I made an excuse for leaving the monastry the next day, without giving any suspicion of the cause, or letting any body into the secret of the Marquess, and disguised as you see found means to be received by the housekeeper, as a servant; I came here in three days after you, and have had the opportunity of being confirmed by your behaviour, of what I before believed, that you were far from being an assistant in his design.'

"Here the sorrowful Charlotta finished her little account, and I testified the joy I felt in seeing her, by a thousand embraces, and all the protestations of eternal friendship to her, that I could make. All the times we had any opportunity of talking to each other, were spent in forming schemes for my escape, but none of them appeared feasible; however the very contrivance was a kind of pleasure to me, for tho' I began to banish all my fears of the Marquess's offering any violence to my virtue, yet I found his passion would not permitt him to suffer my departure, and I was almost distracted when I had no hopes of being in a capacity of hearing from you, or writing to you. In this fashion my dearest D'Elmont have I lived, sometimes flattering my self with vain projects, sometimes desponding of being ever free. But last night, Charlotta coming up, according to her custom, told me in a kind of rapture that you, and my brother were in the house; she, it seems knew you at Paris while her mother was yet living, and to make her entirely easy as to the Marquess, I had now made her the confident of my sentiments concerning you. I need not tell you the extacy this news gave me, you are too well acquainted with my heart, not to be able to conceive it more justly than language can express; but I cannot forbear informing you of one thing, of which you are ignorant, tho' had prudence any share in this love-directed soul, I should conceal it. My impatience to behold you, was almost equal to my joy to think you were so near, and transported with my eager wishes, by Charlotta's assistance, I last night found the way into your chamber. I saw you, Oh D'Elmont! My longing eyes enjoyed the satisfaction they so much desired, but yours were closed, the fatigue of your journey had laid you fast a sleep, so fast, that even fancy was unactive, and no kind dream, alarmed you with one thought of Melliora!"

She could not pronounce these last words very intelligibly, the greedy Count devoured 'em as she spoke, and tho' kisses had made many a parenthesis in her discourse, yet he restrained himself as much as possible for the pleasure of hearing her; but perceiving she was come to a period, he gave a loose to all the furious transports of his ungoverned passion. A while their lips were cemented! rivetted together with kisses, such kisses! as collecting every sence in one, exhale the very soul, and mingle spirits! Breathless with bliss, then would they pause and gaze, then joyn again, with ardour still encreasing, and looks, and sighs, and straining grasps were all the eloquence that either could make use of. Fain would he now have obtained the aim of all his wishes, strongly he pressed, and faintly she repulsed. Dissolved in love, and melting in his arms, at last she found no words to form denials, while he, all fire, improved the lucky moment, a thousand liberties he took. – A thousand joys he reaped, and had infallibly been possest of all, if Charlotta, who seeing it broad day, had not wondered at Melliora's stay, and come and knocked at the chamber door, which not being fastend, gave way to her entrance, but she made not such hast, but that they had time enough to disengage themselves from that close embrace they had held each other in. "Heavens! Mellio-ra," cried the careful interrupter, "what mean you by this stay, which may be so prejudicial to our designs, the Marquess is already stirring, and if he should come into this room, or send to yours, what might be the consequence?" "I come, I come," said Melliora alarmed at what she heard, and rising from the bed-side. "Oh, you will not," said the Count in a whisper, and tenderly pressing her hand, "you must not leave me thus!" "A few hours hence," answered she aloud, "I hope to have the power to own my self all yours, nor can the scheme we have laid fail of the effects we wish, if no discovery happens to post-pone it." She was going with Charlotta out of the chamber, with these words, but remembring her self, she turned hastily back, "let not my brother," resumed she, "know my weakness, and when you see me next, feign a surprize equal to his own."

It is not to be supposed that after she was gone, D'Elmont, tho' kept awake all night, could suffer any sleep to enter his eyes; excess of joy, of all the passions, hurries the spirits most, and keeps 'em longest busied. *Anger* or *grief,* rage violently at first, but quickly flag, and sink at last into a lethargy, but *pleasure* warms, exhillerates the soul, and every rapturous thought infus-es new desires, new life, and added vigour.

The Marquess De Saguillier was no less happy in imagina-tion than the Count, and it was the force of that passion which had rouzed him so early that morning, and made him wait impatiently for his guests coming out of their chambers, for he would not disturb them. As soon as they were all come into the drawing-room, "I know not messeiures," said he, with a voice and eyes wholly changed from those he wore the day before, "whether you have ever experienced the force of love to that degree that I have, but I dare believe you have generosity enough to rejoyce in the good fortune I am going to be pos-sessed of; and when I shall inform you how I have long lan-guished in a passion, perhaps, the most extravagant that ever was, you will confess the justice of that god, who soon or late, seldom suffers his faithful votaries to miss their reward." The Count could not force himself to a reply to these words, but Frankville and Camilla who were entirely ignorant of the cause of them, heartily congratulated him. "I am confident," resumed the Marquess, "that dispair has no existance but in weak and timerous minds; all women may be won by force or stratagem, and tho' I had, almost, invincible difficulties to struggle with, patience, constancy, and a bold, and artful management at length surmounted them. Hopeless, by distant courtship to obtain the *heart* of my adorable, I found means to make my self master of her *person*, and by making no other use of the power I had over her, than humbly sighing at her feet, convinced her my designs were far from being dishonourable; and last night, looking on me, with more kindness than she had ever done before, 'My lord,' said she, 'your usage of me has been too noble, not to vanquish what ever sentiments I may have been possest with to your prejudice; therefore since you have company in the house, who may be witness of what I do, I think I cannot chuse a fitter time, than this, to bestow my self, before them, on him who most deserves me.' I will not now," continued he, "delay the confirmation of my happiness so long, as to go about to describe the extacy I felt, for this so wished, and so unhoped a condescension, but when, hereafter, you shall be told the whole history of my passion, you will be better able to conceive it"; the Marquess had scarce done speaking, when his chaplain came into the room, saying he believed it was the hour his lordship ordered him to attend; "It is! It is," cried the transported Marquess. "Now my worthy guests you shall behold the lovely author of my joys"; with these words he left them, but immediately returned, leading the intended bride. Monsieur Frankville, tho' he had not seen his sister in some years, knew her at the first glimpse, and the surprize of meeting her – meeting her in so unexpected a manner was so great, that his thoughts were quite confounded with it, and he could no otherwise express it, than by throwing his eyes wildly sometimes on her, sometimes on the Count, and sometimes on the Marquess; the Count tho' apprised of this, felt a consternation for the consequence little inferior to his, and both being kept silent by their different agitations, and the Marquess, by the sudden change, which he perceived in their countenances, Melliora had liberty to explain her self in this manner. "I have kept my word, my lord," said she to the Marquess, "this day shall give me to him who best deserves me; but who that is, my brother and Count D'Elmont must determine; since heaven has restored them to me, all power of disposing of my self must cease; 'tis they must, henceforth, rule the will of Melliora, and only their consent can make me yours"; all endeavours would be vain to represent the Marquess's confusion at this sudden turn, and 'tis hard to say whether his astonishment, or vexation was greatest; her brother he would little have regarded, not doubting but his quality, and the riches he was possest of, would easily have gained his compliance; but Count D'Elmont, tho' he knew him not (having, for some disgust he received at Court, been many years absent from Paris,) yet he had heard much talk of him; and the passion he had for Melliora, by the adventure of Alovysa's death had made too great a noise in the world not to have reached his ears; he stood speechless for some time, but when he had a little recovered himself, "have you then deceived me, madam?" said he; "No," answered she, "I am still ready to perform my promise, whenever these gentlemen shall command me. – The one my brother, the other my guardian, obtain but their consent, and –" "Mine, he can never have," interrupted Frankville hastily, and laying his hand on his sword. "Nor mine," cried the Count, "while I have a breath to form denials, or my arm strength to guard my beautious charge"; "Hold brother, – Hold my lord," said Melliora, fearing their fury would produce some fatal effects, "the Marquess has been so truly noble, that you rather ought to thank, than resent his treatment of me, and tho' I see rage in *your* eyes, and all the stings of disappointment glowing fierce in *his*, yet I have hopes, a general content may crown the end. – Appear!" continued she, raising her voice, "Appear! thou lovely faithful maid! Come forth and charm thy roving lover's heart again to constancy, to peace, and thee!" She had no sooner spoke, then Charlotta entred, drest like a bride indeed, in a suit of cloaths, which she had brought with her, in case any happy opportunity should arise for her to discover herself. If the Marquess was before confounded, how much more so was he now? That injured lady's presence, just at this juncture, and the surprize by what means she came there, made him utterly unable to resolve on any thing, which she observing, and taking advantage of his confusion, run to him, and catching hold of his hand; "wonder not my lord," said she, "to see Charllotta here, nothing is impossible to love like mine; tho' slighted and abandoned by you, still I pursue your steps with truth, with tenderness, and constancy untired!" – Then, perceiving he still was silent, "come, my lord," continued she, "you must at last take pity on my sufferings; my rival, charming as she is, wants a just sencibility of your deserts, and is by that less worthy even than I; Oh, then remember, if not to me, what 'tis you owe your self your own exalted merits, and you will soon determine in my favour, and confess that she, who knows you best, ought most to have you"; she spoke these words in so moving an accent, and they were accompanied with so many tears, that the most rocky heart must have relented, and that the Marquess was sensibly touched with em, his countenance testified, when sighing, and turning his head a little away, not with disdain, but remorse, for the infidelity he had been guilty of, "Oh cease," said he, "this flood of softness, it gives me pains I never felt before, for 'tis impossible you can forgive." – "Oh Heaven!" cried the transported Charlotta, "all you have done, or ever can do of unkindness, is by one tender word made full amends for; see at your feet," continued she falling on her knees, "thus, in this humble posture, which best becomes my prostrate soul, I beg you to accept the pardon which I bring, to banish from your mind all thoughts that you have injured me, and leave it free from[1] all the generous joys the making others happy must create." This action of Charlotta's joyned to the reflection how strangly every thing happened to prevent his designs on the other, won him entirely, and raising her with a tender embrace, put it out of her power to regret his ever being false, since his return gave her a tast of joys, which are not, but in reconciliation to be found.

The Count, Monsieur Frankville, and the two ladys who had waited all this while in an impatient expectation for the

---

1  *Sic*, though the sense seems to require "for."

end of this affair, now paid their several congratulations, all highly applauding the constancy of Charlotta, and the timely repentance of the Marquess. These ceremonies being over, the Marquess desired Charlotta to acquaint him by what means she had gained admittance to his house unknown to him; which curiosity she immediately satisfying, engaged a new the praises of the whole company, and more endeared her self to her beloved Marquess's affections.

Tranquillity now reigned in those hearts which lately heaved with various and disturbed emotions, and joy sat smiling upon every cheek; entirely happy in their several wishes, they could now talk of past woes with pleasure, and began to enter into a very delightful conversation, when Frankville on a sudden missing Camilla, and asking for her, one of the servants told him she was gone to the sick page's chamber; this news gave him some little alarm, and the rather because he had observed she expressed a more than ordinary tenderness and care for this page all the time of their journey; he ran immediately to the room where he heard she was, and found her lying on the bed, with her arms round Fidelio's neck, and her face close to his; this shocking sight, had certainly driven the rashness of his temper to commit some deed of horror, if the amazement he was in had not prevented it; he drew his sword half out, but then, as if some spell had charmed his arm, remained in that posture, fixed and motionless as marble. Camilla half blinded with the tears which fell from her eyes, saw not the confusion he was in, nor considered the seeming reason he had to be so, but raising her head a little to see who it was that came into the chamber, "Oh Frankville!" said she, "see here the ruins of love; behold the tyranny of that fatal passion in this expiring fair! But hast," continued she, finding him ready to faint, "let Count D'Elmont know, the faithful, generous Violetta! dies. – She dies for him, and asks no other recompence, than a last farewell." – "Violetta," interrupted Frankville, "what means Camilla?" "This, this is Violetta," resumed she, "who like a page disguised has followed the too lovely Count, and lost her self." The rage, which at his first entrance had possest the heart of Frankville, now gave way to grief, and coming near the bed, he began to testify it, by all the marks which an unfeigned concern could give; but this unfortunate languisher, finding her strength decay, prevented him from making any long speeches, by renewing that request, which Camilla had already made known, of seeing her dear lord before she died, which Frankville making hast to fulfill, she called to him as loud as her weakness would permit to come back, and as soon as he was, "Camilla," said she, "has informed me of my lord's good fortune in meeting with the charmer of his soul, I would not deprive him of a moments happiness. I therefore beg she'd give a dying rival, leave to wish her joy, and as neither my death, nor the cause of it can be a secret, to any of the company here, I desire they all may be witnesses with what pleasure I welcome it"; Frankville fiery as he was, had a vast deal of compassion in his nature, and could not see so beautiful a young lady, and one whom he had so many obligations to, on the account of his affair with Camilla, in this dispairing, and dying condition without being seized with anguish inexpressible; but all the pangs he felt were nothing, compared to those he gave D'Elmont in the delivery of her message; he ran into the room like a man distracted, and in the hurry of his grief, forgot even the complaisance he owed to Melliora, but she was too generous to disapprove his concern, immediatly followed with her brother, the Marquess, and Charlotta. "What is it that I hear, madam?" cried the Count, throwing himself on the bed by her, "can it be possible that the admired Violetta could forsake her father, – country, – friends, – foregoe her sexes pride, – the pomp of beauty, – gay dresses, and all the equipage of state, and grandeur, to follow in a mean disguise, a man unworthy of her thoughts?" "Oh! No more," said she weeping, "you are but too, too worthy adoration, nor do I yet believe my love a crime, tho' the consequence is so; I might in Rome, with honour and innocence have dyed, but by my shameful flight, I was the murderer of my father – that, – that's a guilt, which all these floods of penitence can never wash away – Yet, bear me witness heaven, how little I suspected the sad event, when first, unable to support your absence, I contrived this way, unknown, to keep for ever in your sight; I loved, 'tis true, but if one unchast wish, or an impure desire, er'e stained my soul, then, may the purging fire to which I am going, miss it's effect, my spots remain, and not one saint vouchsafe to own me." Here the force of her passion, agitating her spirits with too much violence for the weakness of her body, she sunk fainting in the bed. And tho' the Count and Camilla felt the most deeply her afflictions, the one because they proceeded from her love to him, and the other as having long been her friend, and partner of her secrets, yet those in the company who were most strangers to her, participated in her sufferings, and commiserated the woes they could not heal, and assoon as she recovered from her swoon, the generous Melliora (not in the least possest with any of those little jealousies, which women of narrow souls harbour on such occasions) came nearer to the bed, and taking her kindly by the hand, "Live, and be comforted," said she, "a love so innocent shall never give me any disquiet. – Live and enjoy the friendship of my lord, and if you please to favour me with yours, I shall esteem it, as it deserves, a blessing." "No madam," answered the now almost expiring Violetta, "life, after this shameful declaration,[1] would be the worst of punishments, but, not to be ungrateful to so generous an offer, for a few moments I accept it, and like children, placing their darling play things on their pillow, and then contented to go to sleep, so I would keep your lord, would view him still while I awake to life, then drop incensibly into a slumber of eternal peace." This mournful tenderness pierced D'Elmont, to the very soul, and putting his arm gently under her head, which, he perceived she was too weak to raise when she endeavoured it, and laying his face on one of her hands, could not forbear washing it in tears; she felt the cordial drops, and, as if they gave her a new vigour, exerting her voice to the utmost of her strength; "this is too kind," said she, "I now can feel none of those agonies which render death the king of terrors, and thus, thus happy in your sight, – your touch – your tender pity, I can but be translated from one heaven to another, and yet, forgive me heaven if it be a sin, I could wish, methinks, to know no other paradise than you, to be permitted to hover

---

1  Chaste and dying, Violetta has nevertheless transgressed against the expectation that
   women not declare their love.

round you, to form your dreams, to sit upon your lip all day, to mingle with your breath, and glide in unfelt air into your bosom." She would have proceeded, but her voice faultered in the accent, and all she spoke distinguishable was, "Oh D'Elmont receive in this one sigh my latest breath" – it was indeed her last, she died that moment, died in his arms, whom more than life she prized, and sure there are none who have lived in the anxietys of love, who would not envy such a death!

There was not in this noble company, one whose eyes were dry, but Count D'Elmont for some time was inconsolable, even by Melliora; he forbore the celebrating of his so eagerly desired nuptials, as did the Marquess and Monsieur Frankville theirs, in complaisance to him, 'till after Violetta was interred, which the Count took care should be in a manner becoming her quality, her merit, and the esteem he professed to have born her. But when this melancholly scene was past, a day of joy succeeded, and one happy hour confirmed the wishes of the three longing bridegrooms; the weddings were all kept in a splendid manner at the Marquess's, and it was not without a great deal of reluctance, that he and Charlotta suffered the Count, Monsieur Frankville, and their ladies to take leave of them; when they came to Paris, they were joyfully received by the Chevalier Brillian and Ansellina, and those who in the Count's absence had taken a liberty of censuring and condemning his actions, awed by his presence, and in time won by his virtues, now swell his praises with an equal vehemence. Both he and Frankville, are still living, blest with a numerous and hopeful issue, and continue, with their fair wives, great and lovely examples of conjugal affection.

*Finis.*

# Appendix: Some Eighteenth-Century Responses to Eliza Haywood

[Two poems praising Haywood appear at the beginning of the second part of *Love in Excess*. This appendix adds other poems of praise or blame, two early accounts of Haywood's career, and Clara Reeve's 1785 prose appraisal of the fiction written by Haywood and the two writers commonly associated with her as authors of explicitly sexual fiction and scandal romances, Aphra Behn and Delarivier Manley.

Haywood was a woman as well as a writer whose subject was love. Since contemporaries respond first to her gender, an uneasy gallantry colours their praise. By 1722, the earlier poems by Savage and Unknown Hand join "Verses Wrote in the Blank Leaf of Mrs. Haywood's Novel" at the start of the novel, replacing the Dedication. Its awareness of Haywood's inexperience suggests that it originates close to the author or her bookseller, perhaps from Chetwood or Aaron Hill. In the first *Female Spectator*, Haywood credits it to "a justly celebrated Poet." Unusually, the poet addresses the recipient not as her lover but as her male friend. Addressing "my fair" but wishing her "an happy D'elmont," he commends Haywood's novels for serving "The cause of honour, and the cause of love." *The Ladies Journal* also registers Haywood's presence. Its author invites the language of gallantry by presenting himself in his first number as a "Champion" who, "tho' he wears not a sword, yet he always carries about him a little instrument, called, a pen, as sharp as the best point of them all." Accepting his invitation, Love More, an anonymous correspondent, complains in gentlemanly verse "Writ on a Blank Leaf of a Lady's Love in Excess" that he lacks Haywood's mastery of language. He can only hope that his unresponsive lady will recognize his suffering in Haywood's exemplary account of D'elmont's. But since he modestly recalls that heroes are women's most eminent admirers, he cedes little male authority to the novelist. James Sterling is less coy. In a poem "hastily inserted in the fourth volume of Secret Histories, Novels, and Poems when that collection had reached its third edition (1732)" (Whicher 16n22), he directly addresses the mastery the fashionable woman writer paradoxically embodies. Playfully adapting the tag "arbiter of fashion,"[1] he memorably dubs Haywood the "Great arbitress of passion." Whether viciously personal or contemptuously Olympian, poems of blame caricature the professional novelist of love as a prostitute. Richard Savage seems to betray his professional jealousy even when he praises Haywood's *Rash Resolve* (December 1723), for he contrasts his own "unfriended" muse with Haywood's "rising name." In his *Authors of the Town; A Satire* (1725), it seems that he rather than Haywood "burns with envy's blaze." He attacks Aaron Hill, satirizes the poet John Gay (another very successful former friend), and condemns his former lover Haywood as "a printer's drudge" and ranting actress, the infernal opposite of his heavenly current mistress. More impersonally, Jonathan Swift satirizes the woman writer so generally that the target of his "Corinna" is uncertain. The name "Corinna" belongs ambiguously both to an ancient Greek poet famous for her lyrics and to the poet Ovid's mistress in *Amores*, which is perhaps why it also appears in condescending poems of praise written by men for women writers.[2] Swift's "Corinna" is often read as an attack on Delarivier Manley, a writer whom contemporaries associated with Haywood, but Swift elsewhere refers sympathetically to Manley, who succeeded him as editor of *The Examiner*. Haywood seems as likely a candidate.[3]

In the most famous and comprehensively misogynist attack on Haywood, the satiric portrait of her in *The Dunciad* (1728), Alexander Pope is characteristically both general and acutely personal. Motivated by slights to women in his circle, especially Martha Blount, Pope targets Haywood's offending scandal

---

1  Tacitus applied the phrase *arbiter elegantiae* ("judge of elegance") to Petronius, the Roman courtier who probably wrote *The Satyricon*, a Latin satire about a man cursed with impotence by Venus!

2  Dryden applies the name to Elizabeth Thomas (1675-1731), possibly one of Swift's targets (Heinemann, "Swift's 'Corinna' Again"; McWhir); on such poems, see Lipking.

3  See Elwood, "Swift's 'Corinna'"; Rogers's helpful edition of Swift's poems annotates with Manley in mind, but see also the Haywood entry in Blain *et al.*, *The Feminist Companion*.

novels as part of his comprehensive attack on hireling writers. His Haywood is a cow-like concubine offered as a prize in a mock-epic pissing contest between two rival publishers, William Chetwood (who published *Love in Excess*) and the notorious Edmund Curll. Though Haywood had two children and no husband in evidence, Pope's "Two babes of love" (illegitimate children) are books, or are *also* books, the books his note refers to as "those most scandalous books, called *The Court of Carimania* and *The New Utopia.*" The prolific author who wrote them is caricatured as an offensively teeming and lactating woman. In the event, impudence carries the day for Curll, who "the pleased dame soft-smiling leads away" (*Dunciad Variorum* [1729] 2.182); his public performance disabled by his bashfulness, Chetwood makes do with the second prize, a chamber pot. Within a patriarchal society, women are vessels. When a woman transgresses against entrenched expectations by writing, she finds that the language of gallantry sours into contempt for the vessels into which men discharge fluids.

Nevertheless, Pope slanders no frail damsel. Haywood deployed the same caustic blend of gossip with gender stereotypes when she vividly represented "Marthalia's" alleged sexual impropriety in *Memoirs of a Certain Island adjacent to the Kingdom of Utopia*. Nor is Pope impartial. Pilloried with Haywood in *The Dunciad*, her publisher William Chetwood wryly comments in *A General History of the Stage* (1749) that "she need not blush in such good company." A writer and theatrical jack-of-all-trades who had knocked around with her in Dublin and London, he cites the 1715 Dublin production of *Timon of Athens; or, The Man-Hater* in which Haywood played Chloe. His brief appreciation of her early career offers what Haywood surely deserves, not pity but sympathy and respect.

In *Biographia Dramatica* (1764), David Erskine Baker too objects to Haywood's satire of particular persons in her scandal-romances, but he rejects scandalous inferences drawn from her fiction. They led her, he suggests, to suppress biographical information. And though Clara Reeve represents Haywood's career through a familiar narrative pattern, the reform of the fallen woman, she like Baker emphasizes Haywood's contributions to the domestic fiction that replaced amatory fiction by mid-century. Contemporary accounts do more justice to Eliza Haywood than most subsequent histories of the novel.

Early eighteenth-century editions are modernized on the same principles as Haywood's novel; later editions are modernized lightly where a reader might be puzzled. I reverse italic and Roman type in poems originally printed in italic.]

## Some Eighteenth-Century Responses to Eliza Haywood

### 1. Anonymous

*Verses Wrote in the Blank Leaf of Mrs. Haywood's Novel* (1722)

Of all the passions given us from above,
The noblest, truest, and the best, is love;
'Tis love awakes the soul, informs the mind,
And bends the stubborn temper to be kind,
Abates the edge of ev'ry poi'nant[1] care
Succeeds the wishes of the trembling fair,
And ravishes the lover from despair.
'Tis love Eliza's soft affections fires,[2]
Eliza writes, but love alone inspires;
'Tis love, that gives D'Elmont his manly charms,
And tears Amena from her father's arms;
Relieves the fair one from her maiden fear,
And gives Melliora all her soul holds dear,
A generous lover, and a bliss sincere.

Receive, my fair, the story, and approve,
The cause of *honour*, and the cause of *love*;
With kind concern, the tender page peruse,
And aid the infant labours of the muse.[3]
So never may those eyes forget to shine,
And bright Melliora's fortune be as thine;

---

1   Poignant; that is, sharp, piercing.
2   A poetic inversion of normal word order: it is love that fires Eliza's soft affections.
3   The reader's sympathy for Haywood's lovers aids Haywood's muse, perhaps called "infant" because *Love in Excess* is her first novel.

On thy best looks, an happy D'Elmont feed,
And all the wishes of thy soul succeed.

## 2. Richard Savage

**a.** *To Mrs. Eliza Haywood, on Her Novel, called The Rash Resolve*
(1724)

>Doom'd to a fate which damps the poet's flame,
>A muse, unfriended, greets thy rising name!
>Unvers'd in envy's, or in flatt'ry's phrase,
>Greatness she flies, yet merit claims her praise;
>Nor will she, at her with'ring wreath, repine,
>But smile, if fame and fortune cherish thine.
>The sciences in thy sweet genius charm,
>And, with their strength, thy sex's softness arm.
>In thy full figures, painting's force we find,
>As music fires, thy language lifts the mind.
>Thy pow'r gives form, and touches into life
>The passions imag'd in their bleeding strife:
>Contrasted strokes, true art and fancy show,
>And lights and shades in lively mixture flow.
>Hope attacks Fear, and Reason loves Control,[1]
>Jealousy wounds, and Friendship heals the soul:
>Black Falshood wears bright Gallantry's disguise,
>And the gilt cloud enchants the fair-one's eyes.
>Thy dames, in grief and frailties lovely shine,
>And when most mortal half appear divine.
>If, when some godlike, fav'rite passion sways,
>The willing heart too fatally obeys,
>Great minds lament what cruel censure blames,
>And ruin'd Virtue gen'rous pity claims.
>Eliza, still impaint Love's pow'rful Queen!
>Let Love, soft Love! exalt each swelling scene.
>Arm'd with keen wit, in fame's wide lists[2] advance!

---

1 Corrected following *Poetical Works*, ed. Tracy (p. 50 & n.); *Works* (1777) reads
   "Hope attacks Fear and Reason, Love's control."
2 The arena within which knights tilted for honour.

Spain yields in fiction,[1] in politeness, France.
Such orient light, as the first poets knew,
Flames from thy thought, and brightens ev'ry view!
A strong, a glorious, a luxuriant fire,
Which warms cold wisdom into wild desire!
Thy Fable glows so rich thro' ev'ry page,
What moral's force can the fierce heat assuage?
    And yet—but say, if ever doom'd to prove
The sad, the dear perplexities of love!
Where seeming transport softens ev'ry pain,
Where fancy'd freedom waits the winning chain!
Varying from pangs to visionary joys,
Sweet is the fate, and charms as it destroys!
Say then—if Love to sudden rage gives way,
Will the soft passion not resume its sway?
Charming and charm'd, can Love from Love retire?
Can a cold convent quench th' unwilling fire?
Precept, if human, may our thoughts refine,
More we admire! but cannot prove divine.

**b.** From *The Authors of the Town; A Satire* (1725)

    A cast-off dame,[2] who of intrigues can judge,
Writes scandal in romance—a printer's drudge!
Flushed with success, for stage-renown she pants,
And melts, and swells, and pens luxurious rants.
    But while her muse a sulph'rous flame displays,
Glows strong with lust, or burns with envy's blaze!
While some black fiend, that hugs the haggard shrew,
Hangs his collected horrors on her brow!
Clio,[3] descending angels sweep thy lyre,
Prompt thy soft lays, and breathe seraphic fire.
Tears fall, sighs rise, obedient to thy strains,
And the blood dances in the mazy veins! ...

---

1  Spain was famous for both chivalric fiction and Cervantes' enormously influential parody of it in *Don Quixote*.
2  Savage presents his former lover, Haywood, as a jilted mistress expert in love affairs.
3  Apparently Savage's current lover, Martha Fowke Sansome, named for the classical muse of history to suggest that she (unlike Haywood) writes the truth.

**3. Anonymous letter from *The Ladies Journal* (Dublin, 1727),
39-40 (No. 5, Thursday February 16, 1726-7)**

To the Author of the Ladies Journal

Sir,

I am one of that infinite number, who wait impatiently for the
return of every Thursday, finding that to be the day on which
you have chose to publish your ingenious and agreeably
instructive paper; in the perusal whereof I confess to have
reaped a great deal of pleasure. Sir, I entirely concur with you,
in your opinion of the excellence of the fair sex above ours,
nor is it a small addition to their praise, that the most famous
warriors and greatest conquerors have been their most eminent admirers; an infinite number of instances might be
brought to confirm the truth of this assertion. I shall at present
only mention one, our great Edward the third is no less famous
for his military atchievements than his devotion to the ladies,
and in particular to the celebrated Countess of Salisbury, to
whom we owe the institution of the most noble order in the
world,[1] on which perhaps I may hereafter enlarge, if you think
the following lines worth publishing.

*Writ on a blank Leaf of a Lady's* Love in Excess

Ingenious Haywood writes like one who knew
The pangs of love and all it's raptures too;
O could I boast that more than common skill,
Which guides her fancy and directs her quill
When she so lively to her reader shows,
A tender heart oppressed with amorous woes;
My passion I so clearly would display,
And to your view my soul so open lay,
Describe in words well chose and apt to move,
The agonizing torments of my love—

---

1   The order of the garter, the oldest English order of knighthood; by popular legend,
    it began after Edward III restored to the Countess of Salisbury a garter she lost dur-
    ing a dance.

The thousand wrecking sighs that rend my breast,
And pangs of jealousy, that foe to rest,
With all the train of ills which constant wait
On the distressed dispairing lover's fate—
That you, unkind and cruel should confess
Count Delmont never loved to such excess.
Love makes many poetasters, one of whom is Sir,
Your Humble Servant,

*Love More.*

### 4. Jonathan Swift

*Corinna* (1728)

This day (the year I dare not tell)
    Apollo[1] play'd the midwife's part;
Into the world Corinna fell,
    And he endued her with his art.

But Cupid with a Satyr[2] comes;
    Both softly to the cradle creep;
Both stroke her hands, and rub her gums,
    While the poor child lay fast asleep.

Then Cupid thus: "This little maid
    Of love shall always speak and write;"
"And I pronounce," the Satyr said,
    "The world shall feel her scratch and bite."

Her talent she displayed betimes;
    For in twice twelve revolving moons,
She seemed to laugh and squall in rhymes,
    And all her gestures were lampoons.[3]

---

1  The god of poetry and learning, who endows Corinna with the art of writing.
2  The god of love decrees her subject, love; one of the rowdy goat-footed classical
   beings conventionally associated with biting satire, the satyr decrees her devotion to
   satire (then spelled "satyr").
3  A lampoon is "A personal satire; abuse; censure written not to reform but to vex"
   (Johnson).

At six years old, the subtle jade[1]
Stole to the pantry-door, and found
The butler with my lady's maid:
And you may swear the tale went round.

She made a song, how little miss
Was kiss'd and slobber'd by a lad:
And how, when master went to p[iss],
Miss came, and peep'd at all he had.

At twelve, a wit and a coquette;
Marries for love, half whore, half wife;
Cuckolds, elopes, and runs in debt;[2]
Turns authoress, and is Curll's[3] for life.

Her commonplace-book all gallant is,
Of scandal now a cornucopia;[4]
She pours it out in Atalantis,[5]
Or memoirs of the New Utopia.[6]

---

1   "A sorry woman. A word of contempt noting sometimes age, but generally vice";
    literally "A horse of no spirit; a hired horse; a worthless nag" (Johnson). Swift like
    Pope resents the professionalization and commodification of writing; hence the
    gentlemanly (and readily sexualized) contempt for the much-used hireling.
2   In Swift, the typical progress of the coquette duped by love stories; see his "Phillis;
    or, The Progress of Love."
3   Edmund Curll, the notorious bookseller who also wins Haywood in Pope's *Dunci-
    ad.*
4   The mythical horn of plenty.
5   Delarivier Manley's most famous scandal romance was *Secret Memoirs and Manners of
    Several Persons of Quality, of Both Sexes. From the New Atalantis, an Island in the Medit-
    eranean* [*sic*] (1709), commonly called *Atalantis* or the *New Atalantis.*
6   Haywood's first scandal romance was *Memoirs of a Certain Island Adjacent to the King-
    dom of Utopia* (1724).

## 5. Alexander Pope

From *The Dunciad, Variorum. With the Prolegomena of Scriblerus* (1729)

[Pope first published his mock-epic attack on Grub-Street writing in 1728; in later editions, he elaborated the mock-scholarly apparatus, added a *New Dunciad*, and finally produced a four-book version. This passage (taken from the 1729 *Dunciad Variorum*) comes complete with the notes of a pedantic mock-editor, Martinus Scriblerus. Although the conventions are Homeric, the passage parodies the epic contests in which heroes compete for prizes. The goddess who presides is Dulness; the heroes are the rival booksellers William Chetwood (who published *Love in Excess*) and Edmund Curll; the event is a pissing contest; the prizes are Haywood herself and, for the loser, a chamber pot.]

> See in the circle next,★ Eliza★★ placed,
> Two babes of love¹ close clinging to her waste;
> Fair as before her works she stands confessed,
> In flowers and pearls by bounteous Kirkall² dressed.
> The Goddess then: "Who best can send on high
> The salient spout, far-streaming to the sky;
> His be yon Juno of majestic size,
> With cow-like udders, and with ox-like eyes.³
> This china-jordan,⁴ let the chief o'ercome
> Replenish, not ingloriously, at home....
> (2.149-58)

★In this game is exposed in the most contemptuous manner, the profligate licenciousness of those shameless scriblers (for the

---

1  Illegitimate children.
2  A contemporary engraver, as Pope notes (see *Dunciad*, ed. Sutherland); his frontispieces include the one for the 1722 edition of *Love in Excess*.
3  "Ox-eyed" translates a Homeric epithet for Juno (Hera), the Queen of Heaven; Homer's heroes compete for captured women and heifers alike, so Pope makes Haywood at once a goddess (object of love), a concubine, and a cow.
4  Chamber pot.

most part of that sex, which ought least to be capable of such malice or impudence) who in libellous memoirs and novels, reveal the faults and misfortunes of both sexes, to the ruin or disturbance of publick fame or private happiness. Our good poet (by the whole cast of his work being obliged not to take off the irony), where he could not show his indignation, hath shewn his contempt as much as possible: having here drawn as vile a picture as could be represented in the colours of epic poesy.—Scriblerus

**Eliza Haywood**] This woman was authoress of those most scandalous books, called *The Court of Carimania* and *The New Utopia....*

## 6. James Sterling

*To Mrs. Eliza Haywood on Her Writings* (1732)

If but thro' fine organs, souls shine forth,
And polished matter marks the mental worth;
Sure spirit free, by no dull mass controuled,
Exerts full vigour in fair female mold—

Let tyrant man, with Salic laws[1] submit,
Nor boast the vain prerogative of wit:
See! from Eliza in a flood of day
With vast effulgence streams the pow'rful ray!
But Nature, in an elegance of care,
At once creates our wonder and our fear;
So delicate's the texture of our brain,
We wish it less refined, and nearer man;
For weak's the clock with over-curious springs,[2]

---

1  The widely adopted law code of the Salian Franks prevented women from inheriting property, including the French throne. Haywood challenges the law by showing that wit is not a male prerogative.

2  We wonder at Haywood's writing but fear that such subtle elegance will weaken the texture of her brain, as an over-elaborate mechanism weakens a clock. The English were famous for fine clockwork.

And frail the voice that too divinely sings—
See! Handmaid-Nature guides her godlike fires,
Each grace adorns what ev'ry muse inspires;
The charming page pale Envy's gloom beguiles,
She low'rs,[1] she reads, forgets herself and smiles:
Proportioned to the image, language swells,
Both leave the mind suspended, which excels—

Great arbitress of passion! (wond'rous art)
As the despotick will the limbs, thou mov'st the heart;[2]
Persuasion waits on all your bright designs,
And where you point the varying soul inclines:
See! love and friendship, the fair theme inspires,
We glow with zeal, we melt in soft desires!
Thro' the dire labyrinth of ills we share
The kindred sorrows of the gen'rous pair;
Till, pleased, rewarded vertue we behold,
Shine from the furnace pure as tortured gold:[3]
You sit like Heaven's bright minister on high,
Command the throbbing breast, and watry eye,
And, as our captive spirits ebb and flow,
Smile at the tempests you have raised below:
The face of guilt a flush of vertue wears,
And sudden burst the involuntary tears:
Honour's sworn foe, the libertine[4] with shame,
Descends to curse the sordid lawless flame;
The tender maid here learns man's various wiles,
Rash youth, hence dread the wanton's venal smiles—
Sure 'twas by brutal force of envious man,
First learning's base monopoly began;
He knew your genius, and refused his books,

---

1   That is, lours, scowls.
2   Haywood moves our hearts as tyrannically as our wills move our limbs.
3   Tormented by refining in a furnace; but literally "twisted" or "stretched," suggesting finely worked gold.
4   Someone devoted to pleasure, especially sexual pleasure, and so free from the constraints of honour; a seducer. Touching the reader's feelings with a noble passion, Haywood reforms the seducer, alerts the maiden to his tricks, and teaches young men to avoid the mercenary smiles of prostitutes.

Nor thought your wit less fatal than your looks.[1]
Read, proud usurper, read with conscious shame,
Pathetic Behn, or Manley's greater name;[2]
Forget their sex, and own when Haywood writ,
She closed the fair triumvirate of wit;[3]
Born to delight as to reform the age,
She paints example thro' the shining page;
Satiric precept warms the moral tale,
And causticks burn where the mild balsam fails;[4]
A task reserved for her, to whom 'tis given,
To stand the proxy of vindictive Heaven.

## 7. William Rufus Chetwood

From *A General History of the Stage; (More Particularly the Irish Theatre) From its Origin in Greece down to the Present Time. With the Memoirs of the Principal Performers, that have appeared on the Dublin Stage in the Last Fifty Years* (Dublin, 1749), 57. [note to a 1715 performance of *Timon of Athens; or, The Man-Hater* at the theatre in Smock Alley, Dublin]

Mrs. Haywood has made herself eminent to the polite world by her writings; she is still alive. Her numerous novels will be ever esteemed by lovers of that sort of amusement. She is likewise authoress of three dramatic pieces. 1st, *The Fair Captive*, a tragedy. 2d, *A Wife to be Let*, a comedy. Mrs. Haywood performed the capital part in this play. 3rd, *Frederick, Duke of Brunswick*, a tragedy. She also joyned with Mr. Hatchet, in making songs to Mr. Fielding's *Tom Thumb* which were com-

---

1   The male reader guiltily recognizes that men, out of jealous fear of women's intellect and beauty, have usurped rather than inherited their monopoly of learning (formal education was largely male).

2   Aphra Behn admired for her pathos, and Delarivier Manley, at this time still more famous than Behn.

3   A coalition of three people who govern together. Literature ("wit") is ruled by these three women writers as Rome was ruled by the original triumvirates (first by Julius Caesar, Pompey, and Crassus; later by Mark Antony, Lepidus, and Octavian).

4   A balsam was a soothing ointment, a caustic a burning one. Haywood's examples of love inspire emulation; her corrosive satire serves heaven by scourging the wicked.

posed by the ingenious Mr. Frederick Lampe, and performed often with the title of the *Opera of Operas*. As the Pen is her chief means of subsistence, the world may find many books of her writing, tho' none have met with more success than her *novels* more particularly her *Love in Excess*, &c. Her dramatic works have all died in their first visiting the world, being exhibited in very sickly seasons for poetry. Mr. Pope has taken her for his goddess of Dulness in his *Dunciad*, but she need not blush in such good company.

## 8. David Erskine Baker

From *Biographica Dramatica; or, A Companion to the Playhouse*, 2 vols. (1764; new ed. 1782), 1: 215-16.

HEYWOOD, Mrs. ELIZA. This lady was perhaps the most voluminous female writer this kingdom ever produced. Her genius lay for the most part in the novel kind of writing. In the early part of her life, her natural vivacity, her sex's constitutional fondness for gallantry, and the passion which then prevailed in the public taste for personal scandal, and diving into the intrigues of the great, guided her pen to works, in which a scope was given for great licentiousness. The celebrated *Atalantis* of Mrs. Manley served her for a model, and the court of *Carimania*, the *New Utopia*, and some other pieces of a like nature, were the copies her genius produced. Whether the looseness of the pieces themselves, or some more private reasons, provoked the resentment of Mr. Pope against her, I cannot pretend to determine; but, certain it is, that that great poet has taken some pains to perpetuate her name to immortal infamy; having, in his *Dunciad*, proposed her as one of the prizes to be run for, in the games instituted in honour of the inauguration of the monarch of *Dulness*. This, however, I own I cannot readily subscribe to; for, although I should be far from vindicating the libertinism of her subjects, or the exposing with aggravation to the public the private errors of individuals, yet, I think, it cannot be denied, that there is great spirit and ingenuity in Mrs. Heywood's manner of treating subjects, which the friends of virtue may perhaps wish she had never entered on at all; and that in those of her novels, where personal character has not been admitted to take place, and where the stories have been of her own creation, such as her *Love in Excess, Fruitless Enquiry*, &c. she has given proofs of great inventive powers, and a perfect knowledge of the affections of the human heart. And thus much must be granted in her favour, that whatever liberty she might at first give to her pen, to the offence either of morality or delicacy, she seemed to be soon convinced of her error, and determined not only to reform, but even atone for it; since, in the numerous volumes which she gave to the world towards the latter part of her life, no author has appeared more the votary of virtue, nor are there any novels in which a stricter purity, or a greater delicacy of sentiment, has been preserved. It may not, perhaps, be disagreeable in this place to point out what these latter works were, as they are very voluminous, and are not perfectly known to every one. They may therefore, though somewhat foreign to the purpose of this work, be found in the following list, viz.

*The Female Spectator*, 4 vols.
*Epistles for the Ladies*, 2 vols.
*Fortunate Foundling*, 1 vol.
*Adventures of Nature*, 1 vol.
*Hist. of Betsy Thoughtless*, 4 vols.
*Jenny and Jemmy Jessamy*, 3 vols.
*Invisible Spy*, 2 vols.
*Husband and Wife*, 2 vols.
and a pamphlet entitled,
*A Present for a Serving Maid.*

When young, she dabbled in dramatic poetry, but with no great success; none of her plays either meeting with much approbation at the first, nor having been admitted to repetition since. Their titles were as follow:

1. *Fair Captive.* T. 8vo. 1721.
2. *Wife to be let.* C. 8vo. 1724.
3. *Frederick Duke of Brunswick.* T. 8vo. 1729.
4. *Opera of Operas* (joined with Mr. Hatchet.) 8vo. 1733.

She had also an inclination for the theatre as a performer, and was on the stage at Dublin in the year 1715. She also acted a principal part in her own comedy of the *Wife to be let*; and her name stands in the drama of a tragedy, entitled, *The Rival Father*, written by Mr. Hatchet; a gentleman with whom she appears to have had a close literary intimacy.

As to the circumstances of Mrs. Heywood's life, very little light seems to appear; for, though the world was inclinable, probably induced by the general tenor of her earlier writings, to affix on her the character of a lady of gallantry, yet I have never heard of any particular intrigues or connections directly laid to her charge; and have been credibly informed that, from a supposition of some improper liberties being taken with her character after death, by the intermixture of truth and falshood with her history, she laid a solemn injunction on a person, who was well acquainted with all the particulars of it, not to communicate to any one the least circumstance relating to her; so that probably, unless some very ample account should appear from that quarter itself, whereby her story may be placed in a true and favourable light, the world will still be left in the dark with regard to it. All I have been able to learn is, that her father was in the mercantile way, that she was born at London, and that, at the time of her death, which was on the 25th of February, 1756, she was about sixty-three years of age.

With respect to her genius and abilities, her works, which are very numerous, must stand in evidence; but I cannot help observing as to her personal character, that I was told by one, who was well acquainted with her for many years before her close of life, that she was good-natured, affable, lively, and entertaining; and that, whatever errors she might in any respect have run into in her youthful days, she was, during the whole course of his knowledge of her, remarkable for the most rigid and scrupulous decorum, delicacy, and prudence, both with respect to her conduct and conversation.

## 9. Clara Reeve

From *The Progress of Romance, through Times, Countries, Manners; with Remarks on the Good and Bad Effects of It, on Them Respectively; in a Course of Evening Conversations,* "Evening VII" (1785)

[Now best known for *The Old English Baron*, a Gothic novel first published as *The Champion of Virtue: A Gothic Story* (1777), Clara Reeve (1729-1807) published her study of the development of fiction, *The Progress of Romance*, in 1785. It takes the dialogue form popular in the eighteenth century; Euphrasia and her friend Sophronia discuss the subject in a series of evening meetings with Hortensius.]

*Euphrasia.* ... Let us next consider some of the early novels of our own country.

We had early translations of the best novels of all other countries,[1] but for a long time produced very few of our own. One of the earliest I know of is the *Cyprian Academy*, by Robert Baron[2] in the reign of Charles the First. – Among our early novel-writers we must reckon Mrs. Behn. – There are strong marks of genius in all this lady's works, but unhappily, there are some parts of them, very improper to be read by, or recommended to virtuous minds, and especially to youth.[3] – She wrote in an age, and to a court of licentious manners,[4] and perhaps we ought to ascribe to these causes the loose turn of her stories. – Let us do justice to her merits, and cast the veil of compassion over her faults. – She died in the year 1689, and lies buried in the cloisters of Westminster Abbey. – The inscription will shew how high she stood in estimation at that time.

*Hortensius.* Are you not partial to the sex of this genius? –

---

1   In addition to early romances and picaresque tales, they mention, as "a very unexceptionable and entertaining work of its kind," *La Belle Assemblée*, written by Madeleine Angélique de Gomez (1684-1770); Haywood translated this collection of tales and another from the same author, *Entretien des beaux esprits.*

2   Robert Baron, *Erotopageion; or, the Cyprian Academy* (1647), a romance.

3   Reeve ends *Progress* with lists of books that can be safely recommended, one to children and the other to young ladies.

4   The court of Charles II, notorious for sexual licentiousness.

when you excuse in her, what you would not to a man?

*Euphrasia.* Perhaps I may, and you must excuse me if I am so, especially as this lady had many fine and amiable qualities, besides her genius for writing.

*Sophronia.* Pray let her rest in peace, – you were speaking of the inscription on her monument, I do not remember it.

*Euphrasia.* It is as follows:

Mrs. A P H R A   B E H N , 1689.
Here lies a proof that wit can never be
Defence enough against mortality.

Let me add that Mrs. Behn will not be forgotten, so long as the tragedy of *Oroonoko* is acted, it was from her story of that illustrious African, that Mr. Southern wrote that play, and the most affecting parts of it are taken almost literally from her.[1]

*Hortensius.* Peace be to her *manes*![2] – I shall not disturb her, or her works.

*Euphrasia.* I shall not recommend them to your perusal Hortensius.

The next female writer of this class is Mrs. Manley, whose works are still more exceptionable than Mrs. Behn's, and as much inferior to them in point of merit. – She hoarded up all the public and private scandal within her reach, and poured it forth, in a work too well known in the last age, though almost forgotten in the present; a work that partakes of the style of the romance, and the novel. I forbear the name,[3] and further observations on it, as Mrs. Manley's works are sinking gradually into oblivion. I am sorry to say they were once in fashion, which obliges me to mention them, otherwise I had rather be spared the pain of disgracing an author of my own sex.

*Sophronia.* It must be confessed that these books of the last age, were of worse tendency than any of those of the present.

*Euphrasia.* My dear friend, there were bad books at all times,

---

1   First acted in 1695, Thomas Southerne's adaptation of *Oroonoko*, Behn's best-known novel, became one of the most popular plays of the eighteenth century.

2   The remains or the spirits of the dead (Latin, pronounced *man-ace*).

3   Her *Atalantis*, "the capital [chief] work" mentioned below.

for those who sought for them. – Let us pass them over in silence.

*Hortensius.* No not yet. – Let me help your memory to one more lady-author of the same class. – Mrs. Heywood. – She has the same claim upon you as those you have last mentioned.

*Euphrasia.* I had intended to have mentioned Mrs. Heywood though in a different way, but I find you will not suffer any part of her character to escape you.

*Hortensius.* Why should she be spared any more than the others?

*Euphrasia.* Because she repented of her faults, and employed the latter part of her life in expiating the offences of the former. – There is reason to believe that the examples of the two ladies we have spoken of, seduced Mrs. Heywood into the same track; she certainly wrote some amorous novels in her youth, and also two books of the same kind as Mrs. Manley's capital work, all of which I hope are forgotten.

*Hortensius.* I fear they will not be so fortunate, they will be known to posterity by the infamous immortality, conferred upon them by Pope in his *Dunciad.*

*Euphrasia.* Mr. Pope was severe in his castigations, but let us be just to merit of every kind. Mrs. Heywood had the singular good fortune to recover a lost reputation, and the yet greater honour to atone for her errors. – She devoted the remainder of her life and labours to the service of virtue. Mrs. Heywood was one of the most voluminous female writers that ever England produced, none of her latter works are destitute of merit, though they do not rise to the highest pitch of excellence. – *Betsy Thoughtless* is reckoned her best novel; but those works by which she is most likely to be known to posterity, are the *Female Spectator,* and the *Invisible Spy.* – This lady died so lately as the year 1758.

*Sophronia.* I have heard it often said that Mr. Pope was too severe in his treatment of this lady, it was supposed that she had given some private offence, which he resented publicly as was too much his way.

*Hortensius.* That is very likely, for he was not of a forgiving disposition. – If I have been too severe also, you ladies must forgive me in behalf of your sex.

*Euphrasia.* Truth is sometimes severe. – Mrs. Heywood's wit and ingenuity were never denied. I would be the last to vindicate her faults, but the first to celebrate her return to virtue, and her atonement for them.

*Sophronia.* May her first writings be forgotten, and the last survive to do her honour!

...

# Select Bibliography

In addition to helpful studies and backgrounds, this list includes items cited parenthetically or consulted for the Chronology and Appendix.

## Haywood's Works:

Scholars still rely on editions and collections published in Haywood's lifetime (see Chronology). Several of her early works appear in photographic facsimile in Garland Publishing's Foundations of the Novel or Flowering of the Novel series, and *Anti-Pamela* appears in Garland's collection of Richardsoniana. Although some modern editions and facsimilies are, like these series, available only in university and research libraries, it is getting easier to read Haywood:

*The Adventures of Eovaai, Princess of Ijaveo.* 1736. Ed. Earla A. Wilputte. Peterborough, ON: Broadview Press, 1999.

*Bath Intrigues: In Four Letters to a Friend.* 1725. Intro. Simon Varey. Augustan Reprint Society No. 236. Los Angeles: William Andrews Clark Memorial Library, 1986.

*The British Recluse* and *Fantomina. Popular Fiction by Women 1660-1730: An Anthology.* Ed. Paula R. Backscheider and John J. Richetti. Oxford: Clarendon, 1996.

*The Distress'd Orphan; or, Love in a Mad-House.* 2nd ed. 1726. Int. Deborah Nestor. ARS Nos. 267-268. New York: AMS, 1995.

*The Female Spectator.* Ed. Gabrielle M. Firmager. Bristol: Bristol Classical Press, 1992 [selection].

*Four Novels of Eliza Haywood.* Introd. Mary Anne Schofield. Delmar, NY: Scholars' Facsimiles and Reprints, 1983.

*The History of Miss Betsy Thoughtless.* 1751. Ed. Christine Blouch. Peterborough, ON: Broadview Press, 1998. *and* Ed. Beth Fowkes Tobin. Oxford and New York: Oxford UP, 1997.

*The Injur'd Husband* and *Lasselia.* Ed. Jerry C. Beasley. Lexington: UP of Kentucky, 1999.

*Love in Excess; or, The Fatal Enquiry: A Novel.* London: W. Chetwood,

1719-20. *and* 4th ed. corrected. London: D. Browne, Jr., W. Chetwood, and S. Chapman, 1722.

*The Masquerade Novels of Eliza Haywood*. Introd. Mary Anne Schofield. Delmar, NY: Scholars' Facsimiles and Reprints, 1986.

*The Plays of Eliza Haywood*. Ed. with an introd. by Valerie C. Rudolph. New York: Garland, 1983 [facsimile reprints with a brief introduction].

*Philidore and Placentia; or, L'Amour Trop Delicat*. 1727. *Four Before Richardson: Selected English Novels*, 1720-27. Ed. William H. McBurney. Lincoln: U of Nebraska P, 1963. 153-231 [modernized text with notes].

*Secret Histories, Novels and Poems*. 3rd ed. 4 vols. London: A. Bettesworth, 1732.

*Selected Fiction and Drama of Eliza Haywood*. Ed. Paula R. Backscheider. New York and Oxford: Oxford UP, 1999.

*Selections from* The Female Spectator. Ed. Patricia Meyer Spacks, New York and Oxford: Oxford UP, 1999.

*Three Novellas by Eliza Haywood: The Distress'd Orphan, The City Jilt, and The Double Marriage* [1726]. Ed. with an Introduction and Notes by Earla A. Wilputte. East Lansing, MI: Colleagues, 1995.

**Selected Secondary Sources:**

Ballaster, Ros. *Seductive Forms: Women's Amatory Fiction from 1684-1740*. Oxford: Clarendon, 1992.

Benedict, Barbara M. "The Curious Genre: Female Inquiry in Amatory Fiction." *Studies in the Novel* 30 (1998): 194-210.

Blain, Virginia, Patricia Clements, and Isobel Grundy. *The Feminist Companion to Literature in English: Women Writers from the Middle Ages to the Present*. New Haven: Yale UP, 1990.

Blouch, Christine. "Eliza Haywood and the Romance of Obscurity." *SEL* 31 (1991): 535-51.

—. "Haywood, Eliza (1693?-1756)." *Eighteenth-Century Anglo-American Novelists: A Critical Reference Guide*. Ed. Doreen Alvarez Saar and Mary Anne Schofield. New York: G.K. Hall, 1996. 263-300.

Bowers, Toni O'Shaughnessy. "Sex, Lies, and Invisibility: Amatory Fiction from the Restoration to Mid-Century." *Columbia*

History of the British Novel. Ed. John Richetti et al. New York: Columbia UP, 1994. 50–72.

Craft-Fairchild, Catherine. Masquerade and Gender: Disguise and Female Identity in Eighteenth-Century Fictions by Women. University Park, PA: Pennsylvania State UP, 1993.

Defoe, Daniel. The Life and Strange Surprizing Adventures of Robinson Crusoe, of York, Mariner. 1719. Ed. J. Donald Crowley. 1972. World's Classics. Oxford: Oxford UP, 1983.

Doody, Margaret Anne. A Natural Passion: A Study of the Novels of Samuel Richardson. Oxford: Clarendon, 1974.

Elwood, John R. "Swift's 'Corinna.'" N&Q n.s. 2 (1955): 529–30.

———. "Henry Fielding and Eliza Haywood: A Twenty Year War." Albion 5 (1973): 184–92

———. "The Stage Career of Eliza Haywood." Theatre Survey 5 (1974): 107–16.

Fielding, Henry. The Author's Farce (Original Version). 1730. Ed. Charles B. Woods. Lincoln: U of Nebraska P, 1966 [satirizes Haywood as Mrs. Novel].

Firmager, Gabrielle M. "Eliza Haywood: Some Further Light on Her Background?" N&Q n.s. 38 (1991): 181–83 [prints two letters].

Hammond, Brean. Professional Imaginative Writing in England, 1670–1740: 'Hackney for Bread'. Oxford: Clarendon, 1997.

Heinneman, Marcia. "Swift's 'Corinna' Again." N&Q n.s. 19 (1972): 218–21.

———. "Eliza Haywood's Career in the Theatre." N&Q n.s. 20 (1973): 9–13.

Herbage, Julian. "The Opera of Operas." The Monthy Musical Record (May–June 1959): 83–89.

Hollis, Karen. "Eliza Haywood and the Gender of Print." The Eighteenth Century 38 (1997): 43–62.

Hume, Robert D. Henry Fielding and the London Theatre 1728–1737. Oxford: Clarendon, 1988 [detailed account of theatre scene, incidental refs. to EH, Wm. Hatchett, etc.].

Ingrassia, Catherine. Authorship, Commerce, and Gender in Early Eighteenth-Century England: A Culture of Paper Credit. Cambridge: Cambridge UP, 1998.

Koon, Helene. "Eliza Haywood and the Female Spectator." Huntington Library Quarterly 42 (1978): 43–55.

Lipking, Joanna. "Fair Originals: Women Poets in Male Commendatory Poems." *Eighteenth-Century Life* 12.2 (1988): 58-72.

Lockwood, Thomas. "Eliza Haywood in 1749: *Dalinda*, and Her Pamphlet on the Pretender." *N&Q* n.s. 36 (1989): 475-77.

London, April. "Placing the Female: The Metonymic Garden in Amatory and Pious Narrative, 1700-1740." Schofield and Macheski 101-23.

McBurney, William H. "Mrs. Penelope Aubin and the Early Eighteenth-Century English Novel." *Huntington Library Quarterly* 20 (1957): 245-67.

McWhir, Anne. "Elizabeth Thomas and the Two Corinnas: Giving the Woman Writer a Bad Name." *ELH* 62 (1995): 105-119.

Merritt, Juliette. "'That Devil Curiosity Which Too Much Haunts the Minds of Women': Eliza Haywood's Female Spectators." *Lumen* 16 (1997): 131-46.

Pope, Alexander. *The Dunciad, Variorum. With the Prolegomena of Scriblerus.* London: "A. Dod," 1729.

———. *The Dunciad.* Ed. James Sutherland. 3rd ed. *The Poems of Alexander Pope,* Vol. 5. London: Methuen; New Haven: Yale UP, 1963 [thoroughly annotated].

Prescott, Sarah. "The Palace of Fame and the Problem of Reputation: The Case of Eliza Haywood." *Baetyl* 1.4 (Summer-Autumn 1994): 9-35.

Reeve, Clara. *The Progess of Romance, through Times, Countries, and Manners; ... in a Course of Evening Conversations.* Colchester: W. Keymer, 1785.

———. *The Progress of Romance and The History of Charoba, Queen of Aegypt: Reproduced from the Colchester Edition of 1785.* With a Bibliographical Note by Esther M. McGill. New York: Facsimile Text Society, 1930.

Richetti, John J. *Popular Fiction before Richardson: Narrative Patterns 1700-1739.* Oxford: Clarendon, 1969.

Savage, Richard. *The Authors of the Town; a Satire.* London: J. Roberts, 1725.

———. *The Poetical Works.* Ed. Clarence Tracy. Cambridge: Cambridge UP, 1962 [1st complete collection; helpful notes].

———. *The Works of Richard Savage, Esq.... With an Account of the Life and Writings of the Author, by Samuel Johnson, LL.D.* New ed. 2 vols. London: T. Evans, 1777.

Saxton, Kirsten T. and Rebecca P. Bocchicchio, eds. *The Passionate Fictions of Eliza Haywood: Essays on Her Life and Work*. Lexington: UP of Kentucky, 2000.

Schofield, Mary Anne. "'Descending Angels': Salubrious Sluts and Pretty Prostitutes in Haywood's Fiction." Schofield and Macheski 186-200.

——. *Eliza Haywood*. Twayne's English Authors Series 411. Boston: Twayne, 1985.

——. *Quiet Rebellion: The Fictional Heroines of Eliza Haywood*. Washington: UP of America, 1981.

Schofield, Mary Anne, and Cecilia Macheski, eds. *Fetter'd or Free? British Women Novelists 1670-1815*. Athens, Ohio: Ohio UP, 1986.

Spencer, Jane. *The Rise of the Woman Novelist from Aphra Behn to Jane Austen*. Oxford: Blackwell, 1986.

Stanton, Judith Phillips. "'This New-Found Path Attempting': Women Dramatists in England, 1660-1800." *Curtain Calls: British and American Women and the Theatre*. Ed. Mary Anne Schofield and Cecilia Macheski. Athens, Ohio: Ohio UP, 1963. 325-54 [includes checklist of plays by author].

Swift, Jonathan. *The Complete Poems*. Ed. Pat Rogers. New Haven: Yale UP, 1983 [modernized text with excellent notes].

——. *The Works of Jonathan Swift, Dean of St. Patrick's, Dublin ... With Notes and a Life of the Author by Sir Walter Scott*. 2nd ed. 19 vols. London: Bickers and Son, 1883.

Todd, Janet. *The Sign of Angellica: Women, Writing and Fiction, 1660-1800*. London: Virago, 1989.

Tracy, Clarence. *The Artificial Bastard: A Biography of Richard Savage*. Toronto: U of Toronto P with the U of Saskatchewan, 1953.

Warner, William B. *Licensing Entertainment: The Elevation of Novel Reading in Britain, 1684-1750*. Berkeley and Los Angeles: U of California P, 1998.

Whicher, George Frisbie. *The Life and Romances of Mrs. Eliza Haywood*. New York: Columbia UP, 1915.